To David & Tiffany,

Thanks for stopping by

Merry Christmas and

—Pete

Peter J. ххх

FORSAKEN KINGDOM
CITY OF PROPHECY

PETER J DUDEK

Forsaken Kingdom
Copyright © 2008
Peter Dudek

Cover illustration by Andrew Dudek
Edited by Arlene Robinson

Published by Carnation City Press
1580 Lilly Lane
Alliance Ohio 44601

ISBN 978-0-615-23201-0

Library of Congress Control Number: 2008910035

TO MOM & DAD

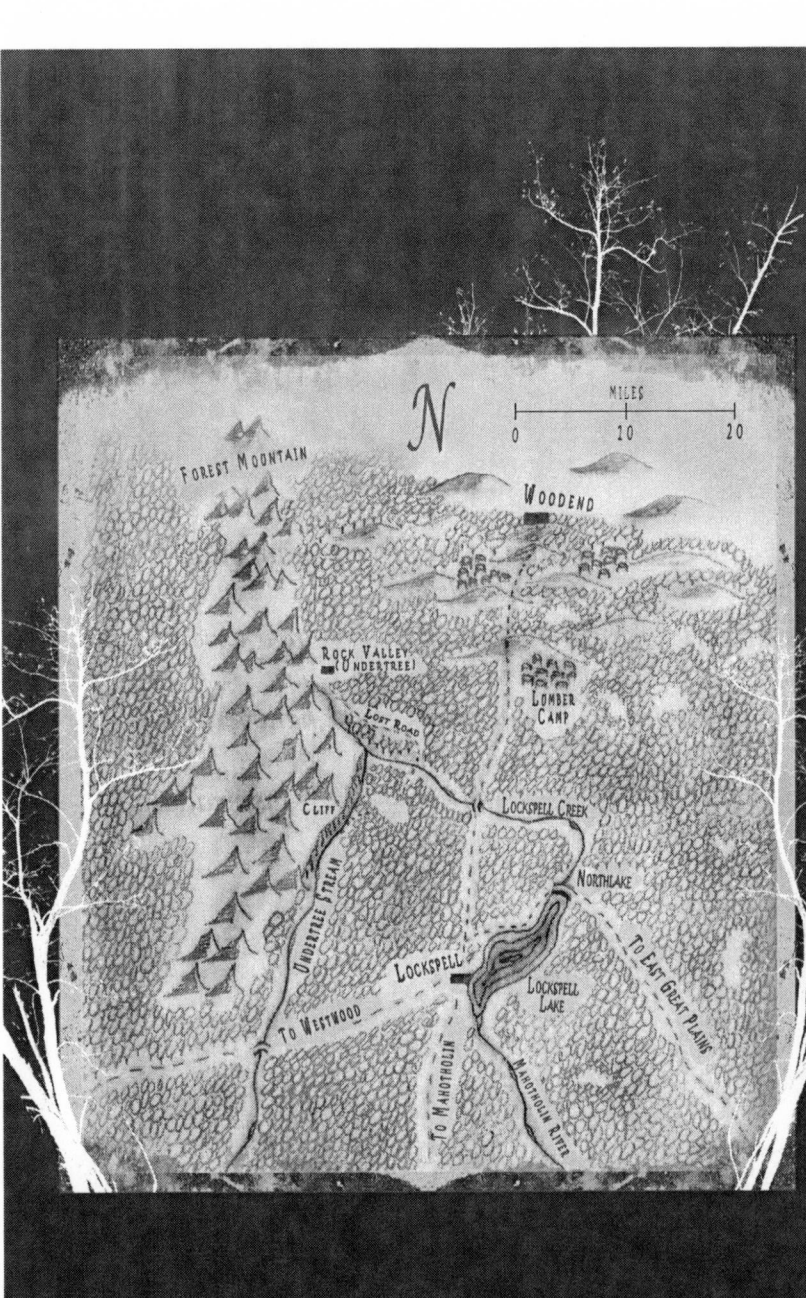

◉NE

The boy moved with great caution toward Willow Road, through a gap between two musty wood houses, looking for trouble. Even though only fourteen, Tarin possessed keen understanding of all the alleys and back-streets of the walled forest city of Woodend. Shyness made him dislike any encounter with his fellowman, so only curiosity could drive him from his safe home, also on Willow Road. And indeed, a powerful curiosity fueled his current mission. Earlier that day, from a side window in his house, he'd heard his neighbor talking to a stranger.

"Some in the forest believe Bolard will return this fall, Clooney," his neighbor had said. "Before the Festival of Colors."

Tarin had almost gasped, hearing this. Three years earlier, Bolard, the city's former governor, was banished due to a sudden heretical decree from a king who, though no one had seen him countless years, still maintained great loyalty from the people of Woodend. Bolard's return would create an uproar, and likely endanger the city's current governor.

"But the Festival be only three weeks away," Clooney had replied.

"Indeed. A lot of people in town are hoping it happens, so we can get rid of that do-nothing Willerdon."

"But is Bolard such a good replacement?" Clooney said. "I heard he went mad."

The neighbor snorted. "That's just what that old geezer up the road likes to tell people. Bill's quite a storyteller, he is."

"I'm headin' to his house this evening," Clooney said. "Maybe I'll get him to bring up the old governor."

"Do as ye please, but don't take every word Bill says as fact."

Shortly after the exchange, Clooney had left, leaving Tarin's mind buzzing with questions about Bolard's madness. This was something he'd been curious about ever since Bolard's exile. Now, this stranger named Clooney was visiting Bill, who might know even more. He had decided to sneak to Bill's house that evening and find out what he could hear. He'd done this before, hiding under the big bush under Bill's front window.

Now, he stood in the shadows between the two houses and looked around in disgust. Bill's house was just across the road, but he couldn't get there without being seen. Although it was getting dark, people were scattered all along Willow Road. Only a few strides away, a woman tried to hush her crying baby while she bartered with a portly butcher for some bloody raw meat. Next to her, lumberjacks stood by a cart full of timber and laughed about something Tarin doubted was worth laughing about. In front of them, a scrawny farmer looked like he was fending off bees while he tried to make a potential buyer see past his vegetables' obvious deficiencies.

Tarin wanted to shout out, "This is Willow Road, not a marketplace! Take your business to the main road where it belongs!" But he was far too timid to make such a bold gesture. It would be futile anyway. The projected winter food shortages, blamed on Governor Willerdon, had sent the people of Woodend into a mad race to secure whatever provisions still existed. He would simply have to wait for the street to clear before venturing to Bill's house.

It took an hour, but at last, the lumberjacks pulled their cart away, the woman left with her baby in one hand and a huge slab of meat in the other, and the farmer gave up his effort to sell his rotten produce. In another half hour, the sun went down. He was just about to step out from between the two houses when he saw Clooney coming up the road, whistling. With a frustrated sigh, he waited.

The balding man approached Bill's house on the now almost-empty street, walked up the narrow dirt path leading to his crooked front door, and knocked. Bill's old and ugly wife opened it, cooed at the arrival of a guest, and let Clooney in with many a useless word about her precious ale, of which she was a well-known brewer.

Tarin would have sneaked over right then, but now, a lampwright was lighting the lanterns along the road. When the skinny young fellow finally passed by, Tarin hurried over to Bill's front window and ducked behind the rhododendron bush beneath it.

He listened carefully, trying hard to focus on the voices within the house. Fortunately, the evening was warm and the window open. He heard Bill rock his rocking chair. "Come now, Clooney," Bill said. "Take some before the wife comes back from the kitchen. She'll guzzle it all before yer lips ever get wet."

"Dern it, Bill," Clooney whispered angrily, "I told ye, I don't drink ale anymore! Quit temptin' me."

"Ah, Clooney, but me and the wife's been saving this batch for years. I wanted a friend to partake with me in the joy of the bottle."

Tarin heard Bill make a gulping noise.

"Put that away," Clooney said. "You promised to spin me a yarn tonight, and a good one at that! I want to hear about old Governor Bolard. About his madness, mind ye."

"'Bout what?"

"Ye see! The bottle's already started to do the thinkin' for ye."

"Fine, fine. . . . Maggie! Come, ye can finish this up."

Tarin heard stomping from deep within the house, then the sound of a door slamming against a wall, and a woman's voice said, "'Bout time ye learned to share, ye old fool." She must have put the bottle to her lips, because the room went quiet. Then she sighed and said, "Ah, this one's aged just perfect."

Tarin heard her patter into another room.

"That be one solid woman," Bill said. "Married her 'cause she was the only one who could hold down more liquor than me!" He burst into laughter.

"The story, man! Please! The one 'bout the old governor. I've heard so many rumors about Bolard, but ye was there. Ye know the truth. What happened to the fellow . . . ye know, 'fore he went crazy?"

Bill hiccupped. "Good question." He broke into a wild cough.

"Ye all right?"

"Give me—" he burped, "a second."

Tarin heard a loud sigh, and then, "Ah, sorry. Think I might've taken one sip too many. I'm feelin' a bit better now, though. So, the story."

All went quiet. Tarin's heart beat fast.

"First, I need ye to open yer dern mind a bit for me. Since ye didn't partake in the ale with me like I asked, that's goin' to be a bit hard."

"Ale or no ale, I've never been one to doubt the unusual, if that's what ye mean."

"Good, very good. . . . It started 'bout three years ago, a few months before Governor Bolard was forced to leave town because of his madness and the Royal Decree."

"Royal Decree, hmm. Don't know much about it. Lived in Lockspell when it was set up."

"It was an order for all the king's followers to give Bolard our little magic lights."

"But why would he do that?" Clooney asked. "Everyone knows the illuminas are all the king's followers have left of him."

"I'll tell ye why." Bill paused for so long, Tarin was afraid he'd fallen asleep.

He hadn't. Bill sighed until, nearly out of air, he whispered, "The phantoms took him." He wheezed, then caught his breath. "They took him while he was out inspectin' the wall one night, after a storm." His speech quickened. "I was with him. He was kneeling, looking at a downed tree next to the north part of the wall. I saw some yellow eyes in the trees behind him. Before I could warn him, those eyes, along with what looked like black fog, darted toward him. The yellow eyes just . . . disappeared into his body. When my senses came back to me, I told him about it. He said I should ease up on the liquor. But only a few days later he began acting real queer, until eventually, he made the Royal Decree."

Tarin felt his skin crawl.

"What do you think that apparition ye saw really was?" Clooney whispered.

There was a long pause, and Bill said, "I think it was one of them beasts. The ones that made the people of Undertree go mad a hundred years ago."

Tarin heard Clooney gasp, then say, "You think it was *them* that destroyed Undertree?"

Bill grunted. "I do. And I have good reason to believe somethin' else. I believe all that happened to Undertree is happenin' to Woodend, even now."

"Do you mean—?"

"Aye. Darkness is comin' back to the forest, old friend. We need to be ready for it."

"But how—?"

"Do you still have it?"

Seconds passed. Tarin saw the window above him grow a little brighter, and began to lift his head to peek through it when something wet smacked his face. He nearly screamed in shock before his reflexes wisely dropped him to his belly. He wiped his face with his hand and brought the slime to his nose. *A tomato?*

"Throw another one," a shrill voice said from the direction of the road. Something flew through the bush and landed on Tarin's back. Another tomato, this one rotten.

"Come on, boy!" the shrill voice said. "We know you're there. Come out or we'll tell Bill."

With how loud this imbecile was yelling, Tarin was sure Bill already knew of his presence. He got up and ran as hard as he could, through Bill's lawn and down the road. A gang of boys around his age followed him. "Let's get him!" the squeaky voice shouted.

The group following him had tormented him before. Tarin had little use for the silliness of childhood. He was known as a loner, and proud of it. This fact wasn't easy for these boys to accept. A tear of anger and fear slid down his cheek, but he couldn't cry. If he were caught like that, they would pummel him for sure.

He ran past a barrel partly full of rotting produce and heaved it into the road as he went by. A moment later, he heard the squeaky voice again.

"Think that can stop us? We're going to put you in that barrel and roll you down the street!"

He saw an opening between two dilapidated old buildings, and remembered it led to an alley that ran between Willow Road and Blossom Street, all the way to the main road. From there, he could double back to Willow Road and home.

A quick turn past a lamppost brought him between the buildings. A few strides, and he was in the alley. It took his eyes a moment to adjust to the increased darkness. Trash was heaped along the backs of the buildings. Rats scurried around his feet. Yet he felt calmer in the narrow fortress the alley created. He hurried on, but made only a few steps when he heard his pursuers stop just outside the alley. The pain in his side told him he couldn't outrun them for much longer. Then, he remembered another narrow alley a short distance ahead.

He ran as quietly as possible until he saw the two three-story brick buildings marking the alley's entrance. He slid into its shadows and ran to an old wagon, ducked behind it and listened. The boys' voices grew louder. He held his breath. A moment later, a group of boy-sized silhouettes rushed by.

Tarin thrust his fist toward the starry sky in triumph and prepared to retrace his steps back to Willow Road. But then he heard something: a man's voice, and another voice, this one a hissing whisper.

He dropped to hands and knees and eased his body around the wagon. In the lantern light, about fifty paces away, he saw two figures standing in Blossom Street, just beyond the alley. One was bald and clean-shaven. The lantern cast frantic shadows while that man urgently gestured to the hissing man, who stood perfectly still. The second man was concealed in a hooded cloak that appeared dull red in the lantern's light. Tarin had never seen garb of such color before. Ignoring the uneasiness ringing in his heart, he began to crawl toward the strangers. The ground was wet and slimy beneath his hands, but he barely noticed.

When he'd crept within fifteen paces of them, he could make sense of their hushed words. He slid behind a barrel and stared at them through its broken slats.

"I told you," the bald man whispered, "the governor's house is on Willow Road, just north of here. I'll give you further directions later. At the hideout, where it's safe."

"There is no danger here," the man in the red cloak hissed. "They would tell us if there were."

The bald man clenched both fists. "Are you deaf? They *are* telling me danger is nearby!"

Tarin gasped as the man looked his way and pointed.

"Something or someone is making *them* uneasy, from both that direction," now the man pointed right, down Blossom Street, "and that direction. And their urgency grows stronger with every moment." He reached into his pocket and pulled out a glowing red object. "Look, much brighter than earlier. Something is amiss. We should leave now."

As the bald man put the red object back into his pocket, Tarin saw something that nearly made him gasp. It appeared the man had more than one shadow. One of them, as Tarin expected, was spawned by the lantern light and strewn across the ground next to the man's feet. But three others stood along the nearby walls, in ways impossible based on the lantern's position. As the red light grew dim within the bald man's pocket, the shadows slid toward the man and disappeared.

Tarin felt his left eye twitch, as it did when nerves overtook him. There was no possible way those shadows had been cast by the lantern light, and the red object's glow wasn't strong enough to create them. With little regard for stealth, he got up and began running back toward the wider alley between Blossom and Willow.

"Who goes there?" the bald man shouted. Tarin ignored him, and was almost back to the other alley when something jumped out from behind the cart where he'd hidden earlier. He stopped running, in fear it was one of the shadows. To his relief, it was only a scrawny boy about his age.

"So there you are," the figure blurted, in a squeak both familiar and unwanted.

Tarin's heart sank, realizing it was the obnoxious leader of that band of ruffian boys. He was now trapped on both sides. But just as he decided the scrawny boy was less of a threat than the strangers behind him, he saw the boy look up and put his hands to his mouth, then retch once, then twice.

Tarin skipped out of the way in time to avoid the explosion of vomit.

The boy looked at him, now with terror in his eyes. "What's happening to me?" He took a few steps back, vomited again, and staggered away.

Tarin turned around and his arms fell limp along his sides. Not three feet away from him stood the red-cloaked stranger. He couldn't see his eyes, but could feel them glaring at him from within the hood's shadow. As he drew away in terror, the stranger snarled and reached out.

Tarin ducked, but then heard the sound of running feet from the roadway where the stranger had just been.

"Get back here!" the bald man shouted, fidgeting and looking over his left shoulder. Tarin saw a white light bouncing along the walls, as if someone carrying a lantern fast approached.

Snarling again, the stranger ran with unnatural speed back to Blossom Street. A moment later, both men darted to their right. Tarin watched as their pursuers swept past the alley, a white light seeming to emanate from their hands. With energy fueled by fear, he ran back the way he came and didn't stop until he was home.

Two ◆

Governor Willerdon stood in his study, grasping a parcel of paper and staring into the moonlit night through the room's only window. The paper had the words *To Will* written on the front, a name only those close to him used. He looked through the window and down, into the scrawny trees that grew against the wall built against his house. Lifting his eyes, he saw alternating fields of corn and soy at the base of Woodend Hill. Some had been harvested; the rest rotted in ponds created by the summer's excess rains. He frowned and searched his pocket until he felt a familiar coolness. His fingers wrapped around it, loosely at first, but soon with more force.

The sight of those devastated fields made him angry: angry with the one who had made him governor. Or at least, angry with the one whose laws specified that the governor was responsible for a city's success or failure. When he could bear his thoughts no longer, he pulled the phial from his pocket and thrust it through the window and toward the fields.

"Do you see that, my king?" he blurted. "Do you see those fields? They're mostly drowned, and many fear the city will starve this winter."

The light glimmered dully with a white luminance. Will grunted and brought the object close to his face. "And are you aware, my king, that something lurks along the road to Lockspell? Something killing travelers at random and eating them? For weeks I've been keeping this hidden from the townsmen, but it will soon find its way into the rumor mill. When this happens, trade between Woodend and the rest of the forest might stop, sending us into even deeper poverty."

He felt a pain in his neck as his tension grew yet stronger. "And have you heard the rumors about Bolard being back in the forest? In case you've forgotten, he did promise to return someday after we exiled him. And . . . the townsfolk are starting to talk."

Will half-expected the phial to grow warm, or maybe brighter, some sign the king understood Woodend's plight. But as he watched the object, it changed in neither brightness nor warmth.

"Does this mean nothing to you, then?" Will implored. "Is this such a small matter in your kingdom that you cannot even grace me with some miniscule sign to demonstrate your concern?"

The light swirled along the phial's walls in apparent indifference. Will pulled back his arm and contemplated throwing the object outside. Perhaps if it landed in one of the pools in the field, or that rouge animal mauled it, the king would have a better view of his problem!

He held the position for a few moments, his heart racing, his ire burning. But he didn't throw the illumina. What would it solve but to force him outside the city's walls to fetch the silly object?

Groaning, he returned the phial to his pocket and stepped away from the window. Only then did he remember the parchment in his other hand. His heart sank even farther in his gullet. On top of his list of already insurmountable difficulties, he had to deal with what the parchment contained.

Footsteps lumbered up the stairs from the first floor, then thudded down the hall toward his study. He turned to face the door, tucked in the white linen shirt under his vest, and waited.

Someone knocked, and he carefully slid the letter into an inner pocket. "Please, come in."

The door opened. The man in the doorframe wore a deep brown cloak that fell to the tops of high leather boots. A hood concealed his eyes, and all Will could see of his face was his bearded chin and sun-parched lips.

"Governor, I come with news from the forest road to Lockspell." He threw off his hood and stepped into the room, revealing the hat with a single white feather he wore.

Will beckoned toward a chair next to his desk. "Good evening, Raulin. Please, have a seat."

Raulin closed the door and sat, placing his cloak on the back of the chair. Will noticed his hands were shaking. Unease swept through his body as he took his place behind his desk. "What news has my head guardsman for me this night?"

"The animal has slain again."

Will closed his eyes and lowered his head. "Have you identified the victim?"

"No, but we think it might've been a fisherman from one of the southern towns, most likely Northlake. We found an empty pail nearby, and some dead fish. Probably planned to barter them here in Woodend."

"Was he . . . like the others?"

Raulin nodded. "Little left. Mostly torn and bloody clothes."

Will rubbed his temples. "What could be doing this? Weeks now, and still no answers."

"I've told you, I believe we have a rouge bear. What else could it be?"

"But what about the other signs?"

Raulin raised his brows. "What are you saying? That we have some sort of monster lurking in the forest?"

"Don't speak madness," Will blurted. "I'm not suggesting it's anything unnatural. I'm just confused by the evidence you and your guards have gathered."

"I've only told you what we've seen."

"Yes, yes. I know. And due to the odd nature of your findings, I'm doing everything in my power to keep this from spreading into the streets. I don't need a panic about some insane animal that feasts upon lonely travelers along the forest roadways. Trade with the other towns would be ruined. And I have enough problems to deal with." He pulled the paper from his cloak and tossed it onto his desk. "Like this."

Raulin read the letter and frowned. "So it is as we feared? Jebin is leaving?"

Will nodded. "Sheriff Jebin was one of the few men in my circle the people respected. His mere presence kept them from completely loathing me. They trusted him, and since I'm his friend, they tolerated me. Now I don't know what's going to happen. Especially with the rumors about Bolard getting louder."

Raulin dropped the parchment into Will's outstretched hand and looked away. "Sadly, you're right. The people feel you're weak. That you strive too hard to keep the peace, even if it means hiding the truth. Jebin always fights for what he believes right, regardless of personal consequence."

Raulin looked at the governor, his face showing anger. "I must confess, I am disturbed you hide information about this beast from the people. I'm sure Jebin would be as well."

Will glared at Raulin and felt his body go rigid. "Have I lost even your loyalty, guardsman?"

Raulin sat still, meeting his eyes in a hard stare.

He prepared to order the man out of his study, when the guard's expression softened and he stood and offered a bow, then said, "Though I disagree with you on occasion, it is the king's will I give you my loyalty and respect. You have both, Governor. Now, may I take leave? I must return to the forest and ensure the dead fisherman was given a proper and concealed burial. Then I will send word south that we found a victim of a bear attack. So his family, if he has one, will know what happened to him."

"Yes. You have my leave. And ... thank you. You're one of the few people I still trust in this forsaken town."

He listened to the steps fade away, then sighed at his cluttered desk. Straightening it could wait; the hour was late, and he was exhausted. He returned Jebin's letter to his pocket, extinguished the lantern on his desk and left for his bedroom. He hoped his wife was already asleep. If Lianna heard Raulin enter, she would want to know why he'd come. And he wasn't in an explaining mood.

✝ ✝ ✝

"Look at them guards. They're scared of that ol' bear. Pathetic!" Kane, an old and calloused Woodend lumberjack, had said this in the thick northern accent still common among many of the forest dwellers.

Jak, Kane's nephew, saw one of the guards turn toward his uncle. "Pipe down and dig if you want to earn your wages," the guard ordered. "I'm sure it's more than your typical business brings you in an entire week."

"A'least I'm not scared of the forest like ye are!" Kane spouted back. "Guards of Woodend? I'd sooner have a newborn pup protectin' me than the lot of ye."

The guard took a step toward Kane. Jak held out his hand. "Pay my uncle no heed. It's just his way."

Kane stopped digging and pointed his shovel at the guard. "And I've been known to kill men who keep me from my supper. Now pipe down so I can finish this job, or I might have'ta show you what this old arm of mine can still do." He twirled the shovel in his hand. The guards snickered.

"That's it," Kane said. "I've had it."

Jak grabbed him by the shoulders. "Please, Uncle. Let's finish the job and get our money. It'll buy us a nice supper at the inn's social hall."

The side of Kane's mouth quivered. "Always the peacekeeper, boy, aren't ye?" He stuck his shovel into the dirt and spat. "But let me tell ye, yer goin' to have to learn to stand up to fools like that if yer ever goin' to make it in this world. It's the only way ta get things done. Fer instance, if it weren't for people like me, always houndin' the governor about what a worthless coward he is, who knows where this town might be?"

Jak took up his shovel and returned to the hole. "And what's wrong with the town?"

Kane uttered a frustrated sigh. "Can't ye see, lad? Ever since Willerdon took charge, trade's down, farmin's down, no one's settin' up any new lumber camps or replantin' the old ones. And it's all because that governor won't stand up and make the people! Those old coons need to be pushed around a bit, or they're worthless."

He pointed his thumb back toward the guards. "Like our mighty protectors back there. Scared of a bear? Pathetic!"

Jak scooped up a rock the size of both his fists and tossed it to the side. "I don't think all that's the governor's fault. The people are getting lazy. But don't worry. With the rains we had this year, and the food shortage we'll have this winter, by next spring they'll all be begging to work."

"That ain't the only reason I got problems with Willerdon. Ye don't know his history like I do. Ye haven't lived here long enough."

Grinning, Jak used his shovel to help his uncle pull out a heavy clod of earth. "I see you have another tale for me, Uncle. Do tell."

Kane stared into the hole. "No storytelling here, just truth. Willerdon's a governor because of cowardice, pure and simple. Ye see, every now and then, there's a man who comes and tries to make changes. Changes for the better, mind ye. But when he does, people don't like it. And if they get angry enough, there's blood spilled. Of course, that's all natural. There comes a time in every life when we need ta pick a cause ta fight for. A few years ago, there was a time like that in Woodend. Willerdon was one of the few who didn't pick a side. Because of that, innocent people died, a great man was exiled, and this town lost its will to survive. Soon, we'll become a ghost town. It's happened before, and it'll happen again."

Jak wiped sweat from his forehead. "So you're angry with the governor because he remained neutral in some fight a number of years ago. Why's that so bad?"

Kane rolled his eyes and muttered to the sky, "Young folks. No fightin' spirit at all." He grabbed Jak's shovel and pulled him close, lowered his voice to a rough whisper. "Nephew, sometimes we need to fight for things, whether they're right or not. I can't condone a man leadin' this town who has no fightin' spirit! Especially because of what's goin' on down south."

Jak shook his head in confusion. "What's—?"

"Rumors, Jak. Dark rumors. About enemies in the Maplelake Forest. If they're true, we're goin' to need a bulldog as governor in the upcomin' years, not a pussycat. War's comin', I know it."

"What do you mean?" Jak said. "This forest hasn't seen a real battle for hundreds of year—"

"Ah, is yer tame little heart startin' to beat with a fervor for knowledge?" Kane slapped his neck as a mosquito swarmed around his head. "Let's say we meet at the inn tomorrow night. I'll introduce ye to me source. Salahan comes from the south. Far south. Place called Macalum. Apparently there's a lot of interestin' goins-on down there. So be where I said when I said to. I'll invite Salahan, and we'll talk."

Jak's eyes gleamed in the lantern light. "I'll be there."

THREE

Something landed on Tarin's belly, and he awoke with a start. An instant later, he shoved his fat, furry cat onto the floor. The cat began to moan and pace.

"Be quiet, Rounder. I'll feed you when I'm ready."

Rounder hissed and plodded out of the bedroom while Tarin walked to the window, scanned the section of Willow Road he lived on for anything unusual. Seeing nothing, he closed the curtains and headed to the dresser.

"What in Arvalast was going on last night?" he whispered while he put on his shirt. "I've never seen anything like those three shadows before." Chills tingled up his back, chills he tried to ignore while he tugged on some brown breeches.

"Good morning."

Tarin spun around at the voice. Ella, his seventeen-year-old sister, stood at the door. He grunted, and decided to make his bed.

"I see you're having a fine morning, my darling little brother."

He beat the lumps from his pillows. "You need something?"

Squealing, "Just a hug!" she rushed into the room and pulled him into her arms. In one awkward motion, he dove away, rolled across the top of his bed and fell off the other side, then poked his head over the top of his mattress. "You know I don't like to be touched!"

Ella lifted her nose. "That's precisely why I did." She retreated to the doorway. "When you're finished in here, come down to breakfast. Father wants to see you."

He climbed onto his bed and brushed at the wrinkles in his blankets. "What does *he* want?"

"You'll have to find out yourself." She checked her appearance in the dusty mirror near the door, then left the room.

He crossed his eyes at her back and stuck out his tongue, then finished his bed and slouched down the stairs, Rounder following.

Kandis, their burly lumberjack father, sat at the dining room table. "Tarin! Come, have some breakfast. Got something to tell you."

Tarin kept his usual silence, but went to the table.

"So," Kandis said, "I heard you were out late last night. Eavesdropping at old Bill's again?"

Tarin wedged a fork piled with eggs into his mouth and nodded.

"That old codger can really spin a yarn, but I've got one for you. Care to hear it?"

Tarin gobbled up more eggs and offered another nod.

Kandis put a large piece of bacon in his mouth, chewed and swallowed. "Now . . . I'm not sure if you heard, but we have some interesting visitors in town. Outsiders, from the north. Two of them. They dress rather funny. Big cloaks and hoods. Though they keep the hoods off most of the time."

Tarin nearly choked. "Are their cloaks red?"

Kandis raised a brow. "Nothing gaudy as that. Brown. Why do you ask?"

"Oh." He shifted his gaze to the nearby fireplace. "No reason."

"I heard they carry swords under those cloaks. Interesting, don't you think?" Kandis tossed a piece of bacon to Rounder as he spoke. "Don't know much else about them, except they say they're heralds to," his voice quieted, "the king."

Tarin looked his father in the eyes. "The king himself? But why would he send heralds here to Woodend?"

Kandis smiled and reached into his pocket, pulled out a shiny glass phial. "Perhaps because I asked him to."

Tarin leaned away from the table, remembering a similar phial in the hands of the bald man he'd seen the previous night. But unlike his father's illumina, which he'd known of since he was a boy, the bald man's had glowed red, not white. Why, he didn't know, nor did he care at the moment. But whatever the color of the little objects, they made him uneasy.

"Please, put it away," he said. "All those things do is cause problems. Remember the old governor and the Royal Decree? He demanded that everyone who had one of those give it up. And when they didn't, there was nothing but trouble."

Kandis lowered his head and sighed. "Governor Bolard was a confused man. Illuminas didn't create all those problems. It was something else."

He put away the phial and stood. "You're almost fifteen, and I feel like I can speak to you as an adult. I don't want to scare you, but I've been uneasy about something for a long time. It's almost as if a darkness is spreading throughout the city. I had this same feeling three years ago, just before the

Royal Decree and Bolard's madness. That time, the king used Sheriff Jebin to drive away the darkness. But now, it appears he's sent his own heralds to intervene. You know what that means, don't you?"

Tarin didn't reply.

"It means that *this* time, something even worse is about to happen." He patted his pocket. "I'd feel a lot better if you had your own illumina. You're old enough now, you need to understand how I know all this."

Anger spiraled up through Tarin's body. He loathed it when his father tried to guilt him into accepting an illumina. He didn't want one. They only brought trouble. When he wanted information or understanding, he went out and got it through whatever means he deemed appropriate. And subtle.

Kandis stood and began to pace. "I can see you're uneasy. Don't worry, I'm not trying to make you accept one. But there is something I'd like you to do for me." He stopped pacing and looked at him. When he spoke again, his voice was a whisper. "Son, you've always had a flair for figuring things out, even things you have no business knowing. Don't tell your mother, but if you want, you have my permission to find out as much as you can about these two heralds. Even if it means a little eavesdropping."

Kandis winked and left the room. Tarin could scarcely believe what he'd heard. His father actually considered his eavesdropping obsession a *talent?*

Rounder scuffled next to him and rubbed against his leg. "What do you think, Rounder?" he said. "Should I eavesdrop on the northerners?"

Rounder looked at him with disinterest.

"It'll be tricky. I've never spied on messengers from a king before."

The cat belched and fell to one side. He reached down and scratched the cat's belly, then peered out the window. The sounds of the village filled the room as people walked by the house and carts clattered along the road. He whispered, "I just hope I don't get bothered by the village idiots, especially those ridiculous boys who chased me last night."

However, the young ruffians weren't the only people of whom he was leery. The bald man and red-cloaked stranger were still heavy on his mind. And the shadows.

He continued to stare out the window, wondering if he should chance going outside. But the sun was bright, the sky blue. Certainly it would be safe as long as it was light.

He left Rounder on the floor and grabbed his old leather jacket, donned it as he slid out the front door and hurried down the street. Just before he reached the main road, as was his way, he scurried into an alley.

✝ ✝ ✝

Sheriff Jebin looked out across Lockspell Lake. Across the rippling water, smoke plumes drifted from chimneys scattered along the distant shore. There lay the tiny fishing settlement of Northlake. He'd never been there, but knew the only way to reach the settlement was to travel a narrow forest road connected to the highway between Lockspell and Woodend.

"Sir Jebin?"

Jebin pulled his eyes away from the flock of geese descending onto the lake, and turned to see a thin man whose formal dress of a white vest over a red-collared shirt spoke of royalty.

"I am the governor's liaison," the man said. "Thank you for your patience. I can take you to Governor Dierop now."

Jebin followed the man into the lakeside town hall, through a sky-lit chamber full of portraits and paintings, and finally into a room with a window overseeing what he recognized as Lockspell's main road. A gnarled old man sat behind a mahogany desk. Each of his fingers rested upon its partner on the other hand. He stared at Jebin with a glint in his eye.

"You bring me a boy, Diggory?" the man said. "Someone so young is to lead my town after me?"

Jebin stood tall and met the old man's eyes with confidence. "I'm hardly a boy, good sir."

Governor Dierop smiled and waved Diggory out of the room. "Please, Sir Jebin, sit."

He obliged.

"As you know, I plan to retire at the end of the month. I ordered my colleagues to search this forest for a worthy replacement, a man who would ensure that Lockspell remains prosperous and peaceful. As the primary trading post for all of Maplelake Forest, in my eyes, that makes it the most important city in the region. You've been selected out of many worthy candidates. As I understand, you've already informed your present governor of your intentions?"

"I have," Jebin said. "The letter likely reached Governor Willerdon yesterday. I'm sure he's already making preparations for a new sheriff."

"You've already brought your family here. They like the city?"

Jebin smiled. "They *adore* the city. As I'm sure you've heard, Woodend recently went through some tumultuous times. The quality of life here is better. But through the leadership of Willerdon and myself, I feel it is stable enough for me to move on."

"And you shall," Dierop said, then stood. "The council of this town selected you because of your strong leadership during Woodend's time of trouble. They feel you will be equally diligent in your efforts here."

Dierop glanced sideways out the window and narrowed his eyes. "I plan to leave Lockspell shortly after I turn the governorship over to you. Within a month." He patted his chest. "Leading the city is becoming too strenuous for this old heart. I will regret it." As he spoke, he walked to the window and closed the shutters on either side. The room darkened.

Without proper light, the study was foreboding. Feeling uneasy, Jebin said, "Where do you plan to go?"

Dierop walked to the map and pointed to its upper left side. A red line extended from a place labeled Macalum, near the bottom, up toward the top, which was filled with circles representing trees and labeled Maplelake Forest. Where Dierop pointed, a great ocean touched the western regions of Maplelake.

Dierop sighed. "I plan to go there when I leave Lockspell. I hear it's . . . warm." He moved his finger to the red line, traced it down to its source. "I will most certainly not be going there. He touched the "M" on Macalum. "Though it would be even warmer, I abhor the south."

Jebin looked at the man. Dierop suddenly appeared so . . . feeble. Tired. *But also, so afraid.* "Why do you loathe the south?" he asked. "Are there rumors of trouble there?"

Dierop lifted his hand. "Please, sir, don't speak to me about rumors. Most of what I hear every day is a rumor, about some horrible event or dark terror on the verge of destroying the world. After all, merchants from all of Northern Arvalast frequent this town, and they are known for their embellishments."

He left the map, walked over to Jebin and laid his hand on his shoulder. "No, there's no mystery. I only hate the south because all goods that come from there are terribly overpriced." He smiled and patted Jebin's back. "Diggory will now see you back to the inn, and he'll give you and your family the grand tour of Lockspell."

Jebin stood, and bowed.

Diggory was waiting. As he turned to follow Diggory to the door leading to the main road, he glimpsed Dierop out of the corner of his eye. The smile was gone, in its stead a haggard worry. Yet the unrest this brought Jebin was trifling compared to an already heavy burden within his heart. Taking this job was the right decision for him, and for his family. He just wished he didn't feel so much like a traitor to Woodend.

Four

Tarin crouched behind a crate of hay and stared at the two-story inn on the other side of the main road. He'd never been inside it, but knew it held a large social hall. Townsmen and a few merchants mingled near the front door. Farmers were setting up their produce stands. He hoped the crisp morning sunshine would offer him a glimpse of two cloaked men, or perhaps the glimmer of their swords.

After an hour of patient waiting, he shifted his weight to find a more comfortable position when something wet, squishy, and memorable smacked his face. He wiped the slime from his eyes and saw three boys standing in the middle of the road.

"Hey, tomato face!" one of them chanted.

"Thought you might be hungry for more!" another added.

The third just stared, and his face, a familiar face, grew pale in recognition.

The boy who vomited last night! Tarin thought.

Another tomato splattered on his nose. He clenched his fist and felt blood surge into his head.

"Hey, Sarky," one of the boys said to the pale boy. "I'm out of tomatoes. Got another one?"

Sarky ignored him.

The boy slapped Sarky on the back of the head. "Hey, you deaf? Gimme another one!"

Sarky looked confused, glanced nervously at Tarin, then reached into a large pocket on the front of his shirt and flipped a tomato to his companion.

Tarin prepared to charge when a cloaked man with shoulder-length blond hair swept toward the boy with the tomato and snatched it from his uplifted hand.

"Hey," the boy yelled. "Give that back!"

"Certainly," the man said, then squeezed the tomato and let its juice spray onto the boy's head. "Have what is yours."

The boy turned to Sarky and the other boy, seething. "Did you see what that fellow just did to me?"

"Yeah," the other boy said. He drew his own tomato from beneath his shirt and pulled back his arm.

Tarin braced, even as he wondered at the man's strange accent.

Another man, this one's appearance nearly identical to the first but with dark hair, snatched the missile from the boy's hand. "Ah," the new man said with the same accent as the other. "A beautiful, ripe tomato. And I was so hungry." He took a large bite from the fruit, chewed to let his saliva mix with its juice, then set the moist object back onto its owner's hand. "Do try some. Quite delicious."

The boy shook with disgust and let the tomato fall to the ground. "Let's get out of here! These men are crazy!"

He and the other boy ran down the main road. Sarky, though, charged directly toward Tarin. Before Tarin could react, Sarky grabbed his shoulders and looked him in the eyes. "What happened last night? What was in that alley with you?"

Tarin tried to back away, but Sarky held tight.

"You saw the same as I did," Tarin blurted. "Some stranger in a red cloak. I don't know who he was or why he was there."

"There was something else!" Sarky shot back. "I didn't see it, but I could feel it. It made me sick, that's why I threw up. I couldn't help myself."

"Is that lad annoying you?"

Tarin looked up and saw the black-haired man pointing at them.

Sarky spun around. "I'm not doing anything of the sort, you ruffian! I'm . . . I'm just . . ." Tears filled his eyes, and he ran away.

The man with light hair walked up to his counterpart and snickered. "Was that a lad or a lass? His face would suggest lad, but his voice, a lass."

The black-haired man crossed his arms. "Perhaps it's a lass with a most disturbing face? Or maybe a lad with a most unfortunate voice."

"How can a voice be unfortunate?"

"Because it leads me, an exceedingly quick-witted soul, into a state of confusion."

"Indeed. Most unfortunate. But more unfortunate is the lad behind the barrel who seems to have received tomato to the face."

Tarin saw the man's eyes turn his way.

"Boy, come here."

Tarin debated whether to heed the command. But with Sarky's outburst of fright at seeing the man, he was more curious than ever about his strange encounters the previous night. He walked out from behind the crate and approached the men, excited to see the shapes of swords beneath their cloaks.

"I am Ristun," the black-haired man said. He held out his hand toward the other man. "And this is Dralo."

The blond man bowed his head.

"We are here on special business from yonder," Ristun pointed north. "Lands you likely know little about." He looked at Tarin with a glint in his eye. "Now tell me, why were those boys so merciless to you? Have you offended them?"

Tarin didn't want to be silent, but his mouth grew dry and his hands trembled beneath rivulets of sweat.

Dralo noticed. "Why do you shake?"

Ristun chuckled and placed his hand on Tarin's shoulder. "Are we that terrifying?"

Tarin pulled away and gave the man a look he hoped was intimidating.

"Hmmm," Ristun said. "That's not the kindest way to react to a stranger's attempt to earn trust."

Dralo knelt to Tarin's eye-level and held him in a gaze both kind and powerful. "There's something about you, young man. Something that makes me . . . uneasy."

"Dralo," Ristun said with surprise. "I've always considered you a brave soul. What has stolen away your courage that you might be afraid of a mere lad, and a quaking one at that?"

Tarin watched as Dralo lifted his eyes back toward the alley. "It is not the lad who makes me uneasy, Ristun."

Tarin felt a prickle begin on his skin. Before he drew up enough courage to turn and look himself, Dralo returned his gaze to him. And then, inexplicably, he smiled. "We'll want to tell Gildareth about this one."

"Gildareth comes tomorrow," Ristun said, "correct?"

"Yes. He'll meet us in the social hall. That is, if he isn't hindered." He glanced at Tarin. "I wonder, boy, do you know what might be stalling our comrade? You live here, and I assume you know the region fairly well."

All he could manage was to sputter, "Bear?"

Dralo's eyes narrowed. "You have not, perhaps, seen anything strange in the area lately, have you?"

"What . . . what do you mean, *strange?*"

Dralo stood and peered down at him. "Think no more about it. Your name, lad, what is it?"

"Tarin, sir."

"I see. It's good to meet you, Tarin." He bowed and walked toward the inn. Ristun followed, leaving Tarin in the middle of the road, awestruck by his encounter with the two northerners but abandoned with yet another question: *Who is Gildareth?*

He heard a cart approaching and retreated to his crate. From behind it he peeked into the alley, just to make sure no shadows clung to the walls, then looked back toward the road. A book he hadn't noticed before rested where he'd just stood, and the cart was quick approaching it.

Thinking Dralo or Ristun must have dropped it, he hurried back to the road, grabbed the book and ran back to the alley. The cart rattled along behind him.

He sat behind the crate and wiped some grime from the book's worn leather cover. *The Annals of Illuminara*, it said in large letters, then in smaller letters below, "As Recorded by Ollervand, Guard of the Citadel."

Tarin's skin tingled harder now.

✝ ✝ ✝

T hen Farmer Gibby says, 'No, I can't sell you any extra beef this year. We had a bad summer and the cows are too lean. And I've promised the Keder family I'd save them the rations you're asking for.' So I tell him I can't help that the Keder woman decided to thrust her and her husband into poverty by having seven children! Seven, Governor! If you ask me, the Keders deserve to starve this winter. Anyway, I have myself and my cats and my—"

"Come now, Gertrude," Will said wearily to the pig-like woman across his desk. "You can't mean you actually want the Keders to starve."

"Of course not!"

Will rubbed his temples. "But you just said—"

"I said they deserve to starve. But they won't. Nor would I let them. I have some old cabbage in the pantry. And because I'm such a caring woman, I plan to have the Keders over every day this winter for some warm cabbage stew. If they help me clean my house."

"But don't you think the beef Gibby's selling them would better suit a large family?"

She crossed her arms on her rotund belly. "Perhaps. But then, dear governor, what would I eat? And what would my babies eat?"

"I wasn't aware you had any children."

"I speak of my animals, sir." She leaned down over the desk. "They *are* my babies."

She smelled so strongly of perfume mixed with sweat, Will nearly gagged.

"You do realize," she continued, "I'm an influential person in this city. You don't want to lose my support at a time like this."

Will leaned back in his chair. "I'm not sure I understa—"

Gertrude laughed. "Come now, Willerdon. Don't be naive. It's Jebin they wanted for governor. For some reason, he chose to allow *you* to rule after Bolard was cast away. But things haven't gone well since you took office. People blame you for the food shortages we're going to have this winter."

"I cannot control the weather, madam."

"But," her lips twisted into a horrible smile, "you *can* ensure that the people who matter most aren't affected by this shortage. People who could make your governorship easy . . . or difficult."

Will's throat tightened. "I'll see what I can do."

"Excellent! I've always liked you, Governor. So caring. Always quick to listen to reason." She stood, waved her hand, and lumbered out of the room.

He grimaced and shook off the needles her presence had somehow lodged into his skin. "What she really means," he mumbled to himself, "is that I'm easily manipulated—that I'm a coward."

He shuffled through his jacket, pulled out a key and opened one of his desk drawers. A stack of bound paper rested inside, under a parcel containing his day's agenda. Just visible beneath the thin top sheet, "Royal Decree" appeared in flowing letters. With a sigh, he crossed "Meeting with Gertrude" from the agenda and looked at the next entry: "Meeting with Mr. and Mrs. Keder." His eye twitched.

The door to his office swung open. He half expected to see the Keders, but his wife and son stood in the doorway. "Lianna, Dibbs, what—?"

"Will," Lianna said as she pulled the ten-year-old Dibbs into the room. She closed the door behind her. Dibbs staggered. Lianna steadied him.

"Look at this," she said, and lifted the boy's shirt.

Will narrowed his eyes and drew closer. "What are those marks?"

She ran her finger over the four shallow-but-long nicks across Dibbs' back. "He said he got them last night. He says he had a nightmare, but won't tell me anything else."

Will took Dibbs' shoulders. "Son, what happened?"

"You . . . wouldn't understand."

There was a knock at the door. Will looked up. "What now?"

Dibbs stepped back into his mother's arms. "You're too *busy* to understand."

Lianna glared at Will. "Can't you put aside your meetings today and help me figure out what happened?"

"Governor Willerdon," a man's voice said from behind the door. "It's the Keders. May we come in?"

Will stood. "Dibbs doesn't seem to want to talk about it, and I won't waste time trying to make him. I'll meet with the Keders. It won't take long. Perhaps in the meantime, you can encourage him to talk to me."

Scowling, Lianna hurried Dibbs out the side door leading from Will's office to the master bedroom. Will thought about going after her, but the renewed rapping at the door stopped him. With a sigh, he opened the door. "Good afternoon, Mr. Keder, Mrs. Keder. Please, come in."

FIVE

An owl hooted overhead, and Tarin looked up to see the sun setting. Had he really been here all day in this alley, poring over *The Annals of Illuminara?* The time had gone so fast! Yet, he knew why.

The mysterious book held tales of monsters, wars, kings and prophecies. He had no idea what all the stories meant, or even if they were true, but they fascinated him.

He stood and peered into the nearly empty main road. Just an old man in a heavy leather coat and a young fellow holding an axe. Both stood next to a cart full of timber. Neither seemed interested in anything but their conversation.

He moved to enter the main road, but stopped when the old man said, "Let's leave the cart here for now, Jak me fine nephew. I'm not one to break me word. I promised an interestin' tale, and that's what I'll deliver."

An interesting tale? Tarin's ears perked up.

The man named Jak threw his axe into the cart, and followed his uncle into the inn.

Tarin darted to the side of the building and peeped into a window. Then he muttered "Dern it all!" He was looking into a hallway. He couldn't see a thing from here. He wouldn't enter the place though. It was too full of people. He'd need to find another way to spy.

He ran a few yards and looked into another window. Still the hallway. He continued around the back of the building, where the walls were taller to accommodate the social hall. He peeped through the first window he came across. Inside was a large room full of people drinking ale and smoking pipes. In the center of the room was a huge fire pit with four pillars holding up a spherical chimney. At the far end of the room was a bar with stools. Nearly half were full.

A fat bartender was sweeping the room with his eyes, presumably looking for empty glasses, when Tarin saw him notice the newcomers.

When he saw which table the barkeep directed them to, he cursed. It was on the opposite side of the social hall, too far away to overhear.

He ran down the street, rounded the corner of the inn into an alley, and found a smudged window near the table his storytellers were headed. He held his breath and carefully lifted it just far enough to hear the bustle inside the room, then squatted down, but not so far he couldn't see over the lip of the windowsill. Through the foggy glass, he watched Jak and his uncle take a seat at the table. The older man lifted his hand to the bartender and said, "Give me the strongest stuff ye got."

"That'd be our Bull Slayer, Kane, and you know that well. Always makes you a bit sick, though. Sure you want it?"

"'Course I do!"

"I'll take some regular ale," Jak said.

"I'll let ye try some of my Bull Slayer," Kane said. "Maybe it'll loosen ye up a bit. Help ye be brave, maybe even get a girl."

Jak squirmed. "Can we just begin the stories?"

Kane stretched his arms, then crossed his legs. "Not yet. We'll wait for Salahan. Ye remember, the fellow I mentioned last night? He said he'd meet us here 'bout this time."

The ale came, as well as the Bull Slayer, and Jak and Kane indulged themselves with dull talk of business and worthless banter about distant relations. Tarin decided partway through the trite conversation to lie down on the alley floor and wait for Salahan. A discarded bag of chicken feathers, likely left in the alley by some butcher, sufficed as a pillow, and the darkening sky and twinkling stars lulled him into complacency. When his eyes began flitting closed and open, he heard a loud voice holler from inside the inn, "Salahan, old boy, over here!" He jerked upright and rubbed his eyes.

"I brought me nephew here so ye can teach him a bit about what's goin' on outside the forest. And I knew there's not a better fella to open his eyes to the real world than ye."

"You flatter me, Kane," Salahan said with a hearty laugh. "But even I know little about the whole of Arvalast, save for rumors I hear in my travels. And I've yet to witness or experience anything to suggest my sources speak truthfully."

Salahan spoke with an accent Tarin had never heard before, and sounded too articulate to be friends with the imbecilic Kane. He lifted his head and peeped through the window. The man sitting next to Jak had dark skin against a colorful button-down shirt. His head was shaved, and tiny gold earrings dotted each ear. Tarin smiled. Such an interesting-looking man would have intriguing stories.

"All right, just tell Jak what ye told me," Kane said. "Tell him 'bout the warrior from Macalum ye met in Mahotholin."

"First," Salahan said, "some of the geography outside Maplelake Forest. Lad, you're familiar with Mahotholin, yes?"

Jak nodded. "Indeed, sir, though I've never been there. It's the southernmost town in our forest."

"Good, because it was there I encountered the warrior from Macalum. Now, are you familiar with Macalum?"

"All I know is that it's a realm far to the south, beyond the Great Plains. Very few from the forest have ever traveled there. Nor do the Macalumese travel here. No need. Merchants enact all business between the two regions."

"That's true. Usually, the people of Macalum don't venture so far north. *Usually*. Things are changing, though. In Mahotholin, I met a man named Varla. He's a palace guard at Macalum's capital city of Farloth. He tells me that war is afoot in the south."

"Aha!" Kane blurted. "Told ye, Jak! There's a lot more goin' on in the world than we know."

"But this doesn't concern us, Uncle. A war so far south would never affect the forest."

"You're correct," Salahan replied. "But let me ask you this. If this forest truly has no reason to fear such a war, why has the Macalumese high governor sent a battalion of warriors, including Varla, to this forest?"

The table went quiet. "I haven't any idea," Jak finally said. "Unless the war is somehow greater than I originally thought."

Salahan took a sip of ale, then stroked his thin braided beard. "Varla told me that Macalum still fares well against their enemies. But, something has indeed happened that makes them concerned for this forest. A year ago, an odd battalion of red-garbed warriors managed to break through Macalum's defenses and travel north, through the mountains along Macalum's southern border. Word spread that this army was somehow inhuman."

"Inhuman," Jak said. "How—?"

"According to the rumors, it cast madness on all who drew too near its camps. I could scarce believe it myself, but nonetheless . . . the high governor found few men brave enough to confront this foe. So he demanded that all guards retreat to the capital city of Farloth and prepare for siege. But . . . here's where it turns strange . . . rather than attacking, the red army bypassed the city and disappeared into the northern plains! For a few months, tales drifted south of a red terror sweeping through the northern grasses and pillaging at will. These were no rumors. The attacks left burnt farms and ruined fields to confirm what was told.

"Eventually, Mahotholin, one of your own cities, claimed to see the red battalion enter the forest. Macalum's food supply was already in danger because of the burnt fields in the plains. It couldn't afford to lose its trade with Maplelake. The high governor feels his enemy has finally realized that if this land is destroyed, Macalum will fall soon after."

Jak squirmed in his chair. "So, you believe there's an entire army of red-cloaked warriors hiding in the woods even now?"

"No, I'm *certain* of it." Salahan's eyes were bright with conviction. "Varla and his band have already hunted down and killed a number of them. But they've yet to find their hideout."

"That's why I told ye we need a stronger governor!" Kane growled to Jak. "Willerdon would never stand against trained fighters like those surely are."

Salahan tilted his head. "Why do you look to your governor for protection? I thought all in Maplelake still trusted in the king ... the one the south long ago abandoned as myth."

Kane slammed his fist against the table. Utensils clanged and others in the hall looked over. Tarin ducked lower to avoid any stray gaze, but kept one eye on Kane.

"I trust in no king," Kane hissed. "I used to, when I was a silly boy like me nephew. I even had one of them illuminas. But the cruel world taught me better. No king, unless he was too weak to rule proper-like, would let his land get so out of control as this forest gets sometimes. Many years ago, I threw out my illumina and trusted in my own strengths and wiles. It's done pretty good for me."

A man approached the table from behind Kane and placed a hand on Kane's shoulder. Tarin's heart flipped in recognition. It was the bald man from last night!

Kane turned around and swatted the man's hand off his shoulder. "What do ye want, ye skin head?"

A smile slid across the man's clean-shaven face. "Though it is indeed possible to trust in man's strength for security, true strength will only come from one source, and that is the king." He turned to Salahan. "And this king is by no means a myth. All the south will know this very soon."

"Foolishness!" Kane blurted. "There is no king."

"Then why," said the man as he reached for his pocket, "does his light still shine?"

Tarin saw something in the man's pocket grow bright red, but the glow wasn't strong enough to disturb any of the inn's guests. He felt awed by the glow, and an odd desire to see the source of the light swept thorough him. The others at the table leaned closer to the glow.

"I can see you all find the king's power quite . . . attractive."

"Show me that light," Kane said, holding out his hand. "Maybe I'll take back some of what I said if ye let me touch it."

"I cannot show you this illumina at the moment." The man opened his free hand toward the center of the room. "It might attract the interest of those not ready to embrace the king's new way." He removed his other hand from his pocket; the light within grew dark.

Jak rubbed his eyes. "Your illumina made me feel . . . strange." He looked up at the bald man. "May I ask, who are you, and how did you acquire such an odd illumina?"

The man smiled. "I'm sure you'll find your answers soon, if you look hard enough." He turned to Salahan. "I see you're a merchant. Be careful upon the road. I hear it's dangerous these days."

He bowed, then strode across the room and out the door on the other side.

"Who be you?"

Tarin sucked in a quick breath. Kane's question was directed at him!

His feet tussled backward and he tripped over himself while Kane hollered curses and tugged at the window, trying to open it farther and succeeding just as Tarin regained his footing and scurried down the alley in the direction of the main road. Had he not run into a wall made of flesh, he would've gotten away.

"I *knew* I saw a face in the window," a familiar voice said.

Tarin stumbled back a few paces and looked up at the hooded face. It was Dralo, the light-haired northerner.

"What have you there?" Dralo asked.

"Uhh, I have . . ." he glanced at the object under his arm. "A book."

"What is it called?"

"The . . . *The Annals of Illuminara.*"

"It isn't yours. A friend of ours will need it soon."

Tarin cautiously lifted the book toward the man. Dralo took it and inspected the cover.

"Did you enjoy your read?"

Tarin wasn't sure what to say, and muttered something not even he understood.

"Alas," Dralo said. "It's clear that you're not gifted in speech, but if I'm not mistaken, you have a sharp mind." He glared at him. "And even sharper eyes." He began flipping through the pages of the *Annals*. "Pray tell, Tarin, did you happen upon a prophecy while reading this?"

Tarin thought for a moment, and his eyes widened in realization. "Yes, sir. I did."

Dralo knelt. "Lad, I hope to meet you again. Perhaps next time you will meet our comrade, Gildareth. He comes tomorrow evening. But for now, farewell."

Dralo turned and hurried down the main road. Tarin peered around, saw the road was finally empty and began to run, hoping to make it back home without any more adventure.

Six

Jebin awoke to the sound of thunder, and looked out the window near his bed. Lockspell Lake hid beneath a curtain of rain. A fishing dinghy busily worked its way toward the nearest dock, its sole fisherman trying to get the craft back to shore before it grew waterlogged.

Jebin felt motion on the other side of the bed. His wife Rosie was awake.

"Good morning, dear," he said, and kissed her forehead. She yawned and glanced outside.

"Another rainy day," she said. "I'm glad we got our tour of the city yesterday. It was so beautiful! Much nicer than Woodend."

"And wealthier," Jebin added. "But that's to be expected with all the merchants who live here. They buy for little, then sell for much. They accumulate wealth, while the rest of the people barely can afford to eat. A rather unwholesome process, I think."

Rosie patted his hand. "But now I'm married to the man who can change all that. A most worthy and noble governor!"

He sighed. "Are you sure I'm as *noble and worthy* as you deem?"

She got out of bed and began changing from her nightgown into a long white blouse. "If anyone deserves this position, you do." She turned and looked him in the eye. "You were the only leader Woodend could turn to during that deplorable decree of Bolard's. If not for you, the king's way would've been destroyed in the city. You're one of the few who had the courage to stand and fight when nearly all others wanted to give in to the Royal Decree. Even Willerdon fell short."

Jebin stood and drew the curtains across the window, walked to a set of drawers in the corner of the room and pulled out a clean shirt. "Will only wanted peace. He never intended to compromise his loyalty to the king. He's a good man, and I know he'll lead Woodend well."

She pulled a blue dress over her blouse and approached him, took his hand in hers. "And you will lead Lockspell even better."

"Rosie," he said softly, "you know I only accepted this position to get away from Woodend . . . to escape the past." He felt a warm tear slide down his cheek. "I'm a murderer, Rosie. I've killed to uphold the way of the king. And by doing so, I violated some of the very morals I profess to follow."

He turned away. Her hand slipped from his. "You were in the midst of a great battle," she said to his back. "You were only defending yourself and your loved ones from a tyrant. The king forgives what happened. You know that."

He sat on the bed. "I know it, but in my heart, I feel only anger from the throne. I cannot escape it."

A door slammed. He quickly wiped his eyes and looked over at the bedroom's entrance. Their seven-year-old daughter, Maddie, stood in the opening, wearing a huge smile. She rushed to the bed and jumped into his arms. "Hello, Father. May I please have a ride?"

He chuckled, hoisted her onto his shoulders, then spun around a few times. Soon they toppled back onto the bed and laughed heartily.

"Father, why are your eyes wet? Are you sad?"

Rosie slid onto the bed and kissed Maddie's cheek. "He's not sad, he was just . . . laughing too hard. Where are your brothers?"

"They're trying to see who can eat the most chicken bones. I think it's a game."

"What! You mean the bones I threw out after supper last night?" Rosie got up and ran out the door. "Get those out of your mouths!" she shouted on her way down the hall. "They're filthy!"

Jebin whistled. "I think she's angry."

"I agree," Maddie said. She stood and began bouncing on the bed. "Know what I saw out my window last night?"

"I can't say. Perhaps a boat, or some rain?"

"Both of those," she said between bounces. "But I also saw something in the air, something huge!"

"A bird?"

"No. Too big for a bird. And it didn't have any feathers. Just lots of hair." She stopped jumping and landed on her butt with a huff and a sigh. "I think it was carrying a deer in its arms."

Jebin looked at her. "The thing had arms? Dear, I think you were dreaming again. Now why don't you go get some breakfast?"

She giggled. "You mean some chicken bones."

"No, no, no. Don't follow your brothers' naughty ways. It makes your mother crazy. Get some fruit." He nudged her gently with his elbow. "Run along."

She jumped off the bed and skipped from the room. For a moment, he pondered her story. Though she often told him of her dreams, this one was amazingly descriptive. He went to the window and peered out toward the lake. All was serene. He shook his head and chuckled. "Easy, old boy. Can't start believing in monsters now. Wouldn't be becoming of a governor."

He retrieved his jacket from a coat stand in the corner of the room. Then he, too, went to breakfast.

✝ ✝ ✝

In the walled city Jebin had fled in self-imposed shame, a father and son sat having their own breakfast. But at the moment, the father was too entranced to eat.

Tarin found it exceptionally easy to talk on this dreary, damp morning. He'd already told his father everything he knew about the northerners, Dralo and Ristun, and was beginning to recap some of what he remembered from *The Annals of Illuminara*.

"There was this great city of Arvalast," he said, "and it was ruled by a great king. But the king never showed himself. He only told the people what he wanted through his high governor, Allestille. Apparently, evil forces from the south were always trying to destroy Illuminara. But they weren't regular folk like you and I. They possessed powers to manipulate people's minds. And they were invisible to almost everyone. Only the greatest warriors of Illuminara, called the spectril, could stand up against the evil forces. And that was only because the king had given the city a special orb of light. It rested in a tall tower, in a citadel in the center of Illuminara."

Kandis reached for an apple resting on the table and bit into it. "Please, continue."

Tarin closed his eyes, trying to recall what he'd read next, but the middle of the book was hard to remember because a couple of drunks had started arguing in the street just then.

"I *think* the *Annals* said that the lord of the south, called Wrathar, realized he'd never win on strength alone. So he snuck some of his strongest warriors into the city. So they could gain access to the people's minds, you see. If I remember right, the warriors were called sentinels. Anyway, the sentinels corrupted the minds of some of the strongest spectril. Eventually the spectril began fighting among themselves. This weakened the city's defenses.

"Wrathar attacked the city for a whole month before he finally managed to get in. He headed straight to the citadel, because he wanted to destroy the orb of light. But when he got there, the tower was already broken into, and the light was gone. But . . . a prophecy was written in blood beneath the shards of glass. It said something about the reawakening of the spectril sometime in the distant future. And oh, it also said that wouldn't happen until three servants of the king prepared the way for three warriors of the light, whatever that means. The three warriors are supposed to create an army that destroys Wrathar and all his followers."

Kandis stuffed the apple core in his mouth and chewed it up.

"Father!"

Kandis spat the partially chewed core onto the table and wiped his mouth, grimacing. "Ugh. Got too interested in your story." He went to the kitchen and came back with a cloth, cleaned up the mess and sat back down. "There. Now I won't face your mother's ire."

Both of them chuckled, then he said, "Interesting story you found in that book. The *Annals*, was it? Remember anything else?"

Tarin shook his head. "It went into much more detail than I just did. *Much.* Though I do remember that, at the end, it said there are other pieces of the *Annals*, and that the reader should seek them out."

Kandis scratched his beard. "I *would* like to know what these other books have to say. And I would very much like to read the one you already have."

He stood and headed toward the front door, lifted his coat from a nearby stool and picked up his axe, which was leaning against the wall. "But, I've got to go to work now. When I get back, I think I'll go to the inn and talk to these northerners myself. They sound like decent enough folk."

"If you think *odd* is the same as *decent*," Tarin replied. "That Dralo is really strange. Says I make him uneasy, though he's twice my size and carries a sword."

Kandis chuckled. "I work with odd people every day." Smiling, he opened the door and headed toward the road. The rain was fast subsiding.

Tarin picked up some toast and began daydreaming about the *Annals*. All in all, it was turning into a pleasant morning. But when footsteps began tapping down the stairs, his heart sank.

"Good morning, little brother."

He hunched his shoulders and took another bite of toast. Something wet and soft touched the back of his neck. He swatted the spot and heard a yelp. His face grew hot.

Ella smacked him across the back of the head. "I was only giving you a kiss. You don't have to hit me."

He stood and faced her. "Why would you ever *do* such a thing! Do you really think I'd want the most disgusting part of your face touching my neck?"

She glared at him. "Your ridiculous loathing of touch is going to really make your life difficult someday. How is anyone ever going to show you love?"

"By leaving, me, *alone*," he growled.

"In that case," she walked over to the chair where their father had been sitting and sat down, "I'll scorn you with my presence."

He clenched his fists and sat back down, having no desire to let his sister gain a victory by driving him from the table. He stuffed the rest of the toast in his mouth and chewed with his mouth open wide. She scowled.

More footsteps came down the stairs.

"Good morning, children," their mother Raina said. "I see you found the breakfast I left out for you. I do say, I'm getting ripe lazy in my old age. I nearly slept 'til sunup! That left me with barely enough time to make breakfast, wake your father, clean the kitchen, make the bed, let out the cat, *and clean up the dog's accident.*"

Raina looked at Tarin. "By the way, please remember to let the dog out before you go to bed tonight. I'm growing weary of finding little dog logs on my kitchen floor each morning."

Tarin groaned. "That should be Ella's job. The dog is hers. Rounder's mine, and I take good care of him."

"Don't argue with me." Raina pulled a towel from her apron pocket. "You stay up latest, so it makes sense that *you* let out the dog." She began cleaning the already clean table.

"That's right, little brother." Ella smirked at him.

"I'm done," he said, and hurried toward the front door. "I'll be back later."

"Don't miss lunch today," Raina called out. "I don't want to have to save you food if you're not coming home to eat it."

He ignored her and ran to the road. Today, he had a special mission: to find out more about this Gildareth fellow the northerners had mentioned, the man they claimed was coming that very day.

SEVEN

Kandis sat on a stump near the edge of the lumber camp. His axe rested on the stump to his left, his lunch pail on the ground to his right. He'd already emptied the pail of its contents, and was now finding it difficult to motivate his legs to stand. He stared out through tired eyes at the well-trodden path leading from the camp to the main forest road, thinking about the sea of tree stumps behind him while he listened to the rhythmic sound of axes against wood, the heartbeat of the lumber camp. Oddly, it was the death of trees that gave the camp its life, and what made it profitable to him and the other lumberjacks of Woodend. As each axe stroke pounded into his ears, he felt his eyes close. Gradually, the sounds grew quieter and more distant.

"Taking an early lunch, are you?"

Kandis started and nearly fell off the stump. He turned and saw Lionnel, his fellow lumberjack and best friend, wearing a sly grin beneath a wool cap.

Kandis looked at the pail. "Guess I did have an early lunch." He sighed. "Pity. I'm still a bit hungry."

Lionnel flipped him a ripe red apple and sat next to him. "Already eaten five of the little devils, and I'm starting to feel sick. I'm also getting sick of the others grumbling about the governor." He gestured toward the assembly of men behind them. Axes were at their sides and lunch pails in their hands as they murmured to each other though sour expressions.

Kandis grunted his thanks and took a deep bite into the fruit. "They should quit griping. Won't help anything. With all the rain, there'd be food shortages this year whether Will was governor or not. And I don't care about all this nonsense about Will being weak because of the Bolard incident. Strength isn't measured in whom you side with, or whether you take a side at all."

After a couple more bites, he finished the apple and sighed. "Five apples, hmm? A wonder you manage to stay so skinny."

Lionnel shrugged. "Guess I just work so hard, I burn off all the food before it turns to belly jelly. Glad, too. Don't want to end up looking like that Gertrude woman back in town."

Kandis shivered. "She's no flower, that's for sure."

Lionnel patted his belly. "I've also been eating a bit less at home, you know. So I can help some of the poorer folk stock up for the winter. Been giving them some of my imperishables, like dried meats and fruits. After all, I only have me and old Bart to feed, and he's not picky. He eats whatever the town kids feed him, which is quite a bit. He's never without bones and slabs of old pork or beef. Me? Apples are good enough to keep me going. Have barrels full in my cellar."

"You've always been a generous man," Kandis said. "I'm sure the king would be pleased if he were to ever visit Woodend and see all the good you've done for the poorer folks."

Lionnel smiled. "Now wouldn't that be something? The king himself in Woodend!" He reached into his pocket and pulled out a dimpled, glowing phial. "You've been ruling for centuries," he said to the phial, "and never visited this forest. How you even lived that long, I've no idea. But don't you think it's time to pay us a visit?"

The phial's glow remained the same, and Lionnel raised an eyebrow. "You really think he can hear us through these things?" he mused as he put it away.

"Don't know," Kandis replied. He got up and picked up his axe. "Why don't you ask the two heralds he sent to town last week?"

Lionnel jumped to his feet. "What! He sent heralds to Woodend? Who are they? What do they look like?"

"I've only glimpsed them. Back on Monday, on my way home from work. Never saw them in town before. One of them noticed me. Said I looked inquisitive. Said he wanted to explain his presence so I wasn't *tortured by my curiosity*. In the next few moments, and they were but moments, he told me that he and the other man were heralds to the king, and that I'd soon know why they were in town."

"Strange talk from a stranger," Lionnel said.

"True enough. He asked me where he could find some good pork stew, and I told him to go to the inn. They headed there, I went home. Next day, I asked Tarin to see if he could find out a bit more about them for me. Figured it would give him something to do, and give me a chance to talk with him a bit if he did discover anything." Kandis sighed a weary sigh.

"Tarin *is* a bit shy," Lionnel agreed. "Though I've got him talking a few times before. I remember one time, I told him about a bear I'd seen in the forest. His eyes lit right up. Asked for the whole story. At the end, he asked me if it had chased me or eaten any of my friends. When I said no, he walked away without a word."

Kandis nodded. "Sounds like Tarin. But don't worry. The mere fact he was willing to hear your story means he must like you."

Lionnel smiled and slung his axe over his shoulder. "Guess I've always had a way with the kids." He turned and looked into the sky. "Midday," he sighed. "Only a few more hours of working light before we're homeward bound—"

A gust of wind blew in, and with it came a foul odor, forcing them to hold their noses. Soon, the other lumberjacks were doing the same.

"What's that stink?" one of them yelled from the other side of the camp.

"Don't know," Kandis shouted back. He peered in the direction of the wind and frowned. "Very odd." He turned to Lionnel. "Care to investigate what died out there?"

"Why?" said Lionnel.

"Because it would be more entertaining than chopping down trees. Besides, it won't take long. It smells pretty close."

Lionnel grinned. "I suppose I could use a longer lunch break. Let's go."

They headed to the northeastern part of the camp, hacked their way through some thickets and entered the woods. After crunching through the underbrush for a few minutes, Kandis sniffed the air and gagged. "Whatever's rotting is farther north."

They continued. Soon they noticed the coniferous trees growing more plentiful, and shortly thereafter, towering pines with gnarly trunks surrounded them. Here, the sunlight struggled through the thick pine needles making up the forest roof.

"Nice place," Lionnel whispered.

"Why are you whispering?" Kandis whispered back.

Lionnel stopped and stared at his friend. "Same reason you are. Never thought I'd say it about the forest, but . . . this place is spooky!"

Kandis looked around. "You're right." He pointed toward a beam of light streaming through the trees. "Look over there, in that bright spot. You see that?"

Lionnel squinted. "My, my, my. Would Bart ever love to be here. That's the biggest pile of animal carcasses I've ever seen. And look on the top! Is that a dead bear?"

Kandis scratched his head. "I do believe it is. But what kills and eats full-grown bears?"

Lionnel grabbed his shoulder. "Let's get out of here."

"No. Let's get a little closer. Maybe we'll find out what killed all those animals."

As he spoke, he took a few steps toward the pile of death, but stopped when he heard the buzzing of flies. The stench grew almost unbearable. He covered his face with his hand to keep from throwing up. Suddenly, he tripped and fell into a depression in the ground. He pushed himself up and looked at where he stood. "Lionnel!"

Lionnel crept forward and peered toward the ground where Kandis stood. "Oh, this doesn't look pretty."

Kandis was standing in a footprint as long as he was tall and as wide as a willow's trunk. It looked like it was made by a hoofed creature, but one with three pointed toes.

He looked around and noticed a plethora of footprints near the carcasses. "From their arrangement," he muttered, "whatever made them stood on two legs."

Lionnel gasped and pointed toward the sky directly above the pile of animals. Kandis looked up. Every branch directly above the pile had been broken off.

"Like something came crashing out of the sky," Kandis said, in wonder tinged with unease. "So, whatever killed these animals can fly—?"

At Lionnel's shriek, Kandis whirled his head in the direction his friend pointed, saw a tapered object the size of a small tree stump next to the severed head of a doe. He covered his face with his sleeve, walked over, grabbed it up and hurried back to Lionnel. "We've got to show the governor this. He'll need to know. It's got to be a predator, which means everyone traveling in the forest right now's in danger."

Lionnel stood dumfounded, staring at the claw as if it might jump from Kandis' hands and lodge itself into his torso. "Everyone's in danger," he whispered. "Us too."

"Right. That means we leave now."

Kandis put the claw beneath his arm, grabbed Lionnel's shoulders with his free arm and pulled him away from the carcass pile. Together, they hurried out of the conifer grove and back to the path leading to the lumber camp. When they got there they collapsed to the ground, panting hard.

"What in Arvalast made those tracks and left that claw?" Lionnel huffed.

"I . . . don't know. But I do know this claw doesn't come from any animal I know of. And the fact it can fly . . ."

Lionnel sat up. "Lovely. We have a giant beast that snacks on bears flying around somewhere over Woodend."

"It appears so." Kandis stood and began walking back toward the camp. "I'd recommend keeping your axe close by for a while."

Lionnel groaned and hurried to his side. Kandis slapped his friend's back. "Let's just get back to the camp, but don't tell the others. Why panic them until we get a chance to talk to the governor? We'll have to tell the people of Woodend carefully too." He smiled. "Maybe this will give the governor a chance to be a hero."

"You think he'll believe us?" Lionnel said.

"How could he not, with evidence like this?" He nodded toward the claw beneath his arm. When we get back to camp, I'll wait outside the clearing until you can fetch a bag for me to hide this."

Lionel nodded as the sound of chopping started to fill their ears. This afternoon, their own strikes with their axes wouldn't join them.

EIGHT

Dibbs sat in his rocking chair in the corner of his bedroom, hoping Father would stay away. How could he explain something he himself didn't understand?

He stared at the lone window on the opposite side of the room. After-noon sunlight glimmered through and lit up the wall next to him with a soft white glow. Dibbs studied the cracks and grooves in the wooden slabs sup-porting the near wall, and wrung his hands together. A fly buzzed around his head, then perched on a wilted flower his mother had set on his win-dowsill last night. Except that it was alive when she did.

Reaching back with a groan, he ran his fingers across his back. Even with a shirt on, he could feel the deep grooves carved there. He'd received the first one a month ago. But it had been small, and he thought little of it. A week later, more appeared, deeper and much more painful. Perhaps that was around the time the nightmares began, the dreams of a strange fog in the shape of a human. Each night it would drift through the window and take form in front of his bed. A face would materialize where the head should be, and he'd see cruel yellow slits form as eyes. Before he could ever scream, all would grow dark. Every morning after, he woke up sweaty, blood oozing from the scratches.

He'd had another dream last night, and though the window the phan-tom had entered was now bright and cheery, he only saw the dark and dangerous portal it had used to enter his world and torture him. Dibbs so desperately wanted to tell someone about his tormentor, but whom? Mother was indeed worried about him, but she didn't seem to believe the nightmares were the true cause of his inflictions. The way she always looked at him when he showed her a new scratch, he knew she thought he was injuring himself. The day before, when she tried to get Father to take notice of his scratches, he thought he might finally believe him. But Father didn't seem to care. The town always took precedence over his own son.

The light streaming through the window represented more to him than the afternoon sun. It symbolized the essence of his pain, the reason his father paid him no heed. His father's loyalty to the king and the king's town kept him and Father apart. And for that, Dibbs loathed both the king *and* his light.

A tear slid down his cheek. That's all he wanted: his father to love him and protect him from the phantom in his nightmares. He *knew* this apparition was scratching him. But how could he make anyone believe it?

Dibbs began rocking faster as he thought about his father's absence. Soon the back of his chair was beating against the wall. The fly flew back outside. He wanted to hit something, anything. Maybe his sister would walk into his room and he could tear at her skin. *Perhaps then Father would attend to me!*

His chair hit the wall, hard. The back of the chair broke off, and he toppled onto the floor. He beat his head against the hard wood, and pain seared through his skull.

"Be quiet up there," his father said from downstairs.

Dibbs wiped wetness from his forehead that turned out to be blood, clenched his hands into tight fists. *Here I am, in complete despair, and all Father can do is rebuke me!*

Knowing his father was downstairs gave him an idea. He marched down the hall to his father's empty study, entered the room and ran to the desk near the far wall. His eyes scanned the drawers. *Which would hold Father's most precious documents?*

He reached for a large drawer on the right side and pulled it open. It was full of paper, and the topmost parcel read "Gertrude's Proposal."

He smiled. *Gertrude's proposal is about to go forever unresolved.*

He grabbed it up and tore at it. Sweat slid down his arms as he shredded the document. It felt good. Incredibly good. He reached for another page, and another. Soon, nothing was left in the drawer and a mutilated pile of paper lay next to his feet.

He tugged open another drawer and saw a lone document resting on the bottom. He pulled it out and read the title.

"Royal Decree," he breathed. The image of a glowing phial was drawn beneath the words.

"An illumina?" His teeth ground together, and his hands quaked in anticipation. *Destroying this one will be most pleasurable.*

Footsteps ascended the stairs leading to the outside hallway, followed by Father's voice, along with the voices of at least two other men.

He slammed his fist upon the Royal Decree. Trapped! There was no time to hide the mess of torn paper at his feet. And unless he could clean it up, he'd certainly be found out.

The men were in the hall now, fast approaching the study door. Panic seized him. Perhaps Father would just stop in for a moment, and not look behind his desk. Then, he would have a chance to clean up before Father came back later.

He looked around, saw the coat rack holding his father's dress suit across the room. He slid into the musty garments' folds just as the men entered, still chatting.

He heard Father walk to his desk, and held his breath. If Father looked behind it, he would see!

Unable to bear not knowing, he peeked around the coat. Father had stopped beside the desk and turned around.

"Please," Father said, holding out his hands toward the two chairs in front of the desk.

The two men sat, and Father took a seat . . . on his desk!

Dibbs sighed, safe, for now. He studied the guests. One was broad-shouldered and had a bushy brown beard. The other was skinny with some stubble on his chin. Both wore leather lumberjack coats, and smelled of pine and moist earth. But there was also another, fouler odor. He wrinkled his noise at the scent of rotting flesh.

"Tell me," Father said, "what is your concern?"

The larger man spoke first. "Lionnel and I found a carcass pile in the forest today. But it was highly unusual."

The skinny man named Lionnel opened up his arms. "It was ridiculously large. I mean, there's nothing I know that would keep that much kill around. Not even the biggest bear in the forest." He pointed to his friend. "Kandis will tell you the same."

"I definitely agree," the man called Kandis said. "That pile wasn't made by any creature I've ever encountered."

Father snickered. "I'm not sure why you came to me with such urgency. A pile of dead animals? No reason to rush to my house and demand a meeting. Such a sight could mean anything. You say one bear wouldn't need to keep so much food? Well, perhaps it's many bears. A whole family! I'd just recommend not working in that area alone. And keep weapons close at hand, just in case you run into the furry little bunch."

Kandis stroked his beard and gave a grim smile. "I didn't think the carcass pile alone would make you understand. So let me tell you more. When we approached it to investigate further, I descended into what I *thought* was a depression in the ground."

"And a depression it was," Lionnel added, "and a lot more. That hole Kandis was standing in was a giant footprint! It had three clawed toes, and a sole as wide as a willow's trunk."

"And here's one of its claws." Kandis heaved a large pointed object from a bag and set it on his lap.

Father's knee began to jiggle. "I . . . how do I know that's even real?" He gave a nervous smile. "This is ridiculous. You two should go back into the forest and look again at this *footprint* of yours. I guarantee it's not what you think. And that thing you have there? Probably just a root." He narrowed his eyes. "You two aren't drinking men, are you?"

Kandis stood, putting the claw beneath his left armpit. "Don't you dare accuse us of being drunkards, sir!"

Father leaned back in surprise, but then stood and faced the lumberjack. "How dare you speak to me like that!"

The two men faced off, silent, neither willing to relax his stiff shoulders. Then, Kandis sighed. "I'm sorry, Governor. I'm out of form. But please, don't insult me by suggesting that my friend and I are drunkards."

Father turned his head away and placed his hands behind his back. When he turned to again face Kandis, his eyes were full of concern. "I . . . I believe what you say about this footprint and the claw, and agree with what you're implying. The matter is simply far more complicated than I can explain."

Lionnel said, "You mean you believe there's some flying monster out in the forest killing animals like a . . . well . . . a monster?"

Father tapped his chin with his finger. "Yes, but there's more." He sat back down on his desk. "It's not just killing animals, I'm afraid."

Kandis raised his brows. "You mean it's slaying people?"

Father nodded. "My guards have reported six deaths along the main road the past few months. Not much is left of the victims except bloody clothing. The last victim was a fisherman from Westlake."

"Anyone from Woodend been killed?"

To Lionnel's question, Father shook his head.

Kandis stood and pointed toward the door. "We must warn the city not to travel through the forest until we've hunted down this monster!"

Father held out his hands, palms forward. "No! We can't do that! It will cause a panic."

"But—"

"The city council is meeting in a couple of days, and I'm going to address the issue there. We'll decide how to tell the town without creating an uproar and destroying trade."

Kandis shook his head. "But people might die in those two days."

"More might die if this gets out!" Father said, his voice stern. "We're already short on food for the winter. If trade stops even for a week, hundreds are going to starve. We *must* address this issue carefully."

Kandis' shoulders slumped. "Would you at least give Lionnel and me permission to gather a few men and hunt this creature? We might be able to destroy it, even before you have need to meet with the council."

Father paced in front of his desk. After a few moments, he turned to Kandis. "If you make your fellow hunters swear to tell no one of this beast until the council makes a decision, you have my permission to form a hunting party. And please, show no one that claw. No one!"

Kandis bowed his head and put the claw back in the bag. "Thank you, Governor."

Lionnel stood, he and Kandis bowed, and both left the room. Dibbs listened as their heavy boots stomped down the stairs. Father stood alone in front of the desk, his eyes glazed over with fear. Then, to Dibbs' horror, his father walked behind his desk and looked down.

"What is this?" he shouted. He bent down and rummaged through the torn paper, then spun and kicked the wall. "Who would *do* this to me?"

Fire in his eyes, his hand swept down and picked up a handful of paper. He crumpled up the paper and threw it in Dibbs' direction. His father's eyes followed the paper as it rolled up to the coat rack and landed at Dibbs' feet.

"Son?" he whispered.

Reluctantly, he slid from behind the coat and lowered his head in shame and fear. His father stomped toward him and knocked the coat rack over. Dibbs looked up at his red face. What he saw made him back against the wall.

"What are you doing here?"

Dibbs shook his head, not sure how to respond. Father grabbed his shirt and dragged him toward the desk. Dibbs tried to pull away, but couldn't. With a grunt, Father pushed him onto his desk and held him down. He pointed at the papers. "Why did you do that?"

Tears welled up in his eyes. "I . . . was angry at you."

"Why? What did I do?"

"It's what you don't do!" he screamed. He shoved his father's hands away and lifted his shirt. "Do you see those?"

Father backed away in surprise.

"Do you *see* them? You just let me get scratched up night after night and don't care!" He swung at his father and missed. "All you care about is the stupid town!"

Father stared at the scratches, then looked in his eyes. "I . . . forgot about your wounds. Your mother showed them to me, but . . . I'm sorry."

Dibbs felt pure rage bubble up in him and yanked his shirt back down. "You're sorry? No, you're not. I hate you, and I always will."

He kicked his father in the shin, then laughed as the man fell to his knees with a surprised howl. He kicked him again, this time in the stomach. It felt both good and terrible, so terrible, he broke into tears. The part of him that hated his father was overjoyed to see him suffering, but at the same time his heart was broken. He'd become a monster worse than his own father, maybe even worse than the creature that scratched him.

"Curse you, Dibbs," Father groaned, meeting his eyes with what looked like hatred. "May the king punish you for treating me like this."

With a scream of rage, Dibbs ran out of the study and hard into his mother, who was standing in the hall. He looked up through blurry eyes, saw deep sadness in hers, and again began to sob as he pushed her aside and stormed into his room.

Going to his drawers, he found a bag and began putting his clothes into it. He would run away from home, and not only his home, but also from Woodend. He never wanted to see either again.

✝ ✝ ✝

Tarin peeked from around a corner and stared at the city gate's wooden frame. The doors between the two much-taller hinge-beams were open, and the gatekeeper stood between them, studying a traveler's documents.

To his dismay, the traveler was just an old fellow in raggedy clothes with a pony, nothing like the king's herald he was hoping to see. Then again, he really didn't know *what* he was looking for, except someone of similar dress and stature as Dralo and Ristun.

He leaned against the wall and prepared for a long day of waiting. Though he wasn't sure what to do when Gildareth came, or if he'd even have the courage to try to speak with him, at the least he'd be able to follow him, maybe even overhear some of his dialogue with Ristun and Dralo.

A couple of hours went by with no sign of anyone interesting entering the city. He grew sleepy and closed his eyes. A moment later, he heard footsteps nearby. He looked around, hoping no one had spotted him. A boy, an all-too-familiar boy, stood a few paces from him, staring with mouth wide open.

"It's you again!" the boy said. He ran forward. "It's me, Sarky. Remember?" He reached for Tarin's hand and clasped it tightly.

Tarin drew back, half-expecting to be hit by a tomato or some other unpleasant object.

"What's wrong?" Sarky squeaked.

Tarin glared at him. He was trying to lure him into some cruel trap. Why else would he be acting so friendly?

Sarky nodded in sudden understanding. "Oh, I see. You haven't forgotten what me and the gang did to you."

Tarin spouted, "It was only two days ago you chased me through the streets threatening to hit me. And the next day, you and your idiot friends threw tomatoes at me!" He waved his hand toward the street. "Your gang's probably out there right now, waiting for you to lure me into the road so they can ambush me."

Sarky frowned and wrung his hands together. "I . . . don't really have a gang anymore. They blamed me for being made fools of by your two outlander friends yesterday. And when they heard I tried to talk to you after they ran off, they thought I was trying to join up with you and your posse. They . . . they called me a traitor. I couldn't tell them the truth, you know. Why I actually wanted to talk to you. Otherwise they would've ground my bones to pulp."

Tarin's anger faded a bit. "What did you want to tell me, anyway? All I remember you asking is if I saw anything odd the night you cornered me in that alley."

"Did you?"

Tarin looked at him, and saw the same terror he had the night Sarky nearly vomited all over him. "I saw a bald man and the same odd fellow in the red cloak. The one who made you throw up."

Sarky shook his head. "*Made* me throw up? That red-cloaked stranger was odd enough, but I've seen weirder things." He looked hard at Tarin. "There was something else out there that made me sick. Something I couldn't see, but I knew it—or they—saw me. I felt as if I was being watched. As if something evil was studying me, trying to look into my mind even." He shivered. "Whatever it was, I imagined it was dark, like a shadow."

Tarin took a step back, his heart thudding against his ribcage. "You say it was a shadow?"

"No. That's just how I pictured whatever was making me ill. I haven't actually *seen* anything."

Rubbing sweat from his brow, Tarin took a step toward him. "Well, *I* have. I saw the shadows you're talking about."

Sarky smiled a small smile, revealing ill-placed teeth, thrust his fist into the air and hollered triumphantly, "I knew I wasn't crazy!"

He leapt forward and threw his arms around Tarin in a tight hug. Tarin shoved him to the ground in disgust and wiped at his shirt. "Don't touch me! I don't like to be touched, especially by lunatics like you."

"But," Sarky said, still grinning, "now we know I'm not a lunatic." He bounced to his feet. "You say there was a bald man in the alley, too?"

Tarin finished brushing off his shirt and looked at him. "He was actually standing near the entrance to the alley, not in it."

"Interesting. Before my gang left me, we'd been following a bald stranger around town. He looked like he was up to no good, and we figured we might see a little action if we watched him long enough." Sarky's lips curled into a sly grin. "We found his hideout."

"What's that to me?" Tarin asked, trying to sound disinterested.

Sarky threw his hands into the air in frustration. "It *means* I know where the bald man's hideout is. So there's a chance we know where the red-cloaked stranger's hideout is, too. It's probably the same place!"

He waited for a response, but Tarin's façade remained strong. "And if we know where both the bald man *and* the red-cloaked stranger are," he persisted, "maybe we can also find out what those shadows are that I feel and you see!"

Hearing this, Tarin's curiosity became a raging monster within him, and he forgot the reason he'd come to the gate, Sarky's past offenses and the fact that he was usually a coward. He stepped forward, grabbed Sarky's shoulders and looked him hard in the eyes. "Let's go. Let's find out."

Sarky grabbed his outstretched arm and pulled him into the main road. A mule-drawn cart nearly ran into them, and the farmer driving it cursed after them as Sarky led Tarin across the road, then shoved him into a narrow passageway between two tall brick buildings.

"This leads to the eastern wall," he explained as they hurried along. "From there, we head north along Tulip Road, until we get to the old cottage next to the wall."

"But wait," Tarin said, "my father said not to go to that part of town—"

Sarky stopped walking and rubbed his hands together. "We'll need to be careful, sure. It's getting late in the day. And that *is* a pretty weird end of town, especially at night." He looked at Tarin, eagerness in his eyes. "But don't be a baby. You ready to find out what those shadows are, or not?"

Even though he was a little nervous about the east end of town, his usual timidity felt weaker than it ever had. Besides, Sarky seemed to know the area well. If there was trouble, he would know how to handle it.

"Let's go," he said.

Sarky pumped his fist in delight, and together they darted into the gap between the buildings.

Nine

A rolled-up tapestry hung from the ceiling, autumn leaves depicted in the fabric. When let down, it covered a magnificent window overlooking Lockspell Lake. But when rolled up as it was now, the noon sun reflected off the water and sent an array of light angels dancing through the spacious living quarters of the governor's mansion.

In the midst of this merry display, Jebin put his arm around his wife and admired the lakeside view. In the other room, he heard poor Diggory pursue their rowdy children in his ongoing-yet-vain attempts to protect the mansion's many valuable items from their wild games.

"Did you ever imagine we'd live in such a place?" Rosie asked as she held him tighter.

Jebin didn't. Nor did he think he deserved such a magnificent dwelling. But not wanting to sully her cheer, he kissed her lightly on the forehead and said, "Not even this place is worthy of such a woman as you."

She laughed and slapped him on the shoulder. "You're such a flatterer." She leaned up to kiss him when their youngest son, Devin, came shrieking into the room and ran into the back of Jebin's knees.

"Father, he's going to smite me!"

Jebin looked toward the door to the kitchen and saw Diggory run out, dripping wet and shaking with anger.

Diggory pointed at the boy, then waved his hands over his dripping red vest. "You little beast! These are my best clothes." He pointed at Jebin. "Governor, your son must be smote. Let's take him outside right now and introduce his buttocks to the rod."

Devin screamed and hid between his father's legs.

"What did he do to you, Diggory?" Jebin asked, trying to hold back his laughter.

Devin tugged at his father's trousers and looked up. Jebin met his tear-stricken eyes.

"Gabin said Diggory's clothes would change color if they got wet," the boy said of his twin brother. "So I filled up the tub and pushed him in."

"He tricked me!" Diggory yelled. "He told me he'd dropped a coin in the water and asked me if I would fish it out. The next moment, I was in the tub headfirst! I could've drowned."

"Devin!" Rosie reached down and pulled him up by his ear. "Get your brother right now!"

The boy whimpered, but obeyed. She glowered at them when they peeped through the kitchen door moments later. "Apologize to Mr. Diggory this instant."

They reluctantly entered the room and whimpered their apologies.

"Is that all?" Diggory asked, staring first at the boys and then at Rosie. "No rod?"

Rosie looked at Jebin for a response. He was still struggling to keep from laughing, but the flare in her eyes forced him to command, "Outside, boys."

They hesitated.

"Right now!"

They started crying. Rosie approached them, then prodded them through a door leading to a little pier next to the lake.

When they were gone, Jebin turned to Diggory. "I'll administer the rod. And if you wish, I'll send them to your house to fetch dry clothes."

Diggory nodded, the red in his face beginning to drain away. "Have them make haste. This is terribly uncomfortable."

He splashed back toward the kitchen, where he took a seat and pouted.

Jebin rolled his eyes, fetched a rod from the fireplace and went outside.

The boys were crying and begging Rosie for mercy. Rosie hushed them, gave Jebin a knowing glance, and returned inside. He knew what he had to do. Evil had to be punished. Though he wondered, was there ever a time a punishment was too severe? A dark thought crossed his mind, and he remembered the night he'd stormed Woodend, shortly after the old governor cast out all those refusing to adhere to his Royal Decree. And he recalled the horrendous mistake he'd made, one that haunted his thoughts without cease.

The boys stared at him, their faces pleading for mercy. He pushed away the pain in his heart and motioned for Gabin. The boy skulked over and bent down. Jebin held up his rod and prepared to lay a few careful blows to Gabin's buttocks. He again remembered his mistake, and the woman.

He grunted in frustration and brought down the rod, harder than he'd ever done before.

Gabin fell to the ground and wailed.

He stared at his son as if seeing him through a dream. But it wasn't his son anymore. It was the woman who lay there, moaning and rolling from side to side as blood poured from a wound in her chest.

Gabin's howl of pain wrested Jebin from his trancelike state.

"You better spank Devin just as hard," Gabin whimpered, furiously rubbing his backside.

Jebin looked over at Devin. The boy was pale and visibly shaking. He blinked and realized that he, too, was shaking. The rod slid from his fingers and he ran, first around the house, then into Lockspell's open main road.

Recognizing him as the new governor, people surrounded him. Carts clattered up and down the road next to him. There was nowhere to go to be alone. He looked south and saw a lone stable. He hurried toward it, bumping into people as he ran, and rushed inside.

In the far corner, dusty sunlight streamed through a single window and lit up a stall containing only tack. The few horses in the stable chewed on hay and watched him stumble into the sanctuary, sit on a saddle that rested on a sawhorse, put his head in his hands and weep.

The night he'd stormed Woodend had started as undeniable success. He and his men had pushed through the gate with little resistance, then drove the guards loyal to Bolard up the main road. As they marched, they sang, and townspeople cheered from their windows. But when they neared the northern end of the city, a new wave of Bolard's men attacked. His men fought valiantly, but many fell on both his side and Bolard's. In the midst of the chaos, he saw Bolard himself leave a nearby house and flee, toward a side street just beyond the battle. A strange fire entered his heart, and a desire to avenge the king for Bolard's treachery. He set an arrow and let the missile soar.

At that instant, a woman had run in front of him, rushing toward a man and small boy who were calling for her from the other end of the road. She never made it to them. Instead, she reached for the object suddenly embedded in her chest and collapsed. The man and boy rushed to her and knelt over her body as it convulsed, then stopped moving. As the man looked up at him, confusion and grief covering his face, he recognized the gatekeeper, Hamlin. The boy's screams of "Mother!" and the anguish on Hamlin's face accused and convicted him. Jebin let his bow fall and backed away.

Eventually he found himself in a dark corner of the city, cold and shaking. There he sat, and realized that in his thirst for vengeance, he had shed innocent blood. Nothing would ever change that. And even now, after running from his errant son, in his heart, he felt the king's rage burn against him for that unforgivable deed three years ago.

He put his hand into his coat and felt for his illumina, found it in an inner pocket near his heart. It was cold, and it made him feel just as cold. He shivered and wiped tears from his eyes. But he couldn't just sit and cry. His family would want to know where he'd fled after hitting Gabin so hard. He couldn't risk them thinking he'd gone insane like Bolard had. He must reconcile with them, especially with poor Gabin. They were all he had left, his only remaining joy in a world of guilt and sorrow.

With a shake of his head and a grunt, he forced himself up, grabbed a horse blanket off a railing to use as a shawl to mask his face, and went outside. The governor's mansion stood tall and proud a short distance up the road. It was magnificent, so much more than he ever deserved. Why had the king allowed him to be chosen to live there and govern this town? Why had Dierop and the council not looked deeper into his life and discover the atrocity he'd committed? Certainly, something would go amiss when he took office. Perhaps the town would fall into poverty or be destroyed by a gale. But for now, anything was better than staying in Woodend, the lair of his most hideous memories.

He'd started toward the mansion when he saw a peculiar sight in front of him. A group of swordsmen in unfamiliar garb stood next to a trade cart, the tallest of the group talking animatedly with an old cloaked man. Jebin drew a little closer, then stopped in surprise. The old man was Governor Dierop.

"I leave for Woodend in the next few days," the tall man told Dierop loudly. "I trust all is in order for your leave. Has the new governor taken power yet?"

"He will in the next week," Dierop replied.

The tall man nodded and turned in Jebin's direction. Jebin lowered his head and pretended to study the potatoes in a trade cart next to him. But that face had given him an odd sensation. Though it was masked behind a trim beard and mustache, the sharp green eyes reminded him of someone. His heart beat a little faster as he listened more intently.

"When are you leaving for Westlake?" the tall man asked.

"I leave in a week," Dierop replied. "You assure me, I will be safe there?"

"You will, by the power of my king."

Thankful that the tall man hadn't seemed to recognize him beneath the shawl, Jebin's racing mind tried to find the link. Slowly, a picture of a phantom from his past materialized within his memory. The noises around him grew faint as he looked into the green eyes of that phantom. Then all went quiet, and his arms fell limp to his sides as those green eyes poured into his. It was Bolard, his old enemy.

The city noises instantly returned, and Jebin slid behind the trade cart so he could peer more closely at the tall man. Though he was much more rugged-looking than when he was exiled three years ago, the eyes, voice and speech were unmistakably that of Woodend's old governor. But what was Bolard doing here, talking to the governor of Lockspell?

Not knowing what else to do, he grabbed a potato and let it tremble in his hand. From the corner of his eyes, both of which were still glued to Bolard, he saw Dierop clasp hands with the tall man, share a few hushed words, then slink out of sight toward the mansion, followed by nearly all the rest of the group, including Bolard. Except for one unusually short soldier, who patted his stomach and called out to the others, "I'm going to gather some nourishment! I'll meet you at the cottage later." His voice, though far from feminine, was high.

One of the other soldiers waved his hand in dismissal. The small soldier grunted, then approached Jebin. Before he could turn and walk away, the fellow came to his side and looked at the potato in his hand.

"Looks delicious," the soldier said. He held out his hand and beckoned for Jebin to hand it to him. Jebin obliged.

The man sniffed it, then rubbed it on his smooth face.

The man, who was proportioned well despite his size and appeared neither young nor old, scratched the brown mop on top of his head and raised a brow. "Feels nice, smells nice, but that ultimately tells me nothing." He peered around, then bit hard into the root. His eyes rolled with pleasure. "Excellent," he moaned. "Simply excellent." He gulped down the rest in a couple of swallows. "Farmer! Where are you? I want to buy."

No one came. He spun in circles, waving his arms. "Buy! Buy! I want to buy!"

Finally, the farmer and apparent owner of the cart ran to them and waved his finger as if rebuking a child. "You must buy first, then eat."

The small man offered a smug smile. "You must be here when I'm here for that to happen. Otherwise, I eat first and buy later."

The farmer turned to Jebin in frustration. "How many has he eaten?"

"Only the one," Jebin said.

He turned back to the little man and held out his hand. "Then you owe me one piece of copper."

The little man shuffled through his pockets and pulled out not one, but ten pieces of copper. "Here," he said, handing the stunned farmer the money. "Now give me nine more." He then reached back into his leather armor and pulled out a gold coin. With a flip of his wrist he tossed it into the cart, where it disappeared into the pile of merchandise. "If you want that coin, you'll have to fish through the food. And while you're at it, give me the nine best potatoes you find. If they really *are* nice, keep the coin."

The farmer's eyes grew wide and he immediately went to work.

"So," the little man said to Jebin as he picked some potato from his teeth, "who are you and what brings you to Lockspell? Your clothes are certainly lacking the luster of any of the natives, and you wear a strange headpiece."

"Perhaps," Jebin said, "I should first ask whom *you* are and from where *you* come. Armor is an uncommon sight to a simple forest dweller like myself."

The man wiped his mouth and looked at Jebin with disinterest. "It might be a more common sight in the near future."

"What do you mean?"

"What I mean," the man said while he watched the farmer pull a few exceptionally large potatoes from his cart, "is that Macalum has sent me and a posse of other warriors to this forest to protect it from potential danger. The governor's most honored captain, Bolard, is from these parts. He's helping us search for a battalion of evil men we fear sneaked in here a few months ago."

"Captain Bolard, you say?" Jebin's heart began to beat hard again. "And he's from here?"

The man looked at him, with interest this time. "You sound as if you know him."

"I've . . ." He cleared his throat. "I believe he was part of the council of a nearby town once."

"More than a councilman," the fellow replied. "He was a governor. Guess he didn't like it though, because he left. Doesn't talk about it often. Gets angry whenever anyone mentions it."

Jebin shuffled on his feet. "So, he's the captain of your battalion? If you don't mind my asking, what plans does he have for you here?"

Jebin turned at the farmer's whoop to see the farmer holding a gold coin and a handful of potatoes.

"Excellent," the little man shouted. "Now give me my quarry and you may keep yours."

The farmer dropped the food into his arms and furiously polished the coin on the hem of his garment.

"Well," the little man told Jebin as he turned to go, "I must be off." He stopped and turned around. "Oh, to answer your question: Bolard plans to lead us to the city of Woodend sometime this week. So we may prepare the city and its governing council for the potential danger in the forest." He tossed Jebin a potato and smiled. "It was good talking to you, sir. May we meet again." He spun on his heels and strode away.

Jebin wondered what danger in the forest could possibly warrant Bolard's return to Woodend. And as a captain of the stout Macalumese guards no less. But he didn't care to think about it right now. All he knew was Bolard was back, almost undoubtedly to get revenge on Willerdon for not siding with him. And even more so, himself. Still, as he stood in the road and glared at all the tall, impressive buildings on either side, he knew he would have to travel to Woodend and warn Willerdon, and soon. The little man said Bolard would leave for the city within the week. Without a warning, Will would be unprepared to stop Bolard from causing trouble.

With heavy heart, he lifted his feet and started back to the mansion. Rosie was waiting at the door with Gabin, tears still moist in his eyes.

Jebin had almost forgotten about the heavy blow he'd administered to his son. He removed the blanket from his head and reached for Gabin. At first, the boy drew back, but Rosie coaxed him. Jebin hugged him until the lad quaked with sobs. Rosie joined the embrace, and soon he felt another body snuggle close. It was his daughter Maddie. Devin also wriggled his way into the center of their arms. For that moment, Jebin's family was knit back together and had forgiven him. But even with them all in his arms, showing him their love and support even in the midst of his foolishness, he couldn't forgive himself for what happened in Woodend. The woman's death had soiled his greatest passion, to be a worthy servant to his king.

Still, he could do his king service. He had to get to Woodend and warn Willerdon about Bolard. Perhaps then he could at least take pride that he still desired to serve the king and his appointed leadership, even though the king would never accept such a criminal as himself as a servant.

After their supper, he sent the boys to fetch Diggory his clothes, which the man accepted with a grunt and a hasty retreat from the mansion. An hour later, Jebin sent the children to bed, and he and Rosie went to the living quarters and closed the tapestry. He took a seat on a rocking chair near the large fireplace against the wall opposite the lake. She rested in his lap.

"Rosie," he said, "I have to return to Woodend for a few days. I must speak with Willerdon."

Tensing in his lap, she lifted her head to face him with distressed eyes. "But why? Why go back to that place, when we need you here to help us set up our new home?"

He rubbed her shoulders and stared at the orange embers in the fireplace. "I heard something on the streets today. Nothing that should affect us, but something that could greatly trouble Willerdon. As his friend—"

She slid off his lap, and looked at him with skepticism. "Tell me the truth. You're not still trying to make amends for the woman, are you?"

He averted her gaze and felt his face grow taut with grief. But he managed to shake it away. "No. It's something I believe would be right to do. Something the king would ask me to do. If he still saw me as his servant."

Her brows lowered. "He still does, my dear. It is you who can't see yourself as worthy."

He opened his mouth in preparation to argue, but she lifted her hand. "You're my husband, and I will always offer you my love and support, even when I feel your mind is in the wrong place. But if you go and do something incredibly foolish, or get yourself hurt in Woodend . . . I might not be so compassionate."

She retreated to the bedroom. He remained in the chair, contemplating her reassurance about the king's measure of him. She would never understand a man's guilt. Nor would she approve of the true reason he was warning Willerdon, which she'd already guessed.

Out of curiosity rather than hope, he pulled the illumina from his pocket and studied it. What appeared to be a gentle luminous liquid swirled within the glass, but it was still lackluster. As far as he knew, it always would be. With a defeated grunt, he stuffed it back into his pocket and followed after Rosie. With a full day's trek ahead of him tomorrow, he needed sleep.

Ten

Will put a pile of greens in his mouth and chewed slowly, listening to his saliva swish around his teeth. Beside him sat his eight-year-old daughter Grace, and across from him, Lianna. Dibbs hadn't come down for supper, nor had Will seen him in over three hours.

"This is delicious, Mother," Grace said, then turned to Will. "Father, who were those men who visited you today?" She giggled. "One was quite strong, but the other looked like a lamppost."

He sighed, too stressed to answer.

"I found a kitten outside today," she continued. "I gave it some milk and named it Chrysanthemum."

Lianna's face flashed with anger. "Grace! I've told you not to feed stray cats. We already have enough of the little beasts crawling around outside the door. I don't want another one."

"But—"

Lianna held up her hand. "Go upstairs for a bit." She looked at Will with furrowed brow. "I need to speak to your father."

Grace frowned, but scooted her chair back, stole a few grapes from the center of the table and pouted her way upstairs.

Will clicked his fork on the table and looked up at his wife. Her face was red, and beneath the table, he heard her foot tap the wooden floor.

"I was hoping you'd talk to me about what happened earlier today with Dibbs," she said. "But it appears you're going to force *me* to bring it up."

He stared at his dirty fork.

"Don't try to scuttle out of this one, Willerdon!"

He pursed his lips together and stared into her fury-filled eyes.

"Why did you curse Dibbs?" she yelled. "Did you see his face when he ran into me? He was heartbroken!"

He opened and closed his mouth in an attempt to say something constructive, something that might explain his feelings, but all he could do was yell, "I need support right now! Not your usual spite!"

Her eyes proved she was as surprised as he at his outburst.

"I can't fix everything!" he continued. "I . . . I try. I try, but I just can't fix everything that's thrown at me."

Crying softly, she stood up and took the seat next to him. "You can still mend things with Dibbs."

He groaned and stared at his knees. She grabbed his shoulders and forced him to face her. "Why do you always do this?" she said. "I hardly know who you are anymore! All I know is you constantly tell me you're overwhelmed, but by what? What's troubling you so much that you haven't the heart to make amends with your own son?"

He threw his hand at the wooden cup in front of him. It flew across the table and slammed into the wall. "Why do you keep pressuring me to talk? Isn't it obvious what's troubling me? I've had it with this heinous place, filled with mindless, selfish idiots. And I'm the one who must cater to their every call, then suffer their constant complaining. And what's in it for me?" He turned hard eyes on her. "Absolutely nothing, Lianna. My life . . . is detestable."

She turned from him and stared at the cup he'd thrown to the ground. "Are we detestable to you?"

"No! You always do this. You twist everything I say in that woman's mind of yours."

He stood and glared at her, then stomped to the dining room window. "Fine! I'll tell you why I'm so upset! Dibbs threw me over the edge today when he tore up those papers. I was like a bulldog that got beaten one too many times. I didn't want to say what I did, but I did anyway! I can't change that," he turned to her, "can I?"

He spun and watched a few townsfolk stroll down the lantern-lit road, looking toward his house as they passed, curiosity on their faces. He leaned against the windowsill and lowered his head.

"Ever since I became governor, these idiot villagers have done nothing but complain. They don't even realize that, right now, I'm protecting them from information that could destroy all business in the town, making the winter even worse. And this at the cost of my own conscience. I had to pick the lesser of two evils, and so I did."

In sudden fury, he punched the window. It shattered into the lawn and sent many more eyes in his direction. Lianna was quaking. Part of him wanted to reach out and pull her into his arms, for comfort, for love. The other part wanted to condemn her for how unsupportive and distant she often was.

He turned his face away from her. "I need more help than I've ever needed before. I've asked the king for aid, and he only responds with bad news. A few nights ago, I pleaded for help. A knock came at the door, and I received a letter."

He reached into his vest pocket and showed it to her. "The king's help came in the form of Jebin's resignation. I now find myself wondering if the king even still reigns in this land, or just lives in the dying breath of a few disillusioned fools."

Lianna thrust her hand onto the table and stood. "Then I am a fool, and a proud fool at that!" She walked up to him and took him in a tight embrace. "And you also are a fool, because I know you still love the king."

Her tears soaked through his vest as his mind spun. Why was Lianna holding him when she should be striking him? His heart started to hurt, and his eyes watered. "Hit me!" he cried. He felt a breeze come through the broken window and his tears began flowing. "Why won't you hit me?"

"I want to! I want to hit you hard enough to knock you to the floor. And I should. But I know you need this more at the moment." Her weeping changed to a soft laugh. "Don't worry, I'll be back to my old self soon. Then you won't get away with all this nonsense of yours. And after I'm done comforting you, you silly fool, you're going to fix that window, talk to Dibbs, and prepare yourself for yet another day of drudgery. But tomorrow, you're going to do it with a smile, because you're going to know the king is with you, and that I'm going to be with you, too. Because I think I at last understand why you've been so intolerable lately."

Love for his wife surged through him like it hadn't since they first married. He heard a laugh, and realized it had come from him. More sobs, then another laugh. He'd never felt like such a lunatic, but if insanity felt this good, he was ready to embrace it and be taken to the nearest asylum.

She held him until, after a half hour of sobbing, laughing, quaking, and the occasional moment of silence, the bottled-up anger had expended itself. Lianna must have realized this, for she returned to her chair, scooted it close to him and looked at him through misty eyes, waiting for him to say something. Waiting, he realized, for him to decide what to do next.

He already knew.

He gently kissed her. "Thank you. I'm going to speak with Dibbs immediately."

She nodded dutifully, but he could see the hope-filled glimmer in her eye.

He headed for the stairs, and at their base, turned back to her. She was holding her illumina, and it was shining, perhaps brighter than he'd ever seen one glow. He had called her a fool, yet she had always had been such a strong servant of the king. After Dibbs, he would have to make amends with her as well.

He felt a warmth in his own pocket, saw a faint glow. Was his illumina coming back to life? His throat grew tight with humiliation. He must make amends with someone else, too. The man he had blasphemed most that night, the man he had forgotten to trust in the midst of his trials.

But first, Dibbs.

He reached his son's room and knocked. "Dibbs. It's Father. I need to speak with you."

There was no answer. Not even a stir within the room. The door was cracked open. He nudged at it and peered inside. The room was empty.

Then he saw it. The dresser against the wall, its drawers pulled out, clothes scattered across the floor in front of it. The quilt on the bed was missing, along with Dibbs' prized walking stick he always kept in the corner of his room. All gone.

He flew downstairs.

Lianna met him when he reached the bottom, still holding her illumina, but now it was dim.

"Dibbs ran away," he sputtered.

The flash of anger across her eyes told him his wife, who moments before desired nothing more than to comfort him, now truly wanted to hit him. He wanted to hit himself.

A thought came to him. "Raulin," he whispered. "Raulin and the guards must start searching for Dibbs. If the boy reaches the forest . . ."

His heart skipped as he imagined Dibbs standing within the shadow of a monster, the one that had already killed so many forest travelers. He felt old rage and despair twist his gut. How could it be coming back so easily? Instinct led his hand into his pocket. His illumina was warm

The fury vanished, and he threw on his jacket and strode toward the front door. "I'll set the guards out to find him," he told Lianna with a quick glance, then ran into the road. Behind him, he heard Grace come down the stairs and ask Lianna what was going on. By the time he crossed the lawn, her voice had trailed off.

He turned toward the main road and ran toward the guardhouse, whose lights glimmered where the two roadways converged at the northern end of the city.

† † †

"We're almost there," Sarky whispered. "Tulip Road is just past those two buildings."

Tarin nodded, impressed at how adept Sarky was at maneuvering through Woodend's alleys and side streets. Almost as good as he, who traveled that way most of the time.

They crept into the narrow space between the musty brick structures and peered at the road beyond. Tulip Road ran north to south, and when it didn't have to weave around one of the buildings next to the city's outer wall, it slid right next to the wall's wooden beams. The sun had set, and Tarin was happy that darkness would conceal them when they ventured out into more open areas.

"The house where I saw the bald man and the red-cloaked stranger is about five minutes' north," Sarky said. There was curiosity in his voice. Eagerness, even.

They darted from shadow to shadow. Five minutes edged by before Sarky pointed at a dingy shack built against the eastern wall. It stood quite high for a single-story structure, and its steep but sagging roof looked like it would leak in a mere drizzle. The walls were rotted in places, and in one spot, missing. Most of what remained was covered in a disgusting white fungus. Through the gaps in the wood, a gentle light flickered.

"That's the place," Sarky whispered. "What should we do now?"

Tarin stared at the largest gap in the wall. "See that hole? We go there and listen."

Sarky nodded, his face pensive. "Sounds like a good start."

They began their cat-like walk toward the shack, but Sarky grabbed his shoulder and held him back.

"Tarin, that last step I took. It . . . made me ill." He put his hand on his stomach. "I swear, before I took it, I was fine, now I feel sick!"

Tarin scanned the area for any sign of the shadows. Though the buildings on the other side of the road looked dilapidated, nothing dark and sinister crawled along their exteriors.

"I don't see anything strange," he said. "You sure you're not just nervous? Or maybe just sick from something you ate?"

"I did have some chicken dung, but I wouldn't exactly consider that distasteful."

Tarin looked at him in horror. Sarky rubbed his belly and smirked. "Kidding. For some reason, hearing you use the word 'distasteful' annoyed me."

Tarin raised a brow. "Why?"

Sarky rolled his eyes. "Don't you ever get out among boys your age?"

"No."

"Well, most of us don't use silly words like that. They sound too . . . formal—" Sarky's eyes suddenly grew wide and his face pale. He gagged, then vomited all over his shoes.

Tarin grimaced. "Ugh. Most people I know don't go around vomiting on their feet all the time either."

Sarky wiped his mouth, still hunched over. "Look around. Something bad's got to be nearby."

He looked around and raised his hands. "There's nothing."

Sarky gagged again.

"Here," Tarin said, and pulled him into the darkness of a dead maple standing against the wall. Then he looked toward the shack. The light glowed weakly through the large hole. "I think I'm going to sneak over there."

Sarky moaned in agreement, but just as Tarin took his first step toward the glowing spot, something dark blocked the dim light. Only for an instant, but it was enough to make him lean back hard against the tree, trying to make himself one with its trunk. Sarky lay on the grass next to him, holding his stomach. "What are you waiting for?" he moaned.

"I saw a shadow," Tarin whispered, his eyes transfixed on the gap in the building.

Sarky smiled. "Good. I thought I might actually be getting sick." He crawled to Tarin and sat up next to the tree. After a few deep breaths, he said, "If you're still willing, I'm ready now. Still sick, but ready."

That shack was calling to Tarin, beckoning him to sneak up beneath that crack and find out what secrets laid just beyond in the dim light, perhaps even the key to what those shadows were. Without responding, he allowed his intrigue to fuel his arms and legs in a scrambling crawl toward the house, ignoring the pain as his hands came down on tiny rocks and twigs on the ground. He could hear Sarky following, also crawling, judging from the slight grunts he was making and the snapping of twigs.

When they got close enough to the house, they stopped crawling and scooted along on their bellies until they were directly beneath the hole. Both of them stilled their breathing and listened.

"Have they left?" a soft voice said from within. Tarin instantly recognized it as the bald man's, the man named Sayin.

"It was only one," a different voice hissed. "And yes, it has gone to attend to the governor in the north. Apparently a victory was won. The son is beginning to embrace our way."

"Excellent," the bald man said. "This will dishearten the governor further. He will be well prepared when the plan is set in motion."

"And what of this lumberjack, Kane?"

Sayin yawned. "His heart and mind are ready to initiate the chaos. He was almost too easy to break."

"They thought so too," the hisser said. "So many in this village are but empty vessels waiting to be filled."

There was silence, then Sayin said, "I will go to the meadow tomorrow and speak with the king. Though I fear that by then, the chaos will have already begun. Pity. I would certainly like to have been here when it happens."

"It will only be the beginning." The hisser laughed as if through a clogged nose. "In the end, a mere droplet in a sea of blood."

"Are the others prepared for the attack on the governor's family?"

"They are. It will take place immediately after the chaos. Again, it will be all too easy, now that the governor's light is all but vanquished. The overthrow will be simple. First here, then the entire forest."

"Then Macalum," Sayin added, "then . . ."

"Then," the hisser repeated, "to the tower, where the king's throne will be restored."

"And what of the prophecy? What if it's *not* a myth?"

"It is a myth. If it were not, it would have already happened, and we wouldn't be poised for victory. No, the *Annals* are but lies, written by the followers of the scourge and believed by the king's foolish phantoms."

Sarky sneezed. Tarin shot him a wild glance, but it was too late. A chair was thrown over from inside and Sayin yelled, "Don't go out there! If you're seen—"

Footsteps pounded onto the road and toward the shack where the boys hid. Tarin doubted it possible to outrun the hisser, based on the speed he'd demonstrated when he first saw him a couple days' prior. So he looked around for a hiding place. Nearby was a tiny building, perhaps a doghouse. He pointed to it, and he and Sarky darted inside.

Spider webs covered their faces, and it sounded as if they had disturbed a nest of kittens. Though scarce enough room for both of them, at least they were hidden. Or in Tarin's case, mostly hidden. His body fit inside, but his face protruded a bit from the door.

A red hood emerged from around the corner of the shack, sniffing in the grass. Two arms covered in red sleeves reached out and pulled the hissing man forward. At least, Tarin thought of the entity as a he: As the hooded body emerged fully from around the corner, its threatening crouch made it appear more animal than man.

The hooded figure took in a deep breath, and then darted to where the boys had been sitting. Two more sniffs, then his head made a slow turn toward the doghouse.

"Sarky," Tarin whimpered. "I think he sees me—"

There was a series of hisses, more like laughs, and then the figure stood to its full height and stared at Tarin. In the dim light, he thought he saw pointy teeth somewhere in the hood, but his mind was in such a state of fear, he wasn't sure.

In panic, he tried to stand. His head hit the top of the door. The man began to approach their hiding place.

"Run!" he screamed to Sarky, and thrust himself from the doghouse. For a single moment, he looked at the man, or whatever he was, and the man looked back, almost challenging him for the chase.

He heard Sarky push out from behind him, but fright kept him from moving. Sarky grabbed his hand and jerked him south, away from the shack and the man.

They ran about ten strides and then darted onto Tulip Road. Tarin heard the man hiss, and charge after them. Panting, he looked back; the figure was moving nearly twice their speed. "We're dead!" he screamed.

"I know!" Sarky cried back. Their combined panic seemed to come out their feet; as one, they tripped over themselves and went tumbling into the hard dirt road.

"What's going on up there?" Tarin heard a man's voice say in the distance.

Sarky looked around wildly. "Help!"

"Help!" Tarin added, also looking around for the source of the voice. Then he saw a man. And not just one, but ten, all of them Woodend guards!

He began to weep with the joy of finally being safe, until he remembered their pursuer. He looked back. The cloaked man was gone. He heard one of the guards yell something, then three of them rushed by Tarin, heading toward the shack.

The rest of the guards ran to the boys and helped them to their feet. The captain, who wore a white feather in his hat, addressed them. "My name is Raulin, guard of Woodend." He offered them a hard stare. "What are you boys doing out so late? And in this part of town? This road is full of dangerous men at night."

"That wasn't any man!" Sarky blurted. "That thing was a monster!"

Raulin looked at him quizzically, and Tarin heard one of the guards whisper something to another guard. He thought he heard the words "thief" and "troublemaker."

"Where do you boys live?" Raulin continued.

Sarky pointed to himself. "I'm the gatekeeper's son. And this is my friend."

"I'm sure your father will want you home," Raulin said. "And you," he glared at Tarin, "where do you live?"

Tarin's throat grew tight, and timidity kept his mouth glued shut.

"He lives near me," Sarky answered for him. "We'll both head back south together."

"Not alone, I won't permit it." Raulin turned to one of the guards. "Accompany them back to the gatehouse, and explain to this boy's father where they were found."

Then he returned his hard stare to them. "Have either of you seen another boy, a bit younger than you, during your little escapade?"

They looked at each other, and then shook their heads in unison.

"Very well." Raulin and the others headed north, but Raulin looked back. "Stay out of trouble."

Sarky waved and nodded.

Meanwhile, their guard glared at them. "Well, don't just stand there. March!" And march they did, grateful to be leaving Tulip Road behind.

Eleven

Tarin sat on a cushioned stool, his feet warming by the cozy fire. This was the first time he'd been in any house except his own in at least a year, and though he still felt terribly shy around Sarky's father, Hamlin, the man's pleasant nature was beginning to cut through his usual timidity.

"Here's a nice cup of tea for you," Hamlin said as he came from the gatehouse's kitchen and held out a steaming mug of sweet-smelling brew.

Tarin took it and smiled. "Thank you."

Hamlin nodded and returned to the kitchen. "I've got a nice treat for you both in the pantry," he said over his shoulder. "Hold on just a bit and I'll fetch it."

Sarky lifted his head from the plush fur rug by the fire. "It can't be true, Father. Are you bringing out the truffles?"

"Seeing as you've finally made friends with a decent enough boy . . ." There was a moment of silence. "Aha! Here they are."

Hamlin trotted into the living room, his round belly swishing up and down beneath his heavy shirt, and set an open box of truffles in front of them. "Tarin, my lad, take a few."

Tarin picked out two. He stuffed the first in his mouth, tasted chocolate bliss spreading over his tongue, then stuffed in the next. He nearly choked as he chewed on the tasty little delicacies. His mother rarely bought sweets, but when she did, they certainly didn't taste this good.

"Like them?" Hamlin asked with a wink while Sarky came over and popped a few into his own mouth.

Tarin nodded furiously.

"They're from the south, far south. Best in all of Arvalast! Take some more, if you promise to stick around."

"But Father," Sarky said, "I can't believe you trust Tarin so much. Because of him, I got into more trouble tonight than I've almost ever gotten into before."

Hamlin chuckled. "Nothing and no one's going to keep young boys out of trouble, especially you. Save maybe that red-cloaked fellow you ran into."

Hamlin chuckled again, then slapped Tarin on the back, hard enough to nearly knock him off his chair. Tarin didn't care, because it brought his face closer to the truffles. As he sat back up, he picked up a few more.

Hamlin walked to the fire and prodded it with a poker, making the room grow a cheery orange, then pointed the poker at Tarin. "I can tell this boy won't be a bad influence on you. Sure, he might be willing to accompany you on one of your quests, like your little adventure to Tulip Road. But he isn't going to prod you to steal or murder cats or scare old ladies by pretending to be wild boars." He fixed Tarin with a stern look. "Will you?"

"No, sir," Tarin said though a mouthful of truffles.

"Then we have it!" Hamlin plodded over to a big wooden chair near the door. "Now tell me, why were you boys caught on Willow Road by the guards? And who was this red-cloaked stranger they saw chasing you?"

"We were looking for the hideout of a burglar," Sarky lied. "My other friends and me saw someone steal something from a farmer's cart on the main road a week ago. Tarin and I felt it our duty to find his loot and inform the guards."

Tarin considered telling Hamlin the truth, that they were hunting the source of the shadows he'd seen. But then he realized how silly that would sound to an adult. Perhaps Sarky was wise to alter the story a bit.

Sarky proceeded to tell Hamlin that the shack they found was empty, and there didn't appear to be any loot when they peeped through the crack. "But then," Sarky said, "we heard someone coming and tried to run away. That's when that red-cloaked villain started to chase us. We were lucky. The guards were out looking for someone else, and scared it off."

"It?" Hamlin asked, retrieving a pipe and match from his vest pocket.

"Well, I'm really not sure if it was a man or woman," Sarky said. "But it was fairly tall. And broad-shouldered. Probably a fellow." He leaned toward Tarin and whispered, "A monster fellow, that is."

"You know," Hamlin lit the bowl of the pipe and took in a bit of smoke, "I've seen a couple of them red-cloaked men strolling through town lately, usually just before dusk." He exhaled and brought the pipe down to the armrest. "They're always heading east, through the less-traveled roads no less. I've always said, trust no one, especially outsiders. And it doesn't take a fool to realize that those are outsiders. Strange, though ... I don't ever remember letting them into the city. They must not have been wearing their cloaks at the time."

He turned his head to look out the nearby window. "Been a lot of strange goings-on outside these walls lately. I hear a lot from the travelers." He frowned. "The few there still are. They're sayin' the roads are growing dangerous, especially farther south toward Mahotholin. And the merchants from the plains? They say no one travels without guards anymore."

He smacked his knee with his hand and looked back at the boys. "If I were you, I'd keep your adventures inside these walls. And by all means, be wary of strangers, especially those red-cloaked men. I've got a sick feeling in my gullet about them, and I'm a good judge of people. Course, there's more reason for me to fear them than just my belly." He smiled and rested his free hand on his knee. "Care to hear an old wives' tale?"

Hamlin must have seen Tarin's eyes light up, because his smile got even wider. "How about you, Sarky?" he asked.

Sarky rolled over on his rug and looked at his father. "Have I heard it before?"

"Not this one."

"Then sure," he put his head behind his arms. "But don't mind me if I fall asleep."

"Pish, posh! This one might actually keep you up." He peeked out the window once more, then turned to the boys.

"Legend says this forest once boasted one of the finest cities in the north. Undertree was clean and wealthy, as beautiful as the lush green trees surrounding its wall and the mountains beyond its western edge. Fresh spring water from the mountains came into the city through a system of canals. It's said that small boats carrying goods or people were a common sight on those canals. Gardens were planted along the sides, and bridges provided for crossing. Some of the canals even flowed under buildings, through openings at their bases. That allowed the water to stream through, or sometimes pool up so people could swim or bathe. Undertree was the jewel of Maplelake, and even outsiders frequented Undertree's streets."

"Sounds like a beautiful place to live," Tarin breathed, enthralled.

Hamlin nodded. "But one day, over one hundred years ago, things began to change. Not sure how it happened, but the people of Undertree grew restless, and eventually cruel. They started polluting the canals, trying to make their neighbors ill, until the whole town reeked of filth. A few people claiming loyalty to the king called for help from the outside. They believed some dark wizardry had descended over Undertree. One of these men was called Clindale. He was a seer, who professed to know the king and his ways. He told the townsfolk that their disloyalty and pride had weakened the ancient blessing the king once placed on the city. Even more,

Clindale said an invisible evil, one that had long watched the city walls for weakness, had at last found entry."

"So what happened when Clindale told them that?" Sarky said, eyes wide.

Hamlin shrugged. "What always seems to happen, son. He was called a madman. And then he and the few who believed him were driven from the city. But he was right. The day he left, a band of outsiders swarmed from the mountains and ransacked the city. Everyone was either killed or forced to flee. The city was leveled, and remains so to this day. Today, we call it 'Rock Valley,' because that's about all that's left now: a valley of rocks. Oh, and weeds and thistles that grow in the broken brick roads. The canals are just pits in the ground. Water won't even run through them."

He pointed toward the other wall. "I'm told the place is about a day's journey to the west, at the base of the mountains. Never seen it myself. Don't think I'd want to."

"What happened to that band of outsiders that attacked?" Sarky asked.

"No one really knows. After they destroyed the city, they disappeared. Most believe they retreated south. Back then, there wasn't much else to destroy. A hundred years ago, Woodend was just a walled village full of straw huts, same as Lockspell. Undertree was where anything of significance happened in Maplelake Forest."

Hamlin's eyes bounced from Tarin's to Sarky's, then back to Tarin's, but then he stared through the window, as if something sinister lurked just beyond the smudged glass. "There's an interesting thing about those outsiders, though. And this is what troubles me. The forest raiders were rumored to have worn red cloaks. Some even say they weren't human, but monsters."

Tarin's heart leaped and he looked over at Sarky, who was now sitting up straight with a nervous glint in his eyes.

A horse whinnied from somewhere beyond the gate, within the dark shroud of the forest canopy. Muttering, "Awful late for a traveler," Hamlin stood and hurried to a narrow door next to the fireplace, took a brass key from his pocket and opened the door. Immediately, Tarin realized it was more than a closet door. As the light of the lanterns and the fire cast away the shadows within, he saw what had to be the wall of the city. He could even smell its distinctive, musty odor of wood in the early stages of rot.

"What's that?" he asked, his curiosity again overpowering his timidity. Hamlin hushed him and peered through what looked like a small gap between two planks in the city wall.

Sarky turned to him. "It's a secret peephole. Father uses it to see what's going on outside the gate or who's coming up the forest road. That way, he doesn't have to let a traveler know there's someone watching from the wall. It's even better than the sliding spy door on the gate."

"A horseman, way down the road," Hamlin said. "He's got a lantern. The way he's riding, looks like some sort of trouble."

Sarky got up and walked into the room, taking a place next to his father. "What's the man doing?"

"Whoa!" Hamlin spun around with wide eyes. "Something just knocked him clean off his horse!" He reached into his shirt pocket and handed a tiny glass phial to Sarky. "Keep this with you just in case."

Sarky frowned at the object in his hand and tried to hand it back.

"Just keep it," he ordered, then turned and hurried out of the little room and rushed to the front door. "I'm going to the gate to get a better look," he called back to the boys. "If I need to ring the warning bell, you boys best hurry north in case there's trouble at the gate. Use the back door." With that, he threw on a jacket and went outside.

Sarky pocketed the illumina and gestured Tarin over to the crack. Tarin did, and looked through the lower portion of the crack.

"Look at that!" Sarky whispered.

Almost a hundred paces down the forest road, a man stood by a horse, thrusting his sword toward the forest. In his other hand was what looked like a lantern. It illuminated his form and that of his horse, but nothing more.

Suddenly, the man stumbled to his side.

"There!" Sarky blurted. "It happened again! But what's hitting him?" He looked up at Tarin. "Could it be the shadows?"

Tarin ignored him; the stranger had regained his footing and begun backing up. Now, he held his sword out in the opposite direction of the town. The light in his hand flickered, then grew brighter. Tarin heard a shout and saw the man make a sideways sweep with his weapon. There, in the greater brightness, Tarin saw them: two yellow slits, glimmering within a dark orb upon the pitch-black, smoky silhouette of a man.

The traveler's sword struck the figure, and it contorted as if hurt, then fell to the ground and writhed. With a final downward thrust, the horseman put his sword, which now seemed to be creating light of its own, through the shadow creature's eyes. The phantom dematerialized into smoke, and as it drifted away, the man sheathed his sword.

"I can't see anything!" Sarky whispered. "What's he fighting with?"

Before Tarin could respond, he heard another shout and looked back through the hole. The man was being thrust from side to side while at least three shadows drifted around him, swinging what looked like black clubs. Tarin squinted harder at the sight, his heart racing.

Then something crawled by the opening, right in front of him.

Before he could react, he heard Sarky groan, "Tarin." The splash of vomit hitting the floor followed.

Tarin wanted to flee, but sudden terror held him fast. Unable to withdraw his eyes from the gap in the wall, he held his breath. A moment later he saw the shadow again, this time crawling along the ground just a few paces from the wall. It seemed to be keeping its dark, smoky belly just slightly above the dirt, and its limbs spread wide, almost like a spider's. With each slow crawling motion, it spread out its long, twig-like fingers and pressed them gently into the earth.

Tarin's mouth went dry as he stood alone next to the crack . . . and the phantom. Like a cloud billowing toward the heavens, the shadow rose to twice the height of a man and stood on long thin legs. Tarin forced his body from the wall, trying not to look at the creature's head. But as if he'd lost all control over where to place his gaze, his eyes lifted and he saw them: two giant, pale eyes, different from the yellow slits he'd grown accustomed too, but even more terrifying. They were empty, yet knowing, and seemed to be searching him. He felt as if some rat had crawled into his head and begun frantically searching for food.

The phantom moved nearer. Tarin's heart pounded harder as the distance between him and danger shortened. But just as it drew within a few paces of the wall, something glimmered behind him. He wrestled his hands from his side and hid his eyes. Immediately, he felt as if he'd been released from a vise.

He turned away from the wall and tried to run out of the room. He tripped over Sarky, nearly knocking a glowing object from his hand.

He looked at the light, and his head cleared. The pungent smell of vomit filled his nostrils, and he realized he'd nearly landed in a pile of the stuff.

"Did you see anything?" Sarky asked, his eyes wide and bloodshot in the glow.

Before he could answer, the nearing gallop of a horse came. Sarky put the glowing object into a pocket in his shirt and forced himself to his feet. He managed a half-grin. "Let's find out why those shadows seemed to enjoy that horseman's company so much."

"But one of those shadows is still out there, near the gate!" Tarin shouted, pointing at the crack in the wall. "It was . . . in my head!"

Sarky's eyes grew wide. "Then we better warn Father."

They sprinted toward the front door, but through the window, Tarin saw it was too late; Hamlin had already opened the gate, and the cloaked horseman was riding through.

TWELVE

"**D**ern you, Uncle Kane," Jak whispered, trying to break the disturbing silence. He couldn't remember an eerier night. Thin clouds veiled the crescent moon, and in the south, deep fog descended upon the forest canopy through the humid air. Most of the buildings along the main road were dark. The only real light came from the lanterns positioned above the road, some of which the lampwrights seemed to have forgotten that night. He watched his shadow grow, then shrink, as he approached each lit lantern, the dark blotches that were his arms exaggerated in length as they swayed from side to side.

Uncle Kane hadn't come home that evening, which likely meant he was in a drunken stupor inside one of the city bars. Kane was already disliked by the guards for his frequent nightly disturbances of the peace, and Jak didn't want this to be the night his uncle was finally locked up. He expected Kane to be at The Rising Moon. It was on a side street near the inn, and already, Jak could see the road in the distance, enshrouded by the shadows of a massive brick house and nearby stable.

He turned onto the road, scampered through a pile of broken glass, and looked up toward the bar about a hundred paces away. Its iron sign hung unmoving in the still air, and a dull light covered the two smudged windows near the entrance. The Rising Moon had to be one of the dingiest and roughest bars in Woodend. Why his uncle liked the place so much was beyond Jak's understanding.

He drew near the bar door when his eyes happened upon a fellow night traveler farther down the road. Encouraged that he wasn't alone, he waved.

The unusually tall and brawny fellow looked at him beneath what appeared to be a dull red hood. Jak lowered his hand. That stare the man was giving him . . . the stiffness of his stance . . . Was he angry, or simply ill at ease upon encountering a stranger?

Jak cleared his throat and hurried up the steps to the bar porch, put his hand on the door latch and glanced back down the road. The man was gone. A tingle crawled up his spine as the latch came down.

The door opened to a smoke-filled room echoing an assortment of grunts and banter. There, in the corner, sat Uncle Kane in a group of unkempt men. Each had a mug of ale, and each looked inebriated. With a sigh, Jak headed there, intent on retrieving his uncle.

† † †

Mist covered the part of the window in front of Tarin's mouth, moisture he'd created in his excitement about the mysterious dark-cloaked horseman Hamlin was speaking with near the gate. Sarky stood next to him, smelling strongly of vomit and sweat. Tarin was so glad the shadow hadn't entered with the horseman, he barely noticed the stench.

Hamlin had just opened the gate and let the man and his large, white-and-spotted horse into the city. After a few hasty words, Hamlin had closed the gate. They'd been talking ever since, but not loud enough for Tarin or Sarky to hear through the glass.

"This is really odd."

Tarin turned at Sarky's comment. "How so?"

"Normally, Father questions strangers through the gate spy-hole. He must've made an exception because the fellow was in trouble. Or maybe he didn't want to wait too long and give whatever was attacking him a chance to catch up and get into the city when the gate opened. . . . The shadow you saw didn't get in, did it?"

Tarin shook his head, his eyes still glued to the stranger outside. Hamlin began to lead the man to a set of stalls across the street.

At the sight, Sarky pulled him from the window. "Let's not give away that we were spying on them."

He pushed Tarin toward a chair, then flopped down on his rug, put his hands behind his head and kept one eye guarding the door.

After a few moments of listening to only his breathing and Sarky's, Tarin heard footsteps outside and saw the door latch move. He bit his lip. The door opened and Hamlin lumbered in, followed by a tall man in a deep brown cloak. A hood was draped beneath his shoulder-length dark hair that, though now unkempt, looked as if it was usually clean and proper. He had a light beard and mustache, again appearing as if they hadn't been cared for in at least a week. His eyes, though tired, glistened green as they met Tarin's. Tarin felt his usual fear of strangers skip away.

"So," the newcomer said, "here are the two fine lads you mentioned." His voice was pleasant, but strong, and carried an accent similar to that of the northerners. The stranger walked over and studied the boys.

"They seem somewhat thin," he said softly, as if to himself. His forehead wrinkled. "Though someday I'm sure they'll be strong as oxen."

Again his eyes moved to Tarin's, and his gaze pierced deep. Tarin felt as if the man was searching, for something in his expression or perhaps something deeper. His heart skipped, and he saw a vision of a tower far in the distance, beyond an endless sea of misty hills. The vision ended almost as quickly as it came, and he saw the man's eyes closed in deep thought.

"May I sit?" the man asked Hamlin, opening his eyes and looking at the gatekeeper, who was adding wood to the fire.

"Please," Hamlin replied, throwing another log into the gentle flames. He pointed to the guest chair next to Tarin, then said, "Sarky, go fetch Mr. Gildareth some milk."

Sarky groaned and got up, not noticing the sudden widening of Tarin's eyes.

"Don't fret, lad," the man named Gildareth said. "For your efforts, I will oblige you and your company with some interesting tales I've gleaned from my many travels."

T̶ ✝ ✝ ✝

Ihe air was far more polluted here than even the inn's social hall. Jak worked his way through the endless smoke, trying not to cough, and took a seat at his uncle's table. Kane glanced at him through glossy eyes and smiled. "This be me nephew," he told the others, slapping him hard on the back and pulling him into a hard hug. "What brings ye to this castle of ill-repute?"

Jak wobbled in his chair when Kane let go, and regained his composure just before toppling off. He carefully took Kane's arm and stood. "Come, we need to be getting home. You need your rest."

Kane pulled his arm away and laughed. "I'm getting rest right now, talking with me friends about the pitiful city and its even more pitiful governor." He held out his hand toward the others. "Tell the boy . . ." He stopped speaking to gulp down a messy swig of ale. Two yellow streams leaked from either side of his mouth. "Tell the boy what ye all think of the governor."

They lifted their mugs and after a few miscellaneous, near unintelligible insults, they chanted in unison, "Curse him!"

Jak grimaced when they all grunted and wiped foam from their mouths, and attempted to steady the nausea creeping up his throat. "Why do you all loath the governor? What has he done to merit your contempt?"

They looked at him as if he were a fool, but said nothing.

From the other corner of the room, near the door, Jak saw a well-dressed bald man stand and begin walking toward them. When the man drew close enough for him to see his face through the smoke, Jak recognized him as Sayin, the odd man his uncle and he had met at the social hall a couple of days before.

"I'll tell you why these men are angry with the governor," Sayin said as his piercing blue eyes glared at Jak with an intensity that didn't fit his gentle smile. "They can sense the king's anger with this governor."

He turned toward the other men at the table. "Kane is angry that such a weak man claims to be the throne's hands and voice in this place, when it's another that should be ruling."

Jak saw Sayin's hand begin to tremble, groping near his waist pocket. He grew sick in his stomach and leaned back in his chair, deciding that Sayin was either drunk or insane.

Kane scoffed and looked into his empty mug. "Ye got us all wrong. We don't care what the king wants."

Sayin's hand began to slide into his pocket, but stopped when Kane slammed his fist into the table and shouted, "But we still can't condone that pathetic Willerdon. How can that weak fool sit back and let the city fall into shambles?"

He spun toward Sayin and met his now-wide eyes and smirk with a face full of fury. "Folks are going to starve this year, the lumber camps are bein' neglected, and worst of all, Willerdon's hidin' somethin' about a danger in that forest, just to keep from havin' ta deal with it."

Kane calmed himself, held out his hands to steady an apparent dizziness, and leaned back in his chair. Sayin hurried to the empty seat to his left.

Jak sensed his enthusiasm exaggerated, but his uncle smiled.

"What danger do you speak of?" Sayin asked.

"A monster of sorts. Don't know much more than that. I just heard from family in Northlake. One of the folks down there was eaten by something in the forest a few days ago. And it was no bear, they say. The marks on what was left of the poor soul proved that. Too big for even the biggest bear claws. I helped bury a dead fellow in the forest a few days past, bet ye anything it was the Northlaker. His remains were in a bag, but I knew something huge must've gotten hold of him from how messed up the contents were."

"Too big for a bear?" Sayin asked.

"Yes. And he seemed like he got flattened from somethin' falling from the sky. This thing's a flyin' monster!"

"And why do you believe the governor is hiding this information?" Sayin said. "How do you know the tale is even true? The people of North-lake are considered rather backward and queer by most. Perhaps they're making it up."

Kane opened his mouth to answer when the bar door flew open and two men walked in, one stout and rugged, the other not weak, but small in comparison to the first.

"Any of you wish to join us on a hunt tomorrow?" the larger man said in a booming voice. "I promise you, it'll be a challenge greater than any of you have ever experienced."

"And what would we be hunting?" an especially hairy brute with a surprisingly high voice spluttered from the other end of the room. "Unless it's bigger than a bear and faster than an eagle, I doubt it'll offer me sport."

The large man stared him in the eyes. "Your greatest challenge is likely convincing people you're a man. That is, until they see the excess of hair upon your body." Some in the bar laughed. Others, including the hairy man with the high voice, looked angry.

The newcomer took another step into the room and held out his hands. "I assure you all, this hunt will not disappoint."

At this, Kane stood and slammed his mug against the table. "It's the monster! He speaks of the monster!" He looked around the room. "I told ye all it was true. My relations wouldn't lie!"

"Shut up, old fool!" the high-voiced brute said. "You convinced a few of us to believe your story, but not even this fellow's rantings'll make the rest of us believe you."

Kane tried to rush the hairy man, but stumbled instead. Jak hurried to help him up.

"The governor's hiding something from ye all!" Kane yelled as Jak pulled him to his wobbly feet.

"It's true!" some of the men from Kane's table shouted.

The smaller newcomer tugged at the arm of his companion. The large man paid no heed. Instead, he pulled from a bag he held on his shoulder a large, pointed object and threw it upon the floor. "This is to help with your unbelief."

There, on the beer-stained floor, rested an animal claw the length of a man's forearm and the width of a young tree. The room fell silent, and the man continued. "For those of you who wish to kill its owner, meet me tomorrow afternoon across from the inn."

He turned and followed his now livid friend out the door. "I can't believe you did that!" Jak heard the man say just before the door slammed shut.

All the men in the bar sat or stood, gawking at the claw. Kane pulled himself from Jak's grip and stumbled toward it, reached down and ran his hand across its dark, striated surface. He picked it up with a grunt and displayed it to the silent group. "See? I state the truth."

The room burst into a flurry of excited conversation, and most of the bar occupants came over to observe Kane's prize. "Should we help with the hunt?" Jak heard someone say. "Kane was right about the claw, which means he's probably right about the beast being a killer."

"How would we hunt something like that?" someone else said. "We'd be the hunted, not the hunters."

"Why weren't we warned about this?" the squeaky-voiced man said.

Kane was now surrounded by many believers in his story. The old man smiled, an eerie, wicked smile Jak had never seen on him before, and his face appeared to glow a dull red. At first Jak thought it was a trick of the light, enhanced by his uncle's drunken state. Then he saw, in the corner of his eye, something actually glowing red. He shifted his eyes toward the source, and saw, still sitting where he'd been moments before, Sayin holding a glowing red phial on his lap. Jak could only see the whites of the man's partly closed eyes, but could hear the strange, soft chant flow from his unmoving lips.

A terrible uneasiness descended upon him. His hands began to tremble when Sayin's eyes flew open and stared at him with what looked like two dark slits. Jak blinked twice, and by the second blink, Sayin's eyes had returned to their normal blue circular state. A cordial smile crossed the bald man's mouth, yet Jak shivered. Sayin again closed his eyes, again only far enough to hide all but the whites, and continued his chant.

Jak's unrest grew so strong, he felt he might vomit. Then he heard them. Or more like *felt* them. Hundreds of silent voices shouting at him, mocking him, screaming for him to leave. He looked at Kane, who stood triumphantly with the claw, his face still as terrible as before. But despite his concern for the old man, he decided his uncle would have to manage on his own the rest of the night. He didn't want any more part in whatever was going on in that bar. Besides, with so many eager ears, Uncle Kane probably wouldn't even leave the bar until sunup.

He worked his way through the crowd and rushed outside. The cool, clean air greeted him, and with it, complete peace.

✝ ✝ ✝

Gildareth was a young man, appearing not much older than thirty, though his keen eyes made Tarin believe him older. He was surprised that when Gildareth spoke to him, he felt no inclination to turn away, as he would with anyone else. Perhaps it was his vain hope that those orbs might reveal some vision of the outside world, that he might see something those eyes had already seen. But no such vision appeared. Instead, Hamlin kept the man occupied with meaningless banter.

"You should spend the night here," Hamlin said after a long speech about Gildareth's fine horse, "and go to the inn tomorrow. Let's see, if you take the road north, you'll get there within a half hour. Of course, I should probably tell you about some of the kitchens on the way. In case you want to get something to eat. There's one called Mr. Fatty Bread, and it's . . ."

Tarin yawned and rubbed his eyes. Would Sarky's father ever shut that flapping jaw of his? When Hamlin began describing Mr. Fatty Bread's greasy biscuits, Tarin decided *enough* and went to the kitchen, where Sarky was stuffing his face with more truffles. Sarky offered him a handful of crumbs.

"What are you doing?" he whispered angrily. "Don't you want to hear Gildareth's stories?"

Sarky held up his finger, chewed a few times, then swallowed. "Of course I do! But not on an empty stomach. Besides, Father never lets guests speak until he's given his account of *allllll* the city's sites. I'm sure you noticed."

Tarin grabbed Sarky's arm and began pulling him back toward the living quarters. "Maybe he's about finished. Let's get back."

"Wait. Do you think we should ask Gildareth about the shadows?"

He paused, remembering both the bizarre sight in the alley and the pale, large-eyed phantom he'd seen just that night. "Yes. But not if your father's around. I don't want him to think we're crazy."

Sarky snickered. "He already thinks I'm crazy. It's you he still believes sane. Though we both know better."

Tarin ignored the comment and looked into the other room. Hamlin was lighting his pipe. Perhaps he was finished with his Woodend report.

The boys entered the room and sat on the rug near Gildareth's feet. He smiled at them, and Tarin didn't try to hide the eagerness in his face.

"Have you boys ever been outside of Maplelake Forest?"

They shook their heads. "I don't think either of us has even been twenty paces outside Woodend's walls," Tarin said.

Gildareth's eyes brightened. "Well, I can hardly tell you stories of the greater world when you don't even understand the wonder of your own forest, or even that of your own city. So I shall begin with lore about Woodend, and its walls that you have yet to venture far from."

Gildareth must have seen Tarin's despair, because he said, "Though Arvalast is a large and magnificent kingdom, there are few jewels left in this world brighter than the forest in which you live, or more precious to the king than this city of Woodend. It is one of the walled dwellings of men in this land, walled because of the dark times. Though this and some of the other towns in the forest are small compared to the large cities of the south, your walls are no less blessed. Like many other cities of Arvalast, they are blessed by the king and were built by a special people: the glorions."

"Interesting," Hamlin said through a plume of pipe smoke. "I wonder if Undertree's walls were so blessed. If so, the blessing wasn't effective."

"Undertree's walls were blessed," Gildareth said as the light of the fire flickered across his bearded face. "Its walls were built well before those of Woodend, and the other forest towns, and were quite strong. But as the people of a walled city grow proud and begin to forget their loyalty to the throne, the walls lose their potency. To your eyes, they might still look strong. But to the eyes of darker things, the walls might almost appear to not exist. Mere wood, nor stone nor brick, cannot hinder all evil that might wish to trespass a city."

At the mention of "darker things," Tarin's palms grew sweaty as his desperation to ask about the shadows increased. But Hamlin was sitting quite comfortable and showing no signs of leaving.

"Traveler," Hamlin said, "what do you say about *our* walls? How strong are they? Assuming your story is accurate."

Gildareth looked at him, the faint lines on his forehead more visible. "From what I have seen thus far, the walls still look strong. But I doubt that's true for the entire structure. That is one of the reasons I was sent, to inspect the wall." He turned his eyes back to Tarin and smiled. "And the hearts of the people living here."

He again gave Hamlin his attention. "This town is pivotal to the throne. Forces are moving in the world. Forces that could pose great danger; to not just the survival of this forest, but to the whole of Arvalast. Your walls, my friend, cannot fail."

Hamlin rested his pipe on his knee. "I must say, if you're right, Arvalast is in a ripe amount of trouble." He gestured toward the spy closet. "I know places in the wall where there're some large gaps between the boards."

Gildareth chuckled and turned to the boys. "Are you afraid of rabbits?"

They looked at each other, befuddled, then shook their heads.

"Then a gap in the wood will pose no danger to you." He turned back to Hamlin. "You see, unless you are worried about keeping out rodents and skunks, gaps in the wood will not be a problem. Beyond your vision lies a protective shroud. This shroud encases the wall with an ancient power once prevalent in the land. The shroud is susceptible to neither rot nor damage. Only the hearts of those living within its protection can weaken it. Often, the condition of the physical wall will indeed reflect the power of the shroud. Yet not always. That is why I must make a careful inspection. To determine if your wall is indeed weak."

The room fell silent. Tarin wished Hamlin would leave, maybe go look at the wall, so he could at last ask about the shadows.

Someone knocked on the door, and all of them started. Except for Gildareth, Tarin noticed. Hamlin got up with a groan and headed to the door. "Who could be calling at such a late hour?"

Sarky nudged Tarin, eager at their chance to ask Gildareth about the shadows while Hamlin was preoccupied with the door. Tarin looked up at the cloaked man and opened his mouth. Nothing came out.

Sarky hit him with his elbow.

He tried again, "Do you know anything about—?"

"Tarin, my boy!"

Fighting a gasp, Tarin looked toward the door and saw his father step into the room. "I thought you'd returned home for the night, Tarin. It's well past midnight!"

He felt blood rush into his face, turned his gaze to a random corner of the room and tried to stutter a reasonable response. He couldn't.

Sarky spoke up. "I asked him to stay the night."

Kandis' eyes grew wide, followed by his mouth. He strode over and patted Tarin's back. "Excellent, lad! It's been years since you've had a friend."

More blood rushed to his head. But at least his father was placated.

Sarky introduced himself, then his father and Gildareth.

Kandis' face grew grave upon hearing that Gildareth had just come from the forest. "How were the roads?" he asked. "Did you encounter anything strange?"

Gildareth laughed. "My travels are never devoid of oddities. So much so, a straight road with no danger is unusual."

Kandis nodded. "I'm glad you made it here safely." He wrung his hands together and raised a brow. "You aren't, perchance, a skilled hunter?"

"In some ways."

"In that case, if you're interested in a most unusual hunt, meet me tomorrow afternoon across from the inn. My friend and I have scoured most of the city today for worthy men to accompany us, but too few seemed interested."

"Where is your friend?" Gildareth asked.

Kandis shifted his eyes toward the fire and frowned. "We had words an hour ago. He doubts whether he'll participate in the hunt."

"What are you planning to hunt?" Hamlin asked.

"That, you can find out tomorrow. If you decide to join me."

"I can't leave the gate, but I wish you the best."

Gildareth stood and bowed at Kandis. "Perhaps I will see you tomorrow. I'll be staying at the inn after the night is over, and I'm interested in this hunt of yours." His voice grew soft. "And I am sure your friend will be back at your side soon. Anger between true friends cools quickly, as long as both have good hearts. I sense you do."

Kandis smiled. "I can certainly vouch for his heart, though mine feels rather calloused at the moment from the day's labors and some reckless actions on my part." He bowed and left, but not before winking at Tarin.

THIRTEEN

Tarin awoke to the sound of a whinny and knocking horseshoes. He and Sarky had spent the night on the rug near the fire, while Gildareth slept in Sarky's closet-sized room across from the kitchen. Hamlin stayed in his room on the other end of the house.

The door to Sarky's room was open, his bed empty. "Gildareth's already up and leaving!" Tarin shouted, recalling the sounds that had awakened him.

Sarky grunted and rolled over. "Huh?"

Tarin slapped him across the head. "Get up! We've got to talk to him before he goes."

Sarky sat up and rubbed his eyes. "I want more sleep. More sleep, I say."

"Shut up, Sarky." Tarin ran to the window. "He's already on his horse. If we don't talk to him now about the shadows, we might never get the chance."

Sarky leapt to his feet. "Dern it! That's right!" He threw a shirt onto his scrawny torso and ran to the door. Tarin followed.

The air outside was humid but cool, and from the puddles on the ground it looked like it had rained during the night. Gildareth had begun to lead his horse north when Sarky sprinted into its path. Remarkably, the beast didn't flinch, but rather tried to find a way around him. Sarky held out his hand. "Stop, sir."

Gildareth pulled back on the reins.

"We've been waiting to ask you something, and since you're heading off, we better do so now."

Gildareth slid off his mount and walked up to Sarky, looked down at him and crossed his arms. There was a hint of a smile on his face. "I knew there was some matter of unrest burning in your heart last night, and I half-expected to be interrupted when I arose this morning. But both of you were in such deep sleep, you didn't hear me prepare the tea, nor wash my face, nor prod you to awaken so I might say goodbye. I thought it perhaps better to leave you be, because a truly important matter would likely not allow for such a powerful sleep."

He turned his green eyes to Tarin next.

"Have you . . . ?" Tarin tried to turn his eyes away, but couldn't, nor did he truly want to. "Have you ever seen shadows during your travels?"

Gildareth smiled. "Many. One in particular just refuses to get off my trail."

"No . . . that's not what I meant."

"I know. You speak of something more sinister." His eyes leapt away from Tarin's and pain washed over his face, followed by concern. He walked to Tarin and knelt to eye level. "You've been seeing phantoms?"

He nodded, relieved Gildareth wasn't looking at him as if he'd gone mad.

Gildareth turned to Sarky. "Have you seen them?"

Sarky's face showed disappointment, and he lowered his head. "No. They just make me vomit whenever I get too close. Tarin's the only one who seems to be able to see them."

Gildareth returned his eyes to Tarin's. "What do they look like?"

He cleared his throat. "Mostly they appear as shadows of men. Only . . . fog-like. As if a gust of wind could blow them away. But I saw one last night that looked different. Rather than the snake-like slits for eyes like all the others, it had great big eyes. Very pale."

Gildareth stroked his beard and placed a hand on the hilt of his sword. His graveness was making Tarin question whether it had been wise to speak of these things. Gildareth must have noticed his concern, because he smiled, and his face seemed less anxious now. "Come here, my young friends."

He and Sarky took the few steps necessary to obey and looked up.

"I am in a precarious position, because there is so much I wish to tell you, yet so little I can at the moment. Knowledge can be good, but also dangerous; if given prematurely. But I can tell you at least a few things, based on what I just learned from you both. First, Arvalast is in the midst of a great war, one both seen and unseen. The unseen has been raging for hundreds of years, and only periodically does it spill into the realm of the seen."

"Is the war about to be seen again?" Sarky asked. "Is that why Tarin saw those shadows?"

Gildareth shook his head. "Tarin, it seems, has been gifted with a special ability."

Tarin's heart leapt.

"Your friend," Gildareth continued, looking over at him, "is seeing into the hidden war with his special eyes. And you," Gildareth said, turning back to Sarky, "you're feeling the unrest caused by this war."

He spread out his hands and lifted his head toward the sky. "All of what you can see lives or dies by what's happening in the unseen panes of this world. Yet few remember that Arvalast is composed of so much more than the trees and the grass and the bright September sun."

Tarin felt a strange sadness descend on his heart. Gildareth's eyes grew moist, and he continued.

"When the king took possession of this land many years ago, there was nothing invisible to the naked eye. All you now see was showered in a canopy of unimaginable beauty created by the power of his light. The sky, the grass, the water, all of it was so much richer and more vibrant in color and feeling. The mere sight of a single leaf would melt one into tears of joy!"

"What happened to change this?" Tarin said.

He lowered his hands and patted his horse. "It began as a rebellion in the hearts of the king's people. They grew discontent in the light and desired to have its power for themselves. Each wanted his own world to rule and dominate. Eventually, those people plotted to march upon the king's citadel in the capital city of Illuminara and take Arvalast for themselves. A few of these dissenters traveled to the forbidden land of Shieth far to the south, seeking an ancient power rumored to dwell there. They found it . . . and unleashed it. It devoured them, both body and spirit, and they returned to spread the malignancy into Illuminara and throughout Arvalast. Those still loyal to the king dubbed it the 'Crimson Light.' All feared and reviled it. Soon, a dark army from Shieth, once held captive by the king's light, swarmed into Arvalast and began a new war against the king. The unseen war."

"This army is the shadows, isn't it?" Sarky said, his voice barely a whisper.

Gildareth narrowed his eyes. "Yes."

"So what happened next in the story?" Tarin asked.

Gildareth knelt and put his hands on Tarin's shoulders. "This is not a mere story. And ultimately, it is for us to determine what happens next."

He held Tarin's gaze for a moment, then bounded onto his horse. He didn't ride away though, just stared down at them. "The king withdrew his kingdom and his light to another place, where it will remain until the day Arvalast is to be restored. All that is evil now tries to enter this kingdom through the only door the king left upon this land: a door of forgotten legend and great destiny."

He pointed up the main road. "The door is said to lie far to the north, beyond your forest and your city. The realm of Macalum, the plains to the south, and Maplelake Forest are all that stand between the darkness and the light. If they fall, Arvalast falls."

Next, he pointed toward Tarin and Sarky. "And your forest is the strongest wall between the door to the realm of light and the king's enemies."

Gildareth looked up the main road, then scratched his head. "All this talk of evil has made me forget where I can find your governor's house. Could either of you direct me to it?" He looked over at Sarky, who Tarin could tell was in no mood to perform such a menial task as give directions. But he still gave Gildareth a quick description of how to get to the governor's house.

Gildareth prodded his horse with his foot. "A friend of mine living in Woodend could tell you all sorts of grim tales about the approaching evil. And perhaps even some encouraging stories about the forces of light still fighting alongside the king to stop the darkness. His name is Bill, and his wife's name is Margaret."

With that, Gildareth snapped his reins, and the horse went charging north.

Tarin looked at Sarky with wide eyes. "Old Bill and Margaret? They live near me! If we hurry, we can get to their house within an hour!"

"Haven't you heard enough?" Sarky asked, his face and voice downcast.

"What's wrong with you?"

"Didn't you hear all that? We're doomed. Those shadows are going to kill us, then go find that door, and then destroy the whole world!" He shuffled his feet. "I kind of like the world, even if the grass isn't green enough or the water tasty enough."

Sarky was right. Tarin hadn't really mulled it over yet, but most of what Gildareth had said was doom filled. But something about what he told them was awakening a fire in him, a desire to learn more so he might better understand the world he lived in. As Gildareth had noted about him, Tarin had always known there was more to it than he could see.

He was staring straight at Sarky, but he could barely see him through his buzzing imagination. "Bill knows some tales of forces of light fighting the darkness," he said. "And no one in town ever takes him seriously. Care to join me on another quest?"

Sarky raised his eyes to meet Tarin's. "Forces of light, huh? Do you really think there's any good in the world if what Gildareth said is true?"

"Of course there is. And it sounds like Bill is our path to knowing about it."

Sarky kicked some pebbles on the ground as he began dragging his feet up the road. "I supposed we can go then."

"Shouldn't we tell your father what we're doing?"

Sarky rolled his eyes. "No wonder he likes you so much. You're responsible. Good for him, but annoying to me. But to appease you, we'll let him know." He grinned. "Besides, if what I'm smelling is correct, he's making breakfast. It'd be a pity to let him eat it all by himself."

Tarin raced Sarky into the kitchen, where they found Hamlin busily preparing eggs over his wood burner.

"You boys see Mr. Gildareth off?"

"Indeed we did," Sarky said, grabbing a few plates from the cupboard. "Charming fellow. Told us some awfully happy stories. Also told us about a friend of his who could tell us a little bit more. Mind if we visit him today?"

Hamlin nearly flipped an egg off the skillet. "You're asking my permission to go out?"

"Yes. Tarin's idea, wouldn't you know."

Hamlin patted Tarin hard on the back. "I knew I liked you, boy! You'll make Sarky a respectable lad yet!"

Tarin felt warm inside at the compliment, and grinned at Sarky's annoyance.

A half hour later, the boys had finished breakfast, packed some dried meat and fruit into a bag for later, and were making their way up the main road. It was a little odd for Tarin, not skirting through the alleys to avoid the people, but Sarky insisted he was in no mood for hiding after last night's adventure. To Tarin's surprise, though still uncomfortable as the street grew busy with farmers selling goods and people walking about on some business far less important than his mission, he didn't feel the usual urge to panic and run away.

They continued along toward the inn, where they saw a few rough-looking people gathering on the other side of the street, the same place Tarin had first met Dralo and Ristun.

"Looks like some of the hunters your father was looking for are already beginning to show their ugly faces. Glad my father decided to miss out on that little adventure." Sarky spoke a little too loud for Tarin's liking. But no one seemed to have heard.

When they were within ten paces of the inn's main door, it opened, and two cloaked and hooded travelers stepped out and headed toward them with a fast stride. Tarin immediately recognized the two northerners, and as they drew closer, Dralo's eyes happened upon his stare. The man stopped and held out his hand.

"Why, I do believe it is our little friend Tarin." He looked over at Sarky and lowered his brows. "You better not have any tomatoes hidden beneath that shirt of yours, or I might have to get angry."

Tarin held out his hands. "No, no, no. We're friends now."

Sarky looked over at him and smirked.

Dralo crossed his arms and glared at Sarky. They all stared at each other until Ristun piped in, "You'll have to pardon Dralo. Our comrade Gildareth finally came this morning, and rather than us being able to have a pleasant morning over some steaming grits, he asked us to accompany him to the roof of the inn. From there, we saw something mysterious in the forest, and he sent us to investigate—"

"Hush, Dralo!" Ristun said. "You shouldn't speak of such things in front of the lads. No need to darken their souls. It's probably just a fire, anyway. And we didn't come to this forest to put out fires of a physical nature."

"Don't worry," Sarky said. "Your comrade Gildareth already told us enough to make a lumberjack cry. Stuff about an approaching darkness that's about to open a sacred door and destroy all of Arvalast."

Dralo's brows lowered above wide eyes. "He told you all that? But why?"

Sarky shrugged. "Maybe it's because Tarin's been seeing phantom shadows from an unseen war. Or maybe because I've been vomiting every time one of them gets too close. Or maybe Gildareth likes to open each bright, new day with a little black yarn, so if a storm wipes out the city in the afternoon, it'll lighten the blow."

Now both the northerners were taken aback.

"Please," Sarky said. "Don't ask if it's true that Tarin sees shadows and that I vomit because of them. Yes, yes, and double yes. It's true."

Dralo reached for the hilt of his sword. "You're being disrespectful, boy."

Ristun kicked Dralo in the shin. "Calm down. We have work to do."

"Investigating the red glow of a fire is not work, it is dull labor. I want to fight, something, anything!"

Ristun pointed to Sarky. "So much that you would battle this lad?"

Dralo chuckled. "I'm not so certain *battle* would be the appropriate word for such an encounter."

Sarky held out his fists. "Don't be so sure about that!"

Dralo burst into laughter.

Ristun rolled his eyes, bowed to the boys, and pulled his suddenly hysterical companion down the road.

"Come back here and get a feel for my fists!" Sarky yelled after them. Dralo lifted his head and howled.

"Shut up," Tarin whispered. "You're embarrassing me."

"I could've beaten him."

"Sure you could've. Now can we please go?"

"Fine." Sarky reached into the bag of food, pulled out some meat, stuffed it into his mouth, and stomped past the inn.

Tarin looked around and noticed a few girls about his age standing next to what appeared to be their grandmother. They were giggling. A sudden burst of anger swept through him and he stuck out his tongue. They frowned and began chatting to each other. He smiled. "Very well done," he told himself aloud. "Very well done."

Another twenty minutes brought them within a few streets of Willow Road. "I wonder where all the people are heading?" he asked Sarky while steady groups of nervous-looking men and a few guards passed by, heading south.

Sarky shrugged. "They're probably off to see what's going on at the inn. That hunt's going to raise quite a stir."

It was then that Tarin noticed his father a few houses up the road. Not wanting to have to explain what he and Sarky were up to, he grabbed Sarky's arm and pulled him to the roadside. Sarky looked around. "What do you see?"

"It's Father. He's coming down the road, probably going to get Lionnel before heading to the inn to see who showed up for the hunt. I don't know about you, but I'm in no mood to explain why we're off to Bill's. He might also want to send me home to visit with Mother for a bit." Tarin sighed. "I'm sure she's ripe worried about me since I've been gone the whole night."

"You're right. Dern adults can be so pesky. Let's just hide."

They hurried to the red and brown walls of a solitary brick house. High weeds grew in what might have once been a yard. Sarky pointed to the partly open front door. "It looks abandoned."

The door made an unpleasant screech as they opened it. The air inside smelled strongly of pipe smoke. "I don't think it's abandoned," Tarin said, looking around at the bed in the corner and fresh ashes next to a pipe on a little stool by a window overlooking the road.

Sarky peered out the window. After a moment, he turned around. "Looks like we're safe. Your father passed by without even glancing this way. But we should wait here for a few minutes, just to make sure he's gone."

Tarin looked around for anything of interest. His eyes happened upon the back wall. Someone had scratched words all over it. He drew closer and stopped. "Sarky, I don't think we should be here."

"Getting a little timid again, old boy? Afraid the codger living here might come back and give us a whooping for snooping about his house?"

Tarin didn't respond. When Sarky finally took his place next to him, he heard the gasp he anticipated.

"This fellow must have the foulest mouth in all of Arvalast!"

"And it's all about the governor." Each word scratched into the wall marked the work of a disturbed and hate-filled individual who wanted the governor and his entire family cursed, killed, and subjected to a number of other unholy pains.

As they continued to read the writing, Sarky's breathing grew louder, and he gagged and grabbed Tarin's arm.

A shadow crossed the window behind them and the room grew darker. Sarky lurched forward and vomited. "Tarin," he whispered as he fell to the ground, "we have to get out of here." He pulled on Tarin's pant-leg. "Quick, look around. Is it safe to run to the door?"

"I can't look," Tarin said, feeling tears swell in his eyes. "I'm scared too."

Sarky heaved again and whimpered. "Try."

Tarin felt his legs become wobbly, and then his whole body. He knew something was behind him, staring at the back of his head, looking into his mind with a malignant curiosity. He tried to turn around, but fear stopped him.

Sarky dry-heaved. "I can't take this anymore." He got up and made to run to the door.

Tarin forced enough courage to turn around. He grabbed Sarky to stop him.

Standing between them and the door was a hideous apparition. Like the shadow phantom he'd seen at the gatehouse, it stood like a man and had two large, pale eyes. He didn't know how he knew it, but he could sense the eyes were searching him, looking for both weakness and strength.

Sarky gagged, and then screamed in a panic and thrashed his arms about.

Tarin saw the creature's eyes move from him to Sarky, and immediately Sarky gagged, then vomited. "What . . . what's it *doing* to me?"

Tarin couldn't take his eyes from the beast. "It's in your head. It wants to see if you're a threat or ally."

Sarky stopped gagging and grunted, "How do you know that?"

The eyes turned back to Tarin. From the spot where a mouth should have been, two yellow cat-like fangs slid from the darkness, and wrath materialized on its blank, translucent face. A voice rang in his mind, telling him he was a coward and of no use to anyone. He was a useless vagabond, put in this town to simply make others feel better about themselves. A terrible grief began to devour him, and he threw his hands over his ears. "No, no, no!"

The wrath on the phantom's face shifted to amusement, and its eyes bugled even wider.

A knock came at the door; the phantom dematerialized and dissipated into the floorboards. Sarky gasped in a few breaths and straightened himself. "I . . . feel a little better."

Tarin looked through his tears and saw a man walk into the house, calling, "Uncle Kane!"

The man caught sight of the boys and nearly toppled backward out the door. He steadied himself and pointed at them. "What are you doing here?"

"Who are you?" Sarky asked.

"I'm Jak. The man who lives here is my uncle. What are you doing in his house?" His eyes grew a little wider. "Are you lads trying to steal something?" He glanced at their pockets, then smiled. "Actually, there's really nothing to steal here except for some pipes. But you boys best be off. My uncle isn't the friendliest man in the world, and if he caught you here, he'd probably beat you."

"I believe you," Sarky said, pointing back at the wall with writing on it. "Your uncle's clearly a lunatic."

Jak looked at the wall, then ran to it. He passed his fingers over the words as he read in a whisper, then turned to them. "Did you boys do this?"

"Of course not!" Sarky said. "I'd never use language like that. Your crazy uncle put that on the wall."

Jak put his head in his hands and moaned, "Uncle's finally lost his mind." He lifted his head and looked at the door. "He must've written that last night, after I saw him at the bar, because it wasn't here when I looked for him in the evening."

"What are you talking about?" Sarky asked.

Jak ran to the door without even glancing at them. "He's probably at the inn, causing trouble for the governor. Better get to him before he gets himself thrown in prison." He'd started out the door when he lifted his nose in the air and sniffed. "What's that hideous smell?"

"You stepped in some of my puke," Sarky said. "Might want to wipe it off in the grass."

Jak gagged, stumbled backward out the door, then struggled to his feet. He hurriedly wiped his boot in the weeds, shot the boys a disgusted look, and then ran down the road.

Sarky glanced around the room. "Hate to ruin his day after he scared away that shadow." He stared hard at Tarin. "It was a shadow, wasn't it?"

Tarin nodded, still a little delirious from the encounter with the creature.

Sarky grabbed his arm and pulled. "Come on. Let's go."

They rushed out into the noonday sun. Tarin relaxed in the light. Still, he couldn't get the beast's cruel words out of his head.

"Am I useless, Sarky?"

"No, you're the best friend I've ever had. Now shut up and run."

By the time they rounded the corner onto Willow Road, Tarin was smiling.

FOURTEEN

It was a full day's journey from Lockspell to Woodend, assuming a traveler kept up a good pace and met no major hindrances along the way. And Jebin hoped he wouldn't. Thus far, the road wasn't washed out, which he was afraid might be the case in places because of the summer's heavy rains. He didn't want to spend even one wasted minute before returning to Woodend, fearing that if he did, others might soon pass through the gate of Lockspell and eventually meet up with him. Others like Bolard.

In spite of his worries, the morning was pleasant while cloaked and hooded in the usual garb of a forest traveler, Jebin walked along the brick path. The path remained paved in that way for a number of miles until it turned to dirt, went uphill, and then angled down to the base of Woodend. But before he reached the more rugged road, he had hours to tread upon the smooth bricks beneath him and admire the hint of color enveloping the leaves of Maplelake Forest.

A squirrel ran across the path in front of him, angrily chattering at another squirrel that had apparently stolen an acorn. He laughed as the two squirrels spiraled up a tree, still chattering. The argument abruptly ended when both animals forgot what they were bickering about and began lunging from tree to tree until they were out of sight.

After another hour, the foliage grew thicker and Jebin's mood more dismal. A cold vise clutched his mind as he dwelled on the dire act he'd committed three years prior, the one that led to the woman's death.

He stepped on a branch, and it cracked. After the crack, he heard another, fainter sound of movement a short distance into the woods. A former woodsman, he knew an animal hadn't made the sound. He kept walking at the same pace, aware that faint footsteps followed him now. A massive oak tree cast a deep shadow along the path a short distance ahead. Chipmunks chattered within its boughs and birds fluttered through its overhanging canopy.

Thud . . . crackle . . . thud came from within the forest.

"Keep on coming," Jebin whispered. "You're in for a little surprise if you're up to no good." He expected the pursuer to be a thief, since forest travelers usually didn't sneak around like this.

Upon reaching the oak tree, he removed his load and placed it next to him on the ground. Whistling merrily, he pulled out some of the dry fruit and meat Rosie had prepared for him, leaned up against the tree and ate. He listened, but there were no more footsteps. He finished eating, yawned deeply, and rested his head against the tree, partly closing his eyes.

At first, there was no sound save for little animals scurrying around and birds chirping. Occasionally a gentle breeze rustled the leaves. Then he heard it. Someone crawling. He carefully directed his hidden gaze toward the source of the sound, a six foot tall thorn bush surrounded by saplings. Again, all went quiet. Then, one of the saplings began to move. The thicket rustled, and he heard the distinct sound of light breathing. He remained motionless.

Out from behind the thorn bush popped a head covered with stubble and thin, matted hair. The head disappeared, then reemerged. The newcomer poked out his head three more times until, finally satisfied, he edged out from behind the bush and crawled toward Jebin.

From his slitted eye, Jebin noticed the man wasn't large, and wore ragged clothes that looked as if they used to be a merchant's for their colorful nature. The scraggly man grew ever nearer and became quieter, moving slower. At last, he came within arm's length of the sheriff's bag and reached for it.

Jebin opened his eyes and reached out, seizing the thief's arm. The man screamed and tried to stand, yelling, "Let me go! I didn't do anything wrong!"

Jebin held fast. "I believe thievery is still a crime in the forest. I would know, because I'm a sheriff of a nearby town. It's called Woodend. You'll be spending some time there soon."

The man quieted. "Why?"

"Because you're under arrest. You're going to jail there."

"Not again!" With a sudden jolt, the man wrenched his arm free from Jebin's grasp, knocked him over, and boldly grabbed his bag before running into the woods at an uncanny speed. Jebin, enraged and embarrassed, yelled, "Get back here!" and darted into the woods after him.

Tree by tree sped by. Jebin couldn't see the thief, but he could hear him running a short distance ahead. At a shout of pain in the distance, he sped down a little ravine, hopped over a creek, and discovered the thief had run into a large thicket and become trapped in its thorny arms.

Jebin couldn't help snickering. "I see you got yourself in a bit of a predicament. Now perhaps you'll allow me to take you to Woodend."

The thief's eyes widened. "I won't go back to jail!" With a mighty struggle, he twisted and pulled. Jebin tried to rush in to stop him, but the thief exploded from the bush and darted west, leaving torn bits of blood-smeared clothing behind.

Weary and frustrated, Jebin turned and headed back toward the road. But each step he took became more and more difficult. Now that he was no longer distracted, images of the bleeding woman, her husband crying over her dying form, returned.

"Why can't I be rid of that memory?" he moaned aloud. "I was only trying to do the will of the king, and she stepped in the way." He stood in the shade of the woods, wondering if he should return to the chase just to have something else to dwell on. But he feared that if he did, he might not reach Woodend before dark.

He had continued on his way when he finally remembered: That thief had his bag and everything he would need in Woodend: clothes, bedding, a document detailing all he'd heard from his spying on Bolard and Dierop. In particular, he couldn't let that get into the hands of his enemies. He turned around and darted west after the man, maneuvering through a maze of roots and multiple briar thickets. With every step he felt better and better as the memory of his crime shrank away.

A narrow creek crossed his path and he lunged over it. A hill rose up before him. He ran up with tremendous speed, reached the top, and bolted back down, working his way through a myriad of saplings and old stumps as he did. But racing through a region of grass higher than his head, his boot splashed down into some mud. A wide stream flowed by in front of him. Beyond it was a tall cliff. He looked down. Footsteps worked their way through the mud and down into the stream.

He listened, but could only hear the water's bubbling. To the south, the creek seemed wider and deeper. To the north, the water was shallower and appeared easier to tread through. Jebin made up his mind, jumped into the knee-deep water and headed north.

The water flowed against him, making it hard to walk. He trudged along for a short distance and soon found some cracked twigs on overhanging bushes. "So, I chose wisely," he whispered, happy he was still on the thief's trail.

He traveled for some time through the water, occasionally catching signs of the thief's earlier presence. The sun rose in the sky as the day approached noon. Soon it grew difficult to see the sun; the cliff on his left grew higher and the trees and thick foliage to his right denser.

The air became muggy, and less light made it through the forest ceiling. Chills crept up his spine as he realized he was in an unfamiliar part of the forest. The sound of rapids approached, and the water grew deeper as huge rocks began jutting out all around him. He looked up ahead and saw that the creek widened and crashed against the many boulders that had fallen from the cliff.

To his right, a narrow path crept out of the greenery and up to the edge of the water. Footsteps were embedded deep within its muddy surface. He plodded over the bank and began to follow them.

The forest grew denser than he'd ever seen, and eventually noon seemed more like dusk. Uneasy, he reached for his pocket. His illumina barely glowed. "Can't the king even give me aid in this small way?" he whispered. Then he remembered why it was dim, and his heart sank.

He looked up, toward the forest roof, and scowled. "I know you're displeased with me. What I did three years ago was terrible. I would change the past if I could. But I cannot. Must I now suffer so much for my crime? Can't you grant me freedom from this constant misery?"

The light became dimmer. Jebin snarled and kicked a branch off the path. "Fine, I'll find my way without the aid of the throne!"

He trudged along for another half hour before noticing a faint glimmer far ahead of him. As he continued, it grew brighter. It began to take on the appearance of a shining red jewel, and its glow made him feel somehow less burdened. As the jewel's aura grew larger, Jebin realized the trees were beginning to thin. Soon, he stepped out into a large meadow, and far on the other side, a diminutive red object seemed to be suspended in space, perhaps some heirloom left long ago on a then-young reed.

Jebin stood for a moment and squinted while his eyes adjusted to the bright noonday light. He looked around. Tall grass spanned in every direction, surrounded by the dark green of more forest and ornamented with that single red light. Not caring what the light was at the moment, he took in a deep breath of clean air, pleased it was no longer muddied with the smell of rotting wood and wet moss. Instead, it contained the fresh scent of grass and flowers.

As he took another step into the meadow, he noticed some bent reeds. He smiled and followed the trail a short distance until he found footsteps in the soft underbrush beneath him.

He tracked them for a while, noticing that they seemed to be avoiding the other end of the meadow, until they abruptly stopped. He looked around. There was some bent grass toward the west. He looked down and saw more footsteps. But these strides were much longer than the previous, as if their maker had begun to run. He trailed them a bit, then noticed something lying in the trodden grass. He picked up the item and realized it was his bag.

He grew suspicious, curious as to why the thief would simply drop his pack. A sudden strange sound crawled up from the easternmost part of the meadow. A gentle song, or was it a chant?

Jebin crouched low in the grass. The chanting grew louder and more fervent, less melodious. Curiosity overwhelmed him, and he cautiously began to crawl through the high grass in the direction of the sound and the red light, making little noise in case the source of the chant wasn't friendly.

After many minutes of crawling through the thorny brush, his heart began to pound; through a patch of high grass, he could finally see who was making the sound. A man dressed in a gray cloak with a hood covering his face was weaving to and fro, waving his arms in the air and chanting in an unfamiliar language. In his outstretched arm he held a phial like an illumina, but it was glowing red, not white.

So the glow didn't come from an ornament, he thought.

The calm the light had brought him when he entered the meadow disappeared, and he felt as if he and this mysterious man weren't alone in the meadow. He looked up. Strange dark clouds billowed above him and blotted out the sun's light. He looked back at the cloaked man, who still chanted and wove through the grass.

His mind raced. Was this man casting some spell over him? Why did he feel so uneasy and fearful? He had never seen, never felt anything like this in his life.

The cloaked man began weaving more fervently, until he wove so hard to his left, he began stepping toward Jebin to steady himself. Not wanting to be spotted, Jebin put his face to the ground and held his breath. He heard the chanter step right up next to him, then change directions and step away. He looked up. The man was now leaning to his right and drifting quickly toward the forest.

Jebin prepared to turn and crawl away when the chanting stopped, and the man thrust the light high into the air and shouted, "Come, oh king! Adhere to your servant!"

King? Jebin couldn't comprehend that this man was calling the king in such a bizarre manner.

Red light poured from the phial, and all went quiet. The clouds above Jebin illuminated with an eerie crimson glow, and began rumbling. The cloaked man's hand looked as if it were on fire. There was a rustling in the trees behind the man, and Jebin's heart plummeted to the hollow of his stomach.

The chanter smiled and turned east, toward the sound. From the darkness of the woods in front of him came slow footsteps. The man dropped to his knees and bowed.

A man enshrouded in a glistening robe of white light walked between the trees and into the meadow. The chanter bowed lower. The glistening stranger looked down at the man.

"I, Lord of Arvalast, have heard your call, wielder of the sacred light." His voice was slow and soothingly calm. "What is your request?"

The gray-cloaked man spoke up, his voice quivering a little. "I, Sayin of Woodend, have much to request of you, my king. For a great injustice has been done in this forest: your forest."

FIFTEEN

Fat Gertrude sat across from Will, babbling about how her neighbor's cat hissed at her whenever she walked past her neighbor's house. All he heard was a shrill horn that seemed to have been thrust into the woman's throat. With his son missing, and the search party still unsuccessful in its hunt, his patience wore thinner and faster than usual.

"What do you want me to do?" he finally said.

"I want you to have the cat taken away, obviously! A beast like that shouldn't be allowed in the city."

He began muttering beneath his breath, "A beast like you shouldn't be allowed in the city."

"What did you say?"

"Oh, I said yes, a beast like that shouldn't be allowed in the city."

Gertrude smiled. "Good! I'll inform Rogan that his cat will be taken away by the order of the governor. I'll bring a guard with me to carry the devil into the forest, where I hope it gets eaten by a hawk."

She stood to leave. Will lifted his hand. "No, no. I'm afraid you misunderstood. I agree the thing is a beast, but we can't just take away an old man's cat!"

She scowled. "Then what do you propose he do with the hisser?"

He rubbed his temples. "I . . . don't know. Maybe we could—"

Someone knocked hard on the door downstairs. He turned his head. Could Raulin and the guards have found Dibbs? He got up to look out the window, but Gertrude stepped in his way.

"You haven't solved my problem yet."

He took her meaty arm and escorted her toward the door. "I'll take the cat into careful consideration, and send you word tomorrow on what should be done."

Astonished more than content, she allowed him to lead her massive body through the narrow door of his office. They went downstairs, and to his great distress, in the living quarters was not Raulin, but a stranger. The stranger was talking with Grace, who'd apparently let him in since Lianna was out helping with the search. Gertrude eyed the stranger with a rude curl of her lip, then took her leave, slamming the door behind her.

Will approached the cloaked and bearded man to greet him when suddenly, the man pulled a coin from Grace's ear. She giggled and clapped. "Show me another!"

"But I have already done three," the man said in a pleasant accented voice. He looked at Will through deep-green eyes. "And I really must speak with your father."

She stuck out her lower lip and moaned.

He laughed and laid his hands on her shoulders. "But I thank you for being such a pleasant hostess and audience while we waited."

Her pout turned to a smile and she skipped to the kitchen, where Will heard dishes splash into a pot.

"She is a wonderful young girl," the stranger said. "You're a blessed man."

Will offered a bow. "Welcome to my home. My name is Willerdon, governor of Woodend." He gestured toward the kitchen. "I see you've already met my daughter Grace. Sadly, my wife is out or I would ask her to brew some tea. You wouldn't want to taste mine, and Grace hasn't yet learned to make it."

"Thank you for your consideration." The man bowed in return. "I am Gildareth, and hail from the north." He looked about, appearing confused. "Forgive me, but I heard you also have a son. May I ask where he is?"

A lump formed in Will's throat. "Yes, I do have a son. His name is Dibbs."

"Is he not well?"

Will turned away, feeling his throat grow tight. "He is missing since last night. My wife and many of our guards are even now searching for him. I fear . . . I fear it's my fault he's gone, but . . ." He paused, looking at the man inquisitively. "What do you seek here in Woodend?"

Gildareth laughed. "A broad question indeed! And one with an even broader answer." He glanced toward the kitchen, where they could see Grace working at the sink. "Is there a place where we could discuss something in private? I don't want to upset your daughter."

Will crossed his arms and sighed. "As long as your tidings aren't about a cat, I don't care how terrifying they are."

Gildareth raised a brow.

"It isn't worth explaining, but if you'll follow me, we'll talk in my study."

They went upstairs. Will took a seat behind his desk, Gildareth across from him. Will looked Gildareth in the eyes, found his unexpected knowing look unsettling, and redirected his gaze to the study window. "So I must again ask, what is your business here?"

"I am a herald to the king, come with his request to enlighten you about . . . important matters."

"You're a herald to the king? How is this so? The king is considered a myth by most, and absent by his followers."

"Are you a follower?"

Will narrowed his eyes. "Wouldn't you know if you were truly his herald?"

"These are dangerous and deceptive times. If you were his follower, you would have the sign with you. Now, have you this sign?"

Will sat for a moment, then drew his illumina from his pocket and set it on the table. "Is this what you wanted to see?"

Gildareth's eyes immersed themselves in the illumina's dim glow. "Good," he said. "Though weak, the light is still within you."

"What?"

The herald lifted his head, his green eyes filled with a quiet merriment, reached into his cloak and pulled out a leather-covered book. He set it in front of Will, who read the cover and looked back up. "*The Annals of Illuminara?*"

Gildareth ran his hand over the silver letters. "Perhaps after I explain some of what this ancient book says about your city, your light will grow brighter." He gestured toward Will's illumina. "Both in the phial, and in you."

Befuddled, Will said, "I have no light within me, as far as I know."

The merriment left Gildareth's eyes. "There are many things you don't understand. But I am about to open your eyes. However you react to this information, many trials, greater than any you have yet faced, are about to enter your life." He set his hands on the desk and leaned forward. "Some have already begun."

Will's stomach spun into a knot. *Dibbs? Could he mean Dibbs?* The man had his full attention.

☩ ☩ ☩

It was the first time Tarin had approached Bill's house with the intent of knocking on the door rather than hiding under the window. Somehow, this made him almost more nervous. Although he knew the old man quite well through his overheard stories, Bill didn't know him at all.

They reached the door and Sarky knocked.

"Hold on!" a woman called from within. Tarin recognized the voice as Margaret's. Soon, a fat old woman with long scraggly hair stood in the frame. She was no taller than they and smelled strongly of ale.

"Just had to turn down the fire for the brew," she said, in a voice kinder than her look. "What do ye lads want?" She smiled at them through crooked teeth, then lifted her finger and winked. "I know! I bet ye heard of Bill's ale and want to try some." She looked both ways, then pulled them into the house.

"Have a seat by the window, dears. I'll be right back." She hurried through a nearby door.

Sarky rubbed his hands together. "Ohhh yes!" I've never been allowed to try ale before."

"That's because we're too young to be drinking that garbage," Tarin said as he stared at a dusty painting of a vase hanging by the window he usually hid beneath. "What would your father say?"

Sarky narrowed his eyes at him. "He won't say anything. Just like you. Right, *friend?*"

Tarin found the window from his new vantage point quite interesting. "Fine. If you want to do something so foolish, do it. But don't blame me if you get into trouble."

"Don't worry, whatever happens to me will be my own fault. But you really should try some too. What if we don't get another chance?"

A couple of minutes later, Margaret entered the room with two small mugs of frothing ale. "Here's some of our best, gentle brew for the young people!"

She handed one to Tarin, which he reluctantly accepted, then one to Sarky.

"Haven't had children here in a long time," she said with a girlish giggle, and retreated to the door she came from. "I'm going to get some nice bread and butter for you dears. Bill will be back from the watershed in a moment. Drink up, lads. It won't hurt ye."

Sarky grinned and downed the entire cup in one gulp. Tarin looked around, hurried to the open window and dumped his behind a familiar bush. There was a loud cough behind him, and he spun around.

Sarky was red in the face and clutching his throat, as if trying to strangle himself. "Help," he wheezed.

"No. You deserve what you got." He returned to his seat, feeling smug.

The kitchen door flew open and a smiling old spider-legged man strode through the opening. "Ha, ha! I see the wench gave ye her usual neighborly greetin'"

Margaret followed her husband into the room, carrying a tray, laughing even harder than he. "I knew ye'd get sick! Tsk, tsk! Ye young people shouldn't be drinkin' of the brew. It ain't good for small bones." She frowned at Tarin. "Why ain't ye sick?"

A boulder dropped into his stomach and his mouth went dry.

"Because he"—cough—"dumped it out like the good little boy he is."

Tarin shot Sarky an angry glance, but Margaret began to clap and said, "Good lad! Nice to know there's young people out there with a bit of common sense." She winked. "And because of that," she lifted the tray of toast, jelly and milk, "ye both will be rewarded."

"Why him?" Tarin asked.

"Because the woman's a softy," Bill grunted.

"Am not, ye old twig!" She gestured toward Sarky. "The poor boy is almost thinner than ye. He needs to eat!"

The toast wasn't the best, and the milk tasted a little sour, but Tarin was too afraid to refuse Margaret's hospitality. So he gobbled the food up as if it were a box of truffles.

"Why have ye lads paid us strangers a visit?" Bill said from his chair next to the window. "Not often do young people visit old folks like us. Just Clooney and a few of the wife's scary old women friends."

Margaret slapped Bill across the back of his head, upsetting some of the strands trying in futility to cover a huge bald spot. He didn't flinch.

"We need information," Sarky said in his usual confident manner. "Do you know a Gildareth?"

Margaret gasped. Bill smiled and nodded, then said, "I've chatted with the chap before, many years ago."

"I want to meet him," Margaret cooed. "He sounds so splendid-like! A fine gentleman, and a fighter from what I hear."

Bill shook his head and shrugged. "She gets all bubbly and foolish whenever she hears about the fellow's adventures." He patted her hand. "Now, now, dear. Calm down. I'm sure you'll meet him someday. And I even bet he'll find an old bat like you quite pretty."

She swatted at him. "Maybe if ye were a little more heroic, I'd be cooing about *ye* instead. Have ye ever done anything adventurous in yer life?"

"I married ye, didn't I?"

Tarin and Sarky both chuckled. Margaret stood and glowered at them, hands on hips. "I see ye gentlemen have formed a little posse against me." She grabbed up the remainder of the food on the tray and left for the kitchen, slamming the door behind her.

"Come now," Bill called after her. "Ye know we love ye, ol' girl."

She poked her head out the door, lifted her nose, and shot back into the kitchen.

Bill placed his hands behind his head and leaned back. "She'll be gone for a few minutes at least. That gives us a chance to talk."

To Tarin's delight, Bill pulled out his pipe, lit it, and crossed his legs. Tarin could hardly believe it. Here he was, actually in the great storyteller's house, welcomed rather than spying.

"What do ye want to know 'bout Gildareth?" Bill exhaled some smoke through his nose.

"Actually," Sarky said with a quick glance in Tarin's direction, "we want to find out more about something we've been running into lately, some shad—"

The front door flew open and a rotund yet muscular old man ran through.

"Clooney!" Bill said in surprise. "What are ye doin' here?"

"We've got us some trouble down by the inn."

Bill brushed ash from his shirt. "But I was just about to answer some questions for these fine lads."

Clooney looked at them. "Ask him whatever ye like, on the way." He ran toward the kitchen. "Margaret! I need to steal yer husband for a bit. That all right?"

"Please do!" came her voice.

Clooney spun back toward them. "What are ye all waitin' for? I said we got trouble. Let's go!" He hurried out the door.

Bill groaned and stood, put out his pipe, stretched, and followed Clooney outside. "If there's trouble, I don't want to be without a sword. I'm going to stop at the armory on the way down there."

"They ain't goin' to let ye in there!" Clooney said, waving his arms.

"I know a secret way in the back, through the cellar. Don't worry, I'll get in."

Clooney groaned, then started toward the main road at a fast pace. Bill and the boys followed.

"I wonder if we're meant to ever figure anything more about the shadows or that ... that *unseen war?*" Sarky said. "I was really hoping to hear some more about the good that's still out there, if any."

Tarin shook his head. "Doesn't seem that way. But I wonder what Clooney's so excited about?"

Sarky shrugged. "Might as well find out."

☩ ☩ ☩

Gildareth leaned back in his chair and squinted at Will. "Have you ever heard of Illuminara?"

When Will shook his head, he said, "That is of little surprise. Few have, except for some old lore masters."

He set the book on the table and opened its cover. On it was a great map. Three landmasses were drawn on it: a large peninsula to the north; an island in the center; and another realm to the south. "Do you see the city on the island?"

Will peered at the map. "I think so. On what the map calls the Dividing Island." He looked up at Gildareth. "It's marked Illuminara, City of Light. That's the one?"

Gildareth nodded. "That is Illuminara. Or at least, it was. Since the time this map was made, the city has changed. No longer is it a city of light." He looked deep into Will's eyes. "Rather, it is a city of darkness; one of evil. Arkoth is its name."

"And why do you say the place is evil?"

Gildareth turned toward the sunlit window. "Wrathar," he whispered, "the lord of Shieth." He closed his eyes. "In the year 3363, Wrathar attacked the island, hoping he would forever wipe Illuminara from Arvalast."

Will shifted his weight and leaned in closer. "Why did he wish to take the city?"

Gildareth's hand fell into his cloak and withdrew a shining phial of light, which he set on the desk. It glowed brighter.

Will stared at it. "I would expect nothing less from a herald of the king," he said, and set his next to Gildareth's. The two lights streamed from each container and embraced each other, making both objects brighter.

"Some claim these phials are merely the works of wizards," Will continued, "for they often seem to grant wishes and give their owners strange power."

"What do you believe they are?"

"Long ago, I heard a tale that there once was a veil of light and beauty that covered the entire land. Then something happened, and the light was stolen away to another, hidden land. All that remains is what can be captured in these phials by the king's true servants. They are a mark, a sign to the rest of Arvalast that the king still rules, although he has been absent for hundreds of years."

"Do you know what these phials of light were called?"

Will peered down at the two objects before him. "They are called illuminas, and likely named after this city you mentioned."

"You're wise, governor of Woodend." Gildareth crossed one leg over the other. "The veil of light you speak of was centered in Illuminara, around the king's citadel. But in 3363, man's loyalty to the king grew so tainted, Wrathar was able to assault Illuminara with a vast army of men and creatures."

He reached for the book, turned a few pages, then pushed it back toward Will. The governor looked down and began to read.

> Thirteenth of October: Year 3363: The citadel is surrounded. I look at the light, and my knees falter beneath me. Its once great brilliance has died, and now all that is left is a faint glow. Nearly all the beauty of the city has been stripped away by the rebellion. The High Governor says to have hope, but I see none. Why has the king abandoned us? Why does he allow Illuminara to fall? Yet I shall fight to the end, as will the few remaining warriors of the king.

Will glanced up at Gildareth. "The king abandoned them?"

"No, his servants abandoned *him*. And those who did not, and lived through the destruction of Illuminara, were forced to flee the Dividing Island and travel deep into the heart of Arvalast. Some of those very men and women eventually reached Maplelake Forest and settled there. It was as far north as any settlers ever came."

"Why?"

"An invisible force has always held men back from traveling any farther north than this small city. You and your people have no idea how close you truly are to the king." He looked out the window. "But others do, and they are coming."

He turned a few more pages in the book. "Look at this page, near the bottom. There is a prophecy I want you to read, one recorded by Ollervand, guard of the king's citadel and one of his closest confidants. You won't understand what I'm about to tell you unless you know of it."

Will nodded, and looked down to read.

> My enemies are just outside the door. I have little time before my end. Though the king hours ago left for the north, a final

herald, herself preparing to leave, informed me the king wished I leave for the north with her. But I knew my duty was at the citadel, and refused. Saddened, she prepared to take her leave. But before she left, she spoke these words:

"When all is nearly lost, and the world has reached its end, it is from the ends of the world that both kingdoms shall reunite. Three will arise: servants of the king. Three more will follow: warriors of the light."

Farewell . . .
Ollervand, Spectril of the King
and Guard of the Citadel

Will read and reread the prophecy, then turned his eyes upward. "I take it the man died not long after writing this."

"He did."

"How was this prophecy not stolen by the enemy?"

"That is a great mystery, but somehow it eventually reached me, and now you. Tell me, do you understand what it's saying?"

Will mulled over the open page. "Apparently, when the world is about to end, six important people are going to come from the ends of the world and reunite two kingdoms."

"So simple, is it not?"

Will bit his lip. "Not really."

"You mean, you don't understand?"

"Vaguely. But how am I to know where the ends of the world are, or what the two kingdoms represent, unless it's speaking literally?"

Gildareth shook his head and rubbed his temples. "Perhaps you need some enlightenment." He reached for his light and held it up.

The governor watched as the light became colorful and began to sparkle. Suddenly, it portrayed the image of a mountain within its clear glass. The view then shifted, sped down the mountain and spun around. There were more peaks next to this one, an entire range covered in white snow that billowed up into the clouds.

The view shifted again. Now, it rushed through a series of hills at the foot of the mountains. Little houses and farms dotted the grassy mounds, and occasionally, a great city sped by. Slowly the hills flattened, and the glass revealed a massive plain covered in high grass. A farm appeared now and then, or a fence surrounding a large herd of horses, cows, or sheep.

Will looked deeper into the glass. Far away, a green color began working its way over the horizon. Ever it grew nearer. It almost appeared as an ocean, but there were no waves. Will's brows rose in realization. "It's a forest."

Gildareth stayed quiet, and Will's gaze stayed on the image.

The view now rushed into the foliage, and down onto the forest floor. It dodged trees and leaped over creeks and rivers until it reached a path that was brick for a time, then became dirt as it traveled up a hill and back down. A gate appeared in the distance.

Will's eyes grew wide. "The gate of Woodend!"

The view burst through the gate and disappeared. The light became a gentle white, and Gildareth set it back on the table.

"You have just seen the known world's end."

Will slumped back in his chair in astonishment. "Are you saying that our forest is the world's end, and that Woodend is somehow involved in the prophecy?"

Gildareth shook his head. "*Woodend* is the world's end. And yes, the words spoken thousands of years ago in the prophecy were referring to this place. I have already told you it is the northernmost dwelling of men in Arvalast. Beyond this is a sacred realm, and a tower, a place leading to the other kingdom of which the prophecy also speaks. That's why I am here. You don't yet realize it, but a war is already raging within this town, and throughout the remaining lands of Arvalast not yet taken by Wrathar and the rebellion. I was sent because soon, three powerful servants of the king will arise from this forest."

He stood, and his eyes narrowed. "And three warriors will follow. Long has the king known this. But not only he. Wrathar, the great enemy of Arvalast, also knows."

He leaned over Will's desk. "Governor, this forest has been attacked twice in the past. Once long ago, before any towns existed beneath the trees. And once just one hundred years ago, in a place called Undertree. The forest's history alone should prove to you the enemy finds this place intriguing."

"Because of the prophecy?"

"Yes, because of the prophecy. But also because Woodend is the last wall between the rebellion and the hidden kingdom where the king still reigns. In fact, it is more likely Wrathar is currently more interested in simply sweeping through the forest to get to the north, rather than destroying the place to keep the prophecy from being fulfilled. Right now, I don't believe Wrathar even considers the prophecy a viable threat. Too few servants of the king are strong enough to fit the heavy roles of the six mentioned in the prophecy."

He took a step back, and glanced back out the window. "This could be a fatal error on his part. But Woodend is growing so weak, even the king realizes it needs aid for the prophecy to come true."

He walked to the window and gestured for Will to follow. Will stood and took a place next to the herald.

"Do you see the wall below us?" Gildareth asked.

The wooden structure rose up against the house and stopped just before it reached the window. "Yes, I see it," Will said.

"This wall was built by a race called the glorions: powerful servants of the king. Walls built by glorions have special power to hold off evil that mere wood cannot stand against. Woodend has one of these walls, as do many other towns and cities throughout Arvalast. But when the king's servants grow weak and complacent within these places, the walls begin to lose their power. That's what allowed the demise of Illuminara, along with many other towns and cities of men."

Will was leery to ask, but he had to. "How strong is our wall?"

Gildareth glanced down at the structure. "Wrathar's full power cannot yet penetrate it. Still, I must warn you. Shadows are in Woodend even now. The longer they are here, the weaker the wall will become."

"Shadows? What are you talking about?"

Gildareth walked to his chair and rested his hands on its back. "Wrathar is not human. Nor are his strongest allies. They are a phantom race, taking on many forms, but mostly that of shadows of men."

Willerdon closed his eyes and fell silent. "You do realize you sound mad?"

"You doubt what I say?"

"Of course I doubt what you say! This whole meeting has led to nothing but foolishness. Suddenly you're speaking of ghosts in my city! What next? Goblins of some sort?"

Gildareth said nothing.

Will rolled his eyes. "I've met plenty of lunatics in my life, sir, and you're beginning to fit the profile." He walked to the study door. "Allow me to escort you outside."

Gildareth's brows lowered. "Have you grown so weak?"

"What?"

He threw the chair across the room and pointed at the governor. "I am astonished at your blindness! There is a war raging within this town, and you have not the courage or the desire to confront your true enemies!"

Gildareth's illumina on the table began to grow bright, so bright, Will had to shield his eyes. Gildareth walked up to him and glared through a face full of fury. Will felt a sudden strange awe of the man, but also a powerful fear. He tried to turn, to flee from his own office, but his feet wouldn't move. Neither could he shield his ears. He was forced to listen to Gildareth's next words.

"The king has chosen this place for his purposes, whether you desire it or not. Wrathar will soon attack openly, and you will believe all I have said. But your faith at this moment is not the king's greatest concern. He chose you as governor, and as such, his grace abounds in you. Yet the past year you have squandered this honor and sent a myriad of complaints to the throne. He is angry, Willerdon. You have let the enemy weaken you and dim your light with small matters, while all along Wrathar has been planning an assault that will decimate this forest, and ultimately Arvalast."

"How have you become so weak, you wonder? Through the constant trickle of the common pains of life. He has sent a deluge of complainers to your house for the past two years. He has made your marriage difficult and damaged your relationship with your wife. He has made your son angry with the king, and with you, by tormenting him in ways you could never imagine."

Will rubbed his hand through his hair. "My son?"

"Yes, that is why your son has run away. Because of your lack of foresight into his trouble. Of course, your concerns over an old enemy's return helped contribute to this blindness, along with the absence of your sheriff."

"How do you know all this?" Will whispered. "How could you *possibly?*"

"The schemes of the enemy are easy to see for those willing to look."

Gildareth's cloak began to shimmer in the illumina's ever-increasing light. "Governor, you must become what the king has made you to be. You must become a servant of the light for this town to survive! For your family to survive."

A tear formed in Will's eye. "I . . . I had no idea."

Gildareth's shoulders lowered. The light in the room began to return to its earlier brightness. "You're beginning to believe me?"

"I . . . don't want to, but yes."

Gildareth placed a hand on Will's shoulder. "You have no idea how important you are. Much has been happening to keep you weak, and though you have many flaws, you are succeeding in some ways. You have a genuine love for your family, which I can feel within the house, and a deep concern for your son. You also care for this town, which is why you have never stepped down from your position even in the midst of much opposition."

Will managed a small smile. "Yes, that's me, captain of resilience."

There was a loud knocking at the door downstairs. "Governor!" a man shouted. "Trouble at the inn!"

Both men looked at each other. Will felt all blood leave his face.

Gildareth smiled and grabbed both his shoulders. "Captain of resilience, go forth! The king will be with you."

"Hurry, Governor!" the man yelled from below. "It's getting really bad! I think a riot might be brewing."

Will looked at Gildareth. "You do realize your news is disturbing?"

Gildareth leaned in closer. "I told you, the king is with you, and his grace within you. Now go."

Will clenched his fists, closed his eyes, and mustered all the strength he had in him, even realizing it wasn't much. He felt Gildareth grab his right hand and put it into his own vest pocket. His fingers brushed against warm glass there. And suddenly, he felt stronger.

"Let's go," he said, and walked out the study door toward the oncoming storm. The man outside, whom he didn't recognize, pointed toward the south and began trying to explain what was happening. Will heard nothing. He just began to walk.

SiXTEEN

Jebin could barely process what the shining man had just said: the shining man was the king. But how could this be? The king was so reticent, he was considered a myth by many. Yet Sayin appeared to have no difficulty believing this. After the shining man's admission, Sayin had begun a long and fervent chant of ecstasy, until he finally fell to his knees and raised his hands toward the shining man, shouting, "May the sky grow bright at the sight of your robe! May the winds and the sea still in the presence of . . ."

The shining man held out his hand. Jebin thought he saw something red sweep through the trees behind the man, but a second glance yielded nothing.

"My servant, you have called many times," the shining man said, "yet now, as the hours draw short, I come."

To Jebin, listening in wonder, the man's voice was like the sound of distant thunder.

When the man said, "Now stand," Sayin obeyed, put his quaking hands behind his back and looked up.

A breeze blew through the meadow, and the shining man's cloak rippled. "Are the plans I have laid out for you in this northern realm complete?"

Sayin's bald head bobbed up and down. "Much is done, and the rest is well into the process of completion." His voice grew quieter. "Breaking the will of the heretics hasn't been simple. Somehow, the walls have remained strong throughout the forest. But Lockspell should be solidly in your hands when you choose to take it, and Woodend is crumbling even as I speak."

"What of the governor? Does he still stand?"

Sayin's lips curled up. "Not for much longer. A plan is in effect today to at last destroy his already-weakened spirit. Two years of the slow dripping of malcontent from the townsfolk have made him ripe for a final blow. Even now, Woodend should be falling into an uproar. One spawned, may

I say, by an opening *your* watchers found in those whose past loyalties lie with Bolard. When the chaos is quenched, which it will be just as planned, Willerdon's family will meet with . . . unfortunate circumstances."

"But what of this new occurrence with his son? He was to be slain with the rest of Willerdon's family, yet my messengers tell me he has run away from his father's home."

Sayin began fidgeting. "A slight mishap, but to our overall benefit. His running away was due to a fierce argument with Willerdon. The governor cursed him, as I was told, and the son's spirit broke. He ran away, and because of this, will temporarily escape death. But I have called upon your servants to take him from the city openly when they find him. It will be but one more blow to the governor after his family is killed. Imagine, during his mourning for his wife and daughter, he will hear of the kidnapping. Or, if the boy is taken first, he will already be in great distress when he loses the rest of them. Together, both misfortunes will surely break him."

"And you know these events will happen as you say?"

There was a moment of silence. Jebin saw Sayin's hands fidget behind his back. "Yes, without a doubt."

Jebin's body had stiffened upon hearing Willerdon's name. Was he already too late to warn the governor of Bolard's return?

A strong gust blew through the meadow, sending the grass that was Jebin's hiding place into a flurry of motion. Jebin felt a sudden presence in the trees behind the shining man, but when he glanced over, as before, he saw nothing.

Sayin began to whimper. "Please, send them away." He bent at the waist, as though the gust of wind had been gale force. "These . . . these ones are too strong. I beg you!"

The shining man closed his eyes. "My messengers agree with what you say. The governor's son shall be taken when my servants find him. But I hear of a matter that has become of interest to my watchers. A boy with keen eyes within weak spirit. Tell me, do you know of such a boy in Woodend?"

Sayin remained bent at the waist. The shining man lifted his hand, and after a moment, Sayin groaned and stood upright. "Thank you, my king."

"What of my question?"

"Yes," Sayin said, rubbing his hands together as if they hurt. "They are correct. Unrest has been growing within me and the hearts of your messengers in Woodend for a few days now. It began when I was showing your servant the path to the governor's house, so he and the others would be prepared for this night's slayings. We saw a boy, then another. Your servant went to investigate based on your messengers' uneasiness. Then those accursed northerners found us. We were forced to flee back to the hideout, taking a roundabout way of course."

"The northerners are becoming a nuisance," the shining man said. "Still, the guardians from the tower are but two, and can be reckoned with when the time comes."

Sayin said, "But I heard there might be a third, my king."

Jebin thought he saw the shining man's face contort into something else, something he'd only seen in nightmares, but a second glance yielded only a calm and gentle expression. "I know of him," the man said. "He too shall be dealt with at an opportune time. As of now, we carry on as planned." He closed his eyes and breathed in deeply. "I was wise to appoint you my herald. You have yielded the crimson light well."

Sayin stood taller.

"There is now another task I wish you to accomplish. The plans for Woodend are already in motion." He opened his eyes. "Even now, I can feel the activity of my messengers, can sense their excitement. The city shall soon fall, and the barrier on the wall will at last crumble. We may enter with our full force rather than riding in on the hearts of willing vessels. Lockspell is our next point of interest, and will not be difficult to overwhelm. The walls are already crumbled and the place ripe for conquest. We shall kill them all, each heretic, be they man, woman or child."

Jebin's jaw tightened and his heart stilled. His family! Were they among the heretics?

"They are your blood and soul."

Jebin started.

"The blood and soul of a heretic."

He looked around for the source of the voice, but whirled back when the shining man began speaking again.

"I want you to begin by enacting punishment on one of my once dearest friends. Jebin of Woodend."

Jebin's mind swam. Where had that voice gone? And what was this man saying? Friend? Was this really . . . it couldn't be!

"His murderous actions three years ago against the gatekeeper's wife merit no forgiveness."

Jebin felt sweat drip down into his eyes. Who else would know of that but the king?

"Though he has longed to see me again smile upon his face, his every plea for grace makes me want to spew fire into his haughty eyes. The man has only my hatred, as does his family."

With the man's last words, Jebin felt as if a sword had been thrust into his chest. Pain greater than any he'd ever endured tore through his spirit with a force so relentless, he could only collapse into the weeds. He wanted to weep, but couldn't.

The man whom Jebin now knew to be king began to explain the logistics of Lockspell's takeover after he and his family were slain. Images of their murder delved deeper and deeper into his mind, until he noticed a strange red aura begin to build above him. He stared at it, and within its glow, saw his family. They were all safe in his arms.

Then, Jebin saw it. Lockspell burning in the distance. But somehow, they were safe. How could it be so? The king had said the town wouldn't be destroyed until his family was dead.

Suddenly he remembered. In the vision, he had saved them. He had forsaken the king and saved them.

His eyes opened wide and the aura disappeared. All sound stopped, and a strange relief poured into him, as though he'd just fallen into a cool lake after many days of thirsting in a desert. His mind returned to him, as well as a sense of purpose he'd not felt since retaking Woodend from Bolard. A voice, one he recognized as his own, began to speak: "*I am free from the barriers the king once had me shackled within. I will now live to do all things to hinder his way.*"

He looked at the shining man and felt nothing but hatred. First, he would save his family from this beast. Then, he would devote his life to destroying all that was allied with the throne, including his old friend Sayin. But not yet. Not while Sayin was with the king.

With his newfound purpose came a strong sense of tact. Openly confronting the king would be foolish. Rubbing his temples, he focused on what was being said. Slowly, the sounds of their talk returned to him.

"They will be prepared to attack Lockspell when word is sent that Woodend's walls are no longer a threat," the king said.

"What about Lockspell's walls?" Sayin questioned.

"They are of no concern. Lockspell will fall easily after Woodend is taken. We will use both cities as supply camps, then we'll fan across the rest of the forest, taking all remaining towns until we have Maplelake Forest firmly established as a northern base. Macalum will be surrounded, a mere island in a sea of our already-conquered lands. When it falls, my eyes can at last turn to the north, and the tower."

Sayin took a step forward and bowed. "We've waited long for this time, and I don't desire to doubt your victory. But . . . do you believe the prophecy of this place has any truth to it?"

"Would I not remember a prophecy that I myself uttered?"

"A foolish question, my king. It is just . . . that boy."

"My servants know what to do with him."

"May I ask one final question?"

The shining man knelt and put his hand on Sayin's shoulder. "Speak."

"Your servants have been seeing a strange beast flying in the forest. It's been slaying animals and even some travelers along the forest highways. As of yet, the residents don't know about the thing, but your servants have seen it. They've been watching it. Could it pose a danger to our plans?"

The shining man stood and looked at the sky. Jebin could see worry in his face, and his heart leapt with joy. Was the mighty and treacherous king afraid?

The king turned his eyes, now calm, to Sayin. "We shall not be hindered by a mere animal. I will inform my messengers to be wary of such a beast, and perhaps even try to tame it." He gestured toward the forest. "Come with me."

Jebin watched the two men retreat to the edge of the meadow. Still within listening range, the shining man called out to the trees in an unfamiliar tongue.

He heard the rustling of foliage. A moment later, two red-cloaked and hooded men stomped into the clearing. Though the king was a head taller than Sayin, these two were a head taller than the king. Jebin withdrew farther into the weeds.

The king exchanged hasty words with the newcomers, then laid his hand on Sayin's shoulder and pointed south.

Sayin shot him a nervous look, but the king's finger remained steadily pointing into the trees. Defeated, Sayin walked into the forest. The newcomers followed. Through the labyrinth of trees, Jebin saw a red glow bob up and down, then disappear.

He returned his attention to the king and lurched back. The man's eyes were ablaze with anger . . . and gazing directly at him! He began crawling away backward.

"Stand," the king's voice thundered.

He felt an unseen power grab him and force him to his feet.

"How long have you been hiding?"

The king's glowing face and deep-blue eyes awed Jebin, but did nothing to quench the fire of hatred he now felt for the man. "Just kill me, as you so strongly desire, and spare my family," he said. "They've done nothing to deserve your wrath."

The king smiled, and again, he thought he saw his face twist into something hideous. But it lasted only a moment.

"Though you were once my servant, the murder of Hamlin's wife was unforgivable. Innocent blood should never be spilled, even in the midst of what you deem good intentions."

"It was an accident!" Tears of wrath and sorrow flooded his eyes, yet he could still see the woman bleeding on the ground, her husband, Hamlin, kneeling over her, wailing. Her young son stood a few paces away, holding his illumina close as his pale face studied his mother's quaking body. But the illumina grew dim while she gasped a few final breaths of life.

"That was no accident!" the king yelled in a booming voice. "You killed the woman out of hatred for my servant Bolard, a man whose only desire was to fulfill my will in your city."

Jebin began to hear strange voices in his head as a grief came upon him, a grief so deep he could scarcely draw breath. His mind still saw the woman, bleeding on the roadway.

The king took another step toward him, his white glow turning a pale red.

"I ordered Bolard to take all the illuminas to spare your town from imminent disaster. My wrath was coming. None was any longer worthy to own the phials, save Bolard, whom I still deemed loyal. It was my will that he take them all, and fill them with a new light, the crimson light I was sending north with my servant Sayin. It was with this light Sayin was to teach Bolard a great power, one I planned to bestow upon your forest, a power that would have reinvigorated the entire region with great blessing. Imagine, my old friend, no more drought, no more strife, no more pain."

The pale pink aura grew bright red. Small rivers of the luminance crawled toward Jebin like skeletal fingers, gripping at him as he stood dumbfounded with guilt and rage as the king continued.

"But you, Jebin, in a foolish action of pride, determined you alone understood my will, and revolted against Bolard."

"I . . . didn't know—"

"You had no desire to know!"

"But—"

"You killed in my name, and for that, I shall now kill in yours!"

A vision came to him. His new mansion in Lockspell was burning. Inside it, he saw the two red-cloaked men, in an upper room still untouched by flames, holding swords above his wife. Tears were in Rosie's eyes, and on the ground next to her . . . he gasped . . . his sons and daughter on the floor, their eyes open in death. He looked up to see one of the sword-wielding men remove his red hood. Beneath it was a familiar head: his head, his hair and beard dripping sweat, his eyes ablaze with insanity.

"No!" he screamed as he watched himself bring the sword down on his wife, her sad green eyes staring up at him lovingly even as he slay her.

"Enough!" he shouted, then spat. A hatred far greater than he'd already had for the king swarmed into him, and he spewed forth curses. All his life he'd been loyal to the throne, and now the throne had handed him over to darkness. Voices of rage screamed within him. He repeated their foul words with greater passion.

The king's red light seeped into his pores. With it, he felt all hope, all love, all joy die within him. Only despair remained. He stopped hurling the curses and collapsed to the ground. As his eyes dimmed, he thought he saw a monster's face hovering above him, enshrouded in a light so red it appeared as blood. As his eyes closed, he heard shouting somewhere in the distance. The monster turned toward the noise.

"The king save us!" came an unfamiliar voice. "It is a sentinel!"

He heard another sound, a deep-throated growl from somewhere high above him. His eyes rolled into the back of his head, the ground greeted him as he collapsed. The grass felt coarse, painful against his cheek. Behind him, he thought he heard the sound of a battle. But all he could see was the image of himself, holding a bloody dagger as he hovered over his unmoving wife.

SEVENTEEN

Kandis heard long before he could see what was happening. Shouts, all men, and all enraged. When he drew close enough to the inn to see what was happening, he realized the feelings he'd been having the past few weeks, those that were warning him of some terrible event about to happen in Woodend, hadn't been misguided.

Lionnel looked at him, and Kandis saw both surprise and fear, but was glad to have his friend back by his side. Though Lionnel had been terribly angry with him for showing the claw to the people in the bar despite the governor's order, the mysterious northerner had been correct when he suggested Lionnel would forgive him.

"Guess these are our hunters," Lionnel said, his voice unsteady. "I recognize many from the bar, along with a few others. Not a pleasant group."

"No, they're not."

"What do we do?"

Kandis inhaled deeply, feeling his leather overcoat tighten around his chest, and rubbed his hand through thick, graying hair. "I say we first speak to the king." Before Kandis even reached down to fetch his illumina, Lionnel was already holding one, silently whispering something, undoubtedly pleading for aid and wisdom on how to deal with the hunters.

Kandis took out his illumina and prepared to whisper his own supplications when a bloodcurdling scream erupted from the direction of the inn. He looked over just as a woman was thrust against the inn's wall. Two guards stood close to her, but were too busy being pummeled by angry fists to help her.

"What's going on now?" Lionnel said.

Kandis' heart thudded in his chest in recognition. "It's the governor's wife!"

They watched an old man run up to Lianna and spit in her face.

"What are we going to do?" Lionnel said, fidgeting with the axe hanging from his waist. Kandis reached for his own axe.

"Don't even think about it," Lionnel blurted. "You have a family. I'll help the guards. You get back home and alert the northern guardhouse to get down here fast."

Lianna screamed again, and the crowd of hunters erupted in laughter. Kandis shook his head and pointed toward the fray. "I have to do something. This is my fault! I should never have shown anyone that claw!"

"But what if something happens to you—"

The woman screamed again. Kandis lifted his axe. "Then I earn a just reward!" Snarling at the band of unruly hunters, he charged down the road.

✝ ✝ ✝

The two boys said nothing as they followed Clooney along the main street of Woodend on their journey to investigate the unrest Clooney warned was brewing by the inn. Bill had only just departed down a side street next to the dark-red-brick armory next to the road. Clooney had since been mumbling grumpily to himself.

After a few more minutes of walking, Clooney quieted; the inn's chimney became visible in the distance, looming above even the tallest buildings, smoke wafting from its top. In the rest of the heavens, all was blue without a cloud to be seen, but the air was becoming heavy. In the south, haze was building.

Beyond the distant southern wall, Tarin saw the forest roof. A light mist rose from the greenery and the leaves showed signs of dulling. Autumn was on the way.

"Festival of Colors is only three weeks away, lads," Clooney said. "Are ye looking forward to it?"

"Am I looking forward to it?" Sarky said with a squeak. "What kind of question is that? It's the best time of the year! The leaves are all red and gold. All that food. Incredible. And the festivities. Amazing! And I hear this year's Festival's going to be better than ever. Old Will's planning quite a celebration." Sarky paused, then said, "I think he's trying to get people to like him more. After all, he's not as popular as old Bolard, even after Governor Bolard went crazy."

Clooney's brows furrowed and he cleared his throat. "Ye shouldn't be so hard on poor old Will. He tries hard ta be a good leader. It's just that the people are, oh what's the word? Harsh. They're harsh on him since he doesn't seem as friendly, or as strong as ol' Bolard. But that doesn't mean Will's a bad gov'nor. It just means he's, well, a different sort'a makeup than Bolard. And that can still be good, even if it don't seem that way to the people."

"I don't really care how Willerdon acts," Sarky said. "As long as he has a lot of food for the festival, he's good by my book." He lifted both fists. "Long live the governor!"

As they drew within sight of the inn, Tarin stopped and tilted his head. Two men with axes were running down the main road. Then he started. One was his father! He prepared to yell out and ask what he was doing, when he saw it. A mob blanketed the road by the inn. A lone woman was amongst them; numerous men screamed at her. Guards began storming up the road from the south, swords drawn.

"Uh oh," Clooney said, watching. "This is gonna get ugly fast."

When the mob saw the guards coming from the south, the shouting intensified. Still charging from the north, Kandis' and the other man drew closer to the uproar.

"Father!" Tarin screamed, and bolted toward the scene. "Stop! What are you doing?"

Clooney caught up to him and held him back. "Ye boys need to run the other direction." He gestured south. "Looks like a full-blown riot's about to start down there."

People from the surrounding buildings began to poke their heads out the windows. Some came outside.

"What's going on?" a fat man holding a young girl said. A woman stood behind him in the doorway.

"Looks like trouble," Clooney said. "Ye better get the word out to the guardhouses."

The fat man nodded, handed the girl back to her mother, and lifted his hands to his mouth. "Get the guards!" he began shouting. He and a few others started marching north, yelling, "Trouble's afoot! Alert the guards!"

Clooney scoured the side of the road with his eyes, then ran to fetch a long piece of wood. He returned and looked at Tarin. "I'll go help your father, see if we can't quiet that group of ruffians before they get too out of hand. Both of ye go back up the hill. Bill should be coming down shortly, if no one caught the old fool in the armory. Tell him to warn the gov'nor."

He turned and began trotting toward the inn, his legs moving fast despite their stocky appearance.

Sarky turned to head back up the hill. Tarin remained frozen.

Sarky stopped. "Aren't you coming?"

"I . . . I can't go back. What if something bad happens to Father?"

Sarky returned and put his hand on Tarin's shoulder, grinning. "Then let's make sure he's all right. I've never been one to do what I'm told anyway."

Tarin looked at Sarky and saw what he needed in those eyes: authenticity. "You'll come with me?"

"Sure. You're my friend."

They followed Clooney.

✦   ✝ ✝ ✝

In the two hours since he'd found his uncle at the inn, Jak noticed that all the men had all been acting strangely. Too quiet, for one thing. But what bothered him more was the anger on most of their faces. There was a lot of whispering, but nothing he could make out. Then it happened. That poor woman, the governor's wife, approached with two guards and asked the group if anyone had seen her son. Uncle Kane recognized her, a shout went up, and they pushed her and her two guards against the inn. Outnumbered, Jak could only stand and watch, trying to think of what to do next.

One of the ruffians slapped her across her already bruised face. "Curse ye and yer family, wench!" Jak grimaced and turned away, but eyes widened when he saw two men storming down the road from up the hill. He blinked twice; they were carrying axes. Running footsteps from the other direction made him turn around. A posse of guards was coming up the hill, toward the confrontation.

His heart sunk. He scanned the group and caught sight of his uncle just in time to see him spit in the governor's wife's face. Bile rose in his throat. His uncle had never treated a woman like that. What had gotten into him?

That question would have to wait. He had to get Uncle Kane away from the group. But if he tried to grab him and drag him away, that might make the already near-insane mob lose their last vestiges of self-control.

"Look!" one of them shouted. "Guards from the south!"

Many of the men began grabbing anything they could find as a weapon: wooden slabs and bricks. But most just held out their fists. The group of guards numbered only around ten. From Jak's quick count of the angry group, the guards were outnumbered five to one.

And simply by standing here, the guards might think he was part of the attacking mob.

This time, the decision was easier. He had to escape the crowd and head north, to the largest guardhouse, and make sure the guards there knew they were needed in the south.

Thankfully, the oncoming guards had distracted the crowd from the woman, and the two guards she was with took advantage of this; they were moving her out of danger. Now it was his turn.

He worked his way through the diverted group of angry men, and soon passed by the two axe-bearing men charging into the mob. He looked back. There was shouting. The mob noticed the two men, and realized they were being attacked from both sides, by the axe wielders from the north and the guards from the south. Like cornered animals, they reacted in fury and waved fists and weapons in the air. Then they spotted the two guards with the governor's wife, sneaking the object of their anger away.

"Stop her!" one shouted. Clubs lifted. One of the guards with the woman pulled out a sword. Jak watched in horror as he stabbed one of the ruffians in the torso.

The stabbed man looked at his bleeding midsection and slumped to the ground. All fell silent. Then, as if battle lines had at last been drawn, a cry went out. The ruffians nearest the guard began beating him. The woman and the other guard tried to help their comrade, but instead fell prey to the same abuse.

Jak knew they would die if not aided. Instinct screamed for him to return to the fray to help. Something stopped him, something he'd not felt in years. He glanced at his pocket and raised a brow. Then, he turned north and ran.

"Riot!" he shouted to anyone who might hear, anyone who, like the two axe wielders, might be willing to help the governor's poor wife.

A stout old man ran past him, holding a slab of wood.

"Riot!" Jak yelled.

Two boys, unarmed, sped by.

"Riot!"

People began streaming out of their houses all around him, many with weapons. Some looked angry, others scared. A few looked wild-eyed and insane. He paid heed to none of them, just kept shouting his warning.

† † †

Kandis saw the man strike the woman's shoulder, then lift the club over the woman's head, prepared to wield a deathblow. He managed to strike the club away just in time with his axe. Then he charged through the crowd, smashing into anyone who dared to get in the way while Lionnel picked up the woman and carried her safely away. The conscious guard dragged his counterpart out of the chaos while Kandis continued deeper into the pandemonium, ignoring the fact that more ruffians were streaming in from all the adjoining roadways, as if summoned. So far he'd yet to deliver a death-blow with his axe. But rage at their attack of the helpless woman led him now. People might well begin dying, and dying fast.

✝ ✝ ✝

"We're almost there!" Sarky shouted. Suddenly, he grabbed his stomach and lurched forward. Tarin ran up beside him.

Sarky lifted his hand to hold Tarin off. "They're here."

Tarin's heart skipped. "Help," he heard himself whisper. "Help!"

"What are ye boys doin'!" Clooney shouted from down the road. "I told ye to go back north!"

"We're in trouble!" Tarin called to him.

"Are ye daft, boy? We're all in trouble!" Clooney said, and ran back toward them.

A small group of ruffians broke away from the main crowd and starting running in their direction.

"Clooney, behind you!" Tarin yelled.

The old man looked back and doubled his pace. "Dern ye young foxes! Now we're in big trouble." He reached them and knelt next to Sarky. "Sick, aren't ye boy? Shouldn't have come back. There's more goin' on here than ye realize." He rubbed his hand through his messy gray hair. "I feel it too, though not as keenly as ye seem to."

Sarky and Tarin looked at each other.

"If I can't hold off these ruffians," Clooney said, "ye both'll be on yer own. Just try to get away fast if things get out of hand." He spun and faced the oncoming foes, holding his club behind his back. "Otherwise, be real quiet. They might leave us alone if we don't go poking a stick into their fire. At least, I hope so."

Tarin looked at the closest approaching ruffian. To his astonishment and horror, the man's eyes were not white orbs, but yellow slits! "Sarky?" he whimpered.

The boy answered with a dry heave.

A shadow slid out of the man's body and began following alongside. Tarin screamed, "Saaarky!"

He heard a splash behind him.

"This . . . worse than usual," Sarky spluttered. He heaved again.

Tarin's body grew rigid. The creature was looking directly at him, and smiling. He'd yet to see one so clearly. It appeared exactly as a man made of smoke, perfectly formed, but moving as a cloud would rather than a living being. Yellow, dripping fangs slid from its mouth, as if its beastly eyes weren't foul enough. *You will die*, Tarin heard a voice say within his own head. He convulsed and fell to the ground in terror.

"Are ye all right?" Clooney asked.

Tarin quivered. The shadow was still coming.

Clooney glanced back at him, and his eyes widened. "Hold on, lad." With a quick jab at his pocket, he pulled out an illumina. Tarin saw a faint burst of light around the glass. The shadow lifted its hands and disappeared back into the ruffian.

Clooney ripped open Tarin's shirt and placed the illumina on his heart. "Have courage, little friend. The king's with us."

Tarin felt a bit better. Until he heard the footsteps.

At least fifteen gnarly men, likely from the grungiest corners of town, ran up to them. The first, the one who'd had the shadow, looked at Clooney quizzically, then grinned. "I see where your loyalty lies," he said in a raspy voice, then punched Clooney in the stomach.

"So much for not pokin' at their fire," Clooney wheezed, then fell to the ground.

Another pulled Sarky up by his hair. "Let's see how well the lad bleeds!"

Tarin looked at the man holding Sarky. His eyes were bloodshot with intensity. Then, the color surrounding the angry black pupils turned yellow and the pupils narrowed to slits.

The eyes looked at him, that same amused look he'd just seen in the other man.

Tarin reached for the light. "Gildareth, help us." He blinked, surprised by what he just said.

There was a flash of light. The man holding Sarky let go and howled in pain. Tarin watched as a dark figure slid from the man and sped away into an alley.

"What happened?" the man groaned.

The others looked around. One pointed at Tarin.

"It was him! That little beast has some sort of weapon there." He reached down and grabbed the illumina.

"It's hot!" He kicked the object off Tarin and pulled the limp boy to his feet. "Ye tried to burn me, ye little wizard, didn't ye?"

Tarin said nothing. What could he say? He had no idea what the man was talking about.

The man lifted his hand to hit him when Tarin heard more footsteps. He glanced up and saw a group of about five guards approaching, clubs in hand.

"What's going on here!" the tallest guard said.

One of the ruffians walked up to him. "Go back to yer little hut and leave us be. This is our business."

"Help," Sarky groaned. A ruffian still held onto his hair.

The tall guard saw him. He lowered his brows. "Let go of that boy."

"What in Arvalast!" another guard yelled. "Sir! Look down there!"

The tall guard shifted his gaze down the road toward the inn, and his mouth dropped open. "Men, there's a riot!" He pushed the man in front of him out of the way, then noticed Clooney in the street, holding his stomach.

He pulled out his club and held it out toward the rest of the ruffians. "Disperse now!"

They didn't move. "By whose authority are ye commandin' us?" one asked.

"By Governor Willerdon's."

They all started laughing. "We don't listen to him," a high-voiced, hairy ruffian said. "He's not our governor. We follow Bolard."

Tarin was worried the guard might flee, based on the expression on his face. Instead, he swung his club at the nearest ruffian and knocked him in the head. The man crumpled.

Tarin was pushed aside. "They can't do that to us! Kill them!" The hairy ruffian pulled aside his shirt. Beneath it was a sheath with a sword. He took the weapon and rushed toward the guards.

The guards peered at each other in bewilderment. The tall guard shouted and reached for his sword.

"Take your weapons, men!" The rest of the guards followed suit.

The tall guard lifted his sword and blocked a blow, then shoved one attacker aside and was preparing to battle another when he looked up in horror. Tarin followed his eyes and saw at least twenty angry men and even a few youth had just emerged from a nearby roadway.

"For Bolard!" they shouted, and drew both clubs and daggers.

The tall guard shouted to his counterparts, "Quick, help me fend off the others!"

Suddenly, his hands went limp at his sides, and his sword slipped from his fingers.

Tarin watched in denial as one of the ruffians smiled at the brave man. He held the hilt of a sword imbedded deep into the guard's torso. The guard's face twisted in pain, and he fell to the ground.

Tarin had never seen a man killed before, and tried not to vomit. Around him, the violence grew in fervor. Suddenly he wondered if his father had met the same fate as the guard, and his whole body began to ache.

"Where's my illumina?" someone nearby whispered. Tarin looked over and saw Clooney crawling toward them.

"That brute kicked it right into my hand," Sarky groaned.

Tarin turned around and saw Sarky sitting up, holding Clooney's illumina in both hands. "It feels warm."

"Thank ye," Clooney said, and took the object. His fingers wrapped around it and it glowed. Grunting, the man managed to stand. Fortunately, they had somehow ended up in a small pocket of no fighting, though they were trapped on both ends of the roadway by swinging metal and wood.

Shouting erupted from farther down the road. The trio turned in unison to see two guards trying to fight off five ruffians.

"I've got to help 'em," Clooney said. He left for a moment and returned with a long piece of wood. "You lads get yerselves out of here," he commanded, then charged toward the fight.

Out of the corner of his eye, Tarin saw two men approaching. They were smiling the same weird smile he'd seen earlier from the first ruffian.

He tapped Sarky's shoulder. "We should leave."

Sarky wasn't paying attention.

Tarin slapped the back of his head. "What's wrong with you?"

"Wow. He's good for an old man."

He followed Sarky's gaze and saw Clooney, as energetic as a man twenty years younger, helping the two guards do battle. "We don't have time to watch Clooney fight. Look over there. See that?"

Sarky turned his head, and straightened. "Those are the freakiest smiles I've ever seen." He put his hand to his stomach. "Uh oh."

Tarin grabbed him and pulled him into the nearest alley. They took a few fast turns between buildings, then through some old broken sheds, and soon found a more open road. They ran as fast as they could toward the east, wanting to get as far away from the riot as possible. But there was a deep pit in Tarin's heart, one that wouldn't be filled again until he knew his father was all right.

✝ ✝ ✝

Clooney swung his club at another enemy but missed. The man grinned and kicked the lumberjack in the shin. Clooney keeled over in pain.

The guards tried to help, but were stopped when more angry men emerged out of the crowd to help the remaining ruffians fight.

Clooney watched as the man approached him. A dagger was in his hand, a malevolent grin on his face.

"You shouldn't have stopped us. Those guards serve Willerdon. The sooner they go, the sooner the governor goes."

"Yer crazy! Ye can't just force the gov'nor away like this."

"Yes we can," said a raspy voice behind Clooney. He looked around and took a step back. It was an old, gnarly man. In his hand was a sword.

The man who'd kicked Clooney smiled and backed off.

"Ye see," the old man said, "I found out last night that the gov'nor's been hidin' some news from the people of town, news about a monster in the woods. Don't get me wrong, I already hated him. But after I heard he don't care if we all get eaten' up, I got really mad. Me and a bunch of fellas who were going to hunt the monster figured it'd be better to get rid of the monster in this town first. All night we've been recruitin' folks from all over, and as you can see, they just keep swarmin' in. All that's left is to get rid of people like you and the guards and finish off Willerdon."

Suddenly the old man's eyes glazed over. "If Willerdon remains, he will destroy us. All who hold the light will." The man's voice had changed, was now deep and guttural. The man looked at Clooney's pocket and snarled, "We know what you have."

The old man pulled back his sword. Clooney prepared to counter with his club, but rather than striking, the old man's face contorted in pain and his weapon fell from his hands as he collapsed to his knees, then onto his face, revealing the dagger in his back.

"Need some help, ol' friend?"

"Bill! Ye finally made it!" Clooney ran over and clasped hands with his friend.

"Now don't get all mushy with me, Clooney ol' boy. We got us some work to do." He gestured toward the south. "I think those guards over there could use our help."

As he spoke, Bill pulled his dagger from the dead man and wiped away the blood on his sleeve. "There's pockets of fightin' all over from what I hear, but this is the worst spot. The northern guards are mopping things up pretty well and workin' their way down here. If we can stem the fighting by the inn, this riot'll be over soon. Here, take this."

Bill handed Clooney a short sword, then pulled out another one. "Got 'em out of the ol' armory."

"So ye actually managed to get yerself in and steal some weapons."

Bill chuckled. "I like to think I borrowed 'em for a special occasion. Now, are we gonna stand around and talk all day, or are we gonna fight?"

Clooney smiled. "Let's go!"

The two friends gripped their weapons tight and charged their enemies.

As they reached the ruffians, Bill bellowed, "Let's have at 'em!" and cut one of them down. Clooney clashed swords with another. The surrounding guards cheered and increased their efforts to battle the enemy.

Other non-dissenters began swarming in from other parts of the town, apparently after cleaning things up in their respective districts. Swords clanged and blood spilled. A hulk of a man with an axe wildly bashed the heads of ruffians with the butt of his weapon, spilling no blood but effectively eliminating them from the battle. After a half hour, nearly all the enemy had been destroyed or knocked out, or had run away.

"We won!" Bill shouted, and held his sword into the sky. But sudden agony swept over his face, then he stooped to his knees and fell over.

"Bill!" Clooney shouted, and ran toward his friend. The ruffian tried to flee, too late. Clooney threw his sword at him, and its deadly tip stuck into his back. The man's hands flew into the air as he collapsed.

Clooney reached Bill and turned him over. "Bill," he moaned. Tears filled his eyes. "Ye can't go. What about Margaret? She needs ye."

Bill looked up, his eyes bloodshot but peaceful. "Clooney . . . don't let 'em win. They want to destroy Woodend . . . just like . . . like Undertree."

"I know, Bill. They're here. I heard one of 'em inside an old man."

Bill shook his head and lowered his brows as sweat beaded up on his forehead. "Not just them," he whispered. "*They're* comin'. The red-cloaked . . . monsters, from the south . . . from the story. I saw two on the way down. That means . . ."

Clooney waited, but Bill was too weak to continue. "We don't have much time before all of 'em come," Clooney said softly.

Bill nodded, and gasped. His eyes went wide. Clooney shook him in desperation, but it was no use. Bill exhaled his last, and his head slumped to one side.

Clooney's shoulders shook with unshed tears, which soon grew too heavy to hold back, and they rained down onto Bill's face while he held Bill close and sobbed.

"Don't worry, my friend. Whatever comes, I'll be ready!" He lowered his head onto Bill's unmoving chest. "I promise."

☩ ☩ ☩

Tarin and Sarky fled down the roadway. Soon they saw a wider road open up toward their right, and followed it. It went steeply downhill for a short distance, then opened into a tiny courtyard.

Clouds drifted in overhead. Tall brick buildings surrounded the open area, making the shadows deep. A dry, abandoned pool rested in the middle of the courtyard, and the boys walked over to it. A bench completely surrounded the empty basin, and they sat down.

When Sarky was able to breathe easily again, he said, "This reminds me of when Bolard made the decree. I was younger then, but I remember the fighting. I can't believe it's happening again."

Tarin nodded but said nothing, trying to push back the horrible memories he had of the time during the decree. They started filling his mind anyway. Trying to shake them off, he studied his surroundings, careful to take in the texture of every brick of the nearby buildings and every crack in the stone beneath his feet. But what his eyes saw was nearly as dismal as his memories. It was as if this part of the town had been long neglected.

The sound of a pebble being kicked came from a narrow road to their north. Footsteps followed. Tarin saw a shadow slide its way along the walls. In fear that had nothing to do with his shyness, he considered jumping into the pool to hide when a boy appeared behind the shadow and walked into the courtyard. He had a bag on his shoulder and was dressed in a traveling cloak.

Sarky looked over at Tarin with a smirk. "Scared you, didn't he?"

Tarin punched him in the shoulder.

"Hey, you there!" Sarky yelled. "Who are you and what're you doing here? Don't you know there's a riot going on?"

The boy walked over to them and stood, staring. After a moment, he sighed and placed his bag on the ground.

"My name is Dibbs." He looked around. "Do you know how to get to the gate from here? I'm trying to avoid the main road."

Sarky grinned. "What's a boy like you doing out by yourself in this part of town? The east end's dangerous."

"That's none of your business. Please, tell me the way to the gate."

"I'm not really sure how to get there from here," Sarky said. "And even if I did, I wouldn't tell you. It's getting late, and you shouldn't be going out into the woods right now. Weird things are out there. Shadows. Monsters. Nasty stuff."

"It can't be worse than here." Dibbs sat down next to them. "Are there really weird things out there?"

"Yes," Tarin said. "We've seen them. Don't know what to call them except shadow phantoms. We're still trying to figure out what they are."

Dibbs eyes grew wide even as his face went pale. "Did you say shadows?"

But he wasn't looking at them anymore. Tarin followed the boy's stare to the alley behind him. His heart stopped.

A figure concealed in a cloak and hood of red stood in the entrance to the alley.

"Run," he whispered to the others.

As they stood, the stranger walked into the courtyard at a fast pace.

"Run!" Sarky screamed. The boys had started to flee toward a westward road when Dibbs yelled, "My bag!" and began running back to where he'd set it down.

Sarky stopped running and shouted, "No Dibbs! Get back here!"

Dibbs reached his bag and looked up just as the stranger hissed and crouched down like an animal, then lunged forward. Three long strides and the entity caught hold of him, pulled him close to its body. "Don't move," it hissed loud enough for Tarin to hear. "You must come with me."

"We've got to help him," Sarky said.

Tarin was too terrified to move.

Sarky frowned, picked up a nearby brick and charged the cloaked stranger. "Let him go!" he screamed, and threw the brick.

The form lunged out of the way with Dibbs still in hand. The brick missed it, and it turned and hissed at Sarky. "Foolish boy!" Before Sarky could run back, it bolted forward with inhuman speed and grabbed him too.

Tarin, horrified, started backing up toward the road. The cloaked stranger peered at him from beneath the red hood, but didn't move to stop him.

He was almost to the road when two strong hands grabbed him from behind. Terror seized his heart when he looked down. The hands were scaly and partially covered by a red cloak.

Tarin was flung up over a broad, rough shoulder. His captor ran to the center of the courtyard. "We must leave," the entity hissed to the other stranger.

Tarin's mind numbed with fear as his captor began to run. "Gildareth ... help me," he managed to whisper. But as he was carried away, no help came.

✝ ✝ ✝

H e wasn't sure how long he'd held Bill in his arms when Clooney realized the fighting around him was dying down. One group was winning the battle. But which one? His survival depended on the answer.

"Get him!" someone yelled. There were some footsteps, and a loud thud. A man groaned and people started cheering.

"Get out of my city!" a loud, strong voice demanded.

"Fight! For Bolard!" someone else bellowed.

There were some timid shouts of agreement followed by a deluge of thuds and some clanging. More cheers.

"He's insane!" someone yelled. "We can't stop him!" Let's get out of here!"

A group of about thirty sinister-looking men broke through the crowd and ran south, past Clooney, then disappeared down the hill. A man followed them, howling in anger. "Cowards!" he screamed. The woman whose distress had started the confrontation stood next to him, arm in arm with a skinny fellow also holding an axe. Though she had cuts on her face and many dark bruises, she looked like she would live.

"The governor is here! The governor is here!" people began shouting.

The woman looked up, and limped through the people taking to the now-safe street. They opened up and made way for her. Clooney watched as she fell into the arms of the governor, who stood next to a tall stranger.

Will looked around at the dead and unconscious as Lianna wept on his shoulder. "What happened?" he said. He turned toward the crowd. "Who did this?"

Clooney shouted over to him. "A bunch of men loyal to Bolard did this, sir. Hopin' they'd get a revolt goin', far as I could tell."

Will held his wife and walked through the crowd to Clooney. He looked pale. "Why is there no more fighting?"

Clooney pointed to the large man with the axe. "This man scared the rest of 'em off."

Will looked at the man. "What is your name?"

"My name is Kandis, sir."

The entire group's attention was diverted down the hill. A man with torn clothes was yelling something as he stumbled toward the crowd.

Clooney looked hard at the figure. It was Hamlin, the gatekeeper.

"They're gone!" Hamlin moaned. "They took them!"

Will handed Lianna over to a guard. "Take her home." He then ran down the hill and helped Hamlin, who was covered with scratches and could barely walk.

"I tried to fight them off, Governor," he said through tears. "But they were too strong." His sad eyes glared deeply into Will's. "They weren't human. They took them."

"Who? Who did they take?"

"My boy. They took Sarky!" He started to sob and collapsed into Will's' arms.

Clooney felt his throat tighten. Sarky had been taken? What happened to Tarin? Tarin was with Sarky!

The man with Will approached Hamlin. Clooney felt his heart leap. "Gildareth," he whispered.

"Something took his son," Will said.

Gildareth knelt beside Hamlin. "What did they look like?"

"Cloaked and hooded in red. That's all I could see of them." He pointed to his scratches. "And they had claws on their fingers. Hideous. Dark."

"Did they take anyone else?"

"Yes, two others."

"Who were they?"

"One carried a friend of my son's." He lifted his eyes up to Will, and his face grew pale. "The other held Sarky in one hand . . . your son in the other."

A wash of disbelief swept across the governor's face, then horror. "No. This can't be."

Clooney saw Will look back at his wife, who was now just a small figure far up the road.

"First my wife is attacked," Will teetered on his feet, "then my son is stolen?" He swayed, and collapsed.

Clooney looked around at all the surprised faces, and heard many people begin murmuring and pointing at Will. Their expressions weren't happy.

Then he looked down at his friend, and for the first time truly realized he'd never hear him tell another story. He lowered his head and wept again.

EIGHTEEN

Hamlin found himself lost in a mob of sobbing women and children, along with angry men ranting about Willerdon's embarrassing display of leadership. Looking around, Hamlin noticed that the governor had disappeared. "Governor!" he shouted. "Where are you!"

"He ran off," a skinny, dirt-smudged young man said as he limped by. "The coward sneaked into an alley a few moments ago. Useless fool."

Hamlin spun in circles, holding his bleeding face in his hands. "Then who's going to help me find my boy?"

Someone grabbed his shoulder. He turned around and saw a burly man he instantly recognized.

"You said three were taken, gatekeeper. Who was the third?"

Hamlin stood dumbfounded, wondering how he would tell the man the truth about Tarin.

"Speak, gatekeeper! Who was the third?"

"It was your son, Kandis! It was Tarin!"

Kandis lowered his head and began to quake, though he made no noise. Hamlin reached out, then yanked back his hand in sudden unease at what the man might do.

Both men stood awkwardly for a few moments, until Kandis inhaled deeply and raised his head. "You said they went into the woods. How long ago?"

"Less than an hour." He paused. "Wait a moment! Are you going after them?"

Kandis had already brandished his axes and was striding away.

"Wait! I'm coming too!" Hamlin called after him. He looked around for something to use as a weapon, saw a bloody slab of wood, picked it up and followed Kandis, the thought of clubbing the beastly kidnappers stronger than the pain from his many bruises and cuts.

It took them nearly a half hour to weave through the bustling crowds converging in the main road. When they finally reached the gate, Kandis knelt and began studying the ground.

Hamlin gazed into the trees past the open gate. He couldn't see much. Beyond thickening clouds, the sun had nearly set, stripping the forest of its few remaining provisions of light. "Those dern red-cloaked freaks couldn't even have the courtesy to close the door," he grumbled. A moist breeze blew from the forest, upsetting what gray hair wasn't already ruffled on his head.

He approached Kandis, who instantly greeted him with the broad, calloused palm of his hand and said, "Don't move. You'll ruin the remaining tracks."

"Why do we need tracks? Didn't the beasts just travel south along the road?"

"Do you honestly think they would simply stroll down the road with stolen children?"

Hamlin had no response.

"Of course they wouldn't. They'd be spotted too easily. Although, with those red cloaks you mentioned, they'll be easy enough to spot once we catch up to them, even in the dark. That is, if your memory hasn't botched that little observation."

"They were wearing them all right! But I wouldn't be too hasty in thinking everything'll be well when we catch up to them. They had claws, in case you forgot, and not like the nails you and me got on our fingers." He lifted his hands like a cat in mid-pounce, then pointed at his face. "Look what they did to me! Look at all these scratches! But don't get me wrong. I want to club them as much as you do. We just got to be cautious."

"Calm down, gatekeeper. I know."

Kandis ran his hand along the ground and jolted upright. "I've found their trail. Let's go."

"Wait, shouldn't we get some torches? It's going to be pitch black in there pretty soon."

"I've been a woodsman for many years, and I know the forest better than I know all the alleys and roads in Woodend. I won't get lost, even in the dark. And besides, if we carry torches, we won't be able to sneak up on our enemies."

Chagrined, the gatekeeper said, "Well then, lead on."

Kandis bounded into the trees, speeding through the foliage with barely a sound. Hamlin followed, and immediately stepped onto a pile of twigs.

Kandis turned around. "Be quiet!"

"Fine!" He carefully dodged the twigs and tiptoed on, muttering, "Lumberjack's are so— *Ahhhh!*" An abnormally large spider web had grabbed hold of his face. He tried to claw it off, but it only seemed to make it more determined to stay right where it was.

"Be quiet back there!"

"Shut up! I got spiders crawling all over me, you madman!"

"I doubt they'll harm you, gatekeeper. Though I wouldn't weep if they did."

Hamlin finally managed to brush off most of the stringy substance. "My name's Hamlin, and I'd appreciate it if you call me that. And watch your attitude. I know you're upset, but don't forget, my son's gone too."

Kandis stood still. "I'm sorry, it's just . . ." He faced Hamlin. "My son's been kidnapped, the town's in an uproar, and it seems the whole world's gone mad. And I can't help to wonder where the king is in all of this."

Hamlin stilled. "So, you're one of those king followers, eh?"

"Yes, I'm a servant of the king, if that's what you mean."

"Do you have one of those illuminas?"

"It's in my pocket."

"Did you ever give it up? I mean, during Bolard's Royal Decree?"

"Of course not!"

"Did Bolard punish you?"

Kandis turned and began walking slowly on. "I was jailed, and my family was treated coldly. All our friends turned against us. We have some new friends now, all of us except my son."

"Why do you think that is?" Hamlin asked, hurrying to keep up.

Kandis kicked a stone into a nearby stump. "Tarin has always been a timid boy. I don't know why. I guess he was just born that way. Though he does have a keen curiosity, which tends to make him bolder than he sometimes ought." Kandis smiled. "I encourage him that way though."

Hamlin placed a hand on the lumberjack's burly shoulder. "Tarin's a fine lad. And I'm proud to say, he's not friendless anymore. Him and Sarky have been getting along quite well. I even think your lad's rubbing off on mine a bit, making him a little more careful and all. Who knows, perhaps Sarky might rub off a little of his recklessness on your boy. They're good for each other." He took in a deep breath. "Don't worry. We'll find them both." He pointed at Kandis' pocket. "And if we're lucky, maybe the king will even find it in his heart to help us."

Kandis reached for his pocket and pulled out his illumina. It glowed gently in the night, only faintly illuminating the surrounding trees.

"What are you doing?"

"If the king's going to help us, it might be wise to ask for his help. You're welcome to join me."

"I . . . really don't know. Maybe you should just do it."

"Come on, gatekeeper, it's for your son."

"It's been a really long time."

"It doesn't matter."

"Fine, I'll do it, but only because of Sarky."

Both men laid their hands on the illumina. It grew brighter. Then, in the distance, they heard rustling, followed by the faint sound of a hiss. Kandis pocketed the light and met Hamlin's eyes in a knowing glance. "Hurry," he whispered. Then winked. "Quietly."

Hamlin nodded, and they moved deeper into the trees.

Nineteen

The winged creature beat its massive papery wings and disappeared beyond the reddening treetops, inexplicably ending its attack on Dralo and Ristun.

Ristun ran to his comrade. Dark blood wet Dralo's brown leather jacket near the left shoulder. He knelt and began wiping a thick red substance from his sword onto the grass.

"It will mend," Dralo managed. "I stuck the creature's underside before it could bite deep."

Ristun knelt next to him and began cleaning his own weapon. "What was that thing? And where did that man disappear to?"

"I don't know. But it's good he did. The beast seemed determined to slay him."

"I noticed. But why so?"

"Perhaps it was under control of the sentinel." He closed his eyes. "Why did the sentinel flee without even a fight?"

"Maybe the creature wasn't under its control, and frightened it away?"

Dralo shook his head. "I have never known a sentinel to fear any animal, however large."

There was rustling behind them. Dralo drew his sword and spun around.

"I saved him! I saved him! Ha ha, ho ho! I, the mighty one, have saved the cruel man from the town on the hill. 'Sheriff,' he says? Oh, so strong he is. Can't even protect himself from a mere animal! Ha ha, ho!"

"Who is that?" Ristun whispered.

"I have no idea, though it appears he's found our missing man."

About fifty paces away stood a scrawny man in the torn clothes of a merchant. He began kicking out his legs as if dancing. Another man lay in the weeds next to his feet.

Dralo moaned. "Why do we always find ourselves among the lunatics of Arvalast?" He again sheathed his sword.

"Hoy!" the stranger called. He ran up to them and studied them with beady eyes. "Scared of something? He, he. I know I'm rather imposing. It's good that monster saw me, or you might've been eaten."

"Do you have your sword?" Dralo asked Ristun.

The stranger lifted his hands. "Just teasing, just teasing. Alas, I know it was thee who scared away the monster. Although, the monster was a mere trifle compared to whom was here earlier."

Dralo grabbed the man by his shirt collar. "You saw the sentinel?" He pointed toward the fallen man. "What did it do to that man?"

The stranger pulled away and scowled. "Fools! I wasn't watching the sentinel's play. I was hiding! That man over there should have done the same, though I'm glad he got what he did. He he! Oh yes, the sentinel found easy prey in him."

"You speak rather flippantly about matters you should not." Dralo took a step forward. "Who are you?"

"Not an enemy, if that's what you're implying. I don't like the sentinel any more than you do. But as to who I am," he scratched the tangled matt of rusty hair on his pointy head, "I have so many names. Let's see. Thief, Fiend, Scrawny Pig, Worthless Scum, Petty Burglar."

Dralo rolled his eyes. "I believe we have the idea. What is your real name?"

"I've already told you many." He brushed some grime from his torn coat. "Call me whichever you wish."

Dralo studied him. Filth was caked into his garment and strewn throughout his hair. "Do you not have a real name, my dirty little friend?"

The man looked up, eyes blazing with anger. "Those are real names, fool! Are they not good enough for a couple of weakling northerners?"

"Do not insult us! We're more powerful than you can ever imagine!"

The man tilted his head and squinted. "Yes, yes. I know what you are. You're servants of the king." He took a step forward. "I'm not afraid of your kind. I deal with glorions all the time. I've even stolen trinkets from them." He searched his pockets. "Aha, look here." He held out a small sheath. "This held a glorion's dagger, once. I took it from him in his sleep."

"Why did you not take the dagger? Certainly you would have acquired a great deal for such an item."

"I, uh, lost it."

"You speak falsely! It was too hot to touch, was it not?"

"Uh, uh . . . no! I simply lost it."

Ristun snickered. "Well, my little friend. Say what you wish, but I wouldn't antagonize my comrade if I were you. He has a long sword and a short temper."

Dralo pulled back his cloak and drew out his weapon, peering at the little man through narrowed eyes as he patted the blade against the palm of his hand.

The man shuffled his feet. "Um, I see, I see."

Dralo lowered the weapon. "Let's get back to the matter at hand. What's your name?"

"I've already told you my names."

"Then which do you prefer?"

"My favorite has always been Thief. So short and sweet, it fits me nicely, don't you think?"

"I rather liked Scrawny Pig, but Thief will do."

There was a groan, and all three men directed their gaze toward the man in the distant patch of grass.

Thief bowed. "Forgive me, I must return to my prize."

"He isn't your prize."

"Yes he is. I saved him, with no help from you two, I might add!"

"You speak nonsense." Dralo pushed past Thief and approached the man.

"Hey, stop!" He took a step forward, but Ristun held him back.

"I told you," Ristun whispered. "Do not antagonize my comrade. You must understand. The man you saved might be of great importance to the throne if the sentinel found so much interest in him. We must make sure he's safe."

"What will you do with him?"

"Bring him to Woodend."

"But he's mine!"

"Ristun!" Dralo yelled in the distance. "Come here!"

Ristun and Thief hurried over. Dralo was kneeling next to the man. Conscious, the man might have looked robust. Now, he was white as a corpse, though breathing steadily.

Thief bent down to get a good look at his quarry. "Not a bad fellow, except for those red eyes. I've seen this before. Grim, quite grim."

Dralo looked up. "Where have you seen this before?"

Thief picked up a large dandelion leaf and blew his nose. He shrugged.

"Speak up! I am in no mood for the games of an imbecile!"

"All right, All right. I've seen it in the south years ago."

Dralo paced. "Where exactly in the south? Mahotholin? The plains?"

"No, farther. In the last country."

"Do you mean Macalum?"

"Yes, yes. That's what some fools call it. You're much too interested in names. Were you never educated? Are you a dolt?

Dralo growled through clenched teeth. "Please, my good sir. Tell me what you know of this sentinel."

"Ah, respect at last." Thief smirked at Ristun. "Well, all my life, after my father died, that is, I was driven north by the shadow's army." He grew quieter. "A king was leading them."

"King?" Ristun said. "There is only one king, and he certainly wouldn't side with evil."

"No, no, you foolish, and growing ever-more so warrior. There are many kings in Arvalast." He fell into a whisper. "The sentinel captains are all kings."

Dralo's took a step toward Thief. "Describe the one you saw."

Thief waved his hands in the air. "He was like all the others! As a glorion, I'm sure you've seen your fair share!" He pointed at the man on the ground. "That sentinel is the one who did this to the sheriff, though the dirty pig deserved it." He looked down at the man and grinned. "Not so strong now, are you, powerful sheriff? Ha, those red eyes hurt, don't they? Burn your soul they do, ho, ho. Maybe now you'll be less likely to try to kill poor Thief." He kicked the man's side and laughed.

Dralo brandished his sword and pointed it at Thief. "Do that again, and I'll scatter your carcass across the meadow!" He turned to Ristun. "Watch this imbecile. I have to go think for a while. Make sure he doesn't harm the man again." He walked away and soon disappeared beyond some high grass.

"Um, sorry," Thief told Ristun. "I'm sometimes, well, not terribly nice. Especially toward people who try to kill me."

Ristun raised an eyebrow. "It happens often?"

"Oh yes. Every few days. In fact, just a week ago I stole a money bag from a merchant in Lockspell and—"

Dralo reemerged from the weeds. "We've got to get this man to Gilda-reth quickly. He has little time left before—"

"Death," Thief said.

"Worse. Far worse. For him, and for us. We should leave."

Thief looked around at the trees as they swayed in the afternoon breeze. "It's getting late. Are you still planning to take him to Woodend?"

"Yes. Gildareth can help him there."

"Hmm. It'll take someone especially powerful to cure the wicked sheriff. He's been smitten badly by the king."

"Please don't call a sentinel 'king.' It dishonors the true king."

"But that's what it is! And perhaps it's more of a king than this *true* one you speak of. His army is certainly greater, and more terrible."

"But the true king is still stronger!"

"Good, I hope you're right. I hate those filthy hissers. They're everywhere, even in the forest."

"Drilockk are here?" Ristun said. "Right now? I thought only their masters were here."

Dralo lowered his head. "We must go, now." He reached down and picked up the man, whose eyes continued to glow a ghastly red.

"You must come with us," Dralo told Thief. "Gildareth will want to hear your story."

"I'm not going anywhere with you. I'll end up in jail!"

"Other than annoying me, you've done nothing wrong."

"Ha. The townsfolk will find something. I'm always ending up in jail. People don't like me. They suspect me of everything. And besides, even if they don't, within a day I'll steal something, and then they'll have a reason to come after me."

Ristun picked up some of the small trinkets that had fallen from Jebin's pack. "Try to control yourself."

"No, no, no. I can't. I don't even want to. I like to steal. It's my lot in life. It's my joy, and my bane."

Ristun pocketed a few coins and what looked like a carved owl. "Then I guess you're right, you will end up in jail."

"No, not again! I'm staying here."

Dralo grunted as he shifted the man's weight on his back. "You have no choice but to come with us. Otherwise I will have to kill you."

Thief lifted his nose. "I'm not scared of you." He began walking away.

"Ristun, get him—"

He stopped speaking when a great shadow swept across the meadow.

Thief halted his stride and peered at the sky through squinted eyes. "What in the name of—?"

A loud roar rumbled through the air.

"The creature," Dralo whispered.

Thief fled back to them and leaned against his knees. "I . . . I've decided to come with you."

"Why the sudden change of heart?" Ristun said as he peered into the sky behind him.

"Oh, I'm just a quite obedient man. Your companion says come, so I come. I'm your loyal servant."

Another roar rolled across the trees and down into the meadow. Thief whimpered.

Dralo gestured toward the northeastern end of the meadow, and led the group into the darkening forest.

TWENTY

Will rounded a corner and entered a dimly lit alley leading west. The wood of the surrounding buildings smelled musty and a large blacksmith's sign creaked above a nearby doorway. He stared at the large iron circle, and watched the metal hammer in its center sway in the breeze.

He struck his fist against a wall. Bolard had to be behind the riot! He should've let Jebin have his way with him after the decree failed. Perhaps if he'd actually taken a side and supported Jebin, the sheriff would've put aside his guilt and led Woodend, maybe even executed Bolard. Then he'd be rid of the menace, and the weight of the city's disapproval of him as the new governor.

Nearby, Woodend's main road ran north to south. He could barely see it through the thickening shadows. A sound came from that direction, faint footsteps pattering down the road from the north. As they drew nearer, he heard heavy breathing, and soon saw a girl of about seventeen stop at the alley entrance. She was dressed in a long blue skirt and brown leather overcoat, and looked nervous as she glanced behind her and turned into the alley. After a few steps, she noticed Will and stepped back in surprise.

"Who are you?" she said.

"I'm . . . nobody important. What are you fleeing from?"

She studied him, taking particular notice of the gold cufflinks on his dirty white shirt. "Governor? Governor Willerdon?"

Will didn't respond.

"Sir, it is you! What are you doing here? Didn't you hear about the riot?"

"Yes miss, that's why I'm here. I . . . never mind." He motioned toward the main road. "Were you running from someone?"

Her face grew white. "There's something here," she whispered. "Odd strangers are lurking around Willow Road where I live. They're going from door to door, sniffing. It appears they're looking for something."

She covered her face with her hand and tried to hold back tears. "When we heard of the riot, my mother and I went to look for my father, fearing he might somehow have gotten involved because of a hunt he was planning. That's when we saw a man running up the hill, screaming about a riot. He told us to not go any farther. We tried anyway, but guards stopped us, so we went home and began beseeching the king for Father's safety . . . and my brother's. He was staying with a friend at the gatehouse. We waited for hours, and no news came from Father. Soon wind of the riot's end reached Willow Road, and people started murmuring in the streets and heading south to see what had happened. Eventually, only a few remained."

Her voice started to quake. "We prepared to leave as well, until we saw them outside the window. At least three strangers in red cloaks. They started sniffing around. Mother ordered me to lock the door and windows, and we hid in my room . . . it's farthest back in the house and up against the town wall. We waited for maybe an hour, and then I suggested to Mother that I run to get help. She refused, but as time wore on . . . we decided to sneak to the front of the house. Just to see if the cloaked ones were gone. Indeed, the streets appeared empty.

"Mother finally agreed to let me try to find help. But she told me to go no farther than our cousin's house . . . to see if she or my aunt had heard or seen anything. So I went. But when I turned down their road, I saw one of the cloaked strangers. It turned toward me and hissed. An awful hiss! Then it started striding toward me. I turned around, toward home. But when I did, there was another one! It hissed, too. I turned and fled toward the main road, hoping there'd be people there who could help me. But no one was around. I found no one until I drew near to this place. Then I thought I heard another hiss, that's why I fled in here and met . . . you." Tears began streaming down her cheeks. "Please, Governor, you've got to come back with me. I'm so scared."

Feeling a renewed sense of purpose, he nodded. "Of course. After all, I myself live on Willow Road." A lump formed in his throat. "What a fool I am! My family's up there too! I've got to get to them!"

"That means you'll help me?"

He stood and nodded, and she reached out and embraced him. "Thank you, Governor!"

The affection took Will off guard. But as her happy tears wet his coat, his compassion got the better of him and he gently returned the embrace. "Shh," he whispered. "What's your name, miss?"

"It's Ella." She sniffled.

"Don't worry, Ella. Everything will be fine."

A quiet breeze carried a hiss into the alley. Will caught a glimpse of a red cloak pass by the alley entrance, then disappear.

Ella began to tremble. "Was it one of them?"

"I ... don't know. We better get moving." He grabbed her arm and headed away from the main road.

They eventually came to a road called Pleasant Hill. They followed it for a while at a brisk step until Ella began to pant.

"I can't keep up," she said between labored breaths.

"We must." He tried to pull her along.

"Please Governor ... no farther."

"Ella! We can't stop. My family's in danger. I've got to get to them."

She collapsed. He let her fall and kept running. "I'll come back for you," he called out, "don't worry—"

Suddenly he felt a terrible burning in his pocket. He stopped and swatted at his cloak, thinking it might be a bee. The burning died away. "Odd," he muttered, and tried to continue.

The heat came back with renewed fervor. He reached into his cloak, but withdrew his hand with a start. It was his illumina, and it was hot. He looked back at Ella, then at the sky. "I'll come back for her, I promise. Right now, I've got to get to my family."

Ella is under your protection as well. The voice, sounding similar to his own, spoke within his mind.

Will looked back at her. "What am I doing?" he muttered. "What have I become?" He ran his hand through his thick sandy brown hair, and returned to her.

"Forgive me child," he said as he knelt beside her. "A madness took me. So much has happened today, I'm not thinking straight. Now, do you think you can walk?"

"I'm so tired, but I'll try." She stood, but wobbled. "I'm sorry Governor. I just can't." She forced a smile. "I'm not usually this pathetic, but I've run more today than I normally do in a month. My legs aren't used to it."

Will knew he couldn't leave the poor girl, yet couldn't abandon his family either. In his heart he cried out to the king, *What do you desire from me? How do I save both the girl and my family?*

He heard footsteps. He didn't want to turn around for fear of what he might see, but forced himself.

Relief washed over him. It was just a man, a young lumberjack from the looks of it, and he was heading toward them.

"Kind sir," Will called. "We could use some help."

The man made an abrupt stop and spun from side to side. "What's that? Who's there?"

Will stood and began waving. "Just get down here! The girl's in need of aid."

The man took a quick glance into the alley he'd just emerged from, and hurried toward them, wiping his brow.

"Don't worry, Ella," Will said, "this fellow can help me get you home."

The man watched his back as he continued his approach. Will saw the man was likely in his early twenties, and seemed strong beneath the leather coat he wore.

"Governor?" the man said when he reached them. "It's . . . a pleasure to meet you in person. But what are you doing here?"

Will beckoned for him to kneel. "Never mind that. We need help."

"Yes sir, sorry sir." He lowered himself next to Ella. "What's happened? Is the riot still going on?"

"Now's not the time for questions, lad. This girl's informed me of potentially unruly strangers prowling around on my road. Odd men in red cloaks."

The man fidgeted and looked around. "She's right. I saw them crawling around the houses up there. Crawling, mind you! And I thought I saw one in that alley I just came from. I've been searching for someone to help me scare them off."

"You'll have to abandon your search for the moment. The girl can't run anymore, and I've got to see if my family's safe. Can you stay with her while I go ahead?"

"You can't go up there by yourself!"

"Please, just stay with her so I can go. Time's wasting."

"Please sirs," Ella said. "I'll be all right. Go, Governor, save your family."

Jak's eyes happened upon Ella's face, and his face reddened. "Who . . . who are you?"

"I'm Ella, Kandis' daughter."

"My name's . . . um . . . oh yes, Jak. It's . . . uh . . . nice to meet you Ella."

Will rolled his eyes. "I don't want to be rude, but there are better times for introductions."

Jak ignored him. "I've decided," his voice grew strong and determined, "to help you both." He turned to Will. "I'll carry Ella so she won't have to run."

"You certainly will not!" Ella sputtered.

Will lifted his finger to his lips. "Now isn't the time to argue either."
More at ease about her situation, he got up and charged north.

✝ ✝ ✝

Iak's heart beat fast, but not from physical strain. He couldn't believe he
was letting this girl's pretty face confuse his usually steady mind. But right
now, he was too tired and apprehensive to shake it off. So he embraced it.
He reached down for her hand.

"I'm not letting you carry me."

He sighed and backed away. "Well and good. But I've got to help the
governor, so I guess you'll just have to wait here."

He turned to leave.

"Wait," he heard. "Just help me up. I think I can run now."

Hiding his smile, he quickly but gently pulled her to her feet. She ran
for a few steps, then stumbled as more cramps stiffened her legs. Before she
fell, Jak pulled her into his arms and began carrying her up the hill.

"Let me down!" she shrieked.

He ignored her and continued running. After minutes of carrying her
up the long hill, most of which she struggled and complained, he at last
stopped near the opening to another road.

"We've made it," he said. "Willow Road."

Will stood nearby, anxiously peering around Chop's Barbour Shop, a
dismal-looking brick building.

"You can put me down now," Ella said as she tried to wriggle free from
his arms.

He gently placed her on the road. She looked up at him, smiled, then
slapped him across his face. "Don't ever pick me up like that again! I'm a
lady, not a rag doll."

His cheek grew red with her handprint, and suddenly he regretted the
ridiculous feelings he'd gotten from her pretty face. "Yes, miss," he replied
sheepishly. "I'm sorry if I appeared a bit rude earlier."

"You two need to keep quiet," Will said. "We don't want those red-
cloaked strangers to see us before we see them. Everything looks clear at the
moment. My house is only a short distance down the road. Quickly!"

They rounded Chop's Barbour shop and headed east. Stars began
twinkling above them as the sun gave way to the pale moon. Faint thunder
in the distance threatened its light.

Will pointed. "There's my house—"

Nearby, something scurried across the street. The three came to a halt
and looked around. But it was only a black and white cat chasing a mouse.

"Where are all the other villagers?" Ella said.

"No doubt still rummaging around down south," Will replied coldly, "spreading gossip as to why I ran off."

"Why did you run off?" Jak asked. "The riot is your responsibility after all."

"Ha! Isn't everything?"

The group continued east, their feet pattering along the brick pavement as Will's house drew nearer. Will halted. The door to his house was hanging open, lazily squeaking in the breeze.

"My family," he whispered. He put his hand into his pocket, felt calm wash over him. He glanced at Jak, saw that he had noted the transformation in him, but simply nodded and continued walking. Jak and Ella followed.

At the door, Will beckoned for the others and pointed at some scratches near the latch. "I'm going in," he said, and walked into the darkness.

Jak turned to Ella. "I've got to follow him. Are you coming?"

A dog barked somewhere in the south. Ella reached out and grabbed his arm. "Yes."

They followed Will as he worked his way through his hall. None of the lanterns lining the walls were lit, or any of the candles on the various tables and shelves.

Thunder rolled outside as they followed him up a set of stairs and into what looked like a study. Piles of papers rested on a desk near a fireplace; books were neatly tucked away on the shelves.

Jak saw a broom lying in the middle of the floor, along with a dustpan. He continued to scan the room. A soiled dust rag hung limply from a shelf.

"My daughter must've been cleaning," Will mused. "My study isn't usually this orderly—"

"Did you hear that?" Ella gasped.

The hiss had come from the roof.

There was another hiss. Will cursed and pointed toward the ceiling, then stormed into the hall. "They're on the roof. Lianna, I'm coming!"

He started for the door when Jak grabbed his shoulder. "Governor, what are you doing? We can't just charge onto your roof without any plan. We don't even know how many are up there."

Will twisted away. His eyes turned to a fireplace poker leaning against the wall, and he snatched it up. Another hiss slid into their ears.

"I'm coming, you filthy snake!" he screamed toward the ceiling. "If you've hurt anyone, I'll tear you to pieces!"

A muffled shriek answered, followed by another hiss and a loud slap. Will slammed the poker against the wall and bolted out of the room. Jak followed him out the door and saw him slam open a narrow door at the end of the hall and ascend a short flight of stairs.

Jak looked at Ella. "I've got to help him."

"Wait," she said. "I'm coming too. I'm not completely useless." She pulled a small axe from her waistcoat. "It's my father's coat," she said with a nervous grin. "He always carries at least one axe with him."

"Smart man . . ." He reached into his own jacket and pulled out a large hunting knife. "The forest can be a dangerous place."

For the first time, she offered him a genuine smile.

He blushed and looked away. "Your legs . . . will you be able to run if you need to?"

She jogged in place for a moment. "They'll suffice."

They sped down the hall and up the stairs after the governor.

At the top of the stairs, they plunged through an open door and into a rainstorm. Ella grabbed his arm and pointed toward the edge of the house. Three large red-cloaked strangers crouched next to a woman and young girl. Behind them was a short wooden railing. Beyond that, nothing but air and a long fall.

Jak brushed rainwater from his eyes and suddenly saw him. Will stood a few paces from the red-cloaked men, holding out the poker with his trembling right hand.

"Lianna! Grace!" he screamed.

"Hello, Governor," one of the strangers snarled from beneath its hood. "It is good to at last meet you."

The little girl tried to squeal something. One of the other beasts swung around and growled at her. She quieted and drew close to her mother.

"Let them go!" Will shouted.

"We cannot do that, Governor." The man tilted his head, which remained concealed in the darkness beneath the red hood. "We have been ordered to destroy them."

Ella screamed. Jak held out his hand, but it was too late. Will, with only a fireplace poker, had charged.

TWENTY-ONE

The evening grew cooler, and Kandis fought a shiver as he made a right after sighting the broken branch, a clear sign the kidnappers had made yet another change in direction. Soon the trail led them from under the trees and into a small clearing with a pond in the center. Cattails lifted their heads from the water all along its shore. Resident frogs chirped and croaked, filling the clearing with their nightly chorus.

Kandis approached the pond and found the ground heavily disturbed. "They must've stopped here to drink. See all the footsteps near the water's edge?"

Hamlin shrugged. "It could've been lumberjacks that made these tracks for all we know."

"Not likely. The camps in this region have been abandoned for quite a while." He peered at the ground. An object glimmered in the moon's dim light. He picked it up.

Hamlin came closer and peered at it. "Looks like some kind of scale. From a fish, maybe."

"It's too large for that. I've never seen anything like it ... except ... Didn't you say the kidnappers had scaly hands with claws on their fingers?"

"Yeah. Oh, I see! Good going, old boy!" He slapped Kandis on the back. "It's got to be from one of them diseased freaks. We must be getting close."

Kandis fell into a crouch and began following the trail around the pond, toward the edge of the clearing. After twenty hunched paces, he stood in surprise. Prints were everywhere, trampled into the ground in a chaotic fashion. Accompanying them, scuffs and rivets skewed the dirt as if a huge sword had scathed the clearing's floor.

"What in Arvalast ... ?" Part of a torn, wet red cloak lay in the center of the trampled ground. He picked it up and his nose wrinkled at its foul odor. "Hamlin, come!"

Hamlin hurried over. "That's one of the beast's cloaks. But what's all that black stuff on it?"

Kandis rubbed the substance through his fingers. "I think it's blood."

The men looked at each other. "Then something attacked the kidnappers," Hamlin said. "But did it also attack . . . our boys?"

Kandis returned to his crouch and to scanning the ground. Soon he found footprints. Not big boot prints, but smaller ones. He followed them. Two other pairs of smaller prints joined them, six in all. The strides seemed long. They'd been running from something.

Kandis followed them until his face brushed against some leaves. He looked up. Dark forest greeted him. To his left, he found huge boot prints, also heading into the forest.

Hamlin drew up next to him, and he pointed down at the smaller footsteps. "All three boys went running into the woods right here." He pointed toward the boot prints. "But they were followed by one of the kidnappers."

"That means there's only one of those beasts left. Maybe the boys outran him! Maybe they're on their way back to Woodend right now!"

"We can't assume that, gatekeeper. The kidnapper might've recaptured them. But what I can't understand is what happened to the other beast. Could the two of them have gotten into a fight?"

"If so, where's the body? All we found was that piece of torn cloth—"

A wisp of cloud swept across the moon as it broke through the surrounding thicker clouds. Hamlin's face went pale. "Kandis!" he whispered. "Look! Up there!"

Something was covering the moon, and moving swiftly. But it wasn't a tuft of cloud. It looked more like a great bird. They heard a terrible, angry roar. They covered their ears and ducked. The thing continued beyond the moon and headed west into what appeared an oncoming rainstorm, then glided out of sight beyond the forest roof.

Hamlin rubbed his eyes. "Did I really just see that?"

The soft rumble of thunder rolled across the sky. "I . . . I've never seen such a thing or heard such a sound in all my time in these woods," Kandis whispered.

Hamlin started backing up toward the pond. "I say we get out of here."

"Pull yourself together. We've got to find the boys. They're in more danger than us, I think."

A noise within the forest hushed them.

"What was that?" Hamlin whimpered.

Kandis placed his hand over the gatekeeper's mouth. Both men became stone, listening to the forest. Moments passed, and nothing happened. But just as Kandis removed his hand from Hamlin's mouth, a hushed voice came from the east.

"The tracks lead this way," it said. "Hurry up, the older ones are starting to grow cold."

Before Hamlin and Kandis had time to react, a small figure burst into the clearing, followed by two larger ones. All three stopped in unison upon seeing them.

"Who are you, and what are you doing here?" the smallest of the three strangers demanded in a shrill voice as he pulled out a sword that matched his size.

"Wait." Kandis held out his hands to show he held no weapon, though his axes were still hidden beneath his cloak if needed. "We mean no harm. We're simply trackers in search of our kidnapped boys."

"That explains the smaller footprints," one of the tall figures, a woman, said.

"You've been tracking the beasts as well?" Hamlin asked. "How did you know about them? Were you in Woodend when they took my boy?"

"No," the third one said. "But we were heading toward Woodend before Dirfin heard something in the woods. We followed the sound and eventually came across a fresh drilockk trail."

"A drilockk trail?" Kandis said. "What are you talking about?"

"You forgot, Varla," the little fellow said. "He's a forest dweller. He's probably never heard of drilockk—"

A distant growl reverberated through the trees from their right. Everyone froze as the noise rolled over the leaves and down onto them. It stopped, and all went quiet.

The little fellow whispered, "That's the sound I heard before we left the road."

"We've heard it too," Kandis said.

"And saw it," Hamlin added.

"You saw it?"

Hamlin looked at the woman.

"Yep. It looked like a bird. Flew right across the moon. Whoosh! Scared me and my friend here to death!"

"Shh," the man scolded. "You don't want to lead it to us, whatever it is."

The small one snickered. "Don't worry so much. I can take care of it if it comes." Tiny chest thrust forward, he patted his sword.

"Sure you can, you little imp," the man muttered under his breath.

"Hey, I heard that—"

The woman stepped between them. "Stop it. You've been arguing all the way from Macalum, and it's beginning to annoy me."

"Sorry, Aliah," the little fellow said. He gave a small bow. "Never would I want to bring grief to your lovely face."

The tall man groaned and shook his head. "Your flattery is never going to win her heart."

"Don't be so certain," the woman said. She patted the small fellow on his head, making his eyes sparkle, and approached Hamlin and Kandis. As she came out of the shadows, they saw she wore a traveling cloak covering a glimmering breastplate. All that graced her head was her long golden hair. Leather boots reached up to her knees, topped by heavy leather pants that continued to her waist, where a sheath for her sword hung beneath the cloak.

She smiled at the two men, appearing noble and wise without losing the aura of a princess. "What are your names, sirs?"

"I'm Kandis of Woodend," he said with a small bow.

Hamlin seemed unable to shut his gaping mouth. Kandis kicked him in the leg. "Oh . . . sorry, miss. I'm Hamlin, gatekeeper of Woodend."

The woman's eyes twinkled. "I am Aliah of Macalum, daughter of High Governor Dirilion. With me are Dirfin of the Eastmont and Varla of the tower guard. We are here with news from Macalum."

"Macalum?" Kandis asked.

"Forgive him, miss," Hamlin replied. "He doesn't get out much. He's a lumberjack, so all that matters to him is what's going on in the forest."

"Unfortunately, he's right," Kandis said. "I have little knowledge of anything south of Lockspell, and I've never even traveled south of Mahotholin."

"That is not a misfortune," Aliah said. "All the happenings in the south are currently dire. That is why we've come." Her voice grew quiet and tense. "We bring news of approaching evil."

"And plan to destroy any drilockk we find here," Dirfin added, a fire burning in his eyes.

Kandis grew tense with excitement. "Perhaps you can help us then. My son is out there somewhere, along with Hamlin's. They were stolen from us earlier by strangers cloaked in red."

"They were scaly," Hamlin added, "and had claws. See what they did to me?" He pointed to the scratches on his face.

"You had a run-in with drilockk, no doubt," Dirfin said.

Varla raised a brow at Hamlin. "They were in your town? How did they get in, gatekeeper?"

"I assure you, sir, I didn't let them in. I don't let anything in I don't trust. And I'd certainly never trust scaly men garbed in nasty red cloaks. Nor queer folk with claws on their fingers." He huffed and crossed his arms.

"Then they must have another way in," Varla said. "We shall find it when we arrive in Woodend. But now, you say your sons are missing, and you're following the same trail we were. Which means we're pursuing the same enemy: two large drilockk.

"One drilockk," Kandis corrected.

"One?" Varla said. "What happened to the other?"

In the background, Hamlin groaned.

Varla looked over and crossed his arms. "And what's wrong with you, gatekeeper?"

"All this talk about drilockk, and I don't even know what they are. And don't let Kandis fool you, he doesn't know either."

Dirfin stared at him, appearing amused at their ignorance. "They're monsters, for lack of a better term."

"And I'm afraid that's all you need to know for now," Aliah said, glancing at the sky. "We've already spent too much time here. Kandis, show us why you think there's only one left, because we clearly saw two sets of their footprints."

Kandis proceeded to explain his observations. A few moments later, Dirfin held up the bloody shred of cloak and sniffed it. "Definitely drilockk blood. But what could have torn it up like this? Other than my sword of course."

"Something I don't want to meet," Varla said. "If it can take down a drilockk and shred its clothes like that, I can't imagine what it could do to us."

"To you," Dirfin argued.

Varla rolled his eyes.

"The boys' path begins over there," Kandis interrupted, pointing. "One of their kidnappers— I mean, a drilockk followed them."

"Then let's pick up their trail," Dirfin said.

The others started into the woods. Dirfin led the way, followed by Varla. Kandis and Hamlin came next. Aliah took up the rear.

"I know you both must have many questions," she said quietly amidst the gentle crunching of the group's footfalls. "But if you want to see your boys again, we must find the one that took them." Her face grew grim. "Be aware, they're in grave danger, as is the entire northern forest."

"You don't need to tell us the obvious," Hamlin said curtly.

She turned to him, and for the first time since her coming, she appeared truly angry. "You forest people have no idea of the evils of this foul world," she whispered through clenched teeth. A pool of water formed over her narrowed eyes.

Hamlin fidgeted with his hands, offered an awkward bow and averted his eyes from her gaze. Kandis stared hard into it. Beneath her regal and confident exterior, he saw pain. Deeply seeded pain.

TWENTY-TWO

A scaly fist plunged into Will's stomach. He stumbled back and dropped the poker. The nearest red-cloaked stranger snarled and brought its fist to its side. Will looked at its hand in revulsion. Horrible dark claws clung to the end of each finger.

The beast concealed its hand within its dull red cloak, lurched its head forward and hissed.

"Help us, Father," a sweet, small voice pleaded from behind the monster.

Will's daughter was quivering near the edge of the roof, her eyes full of tears. Lianna was next to her, equally terrified.

He directed his burning gaze toward the creatures. They stared back beneath their foul red hoods.

How can I stop them! his mind screamed. *What can I do?*

You can do nothing, a quiet voice answered from within.

He blinked and looked around. "What? Who's talking to me?"

You can do nothing, but I can.

Will looked back. He saw nothing, but felt his heart beat faster and a strange anger begin to overwhelm him. *Charge them!* Another voice, foul, but confident, yelled. *You can do it. Find the strength in yourself! Charge!*

No, wait, came the other voice.

Will covered his ears, then became aware of a barely noticeable weight in his vest pocket. Before he could investigate, someone rushed past him and charged headlong into the nearest stranger. The stranger snarled as he and his attacker went hurtling onto the roof's surface. A knife, held by the attacker, glimmered in the moonlight. Up it went, then plunged downward. But before it could deliver its deadly strike, a clawed hand stopped it.

With a quick thrust of a mighty arm, the stranger shoved the attacker into the air and sent him stumbling into Willerdon. Both men collapsed to the ground. Will looked at the man on top of him. It was Jak. Before either could say or do anything, a woman yelled, "You filthy monsters! I'll kill you for that!"

Jak collected himself and sat up. "No, Ella!" But it was too late. She rushed past them with her axe poised for a crushing blow.

The nearest stranger struck her with the back of his hand. She spun around and slumped to the ground, unconscious. The stranger snarled at her fallen body, then turned to the others. "Do it."

At the command, they moved toward Lianna and Grace. Slowly, their filthy fingers spread out and reached for their throats.

"Lianna!" Will bellowed. He got up and prepared to charge again.

That's right, the more powerful voice said. *Go! Get your victory! Save your family.*

"I will!" He looked around for a weapon, but realized all he had were his fists.

You cannot save them alone, the other voice said, again with calm.

He pounded at the air, confused and frustrated at the two voices daring to use his head as their personal platform to voice differing commands. "Silence! Whatever you are, just be quiet!"

Without me, they will die, the quiet voice said. *There is still hope, Will. Believe.*

The weight in his pocket returned.

Do it! the louder voice countered, now in a chorus of other similar voices. *Charge, you coward. Charge!*

One of the strangers grabbed Lianna's neck. She let out a muffled shriek.

See, they're about to die, screamed the chorus of loud voices.

No, have patience, whispered the tranquil voice.

The other beast grabbed Grace.

Will began pulling at his hair. "Patience will kill them!"

The strangers pulled the girls to their feet and began dragging them toward the edge of the roof. Grace began to struggle, but it was no use.

Save your wife and daughter! the loud voices were screaming. *Only you can do it. The king can't help!*

Something snapped in Will's mind, and he remembered. *The king!*

Something in his head began spewing forth curses. At first he held his ears, but it did nothing. Time was running out. Not knowing what else to do, he pointed at the creatures just as Lianna's feet began to dangle over the edge.

"In the name of the king, stop!"

The stranger holding Lianna paused and turned its head. It watched Will from the corner of its hidden eye. "You cannot command us." It began to release its grip on Lianna's throat. Her feet still hung over the precipice.

The words plunged into him like a knife. *It didn't work. Why didn't it work?*

The cursing in his head grew quiet.

Trust me, the soft voice said.

Again, Will noticed the weight in his pocket. His heart grew lighter. He narrowed his eyes and reached into his cloak. Then he turned his wrathful gaze back toward the three strangers.

"The king has made me overseer of this town," he said, "and I have authority within these walls. And by this authority, I command you to let my wife and daughter go!"

The strangers pulled the girls back onto the roof and released them. They joined the third as he hovered, vulture-like, over Ella. "You *command* us?" the third one questioned coldly. "Nay, Governor. We serve no one but our master, not some wretched *man* or his feeble *king*."

It reached into its cloak and pulled out a crooked knife. The other beasts did likewise. "If your king is so strong, let him stop our blades before they plunge into this girl's heart."

"No!" Jak screamed. He stumbled forward.

The monsters lifted their weapons for the fatal strike.

Will knew Jak's attempt to save Ella was futile. There wasn't enough time. His hand burned. He looked at his clenched fist. The cracks between his fingers glowed bright white. His hand was on fire, or so it felt. He looked up, and time seemed to slow. He watched Jak take another step, saw the creatures start to bring their knives down, toward Ella's chest.

The fire moved from Will's hand to his arm. From his arm, it sped like lightning to his chest, then to his heart.

Jak took another step, and the knives grew even lower.

How his heart burned! It burned with anger, and love, and so many other powerful emotions. Some were his own, while others seemed to flow from another source, a more powerful source. His eyes narrowed.

He saw the knives as they readied themselves to gouge into Ella's flesh.

Anger.

He saw Ella lying helplessly on the ground.

Pity.

Jak continued his vain plunge toward his foes, trying to save the girl.

Respect.

Then he saw his dear Lianna and Grace, cowering near the edge of the roof, beyond fear.

Love. Unwavering, powerful love.

His fingers spread open. A light shone from his palm so bright it blinded him, and not just him, but all those on the roof. Knives clattered to the ground as their owners fell back, then to the ground, screaming curses before they stilled.

Lianna and Grace shielded their eyes as they ran past their demobilized captors and into Will's embrace.

Jak swept Ella into his arms and hurried her away from the strangers as they began to get back up.

In the midst of Will's triumph, a terrible voice screamed within his head. *You will die!*

Will clenched his eyes shut, but couldn't shut out the voices.

Die, filth! We'll kill your family! See, they aren't yet safe!

He opened his eyes. The strangers stood in half crouches. The nearest beast had reclaimed his crooked knife, and now stared at Grace and Lianna.

Blood will flow, the voices laughed manically. *And you shall see them die!*

All went silent, but Will suddenly knew what to do. He thrust his illumina into the air. Immediately, the sound of many angry voices screeched at him from all around.

No! Stop! There is no hope!

"Liars!" he bellowed.

The nearest stranger jumped toward Grace. But Will was ready. He aimed his illumina and threw it with all his might. It hit the beast in the head and sent him plunging to the roof. The phial exploded on contact, spilling luminous liquid in all directions. The drops that hit the stranger sizzled, causing it to scream and convulse. Where it hit the red cloak, smoldering holes were forming.

Grace and Lianna held tight to Will, their faces concealed in his sweat-soaked vest. His eyes were glued to the stranger. The red cloak caught fire and the man within continued to screech as he tugged frantically at the corners of the garment and thrust it from its body.

Will's eyes widened. Though the stranger was shaped like a man, it was no man. Scales encased its body, which was girded with light armor on both the chest and waist. On its fingers were curled claws. In place of a nose were two slits, and just below that, a dragon-like mouth. But the most terrible feature was its eyes. Not animal, but completely human, though angry and bent on evil.

The monster returned Will's glare for a moment, then snarled in pain. Some of the liquid was now burning through its scales. In agony it spun around, and to Will's astonishment, it leaped off the roof.

The other beasts, which had been able to avoid the liquid in the illumina, growled and followed the first beast. Will and his family, along with Jak and Ella, were now alone. And to the governor's great delight, the voices in his head were gone.

All five of them sat for many moments, crying and holding one another. Then, footsteps approached. Will spun around, half-afraid one of the strangers had returned. His concerns were instantly silenced by the wonderful sight of a tired, limping man.

"Gildareth!" Will cried. "You can't imagine what just happened!"

The herald sat next to them with a grimace. "What a night," he groaned, and patted Will's back. "Judging from all the hindrances I had on the way to your house, most in the form of shadow, it is no doubt to me you've just been granted a mighty victory. *Granted*, mind you. For if not for the king's intervention, the fate of this evening would have been much different. Always remember, as all his servants must, it is not by your own strength that you are able to fight, but through his."

He turned his eyes toward Jak and Ella. "Ah, young Jak. It is a pleasure to see you here. If not for your presence, things might have turned out much different. And dear Ella, you're a courageous girl. The king knows of you and holds you in high regard."

She blushed, seemed to suddenly notice she was leaning on Jak's shoulder, and pulled herself away. Gildareth chuckled, and turned back to Will.

"I must now ask to speak to you and your wife alone. Perhaps we could go to your study and allow Jak and Ella to attend to Grace?" He looked down at the girl with raised eyebrows. "Would that be all right with you, dear?"

She smiled and nodded.

"Very well then. Let's go inside and start a nice warm fire to chase away the cold and the shadows."

Will, too tired and curious to disagree, obliged.

TWENTY-THREE

Once downstairs, Jak and Ella took Grace into the dining room, and after lighting every lantern they could find, gave her food and drink. They talked cheerily with her, trying to help her forget the horrors they'd all just seen. Will watched until, satisfied, he lit the final lantern, then turned to Gildareth. "Shall we go to my study?"

When they got there, Gildareth walked to the fireplace. "Please sit and rest for a moment. I shall start a fire."

Once the room was full of light and all the shadows had skipped away, he pulled out a chair and sat across from them. "I have much to tell you."

Lianna sat with wide eyes while Gildareth recounted some of what he told Will the day before. As he spoke, midnight passed and the shroud of a new morning spread across the land. The patter of rain on the roof slowed, then silenced.

"So this is why Grace and I were attacked?" Lianna asked after hearing of Wrathar and his plans to destroy Woodend to get to the king.

"I don't fully understand Wrathar's strategy," Gildareth replied, "but it makes sense. He is trying to destroy your husband. Though before today, he seemed to be using more subtle means. For instance, he has been spreading rumors about Willerdon in an attempt to make him appear weak and unqualified to lead."

Lianna laughed. "I don't think the enemy would have to do that. My husband often angers the people enough on his own."

"This is serious business, Lianna," Will said, embarrassed and frustrated. "Please, I need your support. Without it, I won't be able to stand up against this enemy."

"Remember, madam," Gildareth added, "Will demonstrated how courageous he could be if he places his full trust in the king. Have you forgotten the rooftop so soon?"

"No, I haven't forgotten," she said, contrite. "That was the man I remember marrying. When he seemed so full of the king's power, and was swift to stand up for what he believed was the king's will." She paused. "But then he changed. I remember when Bolard began his Royal Decree. Will was furious, and from how he talked about the old governor, I thought he would certainly do something about it. But he didn't. He simply tried to keep peace between the two sides, and acted as if he was on neither, though he definitely wasn't on Bolard's."

She turned toward Will. "That bothered me then, and now."

"I know, dear," he replied coldly.

"And then, when Sheriff Jebin asked him to become governor, he fought against it for so long before finally relenting. I don't know why. He often told me he thought it was the king's will for him to do it."

Will squirmed in his chair. "I was afraid. You've seen what's come of it."

"That's because you haven't put your trust in the king. If you'd always acted the way you did on the rooftop tonight, the town would be quick to follow you and show you respect. They've never seen you that way though, so they don't know what a mighty man you can be."

"Why must you always belittle me?" Will asked. "I've tried! I just haven't been able to get through to these people. And you know as well as I do what's about to happen."

He quieted his voice so Grace, Jak and Ella wouldn't hear from downstairs. "Bolard's coming back to overthrow me. Oh yes, he's coming, Lianna. That's why Jebin got out of here while he could. Maybe we should too, especially after what's been going on lately. A riot broke loose, people were killed, you and Grace were nearly thrown off our roof by who knows what, and . . ." He gasped. "Dibbs got kidnapped."

"What?" Lianna screeched.

"Oh no," Will moaned with widening eyes. "I'd forgotten until now. When Ella came and told me about the monsters on our road, I just . . . forgot."

"You *forgot* that our son was kidnapped?" Lianna stood and ran to him, arms flailing. "You idiot! What happened? Tell me this instant!"

"Those creatures that nearly killed you. There are more of them, and they took Dibbs, and two other boys. . . ."

The realization that part of his family was still in danger overwhelmed him, and he broke into tears. "How could I've forgotten? What have I done?" he sobbed.

Grace ran through the door and into the room, looking frightened. Ella and Jak followed.

"What's going on," Grace cried. "I heard you say Dibbs was kidnapped."

"Your father *forgot* that your brother has been kidnapped!" Lianna bellowed. "He's worthless."

"Don't call him worthless," Grace yelled. "He saved us!"

Lianna held her face in her hands and stormed past Ella and Jak and out of the room.

"Where's Mother going?" Grace asked though misty eyes.

"Please, dear, just leave," Will said.

"But—"

"Grace, leave!"

Her mouth began quivering. Ella shot Will an angry glance and escorted the girl from the room. Jak remained for a moment, looking bewildered, then followed Ella. The door closed, leaving Will and Gildareth alone in the study.

Many moments passed before either spoke.

"Why is this happening to us?" Will finally said. "What have I done to deserve this?"

"Nothing no other man has done."

Will looked up at Gildareth, who appeared too complacent for his liking. "How could you be so cold at a time like this?"

Gildareth didn't reply.

"I'm beginning to wonder if the king truly is benevolent. It seems he enjoys seeing me suffer."

"He helped you tonight, did he not? Without his intervention and his light, you wouldn't even have a wife to argue with or a daughter to shout at."

Will pounded his fist on the armrest of his chair. "How dare you speak to me like that! Are you here to insult me just like my wife? If so, leave!"

Gildareth pulled out his illumina, and its brilliance filled the room. Its brightness both burned Will's eyes and filled his heart with fear. "Put that away!"

Gildareth didn't heed the command. Rather, the light grew brighter. "Mankind is so fickle," he said. "One moment, you're overflowing with the king's power. The next, you're sulking over miniscule troubles."

"Stop preaching to me! Just put that away before my eyes burn out of their sockets!"

Gildareth lifted the light higher, his eyes blazing more brilliantly than the phial. "When you can look into the light of the king and feel no pain or fear . . . when you can march into Shieth and battle Wrathar himself . . . when you yourself burn with a brilliance greater than that of the illumina, then you may speak to me like that, Governor!"

The words, spoken so powerfully, took Will aback. "I'm . . . I'm sorry, sir. But please, put the light away, it's burning both my eyes and . . . soul."

Gildareth returned the illumina to his cloak and returned to his seat. "It is not because you're truly repentant, but out of mercy that I heed your request. The king is angry, Willerdon, and is growing more so with your every foolish action. You would be wise to not insult him or his heralds again. For without his strength, you will soon find yourself in a pit worse than any you could imagine. Believe me when I say this: your current troubles are a delicate flowerbed compared to the fiery hailstorm you would find yourself in, if not for the king's hand of protection covering you and your family even as we speak."

"Who are you?" Will asked.

"I am Gildareth, and I serve the king, and the king alone."

Will continued to stare at him. Never had he felt such awe toward someone. And he was beginning to feel regret about his earlier brash words.

Gildareth grew calmer. "Perhaps there is still hope for you, Governor."

Will's eyes grew sad and misted. "Gildareth, I'm . . . I am truly sorry for my stupidity. I won't disrespect you again, and I'll strive to never again insult our king."

"I know, Governor. I know. And the king is pleased, for these words come from your heart. Now, prepare yourself. Events are about to unfold that will bring you both joy and grief. Please, bring your family into the room, and Ella and Jak as well. They are about to see the power of the king manifest in a way they've never known."

Gildareth sighed and added, "As will you. You need to see this to be able to make it through the upcoming months. I tell you the truth: The months to come will be more painful than anything you've endured before. But if you trust in the king through everything, you and your family will come through the fire unscathed."

Will's heart ratcheted. He hurried into the other room, where after much apologizing and a few hugs and kisses, he convinced his daughter and wife to come with him. They all followed Will into his study and huddled together around Gildareth.

Gildareth peered around the room at all the eager faces, then addressed Will. "The enemy stole your son to draw you into so much despair, you would no longer be willing to govern." He noted Lianna's face growing flushed. "But do not worry," he continued, and gestured toward Grace. "The king has heard the cries of the young one, and has set her brother free. Dibbs shall return to you this night, within the hour."

"He heard me," Grace whispered through a smile.

"How can this be," Lianna asked. "How do I know you're right?"

"I offer you this sign," he replied. "Willerdon," he said, turning to Will. "Hold out your hand."

Will quickly obliged.

"This night, you broke your illumina to stop the enemy. The light of the king was unleashed upon your foe, destroying it and saving your wife and daughter, along with dear Ella. But this doesn't mean the light has left you. Even now, it still burns within you. Behold."

He pulled out his illumina and tilted it above Will's hand. From it, light poured out and formed a new and even more beautiful phial than the one destroyed. Once the light completed its task, Gildareth returned his illumina to his cloak, saying, "My king, if you still deem this man worthy, if his heart is still loyal to you, show us."

An aura surrounded Will. He peered around uneasily, but didn't move. Then, out from the palm of his hand, a liquid light streamed into the new illumina. In moments it was full with a gentle shining.

"I believe you now sir," Lianna whispered in awe.

"Then wait at your door. Your son will be with you soon."

Lianna fled the room and her footsteps pounded the stairs.

"May I go too, Father?" Grace asked.

"Yes, you may," Will said, still gawking at the new illumina.

She ran over and hugged him, momentarily drawing him from his trance. Then she ran to Gildareth and embraced him. "Thank you sir," she said, and left to meet up with her mother outside. Ella followed, but Jak stayed behind, enraptured by Gildareth's sign.

"I have more to tell you, Governor," Gildareth said. "I've been informed that another is also on his way back to Woodend tonight."

Will nearly dropped the phial. "Not Bolard."

"Another. Your sheriff is returning."

Will clenched the armrests of his chair. Gildareth held out his hand. "But not as you might expect him. I must ask you to allow him to stay here for a few days. He's going to need my attention."

"My home is your home."

"Thank you. Now if you would, please, I must be alone for a moment to speak with the king."

Jak and Will left the study. But as Will walked away from the closed door, he glanced back and saw bright light streaming out from the place where it met the floor.

TWENTY-FOUR

Dibbs felt himself thrown to the ground. His head hit the dirt hard, causing his mind to swirl in and out of consciousness.

"Run, Tarin! Don't stop!" someone yelled above him.

"Get back here, you filth," a snakelike voice hissed in response.

Heavy boot-falls sped away from where he lay, followed by a series of snarls and curses.

Dibbs cowered for many moments before gaining the courage to sit up. Though bleary eyes, he saw that his only companion appeared to be the dark forest. He listened carefully, but not even a mouse stirred upon the leafy forest floor.

In spite of his unease, he began to recall what had happened to him. He'd been kidnapped by a red-cloaked stranger in Woodend. No, not a stranger, a monster. For it was certainly not human. Its claws had stuck him many times, and when his skin rubbed against the creature's back, it burned, as if he were embracing the bark of a coarse tree, despite the thick red cloth between him and the monster's flesh. But worse even than the sores he now had from that was its terrible voice, more like a snake's than a man's.

He crawled to a nearby rock and leaned against it, trying in vain to slow his breathing as he recalled the gruesome scene at the clearing they'd stopped at hours before. One of his kidnappers had been devoured by a monstrous creature, something Dibbs had never seen before or even heard tales about. The boys and the other red-cloaked beast had barely escaped its clutches as it satisfied its hunger on the less fortunate kidnapper. Meanwhile, the surviving beast had forced them to march for some time before allowing them to rest at this place, what appeared an abandoned lumber camp.

That rest had been the beast's bane, he now realized. Sarky managed to run off while it was looking away. Tarin had followed close behind.

Apparently, the creature beneath the red cloak was more interested in the other boys, because it left Dibbs by himself and chased after them.

Yet Dibbs didn't feel alone even now. He wondered if that other monster, the one stronger than his kidnappers, was nearby. He could only put together fragments of the beast's appearance since it had been so dark, but that was enough to make him shudder, then look around for a place to hide.

Thinking the brush around the clearing would be safer, he crawled through the underbrush until his hand ran across something hard. He felt it, and realized it was a tree stump. He leaned up against it, and as all he'd gone through filtered through his weary head, tears dripped from his eyes. He didn't like crying, but knew no one was around to hear him. His mother was safely in Woodend, as well as his sister. His father would probably be out searching for him by now.

Or would he be? Doubts flooded his soul as if through a broken dam. This led to a memory that made his heart lurch in his chest.

You ran away from home. Of course he'll leave you here. You deserve it. You were rude to him, and you tore up his papers. You've been treating him terribly lately.

Remorse-fueled tears stung his eyes. He buried his head in his hands and wept.

Then he heard it, footsteps behind him.

"Look," a man's voice cried out. "It's one of the boys!"

He twisted his head around. Five figures emerged from the woods.

✝ ✝ ✝

"Quick, let us in."

Clooney's eyes flew open and he toppled off his chair. The demanding voice, followed by pounding noises, had come from beyond Woodend's gate.

Upon leaving Gildareth, Clooney had decided to check on Hamlin and the gate rather than head home. The poor man might be in no state to properly look after the entrance to the town, considering his son had just been taken from him. As he feared, he found the city's gate unlocked and Hamlin nowhere around.

He locked and secured the gate, but then, exhausted and not knowing where to even begin searching for the gatekeeper, he went into the gatehouse, which was also unlocked, started a fire and slumped into a soft chair. The gentle crackling of the fire and the occasional hoot from an owl in the forest led his eyes to close.

Sometime later, he wasn't sure how long, the loud knock awakened him. He peeped through the spy-hole door, saw a familiar round face, and swung open the gate. Hamlin and five other figures: a woman, a man, two short people, and Kandis stood outside.

"Kandis, Hamlin, where have ye been?" Clooney asked in shock.

"Out looking for our boys," Kandis said with annoyance and rushed in, holding the hand of one of the short people. Clooney looked more closely at the figure and his eyes grew wide. "Dibbs, it's ye!" Then he heard the sound of running somewhere in the forest and looked up. Two shadows approached.

"Quick, everyone in!" he shouted to Kandis and the others. They all hurried through the gate.

"Who goes there?" Clooney yelled as he prepared to close the gate.

"We are friends of Woodend, and we carry with us a wounded man. We must get him to our comrade Gildareth quickly!"

Flabbergasted, Clooney watched as two men dressed in traveler's cloaks hauled a man through the gate. Clooney turned to Kandis and the others, but the tall man spoke first. "My name is Varla. I will carry him if someone shows me the way."

"The governor's house is near mine," Kandis said. "I'll take you there."

The two men staggered toward Varla, Jebin's weight between them. Clooney noticed their garments were badly torn.

"What happened to ye?" he asked.

"We were attacked," one of the men said. "Now quick, close the gate. There is incredible danger within those woods." Then he looked to the sky. "And above them."

Varla took Jebin from the man's shoulder and placed him on his own. After some rushed words, the group decided that Hamlin and Clooney should guard the gate together that night. The two cloaked ones, who introduced themselves as Dralo and Ristun, asked to stay as well. The rest left for the governor's house.

Dralo and Ristun stumbled into Hamlin's little gatehouse and Hamlin pulled out two chairs for them to rest in. Dralo sat first, and as he did, he moaned and caressed his shoulder.

"I best take a look at that," Clooney said. Dralo nodded and pulled off his cloak. Underneath was a white shirt, and at the shoulder, a wide patch of wet blood. Clooney carefully pulled away the shirt, revealing a huge gash. Dralo closed his eyes and grimaced.

"Hamlin," Clooney said, "do ye have any alcohol in here?"

Hamlin smiled. "Sure do. I always keep some handy for a special occasion."

Hamlin ran off and quickly returned with a bottle of alcohol. Under Clooney's watchful eye, he poured some on the wound.

"Owwww!" Dralo howled.

"Can you not handle the pain?" Ristun asked, smiling wearily.

"Don't get cocky over there, lad," Clooney said. "Ye be next."

Ristun's smile turned to a frown.

"I wish I was back north," Dralo said. "The treatments of the king are far less severe than these woodsmen's."

"But ours still do the trick," Clooney said.

He finished with Dralo, bandaged him, and moved on to Ristun, who howled even more than his friend. Meanwhile, Hamlin set up two wooden cots for the guests.

Soon the two strangers were reclining on the cots. But Hamlin wasn't quick to let them sleep. First he recounted, quite loudly, his entire trek with Kandis to Clooney, who listened with wide eyes and an open mouth. Then he turned his attention to the resting warriors.

"So, you two took a mighty beating in those woods. I'm sure you have quite a story to tell."

"Tonight, we do not," Dralo groaned. "Please, put out the light and allow us to rest. You will learn more in the morning."

Clooney frowned at the man, but put out the candles and lanterns while Hamlin extinguished the fire in the fireplace.

✝ ✝ ✝

"There's your house, lad," Kandis said. "And it looks as if someone's been waiting up for you."

As Kandis had approached each streetlamp, it cast an eerie shadow around him, making his heart faint, for his soul was already troubled from the strange sounds in the forest and the loss of his son, which weighed heavily upon him. Yet upon finding Dibbs, he'd felt it right to bring him home rather than tarry any longer in the woods.

At his words, Dibbs raised his eyes to the house. His face lit with a joyful smile at the sight of the woman and girl who stood at the door. It was easy to see they were the boy's mother and sister; he bolted to them and fell into their arms. They cried and hugged and hugged some more until his sister and mother drew him into the house, the mother beckoning to Kandis to follow.

He, though, simply wanted to go home and rest up, and prepare for the next day's search for Tarin. But before he turned to leave, his eyes happened upon a familiar face, and his heart leapt with joy. Ella stood in the doorway, next to a young man he thought he recognized from the forest. But his whole heart was on seeing his daughter safe; he ran as fast as he could to embrace her. In the corner of his tear-filled eye, Kandis saw the young man lower his head and slink away into the shadows.

Twenty-Five

"**R**un, Tarin! Don't stop!"

"Where are you?" Tarin pleaded into the blackness ahead.

"Over here! Follow my voice."

Heavy breathing and hard footfalls followed Tarin while he trudged along with what strength he had left. Something grabbed his foot and he fell facedown next to a bush.

"Shhh. Crawl in here. Hurry, and be quiet."

Tarin recognized Sarky's voice and quickly obliged.

He lay beneath the bush with Sarky, and listened. The heavy footsteps drew closer, then slowed. There was a loud hiss.

Please don't find us, Tarin silently pleaded. The creature growled and moved back and forth, sniffing, searching. Tarin shivered with fright.

The red-cloaked creature took a few steps toward the bush and knelt down. Tarin watched as a hooded face drew up close to his own. From beneath the hood, two nostrils blew out a pungent air, stinging his nose.

Suddenly the creature removed its hood. In the dark, all he could see were its eyes, white with black centers, just like his own, though the face surrounding them seemed contorted.

In a flash of moonlight, the eyes happened directly onto his own, and the creature slid its fat, course tongue across some jagged teeth.

His heart felt as if it would burst from his chest. But just before he fell into complete panic, the monster hissed and stood back up, growled a curse and ran deeper into the forest.

Next to him, Sarky breathed a deep sigh. "That was too close. Let's stay here for a while, until it's safe."

Tarin nodded, realized Sarky couldn't see him, and whispered "All right."

The boys remained beneath the bush for a minute, then another. Even then, neither drew up the courage to budge. The moon disappeared from the sky and the night grew deeper. The smell of dew upon moss covered their noses with its peaceful scent and eventually lulled them to sleep.

When Tarin next opened his eyes, a lump formed in his throat. It hadn't been a dream. He was in the forest, a place he'd never been. And he had no idea how to get home.

The first rays of sun streamed through the leaves above him. Panicked, he looked around. Sarky was next to him, his eyes partially open and moving rapidly, muttering, "Leave me alone, Father. I'll get up when I'm ready."

Tarin slapped him on the head. "Get up! Your father's not around. We're lost in the forest."

Sarky sat up, eyes wide. "All that stuff actually happened? I thought it was just a nightmare."

"It wasn't. We're somewhere in the forest with no food or water, and no way of knowing how to get back to Woodend. To put it simply, we're dead."

Sarky stretched and yawned. "There's plenty of streams we can drink from, and there're berries we can eat." He smiled and winked. "In case you haven't heard, I'm a pretty good herbalist. I can point out what's good to eat and what'll make you sick."

"Somehow I doubt that. And even if it's true, we still don't know how to get home."

"Of course we do. Those monsters took us out through the gate, and followed the road south for a while before turning into the forest. So if we just head north," he pointed toward the rising sun and then moved his hand to the left, "we'll eventually get back to Woodend."

"That won't guarantee we'll make it back. We could miss it well to the east or west."

"Oh, stop worrying. Once we get far enough north, we'll get out of the forest. From there, if the mountains are to our west with no sign of the town, we know we've got to follow the tree line east until we get home. Otherwise, we'll see Woodend Hill to our west and be set. Either way, we win."

"Unless those creatures come back."

"Don't forget, there's only one left." Sarky pointed to the sky. "The other got eaten, remember."

"But by what?"

Sarky's face lost its confidence. "I . . . don't know. It looked like a giant, fat bird. At least, I noticed it had wings."

"That thing could kill us too, you know."

"No, I think it was on our side. Those things sure seemed afraid when they heard it growling."

"And you weren't?"

"Uh . . . no."

Tarin punched the ground. "That thing's out there, and you know as well as I do it could kill us as quick as anything else!"

"Well, then . . . if we hear it roar, we'll duck under a bush or something. That way it won't see us."

Tarin looked deep into Sarky's eyes, and fear made his voice a whisper. "I doubt hiding beneath a bush would help. I don't know what's going on right now, but what terrifies me the most isn't even the monsters that took us or that strange flying beast. I can't stop thinking about those rioters . . . their hideous yellow eyes. I think they were possessed by the shadows."

Sarky turned over a rock, saw a beetle under it, and flicked the bug into a tree. "By the way, whatever happened to that Dibbs boy?"

Tarin suddenly remembered the third member of their party. "I . . . I'm not sure. Was he following us after we escaped that red-cloaked creature?"

"I don't know. But it didn't have him when it ran by, so he must be free. We should go look for him, make sure he's all right. He might be back at that abandoned lumber camp. If so, he won't have any idea where to go."

Tarin stood and looked around. Surely the creatures wouldn't return to the same place they'd fled. "All right."

It took them the rest of the morning to make their way back to the lumber camp. They found no sign of Dibbs. Tarin went over to a stump and rested while Sarky began crawling on the ground, inspecting it for any signs of where Dibbs might have gone. Even if he was just pretending to be knowledgeable at tracking, his friend's actions reassured Tarin.

A bird chirped from a nearby stump, and he looked over. "Hey look, Sarky, I think something's carved into that stump." He went to investigate and was soon reading a message carved into the wood.

Found Dibbs
On way back to Woodend
Search more in morning

K

"It's Father!" Tarin blurted. "He always initials everything as K. He must've been here last night. And look, he found Dibbs!"

Sarky whooped and started prancing around.

"He's searching again right now," Tarin said. "See? It says he's coming back in the morning. All we have to do is stay here."

Sarky stopped dancing. "Dern. I was hoping we'd have to find our own way back. I had such a great plan."

Tarin lifted his brows and frowned.

"Just kidding, old buddy!"

Tarin rolled his eyes.

Hours later, there was still no sign of the search party, and the boys were beginning to grow anxious. And hungry. Sarky set off to look for food, and soon came running back looking gleeful, and carrying a huge quantity of the reddest berries Tarin had ever seen.

Both boys began stuffing their mouths full of them. As their stomachs gurgled with delight, they heard the sound of moving water and followed it until they found a nearby creek. They happily knelt and drank their fill. Their hunger and thirst satisfied, they returned to the clearing and lay down.

Tarin looked up at the sky and watched huge fluffy clouds drift overhead. Right now, he'd probably be lying on the flat roof of his house, imagining the clouds to be familiar people or giant animals. But now, they just looked like clouds, and he was in no mood to think of them as anything else.

Soon, sleep set in. Something wet on Tarin's face woke him up. Around him, all was dark. It was nighttime, and rain was beginning to fall. Above him, the sky lit up. A moment later, thunder rocked the ground beneath him. He sat up, and his stomach told him the berries he'd eaten earlier had made him sick. He heard gagging toward his left and saw Sarky doubled over by a stump, throwing up. This only made him feel worse, and as another lightning bolt shot through the air, he too began vomiting. After finally throwing up the last of the berries, he flopped over a stump and moaned. Sarky came over and did likewise.

"I hate you Sarky," Tarin said in a dry heave.

"I . . . *cough* . . . thought those berries were safe."

Both boys groaned in unison as another clash of thunder shook the outlying trees. Rain started falling furiously and the wind picked up.

"Shelter," Sarky moaned, trying to stand. When he managed to steady himself, he helped Tarin up. Together, they started toward the forest. Just before they reached the trees, Sarky gripped Tarin's wrist so hard it made him yelp.

"That feeling's back." Sarky's voice shook. "And I'm not talking about the berries."

Tarin's hair prickled along his neck, and he looked behind them. But there was nothing. Then, as lightning lit up the old camp, he saw something move on the other side of the clearing. It was completely black, a smoky shadow against the gray-black night. *Oh, Gildareth, they're back. Where are you?* Somehow, and he didn't know why, he sensed the creatures feared the northerner.

Frantic, he turned around and searched for a hiding place. A few paces into the woods lurked the huge trunk of a dead willow tree. Along its side was a gaping hole. At the least, it would provide a place to get away from the rain. He pulled Sarky, who was nearly doubled over in fear and nausea, over to the tree and pushed him inside. He glanced back.

Lightning again lit up the lumber camp. More shadows were making their way into it, moving toward the center. He heard faint hissing coming from another part of the clearing and looked over.

Cloaked figures moved in toward the smoky shadows. He waited. A flash of lightning gave him a clear view, and his fears were realized. The cloaks were red.

He pushed his body back into the hollow as far as he could next to Sarky, hoped it was enough, and closed his eyes. *Gildareth, where are you?*

Why do you keep calling for Gildareth's aid? a small voice whispered within his mind.

He had no answer. All he knew was that Gildareth was the first man he'd ever met that actually made him feel at ease at first meeting. And something inside him told him the man was special, special enough to fend off the darkness now seemingly stalking him wherever he went. Perhaps it was something all northerners could do, including Dralo and Ristun, though he didn't care for them as much as Gildareth.

He heard rustling in the distance, and drew up the courage to peer out of the hollow.

The red-cloaked monsters were lifting up a tall pole on which a piece of leather tarp was centered. They pulled out the tarp on all the edges until it became a large cone, with its tip at the top of the pole. After staking the lower portion of the tarp to the ground, forming a crude tent, they went inside. They must have lit some lanterns upon entering the tent, because light began dancing around within.

The shadows drew up next to the tent and stood just outside the entrance, peering around menacingly through their foul yellow eyes. Tarin waited. Nothing else seemed to be happening outside the shelter. Then, two cloaked beasts came out of the tent and stood at attention at the entrance. Out of the woods, at the far end of the clearing, two more beasts emerged, followed by a much larger one wearing brass shoulder guards and a black breastplate. His red cloak hung loosely on his shoulders, like a cape. But this one wasn't hooded. Rather, this creature wore a tall black helmet on its head. The only openings were for its eyes, which Tarin couldn't see in the dark. He knew this must be a commander of some sort, and the thought of an even stronger red-cloaked beast made his heart tremble.

He watched as it apprehensively looked around before approaching the tent. The shadows standing guard remained motionless, but the two cloaked guards crossed their arms across their chest and bowed their heads in salute.

The commander walked past them into the tent, accompanied by his two comrades.

Within the tent, a snakelike conversation began. Tarin tried to listen, but amidst the thunder and the pelting rain, he couldn't make out much except hissing.

"What's going on?" Sarky whispered.

"I'm not sure."

"What do we do?"

"Right now? Be quiet, and hope those . . . those *things* will soon take their business elsewhere."

An hour passed, the storm drifted away, but the hissing from the tent showed no sign of ceasing. Tarin's mind whirred with curiosity. He couldn't stand just sitting around when whispering was taking place. But no matter how desperately he wanted to draw near the tent and listen in, he couldn't. There was no way to sneak around the shadows standing guard.

Another hour passed, and his muscles were growing tight. Sarky's too, judging from his incessant squirming. Thinking there might be another hiding place he hadn't spotted before, Tarin peeked back toward the tent.

The shadows had disappeared! The guards were gone too. Only the tent remained, lights still flickering within.

If I could just sneak over there and catch a little of what they're saying—

Are you insane? he argued with himself. *Those shadows could still be around somewhere. It's too dark to tell.*

"Tarin." Sarky's cold hand grasped his wrist. "That feeling's gone."

"That means they've left," he whispered.

"What do you mean?"

"The shadows. They must not be around. They're only around whenever you get that strange feeling."

"What shadows?"

"You didn't see them? They were over there by the tent."

"All I ever saw was the tent and those rotten creatures go in it."

Why can only I see them? What's with this? Curiosity returned so strongly, he knew he wouldn't be able to resist. "I'm going over there."

"What?"

"Shhh! I've got to find out what they're talking about."

"What if they catch you? Don't go expecting me to come and save you—"

"I won't. Just stay here. I'll only be a moment."

With that, Tarin crawled out into the rain and began working his way over to the tent. Sarky cursed his friend's impulsiveness, but quietly followed. They reached the tent in moments, and listened.

"They've left to inform the sentinel of your arrival, Captain of the North," a squeaky voice said in hissing breaths.

"Good riddance to the scum! I loathe those foul shadows. If only they'd leave the fighting to us, we'd control Arvalast by now. Their interference has hindered us in Macalum for years. And for what? So they can turn the hearts of the people from the Scourge of the North? Need we care where our enemies' loyalties lie? It's much more pleasant to simply kill them. A heart that doesn't beat can have no loyalty."

The tent burst forth in wild, snakelike, laughter.

"Silence!" the captain shouted after a short time. "Though I desire to strike Woodend now, the sentinel refuses to allow our forces to march until he's finished his plan."

"But Bolard is moving too slowly," another creature argued. "He seems to be hindered by something."

"Sayin has been sent to encourage him to move more quickly." The captain laughed. "Three of ours went with him. Along with a crimson light. The sentinel himself gave it to Sayin in Macalum, upon his declaration of loyalty to us. He shall accompany Bolard wherever he goes, and ensure he doesn't falter from the plan. Though Bolard is a steadfast servant of the sentinel's deceit, the sentinel doesn't trust him. After all, he was deep in the Scourge's grip at one point, before he realized his folly and turned to us. Now he is the key component in securing this forest once and for all. And with its demise, the prophecy will no longer be a threat to the shadows, and we will have established our northern base. Arvalast will be ours, as will the tower."

A chorus of cheers erupted and wooden mugs began to clunk as they were passed around. After a bunch of gulps and slurping, a deep-throated, snarling voice broke the merriment.

"When will the attack on Lockspell finally take place? I'm itching for some bloodshed."

"Quiet!" the captain demanded. "It will come whenever our fearless Lieutenant Shmeed gets the word to march. Unfortunately, some of those filthy drilockk slayers from Macalum keep getting close to the army. But the shadow's spells are hindering them. They will remain hidden until needed."

"My lord, why do we not just kill the drilockk slayers? There are few—"

"Don't worry about them. They are a necessary foe."

"What do you mean?"

"Some fool idea of the king's involving Bolard. Without them, the plan will fail."

"But what do we do with them lurking around?"

"Avoid them or die, you fool!" the captain bellowed. "They should be the least of your concerns. What of this monster that killed one of the scouts that captured the governor's son? Because of this thing, they failed, and the boy is nowhere to be found. And from what I hear, two other boys were captured too, and they are also free. The king is in great unrest about this for some reason. Says Shieth isn't happy either. You know what this means. The Great One might send more sentinels up here to make sure things don't get out of hand. And we don't want that, now do we? One is certainly enough for me, curse him."

The voices suddenly grew quiet.

"Did you hear something?" the squeaky hisser asked. Tarin and Sarky grew as stiff as boards, and Tarin feared they'd been found out. Then he heard running footsteps, coming toward them. He looked over. It was another red-cloaked creature, and it was un-hooded. Like the one they'd already seen, it had a lizard-like, scaly face with human-looking eyes.

Tarin felt Sarky stiffen even more, and knew he was ready to bolt.

Neither of them had to run. The creature ran straight to the tent's entrance without noticing them. Tarin heard the metallic sound of swords being drawn from within. A moment later, two beasts jumped out. "Halt!" one of them shouted. "Who are you?"

"A servant of the Captain of the North. I come with ill tidings from Woodend."

"Send him in!" the captain commanded from inside the tent. The beasts obliged.

"The plot against the governor has failed," the creature panted through hissing breaths. "The governor's wife and daughter . . . They live!"

"How can this be? You were told to kill them!"

"We tried, but the light is stronger than we thought."

"Where are the others?"

"We were forced to jump from the roof after our leader was burned by the light. Neither of them survived the fall. But do not fear, they won't find their bodies."

The tent went quiet. The captain stood and began pacing. "How could the light suddenly be growing so strong? It has been nearly dead for over a year. The sentinel has seen to it, and the shadows have been hard at work within Woodend's failing walls."

"He is here, my lord."

"Whom," the captain asked slowly.

"Gildareth."

Tarin gasped, and the creatures within the tent went quiet.

"Shhh!" Sarky said, jabbing Tarin in the stomach. But it was too late.

"Quick. Search outside!"

Twenty-Six

Tarin looked around. There was a stump a few paces away, but that wouldn't conceal them for long.

A beast emerged from the entrance to the tent. "I don't see anything."

"Keep looking! I know I heard something," the captain growled.

"Come look yourself, you piece of rat dung," the disgruntled beast murmured. Glaring back toward the captain, it pulled out a sword and started striding . . . directly toward the boys!

They remained as quiet as possible, hoping it would change directions. But when it grew but an arm's length away, Sarky bolted to his feet and yelled, "Run!"

The beast jumped back in a start but recovered quickly. "Two spies!" the beast shouted toward the tent. "Get out here! Hurry!" He charged at the boys, sword flailing.

Tarin and Sarky lunged from their hiding spot and headed toward the woods.

In response to the warning, the tent emptied of its vile inhabitants. Three creatures halted and pulled out bows. Tarin heard arrows whiz by his ear. One barely missed Sarky's right shoulder.

"Tarin, we're dead! We're dead! We're dead!" Sarky screamed.

"Shut up and run!" Tarin shouted back, though he agreed with Sarky. Yet he wouldn't give up without at least trying to stay alive.

The forest was too far away. Their pursuers would be on them before they reached it. That option was no longer a choice anyway; three shadows shot from the darkness and blocked the opening in the dense trees. Their yellow eyes glared at the boys.

Tarin's knees faltered, then gave way. Twigs cracked as his body crashed down on them.

Sarky whimpered behind him, "The feeling's back. I . . . I can't move." He too fell.

As the boys groveled, a furious roar shook the old lumber camp. Their pursuers stopped and looked up.

There was another roar, followed by a snarl.

"The winged monster's back!" one of them yelled. "Run!"

The creatures began scuttling around for somewhere to hide from the mysterious foe in the sky.

Tarin managed to look up. A great black figure with massive wings was diving toward the ground. Again it roared, sending a rainfall of saliva down into the lumber camp. Slimy ooze splattered upon the fleeing beasts' scales. As they screamed, the moon revealed the creature's two glowing eyes, shimmering green in the moonlight, much like the gaze of a woodland animal.

His heart thumping, Tarin watched it descend. Its head was the size of a boulder, its body as great as the house he lived in. Covering both was a thick coat of brown, coarse hair riddled with entire briar bushes, remnants of thickets the beast had once trudged through. Its wings were the only region of its body devoid of hair. They were leathery, much like the lonely tent in the middle of the lumber camp, and powered by massive sinews running through thin flesh like the tributaries of an ocean.

But it was the enormous mouth full of pointed teeth glistening with drool that made Tarin wince. As it opened and closed with each roar, fear paralyzed him. But apparently Sarky wasn't as stunned. He got up, despite the obvious pain he was feeling due to the shadows' presence, and ran toward what appeared an unguarded path into the forest, the same spot the shadows still stood.

The creature's head turned toward Sarky, and it dove toward him.

"Sarky!" Tarin screamed. "Stop running!"

Sarky looked up just in time to see three thick, sharp claws mounted upon feet the size of tree-stumps descend toward him. He fainted, and fell into the dirt.

Tarin held his breath, hoping with all his being that his hunch was right.

As though it had sudden amnesia, the monster blinked, looked around, then pulled up and began circling the clearing. Soon its eyes caught sight of a new victim, one in a red cloak, and exploded toward it.

The smaller beast screeched, and ran toward the forest, but in vain. The giant animal grabbed it with its three-fingered hands, one of which was missing a claw, and held tight as it swooped upward, swung the red-cloaked creature into the air, and caught it with its mouth.

Tarin grimaced and turned away. After a moment, he looked back. The creature was hovering just above him, chewing. A piece of a red cloak dangled from one of its teeth while its beady green eyes darted, searching for its next victim.

The captain, who was near the tent, hissed, lumbered around for a moment as if in a stupor, then stood still. "Quickly!" he snarled to his frantic comrades. "Back to the tent! It won't be able to see you there."

At his command, the other beasts fled toward the tent. But the captain inexplicably ran toward the edge of the clearing and dropped to his belly.

As the other beasts entered the tent, the flying monster growled, and in three mighty flaps, descended upon it. Its claws easily tore through the leather, opening a hole into which it lowered its head. In the midst of many a screech and hiss, it began its loathsome feast. Meanwhile, Tarin saw the captain crawl toward the edge of the forest and disappear into its safety.

He felt life come back into his limbs, and heard Sarky groan, "Tarin. Where are you?"

"Over here," he whispered back. "Hurry, crawl over here while it's . . ." he gulped, "eating."

Sarky obliged, and the two boys studied their options. It was either go back in the direction of the tent, or forward into the arms of the shadows still guarding the nearest path into the forest. Both choices seemed certain death.

"That feeling's really bad right now," Sarky moaned as he peered around. "Are they close?"

Tarin nodded and pointed a shaking finger toward the dark figures that only he could see. He managed to hold their gaze for a moment, and could see glee in their eyes. Then he heard a voice in his head.

Choose. Choose your death.

He shivered, and again felt his body tensing to the point of paralysis. Sarky grabbed his shoulder. "Hold yourself together. We can't get out of this unless you're able to move."

"Uh . . . Sarky . . . I can't . . . they're talking to me."

Choose.

"Shut up!" he heard himself shout.

Sarky put his hand over Tarin's mouth and leaned in close to his ear. "That thing's going to hear you. I don't want to be eaten. And though I fear going into the forest and past the shadows I can't see, I'd rather do that than become the droppings of that monster back there. So let's go."

He started pulling Tarin along, but soon Tarin joined him in crawling toward the edge of the woods. Then Sarky stopped.

"I . . . was wrong. I can't go on. I'm too sick." He gagged. "I thought I could, but I can't."

Tarin looked back. The winged monster seemed nearly finished with its meal and was peering around the clearing, looking for stragglers. If they didn't escape into the woods soon, they were dead.

"Gildareth," Tarin whispered. "I wish you were here."

Sarky started.

"What's wrong, Sarky?"

"Whoa ... the feeling went away for a second." He grabbed Tarin's arm. "Are they still there?"

Tarin looked up at the woods. They were, but their hateful eyes had taken on a new look. One of fear. But a moment later, they returned to their original evil state.

Choose.

Sarky groaned. "That feeling's back."

"Gildareth," Tarin whispered, "help."

Sarky shook his head. "What in Arvalast? It's gone again." He put his hand on Tarin's back. "Whatever you're doing ... don't stop."

The boys continued their crawl toward the woods. Every now and then, Tarin spoke Gildareth's name. Each time, doing so seemed to quell Sarky's nausea.

Soon they came within arm's length of the shadows. Tarin looked up and locked eyes with one. Fear stabbed his heart with such force, he felt his body convulse. He tried to look away, but couldn't.

"He cannot save you, filth," the shadow whispered as Tarin tried to crawl past it. "Behold, we come from Shieth, and the power of our lord flows through us. It is a power greater than that of whom you speak. Even greater than the power of the Scourge Himself. Now, boy, feel this power."

The shadow reached down and stuck its hand onto, then *into* Tarin's head. Tarin became dizzy, and thoughts not his own poured into him. He saw Woodend burning, and people being chased by the same red-cloaked creatures that had kidnapped him and Sarky. He saw Governor Willerdon, tied to a pole and being beaten by a hooded man who wielded a whip in one hand and a red, glowing light in the other.

Then he began to feel hatred, hatred for everything. The sun, the moon, the forest, the village, and all people. But most of all, he felt hatred toward one called the Scourge, and a loathing for Gildareth. Just before he began to call curses down on all he once thought good, he saw a glimmer of light within his head, and his own mind returned to him. Without hesitation, he said the first thing that came to him: "Gildareth, help me."

He opened his eyes and came out of the trance. The shadow had pulled its hand out of his head and was shrieking. Its hand was on fire!

Tarin glanced at his own hands. They were red— no, they too were on fire! He screamed.

"Tarin," Sarky sputtered, "you should've heard what you were saying! Didn't know you had it in you—"

Tarin shook his flaming hands at Sarky. "Help me! Put them out!" Then he looked at them in wonder. "Wait a minute. They aren't hurting."

Sarky stared in wonder. "Wow, really—?"

His words became a scream when one of the creatures grabbed him.

Not knowing what else to do, Tarin curled his flaming hand into a fist and punched the black figure in the head. It hissed painfully, released Sarky and backed up.

Tarin tried not to tremble when the shadow extended itself to its full height. Its eyes gleamed down at him with malice, but also curiosity. Then they grew wide, so wide Tarin thought they might engulf the thing's entire head. It drifted back and fled into the woods. The others followed.

The fire in Tarin's hands flickered and went out. Sarky ran over and grabbed them.

"I just can't understand it. Your hands were on fire! And . . . and when they lit up," he grinned until his lips nearly touched his ears, "I could *see* them. I could see the shadows! Can you believe it?"

"You . . . saw them?"

"Yes, I did. *Yessss!* I've got powers. I was so jealous of you. All I could do was feel them. Now I can see them too. This is great!"

"No it's not. They're . . . horrible. You don't realize what just happened to me. They got into my head." He looked deep into the excited boy's eyes. "They took over my mind."

"Well, with what you were saying before your hands lit up, I would've thought you were taking *their* minds over. When you started talking, all my fear left me, and I started cheering for you, buddy. Wow! You were amazing!"

"What . . . did I say?"

"Well . . . you started praising the king and telling them he would soon destroy them and their master. By the way, I didn't even know you were one of his followers. But anyway, after that, you started rebuking them and telling them to leave and that they didn't have power over you and that the king was going to kick them in the face and—"

"I really said all that?"

"Uh, something like that. It sounded a whole lot better coming from you. But when you were done, your hands lit up and I could see them. Wow! It was so amazing. And oh, yes . . . the one with its hand in you caught on fire. Well, its hand anyway. Then it started wailing like a baby. Ha! How pathetic."

"Shhh. Don't say stuff like that."

"Why not? They just got beaten by a boy."

"I don't think it was me, exactly. I . . . well, you know. I'm the pathetic one."

"Not anymore, friend. I mean, best friend." Sarky whooped. "Now you're a warrior!" He jumped into the air and started dancing, humming some stupid tune he'd likely heard at one of the Festivals of Colors.

"They tried to get me after that," Sarky finally continued, "but you stopped them."

I did? Did I really do that? Tarin thought. *Sarky said he saw it, so I must have. Wow, maybe I am as good as he said. . . .*

He looked up to see that Sarky had stopped dancing and gone white, his eyes transfixed at some point directly behind him.

Tarin's muscles went rigid. "Is it . . .?"

Sarky nodded.

He felt warm air blow into his back. He turned his head, and his earlier smugness scurried away.

The winged creature's great, hairy head was but three feet away. Black ooze dripped from its teeth, each one larger than a spearhead. It snorted through the two slits just beneath its eyes, making the hair covering them wave about as if a gale had blown by. Mucous sprayed Tarin's face.

"Uh . . . I think I made too much noise," Sarky squeaked.

Both Tarin and the monster peered at each other. The monster seemed to be studying him, perhaps sizing him up for dessert. Then, to Tarin's horror, it opened its mouth. Its tongue moved around inside like an oversized slug.

Tarin closed his eyes, preparing to feel sharp teeth reach around his body. To his astonishment, the monster let out a tremendous belch. Its foul wind knocked him onto his back.

He waited for the attack, but the animal yawned, stepped back into the clearing, and lazily began flapping its wings. Soon, it lifted into the air, and with a satisfied growl, flew south.

"I guess it wasn't hungry anymore," Sarky snickered nervously. Tarin just lay on the ground, quaking.

Sarky tried to help him up, but Tarin couldn't move. All he could do was hear himself make odd noises.

"Tarin, what's wrong?"

He turned over to Sarky and broke into laughter. Then he exploded into laughter. His eyes grew so full of tears, he felt as if a whole cup of water had been thrown over them.

Sarky began to laugh too. "I've never seen you like this before."

"I . . . almost got eaten!" Tarin howled.

"Not sure why that's funny," Sarky yelped. "But it sure is right now!"

"It spit goop all over me," Tarin managed to squeak out, looking at the black ooze spattering his clothing.

"Sure stinks!" Sarky added.

They both fell and started rolling on the ground, clutching at their sides as the laughter overwhelmed them. Perhaps it was that they hadn't gotten a real night's sleep in two nights. Or perhaps it was some lingering effect of the poisonous berries. Then again, it could have been their continuing ability to escape certain death. But whatever it was, they didn't care, and for the longest time, they just laughed, eyes full of tears and sides splitting. And when they stopped laughing, they both started crying. For what seemed like hours, their emotions erupted in a nonsensical river of tears.

"This is crazy, but it feels . . . good," Tarin said when he was able. "Extremely, wonderfully good."

TWENTY-SEVEN

T*hat had to be the worst dream I've ever had.*

Dibbs rubbed the cobwebs from his eyes and climbed from his bed. He stumbled, grabbed the bed to steady himself. All his muscles were terribly sore. He glanced down at his shirtless torso and saw large brown marks all over. *Bruises? Oh no! It wasn't a dream!*

His heart started pounding. *Sarky and Tarin! They're still out there with those things and . . . and that monster.*

He threw on a shirt and trousers and ran down the stairs. Grace was on her way up, carrying a tray of milk and toast.

"Dibbs! You're up! You slept the entire day yesterday. Mother told me to try to wake you and give you some—"

"Not now, where's Father?"

"Hey! I was trying to be nice. If you want to act like that, then find him yourself. And forget about the food." She huffed back down the stairs, shrieking when he raced past her.

"Father!" he called, sprinting down the last few steps and heading toward the living quarters. Two strange men sat inside, drinking tea.

"Hello lad, and who might you be?" the one with darker hair asked.

Dibbs ignored him and ran toward the small room his father used as a place for visitors to wait for their appointments with him.

"Wait! Don't go in there!"

The man's warning came too late. Dibbs burst in. Instantly, his head began to swim. The atmosphere was so thick, his very soul felt queasy. The windows were covered with curtains, and none of the lanterns were lit. The only light was being held by a bearded man sitting in the center of the room next to a cot. Dibbs instantly recognized the light's source as an illumina.

The man didn't seem to notice his entry. He was perfectly still except for his lips, which were whispering words he didn't understand.

He glanced toward the cot, and his uneasiness was replaced with an even grimmer sensation of disgust. A man lay there, but not just any man. It was Sheriff Jebin! Though this was far from the good-humored, strong sheriff he'd come to know. What lay there was a pale, helpless man who looked as if he'd been crushed by a heavy burden. His eyes were a terrible crimson color, and wide open with some strange fear. At the sight, Dibbs screamed, "Sheriff Jebin! What's happened to you? Help! *Heeeeelp!*"

Just as the bearded man looked up, a strong arm pulled him out of the room and hurriedly shut the door.

"That was foolish," a stern voice rebuked. It was one of the men who'd been sitting in his living room. Not the dark-haired one who addressed him before, but the light-haired one whose face was less jolly. "Come with me."

"Let go of me! Where's Father? And why are you in my house?"

"Your father is at a meeting with the village council and some emissaries from Macalum. We got here earlier this morning, and for the time being, we are your guests." He pulled Dibbs into the living room and pointed to a chair. "Sit."

"What if I don't want to?"

"I wouldn't make him angry," the dark-haired one said from a chair next to a window. "He doesn't like to be annoyed. Please, have a seat."

Dibbs shot an angry glance at the blond fellow and sat, only obliging because the other man said "Please."

"My name is Dralo," the blond man said, taking a seat across from Dibbs, "and that is Ristun."

Ristun gave a friendly nod. "Nice to meet you, son of the governor. And I must say, I'm glad you're finally awake and safe in Woodend. The night before last, you were captured by some dreadfully terrible beasts."

Dibbs was startled at the memory. "What were those? They couldn't have been human."

"Drilockk," Dralo answered. "Terrible monsters from the south. Followers of Wrathar, lord of the land of Shieth, and a great enemy of the king."

"Dralo, he's just a boy. Do not confuse him with such a lengthy answer."

"Then you give him an answer, child master." Dralo crossed his arms and raised a cynical brow.

Ristun smiled and turned to Dibbs. "Dralo is merely in a foul mood. He got no sleep the past two nights. We've been staying at the gatehouse with your gatekeeper and a man named Clooney. Great men, but Dralo says their snoring makes thunder insecure."

"I still don't know how you manage to sleep through it," Dralo interjected.

"I can sleep through anything. Now, where was I? Oh yes, drilockk. Well, Dralo described them accurately, but in simpler terms, they are evil monsters."

The room went quiet. Dibbs shuffled in his chair, then spoke up. "No offense, but I like Dralo's definition better. It's more . . . interesting."

Ristun looked at his counterpart in shock. Dralo's sour expression disappeared, became guarded. "You underestimate these children's intelligence, Ristun," he said. "Remember, his sister liked my description of the beasts better too, and was quite interested as I recounted how they came about."

"Yes, yes. I suppose you're right."

"Why was my sister asking about them?"

Dralo and Ristun looked at each other, then at Dibbs. "Oh," Ristun said. "You haven't heard? You weren't the only child who had a nasty encounter with the creatures. Your mother and sister were close to being thrown off your roof by them, the same night you were found. If not for your father, they might have . . . well, I don't wish to frighten you."

"My father saved them?" Dibbs asked. "How? I mean . . . all he ever does is whine about things and argue with Mother and sometimes talk about the king." He stopped, thinking. "You know, he's rather obsessed with the king. And I wouldn't care, but he's always trying to make me a follower and wanting me to get my own illumina. Yet all he does is treat me badly. How's that supposed to make me want to be the king's follower! And what has the king done for him *or* me? And what's so great about those illuminas, unless you're in need of a candle?"

Dralo leaned forward, eyes narrowed. "If it were not for the king, and your father's allegiance to him, your mother and sister would be dead right now. And it was the light of the illumina that hindered the enemy from fulfilling his quest. You should not speak so lightly of matters you clearly do not understand."

Dralo's stern tone took Dibbs aback, but he wouldn't agree just because he was speaking to an adult. "I don't care what you say! The king has done nothing for us, except make our lives miserable. And the only thing I've ever wanted him to help me with, he's never done."

"I say again, you don't under—"

"No, I think *you* don't understand. I've seen things, horrible things. You think Woodend's safe. It's not. Bad things are going to happen, and the king's not going to stop them. And neither he nor Father cares about anything I have to say! They don't care about me, or the scratches my nightmares give me."

Dralo leaned farther forward. "You had nightmares?"

Dibbs' eyes grew teary. "Almost every night. And the king doesn't take them away from me."

Dralo scooted his chair next to Dibbs' and placed a hand on the boy's shoulder. "You're not alone with these visions, lad. Many are having them."

"Why?" Dibbs asked, shuffling nervously in his chair. "And why is the king allowing them if he's so good, like Father says?"

"He is trying to warn us," a girl's voice answered from the stairs. Dibbs turned around and saw Grace step into room. "I've been having them too. They're about Father, aren't they?"

Dibbs eyes widened. He nodded.

"But there's always a gentle voice telling me everything's going to be all right," she said. "I think it's the king."

For a second, Dibbs' heart stopped. "You . . . you hear a *gentle* voice?"

Grace nodded.

"Well, I don't. What speaks to me is a dragon, and its voice is evil. If that's the voice of the king, I want no part of him."

Dralo's eyes grew wide. "A dragon speaks to you?"

He didn't answer.

"You must believe me. That voice is not of my master."

"And how do you know? What if Grace and all the rest of you are wrong? Maybe the king really isn't as good as you think. Maybe he's been tricking you with nice voices, while all along he's really been setting up Woodend for destruction, and planning to let my father die!"

"Shut up, Dibbs!" Grace's eyes held tears. "Don't speak that way about the king. He's good. I know he's good. You're just listening to lies." She whirled around and stormed up the stairs.

"The girl speaks wisdom," Ristun said after a moment. "She's quite close to the king. Though you likely don't know this."

"Oh, I know. She's always saying how he helps her with all these stupid things. She can say what she wants. And so can Father. But the king doesn't care about me."

A burning thought entered his mind. "And neither does Father. I got kidnapped . . . kidnapped! And where was he? I don't know, but it wasn't in the woods looking for me. Tarin's father came, and Sarky's father too. But where was mine? Attending to the *king's* business, no doubt. Taking care of this stupid town the king left in his hands."

His mouth began to quake. "You know what? It's because of the king that Father didn't come. Once he sets up a governor, he expects him to always put the town first. And that's what Father's been doing the past year. Putting the town first. Above Mother, above my sister, and most of all, above me!"

He stood. "That's why Mother and he always argue. That's why my sister's had to create a pretend friendship with the king. And that's why," he tore off his shirt and pointed at his back, "that's why he doesn't care I'm getting torn apart every night!" He put the shirt back on and threw his wooden chair across the room. "I hate the king! He took Father away from me. I'll never accept him for that. Never!"

He ran out of the room and outside, raced to an empty alley and began to sob.

✝ ✝ ✝

Ella was preparing breakfast with her mother when she heard the knock. Her long brown hair let down over her dressing gown, she walked over to the door. "Who is it?"

"Umm . . . it's . . . it's me."

"Who's me?"

"I mean . . . it's Jak. I just wanted to check up on you after . . . you know, all that fuss a couple of nights ago."

"Who is it?" Raina called out, entering the foyer. "Someone you know?"

"Mother," she whispered, "it's that man I told you about, the one that carried me when I told him not to."

"You mean it's that nice man who saved your life from those creatures? Why, let him in. We should offer him some breakfast."

She stomped her foot and pointed to her robe. "I'm not dressed properly yet."

"Oh hush. You look lovely. Now let him in."

Ella shot her an angry glance and opened the door. Jak stood outside, gazing at the sky. "Come in. Mother says you can have something to eat if you want. But you don't have to," she added quickly. "After all, I'm sure you have work to do and—"

"Oh no, I'd love to eat breakfast with you!" He looked at her eyes for a moment, then shot his own toward the ceiling. "Um . . . you look . . . um, nice."

He rushed by her, face beet red, and headed over to Raina. He offered a small bow and pulled out a single daisy. "Hello, Ella's mother. This is for you."

Raina took the daisy with a beaming smile. "Hello, good sir. And what is the name of my daughter's rescuer?"

"Rescuer?"

"Ella told me all about the bravery you demonstrated on the governor's rooftop two nights past, and how you saved her from those red-cloaked strangers."

"Oh . . . well, I didn't do that much, really." His face became an even brighter hue of red.

"Nonsense," Raina scolded, taking his arm and leading him to the dining table. "You're a hero, and for that, you must eat a hero's breakfast. I shall make you some eggs, bacon and sausage. And how about some fresh milk to wash it all down?"

"That sounds amazing, though you really don't need to—"

"Ella, come sit with our guest while I make the food." She turned to him. "And what may I call you?"

"Please, call me Jak."

"What a nice name. Well, Jak, you just chat with Ella." She hurried to the kitchen, where there was soon the clanking of pans and the sizzling of something that almost instantly smelled delicious.

"It's nice to see you again, Ella," Jak said politely, his eyes carefully studying the nearest window.

"Yes, I'm sure."

"Um, is your father here?"

"Why do you ask?"

"I was just hoping to meet him too."

"No, he's off looking for my brother. He's one of the boys who were kidnapped during the riot."

"You can't be serious! I'm . . . I'm so sorry. Is there anything I can do to help?"

"Unlikely," she said tersely.

Jak shuffled in his chair, and the two remained uncomfortably quiet until Raina returned with a plate full of the promised eggs, bacon and sausage. "Ella, could you go fetch Jak some milk?"

Ella nodded, and headed to the kitchen. When she returned and handed him the milk, his fingers brushed against hers. *They're so warm and rough*, and their warmth seemed to rush through her body.

He looked up at her, his brown eyes gentle and kind. "Thank you."

She almost smiled before coming to her senses.

"Sure," she replied, then fought a gasp. The reply she'd meant as gruff came out sounding sweet. *Come on Ella, hold it together.*

She sat down, and after watching him devour his food like an animal, found it quite easy to forget the feelings she just had.

Over the course of the next half-hour, Raina poured out her heart to Jak about the riot, her concerns for Tarin, and the search that was underway. She also mentioned something that surprised her: Father had mentioned he thought he might have met Jak in the forest before, since they were both lumberjacks. In turn, Jak briefly mentioned the recent death of his uncle, then, in apparent attempt to avoid the subject, offered his own interpretation of the night on the governor's roof, which was riddled with enough embellishments to make Ella sick. Soon, she could handle no more and excused herself to change. When she returned, Jak and Raina were bursting with laughter over some foolish tale about a raccoon he'd mistakenly thought to be a puppy until it attacked him and nearly chewed his hand off. He made sure to show the scars and all.

Finally, after more than an hour of pointless chatter, Jak rose from his chair, saying, "Thank you so much for the meal, ma'am."

"Oh, call me Raina."

"All right, ma'am, I mean, Raina," he said with a chuckle. "I'm off to the woods now." He grew serious. "I plan to catch up with the search party and help in any way I can. Don't worry, Raina, we'll get your boy back soon."

Ella saw a tear form in her mother's eye. "I know you all will," Raina replied. "And the king is with him."

"Indeed he is." Jak shuffled around in his pocket and pulled out a little dirty jar with a cork on top. "Not the best looking one out there, but it'll suffice." He held it tightly in his hand and closed his eyes. "Please look after my new friends Raina and Ella," he said. "And guide me to the search party so that I might help them find Tarin. Keep him and the other boy safe until we can find them." A little luminance managed to beam through the smudges on the glass.

He smiled at Raina and said, "Well, I'm off."

He gave Ella a warm smile. "Your brother's going to be fine."

That warm feeling came back, and she got the strong desire to give the man a hug. She resisted the unthinkable. Still, she wasn't ready to let him out of her sight yet. "I'll show you to the door."

As he walked away and down the street, she noticed how broad his shoulders were. *Ella!* she scolded herself, then shut the door, fighting the sudden desire to giggle.

Twenty-Eight

The council of Woodend consisted of Will as the governor, Councilman Cheeka of the west district, and Councilman Siller of the east district. Together, they formed Woodend's governing society, along with the sheriff. Of course there was no sheriff since Jebin's resignation; Will hadn't the heart to even think about his replacement. Yet, in a sad twist of fate, Woodend's former sheriff was, at this moment, hidden in a room of his home with Gildareth watching over him. Will would've been there too, if not for the insistence of the three emissaries of Macalum that he hold a council meeting that day. They claimed they had information pivotal to Woodend's survival, and that even the sheriff's death would be trivial if what they had to say was ignored.

Also attending was Hamlin, at the request of the Macalumese, who believed the gatekeeper should know more about his son's kidnappers. He'd left the trustworthy Clooney to man his post until his return.

Kandis was also asked to attend, but declined, deciding instead to continue the search for Tarin and Sarky with a few of his lumberjack friends.

Three guards were there, one being Raulin, the chief guardsman.

Lastly, the three emissaries of Macalum were in attendance. Will would ordinarily have Jebin interrogate any official newcomers. In the absence of a sheriff and not wanting to burden Raulin with the task, he'd done this himself over the past two days. The most unusual of the emissaries was Dirfin, the imp of the Eastmont who, as Will had discovered quickly, resented being called an imp, though his people were indeed shorter than the average men of Arvalast; the tallest Eastmontings reached only to an adult man's waist. But Eastmontings were a sturdy, if often temperamental lot, and Dirfin's appearance was made more foreboding by the armor of his people over leather vest and pants. Though today, he wasn't wearing the chain mail over it as he had when first entering Will's house two nights past.

Varla was in the order of the Macalumese tower guard, in fact the overseer of the other guards and chief protector of High Governor Dirilion, lord of Macalum and governor of Farloth, its capital city. Though the man would demand respect whatever he wore, Will admired his garb of light-blue vest with a sapphire cape attached to his neck, the vest embroidered along the neck with snowcapped mountains, the symbol of his land. The mountain symbols ran downward along the opening to the vest until reaching the golden belt, upon which his sheath was attached. Within that was his sword, which he claimed to never part with.

Aliah sat across from Will, her long spun-gold hair and flawless countenance, the pride of her country as Dirfin had already told Will many times. The imp had said some even claimed she was the loveliest woman ever born within the boundaries of Macalum, though she had scolded Dirfin for mentioning it. She had flatly told Will that she preferred the way of a warrior to the life of a princess. Even now, she eschewed the royal robes and dainty crown of a princess, and instead wore the same armor she'd worn while in the forest.

By noon, all had assembled in the secret room beneath the armory, and the meeting was ready to begin. It was rather damp in the underground lair, and it took many lanterns to light the dingy place. Old paintings of past governors hung on each wall, all except for Will's. An artist had yet to come to him requesting to do his portrait. He didn't care. Other things were always on his mind, and ego rarely had a chance to ensnare him.

Moments earlier, all the guests had taken seats in the circle of chairs whose diameter took up the whole space of the room. Will commenced the meeting by introducing Cheeka and Siller, finishing with, "Together, we make up the ruling body of Woodend, with the king of Arvalast as our head."

At this, the emissaries of Macalum leaned forward in their seats a little. Will suspected it was surprise that made them react this way. Acknowledging the king was how all ruling bodies of the king's towns were supposed to refer to themselves, but it had likely been a long time since they'd heard any governor give the king homage.

Their stunned faces gave way to smiles and nods as each member in the room properly introduced him or herself. Then Will stood and began to speak.

"I have summoned the ruling body of Woodend here, along with the acting head of our guard and two of his men, upon the request of our guests from the land of Macalum. I regret to inform you that our former sheriff, Jebin, isn't well at the moment. He is being attended to by an emissary of the king himself, a man from the far reaches of the north named Gildareth. I only hope he can somehow aid Jebin."

Dirfin began to chuckle. Aliah turned to him with a scowl. "And what is wrong with you?"

Dirfin smiled sinisterly. "You saw the sheriff. You know what's wrong. He will need a miracle to survive the red curse."

The room grew eerily silent. Dirfin stood and turned his attention to Will. "Many from our land have fallen prey to the red curse. And the fact that your sheriff has now been hexed means your woods are in even greater peril than we first imagined."

"What is this red curse you speak of?" Raulin asked.

Dirfin prepared to speak, but Varla hushed him. "My counterpart shouldn't have spoken of it."

Dirfin scowled, but said nothing.

Varla gestured for him to sit, then stood. "The red curse is a terrible plague that has long haunted our people. As our enemy moves into our lands, it follows. We have not yet found a way to stop it."

"It now moves northward," Aliah added. "For the drilockk are amassing within your forest. Even last night, we came across their trail. And we fear that your son, Governor Willerdon, and the two other boys still missing, were taken by the drilockk."

With this, Councilman Cheeka nearly bounced from his chair. "What are drilockk?"

"Please be quiet and listen," Councilman Siller said, clearly annoyed at his counterpart's inquisitiveness in the midst of such grave times.

"No, no. It's quite all right," Aliah said in Cheeka's defense. The man's face had fallen into a pitiful expression after Siller's rebuke. "Few in the north have heard of the beasts, much to their fortune, I might add. But the time is coming when all will know of the drilockk, and will fear their name with as much fervency as my own people do."

She looked around the room. "As legend has it, long before the king forsook this land in the wake of his enemy's triumph, a large community of men and women dared enter Shieth, the forbidden lands to the south. There they met a terrible fate, and were warped and twisted by the enemy until they ceased to be human, growing scales rather than skin, claws instead of nails. Their minds were enslaved by the enemy's foulest servants, creatures we dare not speak of. In Shieth, the drilockk multiplied, and eventually became the workhorses of our enemy's army. Macalum, as the final free country in Arvalast, has been in constant warfare with the beasts for many years."

Cheeka gasped. "Then these are beasts not to be taken lightly," he said, his voice now more somber. He pointed at Will. "I heard that some actually attacked the governor's family."

"And mine," Hamlin added, his voice holding unease.

"The guards of Woodend are prepared to fight this foe," Raulin said. He stood and brandished his sword. "If they dare enter this town again as they did when they took the lads, their blood will drip from my sword."

Varla approached Raulin, circled the guard once, and frowned. "You think you're a match for a drilockk? Many of my guards, far more stout than yourself, have fallen to the creatures. Perhaps one you could tarry, maybe even two. But imagine coming against an army of the scaly monsters, each one with claws like daggers and teeth like needles. Then what would you and your few guards do?"

The room fell silent as Varla looked around in challenge. "Die, that's what you would do. For you and your band of stout, yes, perhaps even valiant warriors, would have no chance against an army of the beasts."

Raulin glared at Varla, as did the other three guards.

Varla returned to his seat. "But that is why we are here," he continued. "My counterparts and I, you might say, are drilockk slayers. For that is our job in Macalum, and now our job here: to find, and kill, as many of the creatures as possible. For over a year now, the captain of our force has been mobilizing brave men and women from across our land to fight the beasts. And the offensive is growing. The resistance has already managed to take back some of the towns in southern Macalum, those once occupied by the beasts. Though we cannot overwhelm their armies, we can still catch them off guard, and then retreat as they remobilize. It is a slow and wearisome process. But it forces them to spread their armies all across our land in order to fight our resistance.

"Dirfin aids in the battles in the Eastmont, where his people have all but scoured their mountains of the foes. Aliah and I have fought along our western border. Meanwhile, our captain has valiantly led assaults into the gap within the Dividing Mountains, where Ferion, the gateway city into our land, once stood. Today its once beautiful streets are stained with the refuse of the drilockk. But if our captain has his way, even Ferion will soon be free of the creatures."

"But if all is going well in Macalum," Will said, "how did drilockk reach our forest?"

"All *was* going well," Aliah answered. "An army of drilockk larger than any we had ever seen came through the gap and overpowered the resistance around Ferion five months ago. The drilockk then marched north, the red curse following. We were forced to withdraw into our fortress capital of Far-loth, where my father, High Governor Dirilion, prepared for the onslaught we feared might destroy us. But the army instead turned west, and passed into the Great Plains. Within the vastness of the farm country, we lost all sight of it, and even now are unaware of how such a huge force manages to elude our scouts.

"A month ago," she continued, "the head of our resistance asked my father if he and a few of his most trusted warriors could follow the beasts' trail, in hopes of discovering their whereabouts and perhaps their inten-tions. Father agreed, and the party, which included myself, Dirfin, and Varla, left Macalum."

While she took a sip of water from a cup sitting on a nearby stool, Will was stunned by the elegance this warrior woman maintained even while drinking.

She met his eyes, and continued. "We followed the trail deep into the plains, until it disappeared. Long we looked for signs of the creatures, but found none until we came to the eaves of your forests. There, we discovered evidence that the creatures had entered quite some time ago. Our captain told us to go into the forest and kill all the drilockk we could find."

"Were you successful?" Cheeka blurted, his eyes wide.

She gave a patient nod and answered, "Somewhat. First, we killed all those around your southernmost town of Mahotholin. Yet they were few. Then we followed the trail northward until we reached Lockspell. We set up camp there, and every day, we found and slew more of the creatures. Yet none of them were well organized. We believed them to be scouts. Then, just two nights ago, we followed a group north. Their trail appeared to head directly for Woodend, before another, fresher trail took its place heading south. This led us to believe they'd already accomplished whatever task they had in the north, and were now leaving. So we followed the trail, and even-tually met two from your village, Hamlin and Kandis, and found your son. Now we await the arrival of our captain from Lockspell. He plans on setting up camp in Woodend soon, fearing the beasts have had this town as their target all along."

"And who is this captain of yours?" Siller asked.

Aliah turned her eyes to the councilman. "He is Captain Bolard of the Macalum High Guard."

"Captain . . . Captain Bolard?" Siller stuttered.

"It can't be," Cheeka whispered.

"Governor Willerdon sir," Hamlin squeaked in surprise, "it's not him, is it?"

"What are you all talking about?" Varla asked the room. "You act as if you know the man."

Will slouched in his chair and leaned his head into his hand. "That's because we do. He was once governor here."

"Captain Bolard was a governor of a forest town?" Dirfin asked in shock, and glanced at his companions. "Why has he never told us?"

"Perhaps it's a different Bolard," Varla responded.

"Yes," Hamlin said quickly. "That might be right. Governor, do you think it could be someone else?"

Will didn't respond. He wanted to say yes, but because of the recent rumors about Bolard's presence in the forest, and the lump in his gut that wouldn't go away, he feared the worst.

"Governor," Hamlin repeated. "Do you think it's somebody else, or is Bolard really a guard of Macalum now?"

"I don't know!" Will snapped.

Hamlin shuffled uneasily in his seat.

Will turned to Varla. "When do you think Captain Bolard will be arriving?"

"I don't know. But I will soon find out. I must return to Lockspell and update Captain Bolard on our progress with the hunt. I'm sure he'll want to come here after hearing of the kidnappings."

"It will likely be within a week, then," Aliah added. She turned to Dirfin. "I will stay here. I fear the drilockk might have a hidden entry here, or are somehow sneaking past the gate."

"Impossible!" Hamlin yelled. "None gets past my gate unless I let him. And I can assure you, *no* drilockk have gotten through."

Dirfin stood and brandished a dagger from beneath his cloak. "If you speak that way to my lady again, you will feel the sting of my blade."

Hamlin's eyes grew wide and he leaned back in his chair, putting distance between himself and the angry imp. Raulin and his two guards pulled out their swords and stood between the gatekeeper and Dirfin.

"Dirfin! Put that away!" Aliah shouted.

"But my lady—"

"Silence! I warned you before about that temper of yours. These people have been gracious enough to meet with us, and you have no right to threaten them that way." She turned to Hamlin as Dirfin slumped back into his chair and sheathed his dagger.

"I'm terribly sorry, sir," she said kindly. "I didn't mean to insult you. And I believe you. It's unlikely that the drilockk entered through the gate. More likely, they have a secret way in. And if they do, I plan to discover it."

Will sat quietly, glad the tension was ebbing.

Hamlin smiled and nodded. "Very good, miss. And I shall help you in any way I can. As will our guards, I'm sure." Raulin and the others put away their weapons and returned to their seats.

The room went quiet for a moment, then Varla spoke. "I believe we've told you enough of our mission for now. I must now ask for supplies for my journey back to Lockspell." He turned to Dirfin. "Do you plan on staying with Aliah or coming with me?"

Dirfin's eyes twinkled as they met Aliah's, and he let out a faint sigh. "Um . . ." he squeaked. He cleared his throat. "I will stay with Aliah and look after her. I don't want her to meet up with a drilockk alone, after all."

Varla scowled. "I'm sure you wouldn't, my little friend. And I have a good feeling you plan to *look* after her quite intently. Just don't become a nuisance."

He turned his eyes to Aliah. "My lady," he said, and kissed her hand. "I shall return soon with Captain Bolard, and we shall continue our hunt." He then turned to the rest of the party. "And I promise you, we will find your missing boys. Bolard is quick-witted and wise. He'll know what to do to steal them away from the enemy. As for now, provisions if you please."

Will nodded to Raulin. The guard got up, followed by the other three, and beckoned Varla to follow. They left the room. Will then asked Hamlin to accompany Aliah and Dirfin back to the inn. The gatekeeper was delighted, and in moments they were off. The room was now empty save for Will, Siller, and Cheeka.

"Wow!" Cheeka bellowed. He stood and began pacing. "Looks like we're in for some exciting times. This may even beat the Royal Decree."

Siller stood in a rage. "You fool! Is that what you want? Another time of carnage like during that decree? If this is the same Bolard, we're in for some terrible times, not exciting! Don't you remember his promise? He said he'd be back, and he's going to throw down Will. The governor's in danger, along with his entire family."

"Siller, calm down," Will said in frustration. "We don't even know if it's the same Bolard yet."

"How could it not be?" Siller retorted. "Everything fits. And don't tell me you haven't heard the rumors. Good grief. And even the riot points to Bolard's return. You'd be a fool to think this isn't the same man who nearly destroyed the town three years ago."

"He didn't *nearly destroy the town*," Cheeka countered. "Before he . . . well, implemented that odd decree of his, he was a great man, and an excellent governor. He helped my district in ways no other governor ever had.

Many a shack was replaced with a fine wooden house. The west of Wood-end is more beautiful than it ever has been, though lately it's been going rather poorly for us."

He looked somberly up at Will. "No fault of yours though, sir. It's just been the rain. Most of the people in my district farm the hills to our north, and the excessive rain's just been terrible for the crops. Very little money's come in over the summer, and the lot of them are going to be in tough times when winter hits."

Will nodded. "I know, Cheeka. And I've already been looking into the matter with Siller on how to help the west district. Since most of the people on his side are lumberjacks, and have had a good year, they're willing to buy extra food for the west side, as well as offer them firewood."

Cheeka's lips lifted into a smile. "The people have been thinking you didn't have any sort of plan. They've been, well, grumbling an awful lot about it too. They'll be excited to hear the good news."

"Too few give Will the credit he deserves," Siller said gruffly. "And even with the news you plan on presenting, there're still too many that, I'm sad to say, loathe him. That's why, if Bolard indeed returns, we are in trouble."

Cheeka's smile faded and he slunk back to his chair. "Then what are we going to do?"

"Nothing, for now," Will said. "I have too many other problems at the moment."

"You mean Jebin?" Siller asked.

"He's certainly one of them."

"Does Jebin really have this red curse the outsiders were talking about?" Cheeka asked.

"I don't know, but I need to return home to see how Gildareth— I mean, the emissary from the king is faring."

Siller's brows rose. "Do really think this is a true herald from the king? He could simply be trying to stir trouble, along with his two friends."

Will looked at him sternly. "I have no doubt in my mind he is true to his words. I can't explain why. You'll just have to trust me."

Siller gave a small bow. "As you wish. But be careful." His voice lowered. "I have a sick feeling about all of this. Something awful is on the horizon. I just know it."

Cheeka walked over and slapped Siller on the back. He chuckled. "There you go again, old boy. Always proclaiming doom and gloom. That must be why the east district is always looking so down all the time, even though your side happens to be richer at the moment."

Stiller stiffened and balled up his fist, but Will stood and got in between them. "I think it's time we be off. I'll keep you both posted on Jebin's condition. And please, keep all that was said at this meeting quiet. I don't know what would happen if word got out that Bolard really is returning."

"I do," Siller growled. "Pandemonium. Chaos. More riots."

"There you go again," Cheeka said with a snicker.

"Please shut up," Siller responded wearily.

Will watched, trying not to smile, as the two councilmen argued their way up the stairs and out of the armory cellar. Soon their voices died away and he was alone. He looked around at all the pictures and took in a large breath of the damp air. *I wish I were just a memory like them, rather than the one in charge.* He let his head droop in despondency and slowly climbed the stairs, not looking forward to facing the problems that lay at their top. Inside his pocket, he barely noticed his illumina grow warmer.

TWENTY-NINE

Dralo and Ristun sipped on tea Grace had just brought them. She gladly sat across from them now, enjoying the compliments they'd given her on its flavor.

She had turned ten a few weeks ago, and was often referred to as "pretty," which delighted her. Already these new guests had offered her the same compliment, and she found it easy to smile around them, as she did with most people. Dibbs was the only one who found it easy to turn her smile upside down. How she wished her own brother would be as nice to her. Just a little earlier, she'd gone to his room and offered him a sandwich for lunch, which he'd snatched from her and thrown against the wall. She'd thought Dralo and Ristun might be better company. Now, she realized she'd been right.

The fair-haired one named Dralo, with his well-trimmed beard and neat mustache, was polite to her, and enthusiastic in his storytelling of the many exciting adventures he and his counterpart, Ristun, had participated in. Ristun, in comparison to Dralo, laughed more and seemed less intense.

"All those battles you fought for the king, that's so exciting!" she said to Dralo. "I only wish I could've been there to watch."

"And what about me," Ristun whined. "Am I not amazing too?"

"You're silly," she said.

Dralo chuckled. "She's right, you know. You're a rather silly fellow." He turned to Grace. "Just two days past, he was nearly killed by . . . something big because he wasn't paying as much attention to the battle as he should have been."

"Oh, now you've done it," Ristun said. "If not for me, that battle would have had unfortunate consequences. Namely, you would have been in multiple pieces by the end."

"Then you're a hero!" Grace shouted happily, and gave Ristun a hug. "Saving your friend is quite a good thing to do."

"Um, my dear," Dralo interjected, "it was I who saved Ristun, not the other way around."

"Don't listen to him," Ristun whispered. "He is known to bend the truth on occasion to make himself look better. Not that it helps."

"Now sirs," Grace said, crossing her arms and glaring at the two men, though she couldn't stop a smile from forming on her lips. "Are you two going to argue all day? Because if you do, I'm afraid you'll be sent to bed with no supper. After all, rules are rules, and there is no arguing in this house." She grew pensive. "Well, that *is* the rule. Dibbs and I argue all the time, and so do Father and Mother. So I guess you two are all right. You may keep arguing if you wish. But I must go see to my bird. I have a pet turtledove, you know. I've been raising it since it was a baby." She sighed. "Mother says I'll have to turn it loose soon, so it can have its own family. But I wish I could keep it forever."

"I'm sure it will always remember you," Dralo said cheerily. "Not even animals are quick to forget kindness."

She beamed at him before skipping up the stairs to attend to her turtledove. Behind her, she could hear the men chatting. After feeding the bird and stroking its soft feathers, she began back downstairs.

"This tea really is quite good," Dralo said as she descended the first stair.

She stopped when she heard footsteps approach, and saw Gildareth stride into the living quarters, saying, "Are we alone?"

"Yes," Dralo said. "Grace just went upstairs to attend to her pet."

Oh, I guess they won't want company now, she thought, and considered returning to her room. When she heard Ristun say, "Have my chair, Gildareth, you look terrible," curiosity made her sit on the top stair instead.

Gildareth let out a weary groan. "Thank you. That feels better. I finally broke the curse, though it was difficult. Jebin's heart is extremely darkened by his past, and he believes the king loathes him. This grief of his, I did not break, but the curse itself I eliminated. The man's eyes are again of good color, and he seems more peaceful. But to again be well, he will have to defeat the lies of the enemy himself, and believe once again that the king isn't against him, nor does he hate him for his past, however tainted it may be."

"And did you discover what he's so guilty about?" Ristun asked.

"I did not. Though I believe it stems around an event occurring during Bolard's Royal Decree. Much pain lays in his memories of it . . . much pain."

"And what of this curse?" Dralo prodded. "Is it as we feared?"

"It is," Gildareth said. "It is Shieth's sword, the red curse."

The room fell silent. "But only a sentinel of the enemy can perform that mighty curse," Ristun said.

"Don't forget," Dralo answered, "we saw the apparition in the meadow that might well have been a sentinel. I have feared for quite some time now that a sentinel has been leading the forces against Macalum. Many of its people came under the red curse while we were in the land. And many did not come out of it." He sighed. "If only they knew the king. But that land is so defiled by the lies of the enemy, there's almost no one who can put up any real resistance against the evil there."

"But they believe they *are* resisting the enemy," Ristun added. "For many months, they actually managed to push back the drilockk. But they don't realize that the drilockk are but ants compared to the real threat. And the shadows are so thick in Macalum, and its capital of Farloth, those who can see them are nearly blinded. You and I had nearly no power there."

"Nor do the myriads of others the king has sent to the land," Gildareth said. "That's why Woodend is so important. Though it is darkening every day, it still wields more light than any other place in Arvalast. Which is fortunate, as it is the city of prophecy. Though I fear the enemy will strike soon, perhaps for other reasons than the prophecy. He seeks the tower. To accomplish this, he will attempt to confuse and lie to the people, as I told you. Eventually, I deem, he will attack and kill all in the town who profess loyalty to the king. I am believing more and more that the Royal Decree was an attempt of his either to eliminate the king's light, or to weed out those with the light, so he would know whom to destroy. Though his first attempt three years ago failed, the time is coming for another. That, of course, is why we're here."

"And that is undoubtedly why the red curse has followed us," Dralo said. "The sentinel of Macalum must have heard of our coming and decided to come himself, to hinder us. But why did he attack the sheriff? It sounds as if he was already so grief stricken, he would be of little threat to Wrathar's schemes."

"That is true," Gildareth replied. "But he's the man most responsible for stopping the Royal Decree. And he fought harder than any other to exile Bolard. Afterward, as Wrathar always does to those who have victories over him, he likely sent his messengers to slowly work in Jebin's mind until he was consumed by the enemy's lies. And regrettably, the sheriff didn't turn to the king, or anyone else, for help. Rather, he endured on his own. This is the bane of too many men. They always believe they can cope on their own through times of great testing. Yet always, they fail. Perhaps not immediately, but at some point."

"Do you believe this is Jebin's current state?" Dralo asked.

"Yes, I do. His mind is imprisoned by Wrathar's lies. And I'm unsure if he will ever be willing to receive the key to escape this prison. Yet I know this much. Somewhere, there are people fervently seeking the king on his behalf. It was their pleading that enabled me to free him from the curse. Perhaps it will be they who will also provide him an escape from the enemy's lies. But for now, we must simply wait."

"As we wait," Dralo said, "we have interesting news about a new threat we discovered in the forest while returning Jebin to the city."

"Yes," Gildareth said, "tell me more of this monster you battled after seeing the sentinel in the meadow."

"Ristun saw it first," Dralo said, nodding to his partner. "He looked into the sky, then a growl nearly shattered our ears. Above us, a huge winged beast eclipsed all remaining daylight from the clearing. Its little beady eyes gleamed down at me, and I returned its gaze. Perhaps this was my bane, for it seemed to perceive me as a threat. It began flapping wildly and roaring. I shouted for Ristun to take Jebin away from the sentinel, but as usual, he didn't comply with my command."

Gildareth said, "That thing was too great a foe for you to have sparred with alone, and you know it. Besides, the sentinel had disappeared for some reason. Jebin was safe for the moment."

"I suppose you're right," Dralo replied. "The sentinel had left, but the creature was fast approaching."

"Thankfully, the creature was too slow," Ristun said, "as most large beasts tend to be. I used my illumina to momentarily blind the beast before slashing at it with my sword. And together, we prevailed over it."

Gildareth nodded. "For which I am grateful. But what ever came of Thief, the silly man you briefly mentioned to me the other day?"

"He sneaked away on our way to Woodend," Dralo said.

"He kept antagonizing poor Dralo," Ristun said. "And I must admit, he annoyed me as well. I'm glad to be rid of him."

"I am sad to hear he was disagreeable," Gildareth said. "But I am happy you showed the man mercy nevertheless. Yet your battle with this creature is grave news." He gazed into his comrades' eyes. "Do you recall the lore about the times of conclusion and the reuniting of the kingdoms?"

Both nodded.

"I am sad to say that within *The Annals of Illuminara* there is a reference to creatures such as the one you spoke of, ones that come before great times of unrest in Arvalast. Times when the kingdom of light is in danger. Such beasts are prophesied to wreak chaos among all the living.

And some are predicted to be terrible, more so than even the one you spoke of."

"But these creatures have been referenced by more than the *Annals*," Dralo said. "I've heard tales of strange monsters appearing shortly after the *Annals* were written. Does that mean the prophecy about them has already been fulfilled?"

"Yes and no. In the rural places of Arvalast, there are terrible stories passed down for generations, about a dark time when monsters prowled about, killing all that moved. Then, after Illuminara fell and all of Arvalast was plunged into shadow, the creatures simply disappeared."

"Why is that?" Ristun asked. "Why did they leave after evil's victory?"

"Because there was no more unrest. Light and darkness were no longer at open war. Evil had triumphed. But now, tension is again mounting as Wrathar plans a final assault. Perhaps this is why the beast has come. And if so, we have yet another enemy, or perhaps many, we must be wary of."

Ristun sighed. "As if we do not already have enough."

Gildareth was quiet for a long time, then said, "None of these enemies or beasts even remotely compare to the potential threat we all believe might be lurking in the forest right now." He peered around the room. "At this moment, its spies could be watching us, relaying our every word to their master."

"Do you mean the sentinel?" Dralo whispered. "The one we feared was in Macalum?"

"Let's not speak anymore about it until we're absolutely certain."

"Agreed," Ristun and Dralo said in unison.

Grace, her palms sweaty from the gravity of all she had just learned, heard pots and pans clamoring from the kitchen. *Mother's preparing lunch. I should help.* Her thoughts still swirling, she stood, brushed some dust from her skirt and headed down the stairs, affecting a lightness she didn't feel.

"Hello, dear girl!" Gildareth said when she entered the room. "I hear you've been listening to some stories from Dralo and Ristun. I hope my two companions didn't bore you."

She smiled. "Oh, no, Gildareth, they were quite … interesting." He had no idea how interesting. And how important. At only ten, she knew she had just been privileged to hear about a prophecy few others realized the import of, yet one that made her heart heavy and fearful.

She excused herself to help her mother prepare their lunch, still pondering what she'd heard might mean to her birthplace, and her beloved family.

THIRTY

Grace set a cup of water in front of Gildareth while Lianna set out the rest of the plates for their lunches, then took a seat at one end of the table in the small dining room between the kitchen and living quarters.

"Would you like something to drink too, sirs?" Grace asked Dralo and Ristun.

"Yes, please," they responded in turn, and she left for the kitchen to fill two more cups, careful to remain within earshot.

"Where is your son?" Gildareth asked Lianna after taking a sip of water. "Dibbs, isn't it? I haven't seen him for quite some time."

"Yes, Dibbs. I think he's upstairs. Though I'm not sure you'd want to see him right now. He's in a exceptionally bad mood. Understandably, I suppose, considering what happened to him."

Gildareth glanced at his counterparts, who looked back knowingly. Then he nodded, as though making a decision.

"I'm sure you likely don't want to hear more grim news," he said, "but I'm concerned for your son, as I am for your entire family. As you know, the enemy seems to be targeting you for some reason."

Lianna sighed. "Forgive me if I seem rude, but . . . there you go again. I keep hearing of this *enemy*, yet I know little of him. All I know is, his minions nearly killed my daughter and me last night."

"Is there something wrong?" Grace called from the kitchen.

"No, dear. It's nothing."

Grace filled the other cup, peering apprehensively into the dining room.

"I'm sorry," Lianna continued, now addressing the guests. "I'm sure my tone *is* coming across as a bit rude. It's just . . . I'm under a lot of stress right now." She laughed. "I haven't even sorted out that night on the rooftop yet. It just doesn't make sense. Why would anyone want to kill Grace and me?

Why would this *enemy* you keep talking about have any interest in us, two unimportant townsfolk of a small city?"

She rapped her fingers on the table. "There was only one good thing that came from that night. Well, two, I suppose. First, Dibbs made it back safely. Secondly, my husband acted boldly for the first time in many years." Her voice quaked. "Though I've not been the sweetest wife in the past months, he still fought so hard to save us, and showed so much strength and reliance in the king. I didn't even know he still had any faith left. That's why I was so angry with him that night. His incessant complaining because of his trying to do everything on his own was driving me mad. But now, I don't know what to think. Is Will changing, or is he just going to go back to the way he's been for so long?"

"I wish we had the answer to that question," Gildareth said. "But even the king himself is waiting to discover what Willerdon will do. And for the sake of this town . . . well, let us just trust the king and see what happens, shall we?"

Grace entered the room with the cups of water and set them on the table, receiving thanks from Dralo and Ristun. She then fetched, with Lianna's help, a steaming pot of vegetable soup. With reluctance in her voice, Lianna called on Dibbs, who sulked down the stairs and slumped into his chair, avoiding eye contact with all the guests.

"Well," Lianna said, "I guess we can begin. I don't think Will's going to make it in time." But just before they commenced the meal, Will entered the room, looking haggard.

"*Awwww*," he said half-heartedly, "vegetable soup. My favorite."

Lunch went by with few words. Most of the discussion was between Grace and the three northerners, who told her willing ears more of their many adventures. Dibbs, though, acted disinterested, and even scoffed a few times at the mention of the king.

After the meal, Dralo and Ristun went for a stroll through the town to see how people were reacting to the riot. Gildareth had asked for a meeting with Lianna and Will, privately. With reluctance, Grace left the room and began up the stairs, looking at the place she'd eavesdropped before. Dibbs pushed by her, but she kept her eyes glued to that spot, remembering.

The meeting commenced in the living quarters, where a pleasant fire simmered on the north end of the room. Will filled both his wife and guest in on the meeting with the people from Macalum, but didn't mention Bolard.

"So there's an army of drilockk somewhere in the plains," Lianna said nervously, "or perhaps even in the forest?"

"That's what they seemed to think," Will replied. "But don't get your-self worried. Nothing is certain yet."

"But it seems those emissaries are right! Consider what happened to Grace and I on the roof! There's definitely something out there."

"But we don't know how many," Gildareth interrupted. "And if Wrathar was planning to invade the forest by force alone, he would simply do it. There is more than this army we must be leery of. I find certain situa-tions within your own family far more troubling at the moment."

"What do you mean?" Will asked, narrowing his eyes at the herald.

Gildareth leaned back in his chair and rested his hands on the arm-rests. "It doesn't take keen eyes to see that Dibbs' desires to have nothing to do with the king."

Lianna nodded. "I'm sad to admit it, but you're right. There's simply nothing we can do. We can't force him to declare loyalty to the king."

"You're right." He stopped and sipped from his cup of tea. Will waited for more, perhaps a suggestion on how to persuade Dibbs to stop loathing the king, but Gildareth simply watched him stare at him.

"There's nothing more you've got to say?" Will asked in disbelief.

"I wasn't sent here to give you a solution to this problem. My purpose is to monitor the enemy and ensure the town of prophecy isn't destroyed."

Lianna fixed alarmed eyes on Will. "What prophecy?"

"I . . . didn't want to worry you, dear."

"I don't want to hear excuses. Why haven't you told me about this prophecy?"

"Well, I've been a little busy, if you haven't noticed. Riot and all. Not to mention the council meeting and our little rooftop adventure. I guess it just slipped my mind."

"Don't give me that tone! I hate it when you get sarcastic with me!"

Gildareth took another sip of tea, then retrieved his illumina from his pocket. The light flickered, and Lianna's hard glare at Will fluttered toward the phial.

"You have no need to be angry at your husband," Gildareth said. "By not telling you about the prophecy, he has wisely left its telling in the hands of myself, who happens to be a more clever lore master." He winked at Will. "I would be happy to reiterate the story of the prophecy as laid out in *The Annals of Illuminara*," he pulled out the book, "so both of you will know of the danger this place is now in."

Lianna blushed. "I would like that."

"Go ahead," Will sighed.

Gildareth proceeded to tell Lianna what he'd told Will about the prophecy, the tower, and the end of the world.

"You say the end of the world is Woodend?" Lianna asked after Gildareth finished.

"Yes, it is. And it's pivotal that the six mentioned in the prophecy aren't destroyed upon Wrathar's assault on this forest. Though I don't yet believe he counts the prophecy as a threat, he still seeks to take this forest as a stronghold in which to launch a final attack on the north. Which means the six are in danger. They must be allowed to come into the playing field of this war."

"But three already have!" Lianna said. "You, Dralo and Ristun! The three servants!"

Will gasped. Gildareth merely chuckled. "I thought someone might eventually think that. But I assure you, we are not those mentioned. We are from the north. The prophecy was referring to people from this forest."

"How do you know this?" Will asked.

"I have my sources."

"Then who are these servants?"

"That is yet to be revealed. But we know this much: the servants must come before the warriors."

"And what is the difference," Lianna asked, "between the servants and the warriors?"

Gildareth took another sip of his tea before answering. "The servants are those who will be the first for many a century to place their full and utmost reliance on the king. Their witness will be a rallying point for many other followers of the king, who've been waiting for an example to follow. And from these followers of the king, three special people shall discover in them a quest the king has specifically set apart for them. *They* will become the warriors of the prophecy, and the leaders of the king's army, which will at last awaken from its long slumber and begin to advance against the enemy and reclaim the whole of Arvalast for the throne."

"So you three are the warriors!" Lianna said.

"No. As I told you, the servants must come first."

Lianna blushed a deep red.

"Unfortunately," Gildareth continued, "if Wrathar continues to cause so much strife among the people in this town, even within individual families," he shot a stern glance at the couple, "there will never arise these three servants. That's why I brought you here. Will, Lianna, you must ensure that your family is as close-knit and reliant on the king as ever before. Right now, you're setting a poor example for the rest of the people here. Though you put on an outward appearance that all is as it should be within your family, they can feel a deception. This is the greater plan of the enemy. He needs dissension among the king's followers. An unseen army has already been stirring this for many years now, within these weakening walls."

He gestured outside, toward the city wall, then leaned forward in his chair. "Governor, there is an army in this town. One of shadow. One that can not only destroy you on the outside, but within as well. This is the more dangerous army. And this is the army my companions and I must fight. But we aren't permitted to do it alone. The king desires to see his people begin to rise up against Wrathar, using only his strength as their weapon. You, Will, have already done this once, just two nights past. That was the greatest blow the enemy has received in this town for many a year. And I can feel his dark servants' rising anger at their defeat. But they'll be back, and in greater force. You and your family must stand firm, or you will be destroyed."

"Then what shall we do?" Will asked, the faintest tremble in his voice.

"Seek the king's counsel. You and your wife. Together. Tonight. Ask him what he desires from you. And by all means, be vigilant on behalf of your son. I believe he's on a path of great peril at the moment. And Will, you are the one who must show him the folly of this path."

"But how? Dibbs hates me at the moment."

"Then find out why! You cannot continue to passively sit back and allow your only son to walk into the smoldering fires of Shieth!"

"But Will tries to talk to him," Lianna interjected.

"That's the problem," Gildareth said. "Will tries."

The living quarters became still and quiet. From her hiding spot at the top of the stairs, Grace's heart beat hard in her chest. Now, she was certain she'd heard too much for a ten-year-old girl. Far too much. She rushed to her bedroom and grabbed her illumina. In her hands, it felt warm and soothing. The pace of her heart slowed, and she breathed easier. Then, a soft voice spoke from it. Or was it just in her head? *Fear not*, it said quietly. *For your time to play a part in these matters is still distant.*

Thirty-One

Abird's chirping forced Tarin's eyelids apart. The noon sun shining through the leaves above him kept them open. His next realization: He was wet with dew. *Ugh, lousy morning. How am I going to dry off?*

He heard whistling nearby and glanced around. Sarky, completely naked, stood behind a bush.

Tarin turned away. "Put your clothes back on, you lunatic!"

"Are you crazy? They're soaking wet! I've got to let them dry off in the sun a little bit. Besides, there's nobody around. You should do the same, or you're going to have a pretty uncomfortable hike later."

"What? I'm not taking my clothes off in front of you."

"Oh, you're one of those *private* types, eh? Embarrassed by your bony bum? Hey, fine by me. I'll just dry off here, and you go find yourself a nice sunny spot somewhere else. I won't peek. I promise."

Tarin stood. His soggy clothes clung to him, and already he could feel them chafing his skin. "Fine. Just don't go anywhere until I get back."

"Don't worry. And Tarin, watch out for monsters. Woods seem full of 'em lately." Sarky punctuated this with a snicker.

It amazed Tarin how quickly his friend could get over even the most horrible experiences. But that wasn't him. Before he set out for a bright patch of forest, away from Sarky's range of sight, he glanced around, hoping to see no signs of shadows, no hairy monsters with wings, and especially, no red-cloaked lizard-men.

A half hour later, both boys were dry and dressed and peering into the open sky above the old lumber camp.

"Well, it's getting past noon, which means the sun's pointing west." Sarky pointed toward it and moved his hand a little toward the right. "That means north's that way. We better get going if we want to get anywhere near home by nightfall. Don't know about you, but I sure don't want to be out here after dark again. Last night was awful. I know I was excited about seeing those shadows, but I had a few nightmares last night, and I'm not too keen on seeing them ever again!"

"I'm glad I'm not the only one who can see them anymore," Tarin replied. "Now people won't think I'm crazy."

"Awwww, no one's ever thought you were crazy, just weird."

"Thanks a lot."

"No problem. But don't forget, I got an extra-special ability that you don't have. I can *feel* them too."

Tarin grinned. "Good for you, but I never really needed that talent, now did I? After all, I've been able to see them all along."

"Now don't start bragging."

"It's nothing to brag about! In case you haven't noticed, they seem to have taken an interest in us. How do we know it wasn't because of them that we were kidnapped yesterday? I saw a bunch of them during the riot, and they knew it! Maybe those red-cloaked things are their servants. It sure seemed that way from what they were saying in the tent last night."

Sarky's face became pensive. "They also mentioned their king. You think—?"

"Of course not! That can't be the king that sent Gildareth. That would mean Gildareth is on the same side as the ... what did they call themselves?"

"Drilockk, or something like that."

"Ugh! Fits them sure enough, those filthy lizard-men."

"What king were they talking about, then?"

"I don't know, but I sure don't want to meet up with him. I hope he's nowhere nearby."

With a shiver, Sarky peered around. He pointed toward a tree and screamed, "Look!"

Tarin jumped to his feet and looked around. Sarky started laughing. "Gotcha, buddy!"

"You idiot!" He drew his hand back to punch Sarky, but before he could, the boy fell to the ground, laughing. Tarin kicked dirt at him. "You've got to stop treating this like a joke! Did you forget? We were almost killed a dozen times yesterday. Even you seemed pretty upset last night. You were even crying!"

"So were you. And laughing. First time I've ever heard you do it too."

"I've laughed before."

"Must not have ever done it in front of anybody."

"You just shut up. What are we waiting for anyway? Shouldn't we get moving?"

"Yeah, if we want to get home before nightfall. But . . . something I forgot. What will we do for food?"

Tarin gave a frustrated sigh. "I don't want any more of *your* food. I still remember those horrible berries." He paused for a moment, letting his insult sink in. Sarky, as usual, was unaffected. So he decided to be practical.

"You said it would only take 'til nightfall to get back home. Certainly we can go without food until then. As long as we have water, we'll be fine."

"Yeah, there're plenty of creeks. But I'm starving!"

"Then eat some dirt, or maybe a worm. And there's always your precious berries."

"*Enough* about the berries."

Finally, a reaction. Tarin smirked. "All right, no more berry talk. Lead on."

Together, they pressed into the woods.

The hike north went without incident, and the woods had been merciful. They were in an area where most of the trees were tall and fairly spread apart. Every now and then they'd come across a moss-covered rock, which Sarky would insist on climbing, much to Tarin's annoyance. But as they approached another such rock, Sarky's eyes lit up. "We should get ourselves some decent walking sticks. There's the one for me, right over there."

He ran to a perfectly straight stick of sturdy width. Its bark had all fallen off, making it smooth. He picked it up and tapped it on the ground a few times. "Wonderful! Now you find one."

Tarin looked around. He really didn't want a walking stick, but didn't want Sarky to have one while he didn't. So he lumbered over to the rock Sarky was standing next to and glanced around. Nothing. Then he looked up at the rock and saw a stick, straighter and smoother than Sarky's, resting on its topmost corner. Without saying a word, he found what looked like natural stairs carved into the rock over time. He started to ascend.

"Hey!" Sarky challenged, "I didn't think you liked rock climbing."

Tarin didn't answer, and soon reached the top, which was about four times Sarky's height. He grabbed the stick and lifted it up so Sarky could see, then tapped it on the rock. "Solid."

"Nice selection! Now wait up, I want to climb up there too. It's a great looking rock."

"Fine," Tarin said. "Just hurry up. We don't want to get stuck in the forest after nightfall."

"I know, I know," Sarky huffed as he quickly went up the stairs. "Hmm, that was a lot easier than some of those other rocks."

They rested on the rock for a short while, listening to the forest as birds chirped happily and chipmunks scurried about looking for food for the oncoming winter. Sarky sighed. "It's hard to believe that just last night, we were nearly eaten by a monster and killed by those drilockk things."

"I know," Tarin said. "But danger's still out there. We should get going."

"Yeah, you're right." Sarky stood and prepared to descend the stairs when he stopped and pointed west. "What's that?"

Tarin squinted. "I don't know. Looks like a tower or something."

He looked harder. Indeed, it was some sort of tall structure. At its base, it appeared to have four massive shafts that traveled from the ground toward the forest roof, where they disappeared into the leaves. Crisscrossing beams followed them upward, connecting the legs and appearing to give them support. And in the center of the four poles, something that looked like a staircase worked its way up, doubling back on itself, winding its way toward the top of the structure, which was obscured by trees.

"You're right!" Sarky said. "That's definitely a tower! Hey, I bet it's the old guard tower south of Undertree. Father's told me about it. The earliest inhabitants of the forest built it to keep watch from enemies and fires."

"So there really were enemies back then, just like your father told us?"

"Suppose so. But it must not have helped Undertree too much. It still ended up getting destroyed." Sarky thought a moment. "I think we should go over there and climb it. We might be able to get our bearings straight, maybe even get a glimpse of Woodend Hill."

Tarin looked at him with narrowed eyes. "I thought you already had our bearings straight."

Sarky shrugged. "Never hurts to make absolutely certain, now does it?"

Tarin thought for a moment. He'd never fully believed that Sarky knew what he was doing. And from the tower, he might be able to see Woodend. Then he could make certain they were heading in the right direction. No more of this relying-on-Sarky nonsense.

"All right," he said at last. "I'll go. It doesn't look too far away. Shouldn't take long to get a peek of where we are and set off again."

They found a stream along the way and drank their fill. A short time later, they arrived at the tower. Sarky pranced around its base, chatting wildly about how sturdy it still looked even after so many years. Tarin was skeptical. Now that he was close enough, he could see how high it actually was, far taller than any of the nearby trees. And he was surprised he'd never noticed it from Woodend Hill. He could barely see the top of the stairs, but thought he could make out a trapdoor to some kind of platform.

Sarky agreed. "Probably where the lookouts were stationed. Huh. Wonder what it's like up there?"

Tarin grimaced. "I just hope there's a railing up there, like there is around the three platforms on the way up to it."

"Beautiful, simply beautiful," Sarky cooed. "I can't wait to get up there."

"You think it's sturdy enough for two people?"

Sarky looked at him. "Getting scared? Afraid of heights, maybe?"

"Uh . . . no. I just don't want to step on a weak board and fall to my death."

"I'll go first then. If I break through a board and die, don't follow me, all right?"

Tarin couldn't help but grin at the thought of Sarky plunging through a board. To his surprise, that made him feel guilty. He shook both the guilt and the comical image away. "If you go first, I guess it'll be all right."

Sarky started up the stairs, moving quickly. Tarin followed.

The trek to the first platform was smooth. All the stairs felt sturdy to Tarin, and the railing seemed intact. They stopped on it to look around. They were as high as some of the shorter trees, and perhaps halfway as high as the tallest ones. Tarin looked down and felt dizzy, clutched the railing with such force that his knuckles turned white. He began to sweat.

"What's wrong?" Sarky said with a snicker. "Thought you weren't afraid of heights."

"I . . . don't think I can do this," he panted. "It's . . . too high."

"Then stay here. I'll get a look around myself when I reach the top. Bye now."

Sarky started up the next flight of stairs, and Tarin closed his eyes and managed to regain his composure. He really didn't want Sarky to have yet another reason to make fun of him, so he called out, "Hey, wait up," and continued up the stairs, careful not to look down.

The next platform proved nearly as tall as most of the trees, just shorter than the tallest ones. "Maybe when the trees were shorter, the lookouts could've gotten a good-enough view from there," Tarin said.

"Well, no longer. We have to go higher." Sarky's words held confidence, but he looked a little nervous himself.

"All right, let's just get this over with," Tarin whispered, his hands beginning to shake as they clung to the railing.

Sarky knocked on the wood. "It's still sturdy." To prove it, he jumped, making the platform shake.

"Stop that!" Tarin screamed.

Sarky stopped. "*Shhhh*. There's *danger* nearby. Remember?" Grinning, he scrambled up the next flight of stairs.

Tarin, now shaking with rage along with terror, followed.

His knees were weak by the time he reached the third platform. But, once he got there, his eyes filled with wonder as he at last came completely out of the trees and into the vast blue sky above, which contrasted with the leaves of the forest roof. Dotting the treetops were patches of foliage glimmering in reds, oranges, and yellows. He thought he'd never seen anything so beautiful.

Hand still tight on the guardrail, he turned around. To the west, mountains covered in trees rose into the sky. He'd never seen the Maplelake Mountains so close before. They'd merely appeared as hills from Woodend. But now their true height was stunning, and their beauty, enhanced by the tall cliffs gashing their sides and the periodic glimmer of blue from a waterfall, made his heart skip.

"Pretty, aren't they?"

Boy, Sarky's got a way of taking the wonder out of a moment, Tarin thought. But before he could tell his friend that, a gust of wind blew through the tower, making it sway gently. Tarin realized that here, above the trees, the wind had no barriers. It would be like this the rest of the way up.

"Kind of scary, the wind, isn't it?" Sarky said, no longer trying to mask the trepidation in his voice. "But we're going to have to go to the top. Can't quite see Woodend Hill from here."

"But we know for sure which way's west," Tarin said, pointing toward the mountains. "Isn't that good enough for us to know which way's east?"

"No, we need to see how far east we still have to go. Otherwise, we'll just end up in the wilderness north of the forest and have to travel who knows how long until we get to town. We'll save a lot of time if we make a beeline straight to the city."

"All right, all right. Let's finish this."

This time, Tarin decided to get the edge over Sarky and go first. He went up the first step, then the next. They seemed sturdy enough. Not so bad.

He began moving faster, forcing himself to look only up, toward that trapdoor as it loomed ever closer. He was only a few steps from the top when he heard a cracking. The step beneath his right foot gave way and he toppled forward. He couldn't scream, couldn't even breathe. He just held out his hands, closed his eyes, and fell.

His hands landed on something solid, and he opened his eyes. His left foot was still planted safely on the step below the broken one, and his hands had landed on the steps following it. He breathed a sigh of relief, pulled his right foot from the gap, and clambered past the hole.

"Tarin!" Sarky said, running up the stairs in a panic. "You all right?"

"Hey, slow down! There's a broken step up here."

Sarky stopped just in time to avoid the gap. He peered down. "This isn't so bad. Even if we fell through, it wouldn't be far, considering that the steps double back on themselves just beneath the hole. We'd just break a leg, not die."

"Oh, yes, that's reassuring."

Tarin helped Sarky over the hole, and they both looked up. They had to turn one more corner; the steps changed direction one last time before they reached the trapdoor.

After some careful tapping on each step while they ascended, they finally reached their goal. The wind had died down some too, which made the final ascent a little less nerve-wracking. The trapdoor pushed open easily, and landed on the floor above with a loud bang. They clambered through and crawled onto the final platform.

Above them was once a roof, but it had long since deteriorated, leaving its remnants strewn across the floor. Rather than a railing, walls rose up to a height just short enough that a child could look over. They were obviously built to hold off the wind so a guard could lie on a cot and not get a chill, and if necessary, still allow the guard to look over into the forest below.

Carefully, the boys walked over to the eastern wall, choosing their footing cautiously so they wouldn't trip over the rubble. Then, Sarky saw it.

"Look! Woodend Hill! I can even see the city. See that dark spot?"

"But it's so far away," Tarin moaned. "Is there any way we'll get there before dark?"

Sarky was quiet for a moment, then he smiled an obviously fake smile. "Sure we can. But we have to hurry. Let's get off this thing as quick as we can and start home—"

A sudden shaking made them both grab the guardrail. The tower had been stable since the wind ebbed. Now Tarin felt vibrations through the wood. But not like a wind gust. Rather, something striking wood somewhere below them.

"Stay here," Sarky whispered. "I'll go down the stairs a little and check it out."

He exited through the trapdoor, and Tarin felt his footsteps through the wood as he descended. A moment later, they hurried back. and Sarky scrambled through the door and closed it.

He gestured for Tarin to come over. "Sit on the door with me."

"Why?"

"Someone's coming up the tower."

Thirty-Two ◉

The tower swayed in the wind, but this subtle movement no longer scared Tarin. It was the footsteps below that stilled his heart. Only moments before, the footfalls had been faint; now they sounded like they were already on the third platform, the one just below him and Sarky. And now, he heard faraway but frantic breathing.

The footsteps paused on the third platform, allowing him a moment's ease. There was a little yelp that sounded like disgust, then the feet continued up the tower. Tarin held his breath, hoping the stranger would stop before reaching the trapdoor. What would they do if their combined weight wasn't enough? What if the footsteps' owner was still able to force the door open?

Clump, clump, clump.

The footsteps rounded a bend in the stairs.

Clump, clump. There was a hushed cry, and the stranger's steps seemed to fly up another flight of stairs.

Clump, clump, clump. Feet rushed through the last bend and scrambled up, just beneath the trapdoor. Tarin felt jiggling at the latch beneath him. He stopped breathing.

Sarky shot him a look of pure terror and mouthed, *Don't move.*

There was some more jiggling at the door when—*bang!* The door lurched beneath them, sending them up with it. Their combined weight brought it back down.

Bang, Bang—bang! "You confounded door!" the person below them said in a harsh whisper. "Open!"

Bang.

"Open up, why don't you! Can't you let a poor forest traveler in?"

Thump, thump, thump. The knocks grew softer and the stranger, a man, began crying.

"They're going to get me if you don't open. I've got to hide . . . please open." The breathing grew frantic. *Bang! Bang!* "Curse the tree that made you, you stupid door! If you don't let me in, I'm going to die!"

Tarin felt a push from his side and rolled off the door. Before he realized what happened, Sarky swung the trapdoor open.

"Quick, sir. Hide up here with us." Sarky reached down, and a pale, bony hand grabbed hold. With amazingly little effort, Sarky pulled up a skinny little man wearing faded but still colorful clothes.

Upon stepping foot inside the rundown shack, the newcomer pushed Sarky aside and closed the trapdoor. He began looking around wild-eyed. His lips curled at the sight of something behind Tarin. The stranger rushed passed him, shoving him aside as he did, and picked up a few slabs of old wood. He rushed by Tarin again, more slowly this time, and placed the wood on top of the door.

"Quickly, you little fools, get more wood. We've got to pile as much as we can on the door so they can't get in."

"Hey! You can't order us around like that," Sarky yelled. "This is our hiding spot and we're just letting you stay as our guest, since you were about to die and all. That means *we* make the orders, not you."

The man smiled wryly. "Not if you want to live, you little mudmouth." He turned to Tarin. "If your stupid friend doesn't want to help, why not you? You look stronger anyway." He looked him up and down. "Though you're still pathetically skinny. Don't parents ever feed their children anymore?" He patted his stomach, which appeared an empty void beneath his raggedy shirt. "Father always fed me well when I was—"

Tarin heard a thud, and the man's eyes fell into a blank stare. The man then toppled forward onto him.

Tarin screamed and sank to his knees under the weight of the body, which seemed remarkably heavy considering its small size. Using all his strength, he shoved it off him. The man rolled over onto his back, staring at the rotted ceiling and smiling stupidly.

Behind where the man had just stood, Sarky patted the old board he held. "That'll teach him to insult us, hey Tarin?"

"Did you . . . did you kill him?"

"Of course not! I merely showed him who was boss." He looked at the man and giggled. "Look at him. Drooling out of the corners of his mouth. Yuck!"

The man was indeed drooling, and his mouth was moving as if trying to form words.

"Wonder what he's trying to say," Tarin said.

The man's voice grew a bit louder. "Not ... not again. The head ... hurts. Oh yes ... hurts ... again. Poor head." A huge smile covered the man's face and he closed his eyes. "Sleep time."

Sarky kicked the man a few times in the side to make sure he was truly unconscious, then fetched some wood.

"What are you doing?" Tarin asked.

"You heard him. He thinks something might be coming." He dropped more wood on the trapdoor.

"You mean you believe him."

Sarky shrugged. "I want to be careful, just in case it's those cloaked creatures."

Tarin's heart thudded, remembering. "I guess we won't be getting home tonight then." He hurried to help Sarky add wood to the door. To their west, the sun lowered deeper.

Crickets and frogs chirped around them as they finished adding the last bit of wood to the door. The boys had just sat down on the pile when the stranger bolted upright. Sarky grabbed up his makeshift club.

The man rubbed his head and peered around. "What happened? Why does my head hurt so?"

"I hit you," Sarky responded. "And let that be a lesson to you. We're in charge up here, Tarin and me. So don't go bossing us around."

"Fine, fine." He stood and bowed mockingly. "I am your humble servant, oh lord of the gangly ones. Now, my new little master, how is your ever-so-meek servant to address you?"

Sarky rolled his eyes. "Shut up, you old fool. Just call me Sarky. And that's Tarin. Now drop all this 'lordship' business and tell us why you're needing to hide up here with us." He held up his club menacingly. "Or I might have to ask you to leave our tower the quick way."

"No, no, no. No need for that. I'll tell you everything." His voice fell to a whisper. "But please, we must be quiet my little friends. There is grave danger out there. They were following me. Not my fault, mind you. Those stupid northerners drew the beasts to them. They know when northerners are about. Their masters tell them. How I hate those creatures! I can't seem to escape them anymore, no matter how far I run."

Sarky and Tarin glanced at each other. "You've seen *creatures*?" Sarky asked.

"Yes, creatures. All sort of creatures. But the ones I'm talking about are drilockk. At least, that's what you might call them in the north. I don't know. The beasts have so many names. Most foul. Most hideous."

"Drilockk!" Sarky yelled, making the man squirm. "We were kidnapped by them, then this winged monster came and ate some of them, and we escaped into the woods, and saw these shadows ... well, I sort of saw them. For a moment, anyway. Then—"

"Yes, yes, yes. I'm sure you and your quiet friend," Tarin blushed and looked down, "I'm sure you two had quite a little adventure, just like I have had. But do you want your servant to finish his tale or not? After all, you demanded so fervently for me to tell you why I fled up here."

"Go ahead," Sarky replied. "And quit with the *servant* stuff. I told you, I don't want to hear it."

"As you wish, Master."

Sarky groaned.

"Now, my story starts a couple of days ago. I was traveling through the woods, minding my own matters, when the sheriff of a nearby town tried to kill me for no reason at all."

Sarky's eyes narrowed. "What was his name?"

"Um ... mud-eater, or something like that. Now, continuing my sad tale, the sheriff chased me into a meadow. Like a fox, I hid in the tall grass, hoping the madman wouldn't see me. And he didn't, because he heard the wizard chanting and was lulled by the incantations—"

"Wizard?" Tarin interrupted.

"Yes, wizard," the man said, turning a raised brow toward Tarin. "You sound surprised."

Tarin felt his timidity begin to build, and didn't answer. But by the look of Sarky's fidgeting, his friend was ready to learn more.

"I didn't even know wizards existed," Sarky said. "I mean, I've heard stories and such, but I never thought they were out there."

The man started to laugh. "Then you've never been to the south. It's difficult *not* to find a wizard down there. Many, yes, *many* have taken the crimson light and used its powers for all sorts of things. Some seem good, but all are bad ... yes, *all* are bad."

"What do you mean?"

"It's of no consequence, foolish— uh, I mean, Master. Just remember this. If you see the crimson light, *run*. That stupid sheriff, he didn't run. In fact, he went right over to it and got the red curse from the shadow lord. Figured he'd die after that. But then the northerners came, and there was a flash of light. The shadow left, but then the legendary creature came." He started giggling. "Almost killed the northerners. Wish it had."

"What do you know about this shadow?" Sarky asked, shooting an excited glance at Tarin.

The man gave him a quizzical look. "Don't my masters know about the shadows: the masters of the drilockk?"

He received no response.

"The vulgheid, the lesser sentinel!" he reiterated. "Although I believe that one actually was a sentinel." He looked at them with a calculating expression. "Does this frighten you?"

Tarin stared into the stranger's eerie stare, and could almost imagine shadows sliding across the bloodshot whites of his eyes. "I finally know the name of what I've been seeing," he whispered. "The vulgheid."

"You can . . . you can *see* them?" the man asked in wonder.

"I can see them too, sort of," Sarky added. "And I can feel them coming and—"

"—and I simply don't care." The man returned his attention to Tarin. "So, you're called . . . what is it, oh yes, Turbin."

"Tarin," Sarky growled.

"That's right. Tarin. So, you saw the shadows, Tarin. Tell me, what do they look like to you, just out of curiosity?"

"Just like you've already described them. They look like wispy shadows. Although sometimes their eyes are yellow slits, and other times they're wide, white orbs. All of them have long, spidery fingers."

"Yes, yes. That's what my father told me too." He narrowed his eyes and locked eyes with Tarin. "You have a powerful gift."

"Tarin's power wouldn't be so good without my own," Sarky mumbled.

"What do you mean, you little pile of . . . I mean, Master?"

"Well, he only sees them when they're basically right on top of him, about to kill him."

"Is your little friend lying, Tarin, or is it true you can't feel them as well as see them?"

"No, he's telling the truth. Sarky here seems to be able to feel their presence, even when they're still a good ways off."

The little man considered this. "Hmm, your gift isn't as magnificent as I'd hoped. I guess I'll just have to take both of you with me, since only one can see and only one can feel. More the merrier, I suppose."

"Wait a minute," Sarky blurted. "There you go again, acting as if you're in charge. We aren't going anywhere with you unless we want to."

"I'm so sorry, my little master. But I assure you, you'll want to come with me after I finish my tale, assuming we make it through the night."

"What do you mean by that?"

"Oh, don't worry. Things should be good now that you two are with me. Together, we are . . . well, nearly all-powerful. Yes, no more weak little Thief all alone in the woods by himself. Still, I wonder if either can—"

"Thief?" Tarin said.

"Oh, um . . . I didn't quite hear you. Now, Masters, silence your inquisitive little mouths and let me continue my story."

After shoving away a piece of wood that was jabbing him in the thigh, the man crossed his legs, squared his narrow shoulders, and continued.

"As I said, the two northerners were attacked by the legendary beast, but managed to survive and do battle with it. Meanwhile, I mercifully pulled the sheriff away from the battle and saved him. But when the two big brutes finally chased away the beast, they came after me, and demanded I hand the sheriff over to them. As I said, they were *big* brutes. I didn't want to upset them. And although I feared for the sheriff's safety in their hands, I obliged to their request. Then they demanded I accompany them back to Woodend. And again, I was obedient. But on the way there, I grew weary of their presence and ran away."

He peered around nervously. "But I must admit, I miss their swords. There's so many cruel things lurking around. All little old me needs is to be attacked from the air by that furry, winged monster while I'm safe from the drilockk on the ground."

"We saw that thing too!" Sarky said. He explained how the monster attacked the drilockk tent and ate almost all of the drilockk before flying away.

"Little master, if you don't be quiet and keep your silly stories to yourself, I might never finish the one you most kindly asked me to tell."

Sarky huffed and crossed his arms. Tarin couldn't help but chuckle, which seemed to amuse the man but infuriate Sarky. "So what do you know about the beast?" Sarky fumed.

"Well, the big monster my joyful master has also described is what I believe to be a bostt, a legendary creature told in prophetic books to emerge from the earth in times of great unrest. Father told me much about them, for he battled some of their most hideous kind. Some are even more terrible than the vulgheid, from what he said."

He rose from the platform, walked over to the guardrail and spat off the edge of the platform, then returned to sitting. "Though I'd rather face a whole army of those creatures than to have gone to that forsaken city of Woodend with those idiotic northerners." He laughed. "They have no idea what they're in store for."

"What do you mean?" Sarky asked, still annoyed.

"My business. Yes, mine, not yours."

"Tell me!" He knocked the man on the head with his club, but only hard enough to scrape his scalp.

The man held his head and started sniffling, looking as if he would cry.

"Oh fine!" Sarky said. "Keep your mouth shut about it then, if it's going to make you start sobbing. Just tell us this much. What were you so afraid of when you came barging up the tower and banging on the trapdoor?"

The man continued to whimper. "I . . . was running away from drilockk, the same foul things you said took you from your home. After I ran away from the northerners, I heard noises behind me. I knew it was those horrible drilockk. So I fled hard and far, until I reached this place. I ran up the stairs, and they followed. Last time I saw them, they were on the first platform."

Sarky grasped the piece of wood tighter . "You mean you've led them to the tower? Drilockk are down there right now?"

"Oh no, no, no little master. When I woke up from my little, *headache*, which now happens to be worse, thanks to you, I realized they must've left. Otherwise I'd never have woken up at all."

Sarky scowled at him. "Why not?"

"I'd be dead, my less-than-clever little master, as would you and your friend."

"Stop with the *master* stuff!"

"As you wish, little sir."

"Oh, you're hopeless, you . . . you . . . what's your name anyway?"

"Oh, I have so many. Most not so nice. But you can call me what those nasty northerners did. Don't know why they were so cruel, but they decided to call me Thief. I guess it was better than some of the other foul names they offered. So, you too may call your poor humble servant Thief, though it certainly doesn't fit me well. I've never stolen anything in my life."

"I'm sure," Sarky scoffed. "All right, Thief, so why do *you* think we're safe? If the drilockk followed you up the tower, even if they left for a little while, I think it's safe to assume they plan to come back, maybe with more of their own. And I don't want to be here if they do. Tarin and me, we don't have good relations with the drilockk right now, considering they've already kidnapped us once."

"Ah, yes, I see."

"So what do you propose we do?"

"Do you feel anything?"

"And what do you mean by that?"

"Do you feel the vulgheid? The drilockk are rarely far from their masters."

"Well, no. But I didn't when you were coming up the tower either, and you said they were following you then."

"You were distracted by the fear of my coming, I'm sure. Otherwise, you'd have felt something. Or, perhaps their masters found me too little a threat to accompany their slaves in following me. Though even then, I doubt they would have been far behind. Since you feel nothing now, we're probably safe for the time being. Unless you've been lying about being able to sense the vulgheid."

"Of course I wasn't lying!"

"Fine, fine, little master. Don't explode that little head of yours."

"Stop calling me master!"

"Shhh!" Tarin said. "If you two keep making so much noise, everything in the forest is going to come to investigate. And I'm starting to feel kind of safe up here. It's getting dark, and it'll be even darker if we go down into the woods." He looked up into the sky. "And I feel better being able to see the stars. Somehow, I don't think they like the stars. Or the moon. Or any light for that matter. That's probably why they didn't come up here. They'd be away from the shade of the trees."

Thief nodded. "Yes, other master is wise. He realizes that the wicked vulgheid and drilockk don't like the light. That's why I came up here in the first place. I didn't think they'd follow me into the sunlight."

"Then why did you still seem so terrified?" Sarky asked with a raised eyebrow.

"I wasn't sure they wouldn't follow. Which they did, to a degree. I was only hoping they wouldn't. They're far more aggressive than I remember them being down south. Seems like something's got them stirred up."

Tarin and Sarky glanced at each other, remembering the drilockk commander's thirst for bloodshed, and his annoyance at having to wait for his master's plan to be completed before attacking the forest towns. But before Tarin could tell Thief anything, Sarky gave him a look that said, *Don't waste your time*, and Tarin relented. But he still had a question.

"Thief, you said you've come from far south, and you seem to know an awful lot about the vulgheid and the drilockk. Maybe you could tell us more about them. After all, they seem to have a great deal of interest in me and Sarky."

"And no wonder, considering the powers you have."

"What do you mean? Are you saying there's something special about us?"

"Maybe you're more foolish than I thought, my more soft-spoken master. I've already told you that few except the seers can see the shadows. And if they've found out you can . . . well, too bad for you." He snickered.

Tarin felt a lump form in his throat. "Why do you say that?"

Thief looked at him, and his eyes grew misty. "Because I knew someone else with your powers."

"And what happened to him?"

Thief turned his eyes away from the boys. "They shouldn't be asking these things. Foolish masters. They don't realize what they're getting into."

"Just answer Tarin's question!" Sarky bellowed.

"Ho, lo, they don't want to know. Tee dee, they shouldn't ask me."

"I think he's losing his mind, Tarin. Look at the lunatic. He's singing!"

"Fee, lee, he too could see. Ding, dong, now he is . . . gone."

Sarky stopped laughing as Thief turned toward him, his eyes full of madness. "All who can see and feel them end up dead. I'm afraid, my little masters, that unless you stay with Thief, you too will end up decaying in the grass, just like my father Clindale, the last seer of Arvalast."

THIRTY-THREE

"**Y**our father was Clindale the seer!" Sarky exclaimed. "That's amazing! My father's told me stories about him, and how he warned Undertree of an attack, and that they didn't believe him. What happened to him after Undertree fell?"

Thief rested his head in his hands. "Suffice it to know he died, and that you will too. Unless, that is, I become the master."

"And just how do you *think* you're going to be able to do that?" Sarky challenged. "It's two against one." He held up his slab of wood. "I'm not afraid to use this again."

"No, no. That won't do, my new little servant. Not again, no, not again. This time, I'm ready." He lazily pulled open his outer garment and grabbed a large, rusty knife. "Try to hit me with that wooden stick of yours, you'll find this metal blade stuck in your scrawny neck, my little friend."

Tarin quickly backed away from Thief, Sarky's mouth fell open and he held out his hands in a gesture of peace. "All right, all right. Don't get hasty there. I suppose we could let you be in charge for a little while. It won't be a problem."

"Oh, no, no, no. It certainly won't be." Thief slid the knife inches away from his own neck then pointed to Sarky. "Unless you want that to happen to you or your friend, you will listen to poor little Thief for now on. Yes?"

"Yes, sir, Mr. Thief. Whatever you say."

"Hmm, I like that. *Mr. Thief.* It's got a nice sound to it. Yes, definitely nice. And you," he pointed at Tarin. "What will you call me?"

"Umm ... um ..."

"What's wrong with the scrawny boy, I do wonder? Perhaps he finds me a little too intimidating to speak to. Yes, that's it! I like that too. Fine boy, you may simply cower before me. I'll accept either that, or, if your tongue becomes untied, Mr. Thief, as your friend now calls me. And though I know that you, skinny boy, are called Tarin, I'm going to call you Mouse for now on, seeing how it fits your manners. And you," he said, scowling at Sarky, "I shall call you Rat. Mouse and Rat, my two new servants."

"If I may say so, Mr. Thief," Sarky said through clenched teeth, "if you had that knife all along, why did you act as if you were our servant to begin with, rather than just taking charge?"

"Well, I thought you two might be warriors, considering you were all alone in the woods and still alive. In case you learned nothing from my tale, it is no small feat to remain alive in the forest right now with all the drilockk, vulgheid, and other miscellaneous monsters out there. Plus, you seemed rather intimidating at first, as if you were afraid of nothing. But after talking with you and finding out how ignorant you were about all things evil, I decided it was merely luck that enabled you to survive. That's the only way you could have escaped the drilockk and the bostt. Luck. And despite your seer-like powers, you're definitely not warriors. No, my father was nothing like you both. In fact, I think you might've been lying about your powers all along."

"No we weren't!" Sarky yelled. "Tarin, tell him."

"Um . . . I'm afraid that we actually *were* lying to you, Mr. Thief."

"Tarin!" Sarky yelled in disbelief.

"Ahhh," Thief said, "I thought so. Otherwise . . . well, let's just say if the shadows knew of your powers, you would most definitely have been dead by now. They must see you as worthless, as they obviously see me."

"And how do you know that?" Sarky sneered.

"You never learn anything, Rat, do you? They stopped following me up the tower, didn't they? So they must have no interest in me. And of course, the vulgheid don't appear to be stalking either of you at the moment, do they? So you must not be important either. Still, it would have been handy to have your powers. I could have avoided almost any chance of encountering the nasty things on my way back south. Anyway, I guess I don't need you two anymore. You're of no more worth to me than to the shadows. I suppose you can leave."

Tarin winked at Sarky, and from his expression, knew he finally realized why he had denied their powers. "Well," he said to Thief. "I suppose we'll be off."

"Yes, yes. Leave, my little Mouse and Rat. I need some sleep, and I don't want to be in the forest with all the creatures lurking about right now. I'm staying up here for the night. You two," he headed toward the trapdoor and pulled it open, "can fend for yourselves down below." He smiled sinisterly. "Goodbye."

Suddenly Tarin realized the folly of his plan. "Sir, is it possible that we could hide up here with you tonight? After all, it is a little dangerous down below."

"No, no, no. Not after I threatened to kill you, and you, Rat, harmed me not once, but twice. I can't exactly trust you two now, can I? No, certainly not."

"But we promise—"

"It doesn't matter. Now get going."

Tarin tried to think of something else to convince Thief to let them stay, but the dagger made him check himself. Grudgingly, he slouched over to the door and began to descend. Sarky began to follow suit when suddenly, he grabbed his stomach and lurched forward, nearly toppling onto Tarin.

"Tarin, it's . . . it's back. That feeling."

Thief's face contorted in fear, and he peered over one of the walls and down into the forest. He grew pale and sweat beaded up on his forehead. He took a couple of wobbly steps back, then, in a rage, swung around and shoved Sarky away from the trapdoor and into a wall. "Scum!" he shouted.

He returned to the door and looked through it. "Liar!" he screamed to Tarin. "You two do have powers, don't you? But no, no, no. You didn't want to share them with Thief. And now it isn't gong to matter." He pointed toward the woods below. "*They* must know too . . . they're coming."

Tarin looked up at Thief and could see the fear and anger burning within him. For a moment, a red light from below glimmered onto his face, and when it stopped, Thief was paler than ever. "No, not again," his voice trembled as he gazed into the woods. He looked slowly down at Tarin, his lips twitching beneath his nose. "Hmmm, trapped, it seems. Unless, oh, yes, yes, yes. . . ."

"What?" Tarin said, still clinging to the ladder leading to the trapdoor.

"Unless they get something they want. Then, just maybe, they'll go away."

Tarin realized what Thief was saying and began to try to climb back up. But Thief swept away from the trapdoor and returned with Sarky, holding the dagger precariously close to the boy's neck. Sarky was too terrified to do anything, and looked as if he might throw up at any moment.

"I'm closing this door," Thief said. "If you try to get back up here before I'm sure they're gone, I'll slit Rat's throat. If they leave, I'll let Rat go, whether you come back or not."

"But . . . I can't. I'll get killed!"

Thief held the knife closer to Sarky's throat. "Either you or him! Now be a good little Mouse and use your nice powers to get rid of them."

"I can't! I don't even know how! Last time . . . I just . . . I just happened to be able to scare them off. How do you expect me to be able to do it again?"

"Don't know, don't care. Just do it. I'm closing the door now. It better not open again unless they're gone, or you know what'll happen."

"Tarin," Sarky moaned. "Don't do it."

Before he could say more, the door closed and Tarin was left on the ladder, alone.

✝ ✝ ✝

All was quiet in Woodend as the night grew longer. The lampwrights had already finished lighting the lanterns along the main road. Every house had long since gone dark, save a few containing those who were up late drinking and the gatehouse, which was being looked after by Clooney and Hamlin.

Just a few hours earlier, the search party led by Kandis had returned, bringing news that they hadn't found the boys, but would continue searching in the morning. Weary and exhausted, they'd left for their homes, low in spirit.

Clooney and Hamlin, who were quickly becoming friends, now sat by the cozy fire inside the gatehouse. Clooney puffed on his pipe while Hamlin chatted about how Sarky would make sure he got himself, along with Tarin, back home safely. But Clooney was thinking about Margaret, Bill's poor widowed wife. He'd visited her earlier that day to see how she was faring, and it wasn't well. She'd taken to knitting rather than brewing, and spoke barely a word to him. Thankfully, she had a few old women friends who were staying by her side in her time of grief.

He flicked his pipe with his finger to remove some ash from the opening, and wearily looked at Hamlin, who was still rambling about Sarky. Clooney figured it was his way of trying not to lose his mind with worry.

"Sarky knows those woods better than anyone," Hamlin said. "I'll bet you anything we'll be hearing a knock at that gate later tonight, and find them standing outside."

Clooney inhaled deeply, then let out a billow of smoke. "Let's just make sure it's them. Remember what Dralo and Ristun told us about that flying demon they saw. I sure don't want to catch sight of that thing anytime tonight, or ever for that matter."

A shadow of fear swept across Hamlin's face. "I hope the boys don't run into that thing."

"Well, from the sound of it, ol' Tarin and Sarky managed to escape the beast somehow. That's how the gov'nor's son got free. I'm sure they're still managin' all right. They be bold lads."

Hamlin's cheeks grew rosier from a deep swig of gin. "You're right. They're going to be all right."

"The king'll see to that, I'll be sure of it!"

"Hmm, king, eh?" Hamlin slouched a little in his seat. "I suppose."

"Ye don't trust the king? Why, he's even gone so far as to send Gildareth here. That means he means business."

"I used to trust him. Even still have one of those lights and everything. But that's before . . ." He stopped, and his eyes grew misty.

"Somethin' bad happened 'while back, didn't it?" Clooney said softly.

Hamlin wiped his eyes with the sleeve of his shirt. "Yes. I just . . . don't really want to talk about it."

"That's all right, me friend. But do ye mind if I keep on asking the king to help yer son get back safe? I'll do it in private if ye like."

"No, it's perfectly all right. Kandis asked me the same thing when we first started looking last night, and I said yes, even joined in a little. Only with his illumina, of course. But still, it just reminds me . . . someone. Never mind."

"Well," Clooney drew in another deep breath through his pipe, "let's just keep on watchin' the gate for now. But I suggest we do it in shifts. I'll take the first one, considerin' ye look tuckered out. Why don't ye go to bed and I'll wake ye in a few hours."

Hamlin yawned. "I *am* tired, considering I didn't get much sleep the past two nights. Of course, neither did you, if I remember."

"That's all right. I like stayin' up late. Go ahead and get some sleep."

Hamlin went to bed, falling asleep almost instantly. Meanwhile, Clooney, beginning to feel a little uneasy about something, though not sure what it could be, pulled out his illumina.

"Hmmm, got that nasty feelin' in the pit of me stomach," he said to the illumina. I think ol' Wrathar might be schemin' 'bout now. I just ask ye to keep watch over the town tonight, and especially the lost lads. They're goin' to need ye more than ever, and I don't think either really knows ye too well yet. Ask that that changes soon though. It'll do 'em good to accept yer light and become yer followers."

The illumina grew subtly brighter just as Clooney thought he heard a faint growl outside the gate. Feeling a shiver up his spine, he pulled his chair a little closer to the fire and held his illumina.

✝ ✝ ✝

Tarin stood on the ladder while relentless terror coursed through his body. Soon his trembling made his hands grow too weak to hold onto the ladder, and slowly, their grip slipped and he toppled onto the stairs below. He tumbled until his head hit the corner, where the stairs turned directions and headed down toward the third platform. Pain gushed through his head and made him dizzy.

What have I gotten myself into? If only I'd never run down that alley and seen the shadows. They know, just as Thief said, that I can see them. That must be why I was kidnapped with Dibbs and Sarky. There's no other reason—

The noises came from far down the stairs, as did faint vibrations in the wood as someone, or something, began to ascend from far below.

"How do I escape?" he cried softly to the darkness. "There's no way out of this one. I'm dead." Tears rolled down his face. "There's no one to save me."

Off in the distance toward the north, he thought he saw something like lightning streak through the sky. Whatever it was, it disappeared as quickly as it had come. Then, a familiar face appeared in his mind, smiling at him, beckoning him to summon up his courage and trust. *But trust whom?* he wondered.

A vision of a stone tower stretching into the dark heavens swept past his mind, and in the sky, a bright light shone as strong as the sun. He was surprised that the sudden vision didn't startle him, but he immediately knew it was the king.

The vision passed, and he rubbed his eyes. *Him?* his mind cried in disbelief. *How can I trust someone I've never trusted before? And even if I did, how would that help me now? Nothing can help now. Not even a hundred warriors like . . .*

Gildareth's bearded face appeared in his head again, looking at him solemnly. The only response he could muster was a sigh. *I suppose you probably could help me if you were here. But you're not. You abandoned me right after meeting me. It seemed you only came to town just to get me into trouble. In fact, if it weren't for you, maybe I wouldn't even be in this mess right now.*

The face in his head disappeared, and suddenly, Tarin felt painfully alone. The tower shuddered as heavy footfalls began thundering up the stairs from far below, and Tarin realized he'd been wrong. He'd do anything to see that face again, to have the first person he'd felt truly peaceful around for as long as he could remember standing beside him, ready to do battle on his behalf.

"Gildareth," he whispered. "I'm sorry. I . . . I'm just angry because you're not here. I need help. Any help. Otherwise . . ." The thuds grew louder, and he realized that whatever was coming had reached the first platform. "Otherwise," he whispered, "I'll die."

He heard something hiss from far below. His heart faltered. *If only I'd listened to Father all along and learned the ways of the king. Perhaps I'd be able to escape these things. But even if I trust the king now, I don't have an illumina.*

Suddenly, he again pictured Gildareth. *Now Gildareth I could trust, with or without an illumina. At least I know he really exists, and actually has a sword he can use.*

But wait . . . Gildareth is a herald to the king, which means he must trust him, or he wouldn't be serving him.

Tarin found it hard to believe that anyone as seemingly strong as Gildareth would need to trust anyone. Yet Gildareth's loyalty to some unseen king intrigued him.

He listened for noises from below; it sounded as if whatever was approaching had stopped. He lay still for some time, but all he could hear was the gentle breeze rustling through the treetops.

Then he saw it; a glimmer of red light illuminated the forest canopy directly below him, and he heard a strange, lovely voice lift toward him.

"Tarin. Come to me. I am he whom you seek."

✦

✝ ✝ ✝

It was midnight. Willerdon and Lianna had fallen asleep hours ago. Dibbs had decided to ride out the night in his own room. Gildareth, Dralo and Ristun were bunking in the living quarters, and Jebin still lay silent in the governor's spare room, not yet having awakened from his dark sleep brought on from the red curse.

Grace, though, was having tremendous difficulty finding slumber. Every time her eyelids fluttered shut, she'd hear a wolf howl or an owl hoot and think of the two boys, lost and alone somewhere in the woods, no mothers to comfort them, no fathers to protect them. At last, she decided to get up and get some milk from the kitchen, hoping it would soothe her mind.

She crept out of her room and tiptoed past Dibbs' room toward the stairs. As she descended the first stair, it creaked a little, and she stopped, listening. But there was no sound of stirring, so she continued down each step as softly as possible. Eventually, she reached the bottom and continued toward the kitchen, passing the living quarters where the three guests slept. Taking a few more steps, she reached the entryway to the kitchen, lit a nearby candle, and headed to the icebox to get the milk. She poured herself a tall cup and sat down to drink.

She nearly yelped in surprise when she heard a noise coming from the nearby hall, where Jebin's room was located. Curious, she left her milk, picked up the candle, and headed toward the sound. The candle's light penetrated each corner of the walkway, but she didn't see anything suspicious . . . until her eyes caught sight of the door at the far end of the room, the door leading to the room where Jebin lay. It seemed to be drawing her, that old wooden door, though she didn't know why.

She'd taken a few steps backward when she heard it again, more distinctly this time. A soft groaning, as if someone was in pain.

"Jebin?" she whispered. For a second, she thought she should go back and wake her father, or maybe the guests. But there was another groan, and she knew Jebin must be in terrible pain. She sprinted toward the door and flung it open.

Fear exploded through her body and she stumbled backward, clutching the doorframe to keep from collapsing. In the center of the room, on a little cot, Jebin was writhing, his eyes wide open and his mouth moving as if trying to scream. Standing next to him was a cloud of smoke shaped like a man. The long fingers at the end of its arm were deep within Jebin's thrashing head.

Grace tried to scream, but couldn't. She tried to run, but her feet felt glued to the ground. The candle's light made eerie shadows dance around the room, but the one in the center, the one with its arm in Jebin's head, was unwavering. Its head tilted upward and two hideous black slits within yellow orbs caught her eyes and held them in a malicious stare. A smile slid across the smoky face, and two dirty white fangs glimmered in the candlelight.

"Young child," it hissed, "where is your light?"

Her hand shook violently, but she lifted the candle, and with all the strength she could muster, she replied, "Right here, sir."

"Ahh, such respect you show me. But that light you hold is of no consequence. I wonder, where is his light, the light of your king?"

She realized what the beast meant. "I . . . I don't have it with me. It's upstairs, in my room."

"Pity," it hissed. It withdrew its fingers from Jebin and crouched like a predator before a leap. She took a step back, unable to cast her gaze away from the fangs. She tried again to scream, but nothing came out.

Then, it jumped forward.

Before she could move back, its smoky fingers swept into her body, making her insides squirm. With a maniacal laugh, it plunged its fangs into her head.

A wave of images and nightmares crashed against the walls of her mind with such force, she felt as if she would go mad. Like Jebin had been doing earlier, she now found herself thrashing about, trying desperately to thrust the beast away from her, but to no avail. Strange voices screamed at her, threatening her and her family with death.

Just before she thought she could bear no more, the creature gasped and let go of her, so suddenly she fell back, hitting her head against the ground and dropping the candle next to her. It snuffed out instantly, replaced by a brilliant light.

"Take heart, Grace," a kind and warm voice whispered into her ear. "Everything will be all right."

Strong arms swept her up, and she gazed through blurry eyes at the reassuring face of Gildareth. But her peace wasn't long-lived; the room erupted in screeches, and two brilliant swords began thrashing about. A third sword, blacker than the night of a new moon, fended off blow after blow.

Gildareth held her close, protecting her from any stray swings. Many times the dark weapon came precariously close to her, but each time, a brilliant sword would block the attack.

She closed her eyes as one of the wielders of the gleaming swords was forced to parry a strike right in front of her. A moment later, all went quiet, and the swords stopped their clanging. She opened her eyes and saw the creature back toward the far wall, hissing as if in deep pleasure.

✝ ✝ ✝

The voice was so soothing, all fear left Tarin. As if in a trance, he forgot all his anxieties and stood, wanting nothing more than to hear that wonderful sweet voice again. "Who are you?" he whispered.

"I am he whom your father has spoken of since you were a child. I am he whom has kept the vulgheid of Shieth from destroying your village. And I am he whom sent Gildareth to Woodend, to awaken your soul to my presence."

"You sent Gildareth? That means you are . . . you are . . ."

"Yes, Tarin, I am the Lord of Arvalast. I am the one whom you seek. Now come to me, for I know you seek the illumina, so, like your father, you too might wield great power. But I shall give you something better."

The red light grew even brighter than before, and Tarin, unable to resist, began descending the stairs toward it.

✝ ✝ ✝

The shadow's yellow eyes gleamed, then shot toward Dralo and Ristun. "The crimson light is at work," it hissed. "A new slave is about to be born." It tilted its head upward and let out a piercing laugh, shaking with a wild glee. It lowered its head. "Soon, it will be here too," it said through labored breaths, "claiming more followers for my master."

It looked at Grace, and its cruel stare made her quake in Gildareth's arms. "Ahh, another can see us. Two so far. Rather amazing. Not like in the south, where so few have the ancient gift of the seers. I must inform my master of her." He smiled at the girl, his fangs glistening in the light of the warriors' swords. "She too will make a valuable ally, along with the boy."

"Speak no more to the girl, slave of Shieth!" Dralo howled. "You may not have her!"

Together, the warriors charged, but before they could deal their final blow, the shadow slid through the wall and out of the house. As it did, it hissed one final warning. "You cannot protect the sheriff forever. Mere chance has saved him tonight, but not again."

Dralo and Ristun began beating at the wall with their fists, yelling in rage.

"Friends!" Gildareth called, "don't worry about the beast. We have work to do. Quickly, Ristun, take the girl upstairs to her brother's room. Then wake her parents. You and Lianna watch over the children. Send Willerdon down to meet with Dralo and me. We must seek the king's intervention on behalf of the boy, and swiftly. He is in danger, as is all Arvalast. Though he doesn't realize it, if the enemy has his way with him tonight, Arvalast might fall."

"But Gildareth, how could this be?" Ristun asked in astonishment.

"Now is not the time for questions! Hurry!"

Ristun didn't argue, just took Grace from Gildareth's arms and sped away.

"Ristun!" Gildareth yelled after them. "When you get upstairs, start pleading to the king for the boy! Have Grace and Lianna do the same. We will need their help!"

"It will be done!" Ristun said, and carried her around the corner and up the stairs.

"What's going on?" Grace began to whimper, feeling her head for the wound from the fangs but finding nothing.

Ristun didn't answer as he strode up the stairs.

Thirty-Four

Tarin crawled past the broken stair, and soon stood on the third platform. He gazed at the treetops below and could just make out the source of the light, an orb glimmering somewhere near the first platform. Knowing he was close, he began to run toward the next flight of stairs.

The treetops were just barely below him when he reached the second platform. He sped down through the forest canopy, rounding the final bend as he looked down the flight of stairs leading to the first platform. Five drilockk in red hooded cloaks stood on the platform like guards next to an extremely tall man shining so brilliantly white, Tarin could barely stand to look at him.

Tarin hesitated for a moment, and glanced nervously at the five drilockk. He tried to recall why he feared them so much, because in the presence of the shining man and the brilliant red orb, he found fear an exceedingly odd sensation.

"Fear them not," the tall man said in a pleasant, deep voice. "In my presence, they will not harm you." He took a step forward, and the bright aura surrounding him dimmed slightly.

Tarin saw the man was twice his height, with a smooth face and long, shimmering-white hair. Upon his head was a crown that looked as if it had been woven together by thin branches hewn from a tree of silver. Encased within a gap between weavings, directly above the man's forehead, was a bright red jewel. In its center, small, dull and seeming insignificant, was another jewel, this one the color of the noonday sun. Wrapped around the man's shoulders and flowing down to the ground, concealing his feet, long silver robes seemed to emit a gentle light of their own. A white sash held the robes to the man's waist.

"Tarin," the man said gently as his lips curled into a soft smile. He extended the ring-studded hand holding the red and glowing phial. "All you must do to receive this crimson light, the rarest and most powerful of illuminas, is to bow before me and give me your loyalty."

Tarin stared greedily at the object. Around him, the drilockk hissed their approval and made coaxing motions with their long-fingered hands. His hand began reaching toward it, desperate to feel the cool glass within his fingers.

✝ ✝ ✝

Will ran down the stairs, frightened and disheveled.

"What's going on!" he demanded of Dralo and Gildareth, who were speaking in a language he couldn't understand. "Ristun said to bring my illumina and get downstairs quick!"

"Arvalast is in peril." Gildareth responded, his voice grave. "Begin pleading for one of the kidnapped boys, the one named Tarin. He is about to fall to the enemy and meet a fate worse than even the sheriff's."

Will looked at Jebin, who was groaning as if in pain and mouthing something unintelligible. Then he turned to Gildareth. The herald's illumina, which he clenched in his right hand, was growing brighter as he watched.

He pulled out his own illumina and began to plead for Tarin. But then, he paused. "I should get the boy's father. He would want to know about this."

"No," Gildareth said. "The king has already informed him. Even now, he too pleads on his son's behalf."

Will nodded and gripped his light tighter. It began doing something it had never done before, vibrating within his hand.

Its light began to sweep toward Gildareth's, joining with it and growing even brighter. Soon, the room looked as if the sun itself had entered. From the windows, streams of light poured in.

"Others in the town are seeking the king as well," Gildareth whispered. "It has been long since the light has united as strongly as now. I only hope it is enough."

✝ ✝ ✝

Tarin's mind whirred with wild fantasies in which he was no longer timid and weak but held power over many men, even controlling the drilockk that had kidnapped him. But in the midst of these visions, Gildareth's face appeared, dim at first, but like the sun breaking through clouds, the image grew gradually brighter. On it was an expression of sadness so great, Tarin felt tears come to his eyes. For a fleeting moment, he felt terror.

What's going on? he inwardly screamed. *I don't want power. This isn't me.*

He looked up at the tall, shining man, and an unquenchable fear paralyzed him. No longer was he shining and beautiful. Rather, he appeared as a hideous beast, and the crimson light Tarin had, just moments before, been longing for was now being held by scaly hands with large rings upon each finger, each containing a single red jewel. The creature's head was that of a dragon. The snout was long and full of razor-sharp teeth. Smoke drifted from the two nostrils, and above them, two black slits in deep yellow cavities drilled into Tarin. Upon its back was a cloak of crimson with black markings, writings Tarin didn't recognize. Its front was concealed by a large amber breastplate, with the picture of a broken flask centered within a crown containing a single, glowing gem. The beast's loins were girded in a metal similar to that of the breastplate, and its feet were covered with heavy black boots.

Unbearable though it was to do, Tarin looked up, to its face. Unlike a dragon, it stood erect like a man, and was of powerful build. The woven crown on its head was now blood red.

The drilockk around Tarin snarled and howled curses at him, but the kingly beast held out his free hand to silence them, then slowly withdrew the hand holding the crimson light and hid it beneath his cloak.

"You see me for whom I really am. Yes Tarin, I, king of Arvalast, come in many forms. I am not the beautiful picture your father painted for you all those years, lying to you that I was simply a guardian of those who profess loyalty to me. No, Tarin, I do as I please, and elevate those whom I find . . . exceptional. You, boy, were able to thwart my most powerful servants, the vulgheid, with powers not seen in this land for many a year. They told me of you, and I was pleased. Now I stand before you, and one last time, offer you the opportunity to serve me, just as your dear friend Gildareth does."

Tarin looked into the black slits as they bored into him, and a surge of rage pushed aside all the timidity he'd ever known and all the fear he'd ever faced.

"You're right," he said through clenched teeth. "Gildareth does serve a king." He stood and took a step forward. "And you're not that king!"

The beast lifted its arms and roared. The entire tower began to quake and sway. Tarin found it hard to stand, and one of the drilockk was caught so off guard, it toppled over the barrier at the platform's edge.

The dragon-like beast took a quick step toward Tarin. "You dare to defy me?"

"I'll defy anyone, or in your case, any *thing* that would insult Gildareth! I don't know him or his friends well, but he's the first person I've ever met who takes away my fear. And there's no way a man like that would serve something like you! The king Gildareth serves must be quite kind and very powerful to be able to help someone like me."

As he spoke the last words, Tarin felt a stirring in his heart and a strange desire more powerful than any he'd ever had, including his longing for the crimson light. Willingly, he surrendered to that desire, and, undaunted by his foe, stepped forward and gazed up into its hateful eyes. "If Gildareth deems this king so worthy, then so do I!" Then, with more passion than he ever remembered having, he proclaimed, "*He* has my loyalty!"

The creature stood silent for a moment, then reached beneath the cape slung around its shoulders and withdrew a long black sword. "You, like all the followers of the Scourge, have just sentenced yourself to death."

It drew its sword back and slashed. Tarin stood his ground as it sliced through his body, and though he felt no physical pain, his mind reeled with agony.

The sword passed out of him on his other side, and the beast screamed in sadistic pleasure as Tarin fell to his knees. It pulled back the sword and swung it again, this time into Tarin's heart. Again, Tarin's mind felt as if it would explode with pain. He saw himself being killed in so many ways, it would be impossible to count them all. Then he saw his father being hunted and slain by a bear. He saw his house burn down with his mother and sister trapped inside. He saw the drilockk overrunning his town and massacring every villager within their path.

"These are the horrors that will now come to pass because of your insolence, young fool!" bellowed the source of those grizzly images, who stood before him, triumph in its manic eyes.

Tarin clenched his eyes shut and reopened them, trying to put away the horrible imagery. But when they reopened, he looked around and saw the forest burning, and from a nearby tree hung Gildareth, dead. He watched a small flask that dangled from Gildareth's limp hand slide from its slack grip and fall crashing to the forest floor. The light within spilled out and disappeared into the ground. Helpless tears gushed from Tarin's eyes.

The beast roared in laughter and plunged his sword into him again, and again, and again. He writhed on the ground as the thoughts grew ever more terrible. He began to desire death more than this inner torture, and wished a drilockk would come over with a real sword and eliminate his pain.

The beast's sword approached for another blow when a rush of wind blew through the trees, making the tower tremble. Tarin held up his hands in a vain attempt to fend off the strike ... but it never came. He looked up at the creature, and saw, for the first time that night, fear in its eyes. He followed its gaze and saw something unfamiliar approaching from the northeast. It looked almost as if the sun was coming up, though it was still the dead of night.

The tower began to shake harder. A new fear entered his mind: What if the tower fell?

The light grew ever closer. The drilockk started trying to escape down the stairs, but as each one did, they tripped over themselves. At least one more toppled off the tower, though two or three managed to reach the stairs and begin to descend.

"Stop!" The creature shouted to his cowardly servants. They paid no heed. It then looked at Tarin. "If he thinks he can stop me this easily, he is gravely mistaken."

It planted its feet, pulled out the crimson light, and began chanting. The red light flowed like blood out of its container and surrounded the beast in a glowing red sphere.

As the light from the northeast grew nearer, Tarin realized it wasn't the sunrise, but rather a great orb of golden luminance that was racing toward the tower. From it, he heard voices. Some sounded familiar, and as they spoke, his trembling heart began to feel peace. At the same time, the horrible images that had imprisoned him moments before faded, then disappeared.

The world around him quaked violently, and the tower creaked as if it might break into pieces. Relinquishing his last attempts to control what was happening, he smiled and relaxed. Soon, the light swept upon the tower and encased him and the beast in its brilliance. But within this orb, a tiny red globe stood fast, covering the quaking beast it shielded. Tarin's mind grew even more peaceful, and a soft, familiar voice spoke to him.

Hurry Tarin! Go get Sarky and Thief. Bring them out of the tower. It will not stand much longer.

Without questioning the voice, Tarin nodded and ran as fast as he could up the stairs.

Upon reaching the third platform, he came out of the orb of light. The euphoria he'd experienced while encased in its glow left him. Saddened, he wished he could go back into it, but knew he had to save Sarky though he wasn't all that keen on saving Thief.

He hurried to the top as the orb began to collapse onto itself, climbed the ladder leading to the trapdoor and pounded on it.

"Sarky, Thief! Hurry! The tower's about to come down!"

"Are they gone?" Thief yelled, sounding terrified.

"All but one, I think. Just hurry up or we're all going to die!"

The door burst open. "I told you to get rid of them all!"

"It doesn't matter. The light's stopping it. Just come on!"

"What light, little Mouse? I don't see anything."

Tarin looked down. Though the brilliant orb was quickly shrinking, he could still see it.

"What do you mean *what light*? It's right down there."

"I told you, Mouse, I don't see anything."

"Fine. Just come out of there with Sarky so we can get off this stupid tower before it falls."

"Not if one of the shadows is still down there. No, no, no. I'm sorry, but Rat's going to have to die. You remember what I told you. Come back without getting rid of all of them, lose your little friend. It'll serve him right too, after he dirtied me up so badly."

Thief pointed to a large pink stain on his shirt. "The little beast vomited all over me, again and again and—"

"Shut up, you old fool!" a shrill voice screamed from behind. Thief turned around as Sarky's foot smashed into his head. The dagger he was holding fell through the trapdoor and landed next to Tarin's feet. Tarin picked it up as Thief tumbled out the door, landing with a loud thud next to him. Tarin pointed the dagger toward Thief, who groaned and rubbed his head.

"That's a boy, Tarin!" Sarky said, and hurried down the ladder. "Here, give that to me." Tarin handed him the dagger, and Sarky pulled Thief to his feet and held it against his throat.

"Not again," Thief moaned. "Held captive by my own dagger? I've got to stop dropping it all the time."

"I take it this happens often?" Sarky sneered.

"Yes, yes. All the time."

"Well," Sarky said, "looks like little Rat and Mouse are your masters again. Oh, and by the way, you may now call us Master Sarky and Master Tarin. I don't have a problem with it anymore."

"You're feeling better now, hmmm?" Tarin asked Sarky with a little grin.

"Much better. Whatever you did down there worked."

The tower groaned and swayed to one side. This time, it didn't straighten. Tarin looked down. The light was now an extraordinarily concentrated orb below them, and there was no sign of red. But the floor under them shook harder now.

"I wonder what's causing this shaking," Sarky asked.

Tarin realized Sarky couldn't see the light either. "Doesn't matter what's causing it. I just know the tower's going to come down any moment now, and I don't want to be up here when it does."

"Me neither. How about you, Thief? You want to stay up here?"

"No, no, no, no, NO! I want to follow my little masters to safety. Please, take me along. I don't want to fall."

"Fine, but Tarin goes first. You follow him, and I'll follow you." He patted the dagger a couple of times on the palm of his hand, then nudged Tarin. "Lead the way."

Tarin began running down the stairs. Again, he avoided the broken step while warning the others to do the same. They managed to reach the third platform just as he noticed the light disappear below. He hoped that meant the creature was gone.

They hurried to the second platform, ran to the next flight of stairs, and descended. Just as they came back under the forest canopy, a loud crack, and then a grinding sound came to them. Something came crashing through the trees nearby. The topmost part of the tower had broken off.

Thief screamed and ran even faster.

"We're almost there!" Tarin called out as he reached the first platform. To his relief, nothing was there except a tiny glowing phial resting on the ground where the beast had once stood. Without thinking, he picked it up and shoved it into his pocket. At that moment, the tower ceased trembling, and all went quiet. The trio stopped on the platform for a moment.

Don't stop, a voice said to him.

"We're not safe yet," he told the others. "Let's go."

There was another loud crack as one of the tower's corner beams broke in two. The beam splintered further, and the tower leaned toward the broken support. Knowing they had no more time, Tarin headed toward the last flight of stairs. The others followed.

As they descended, their steps grew more and more difficult as the tower continued to topple to one side. They rounded a bend and headed down the last flight.

Tarin's feet hit the dirt and he sprinted away from the tower. As he ran, he looked back. Sarky and Thief were just behind him. After reaching a safe distance from the tower, they fell down just as the broken corner at last gave way, and the tower began to fall. Down it came, crashing through the trees, breaking into pieces as it did. Finally, it smashed onto the forest floor.

Gasping for breath, Thief smiled. "We're saved," he panted. "My two little masters are wise, yes, very wise to help me out of the tower. You'll see. I'll make you prou—"

"Shut up, Thief," Sarky groaned.

"Yes, Master."

THIRTY-FIVE

Grace peeked around the corner of the hall. In the morning sunshine, Gildareth lay on his stomach on a cot in the living room. His arm was hanging off one side; his leg dangled from the other. Two other cots were positioned across from his. They held two other exhausted northerners, Dralo and Ristun.

She tiptoed past the entrance to the living quarters and peeked around the other corner, leaning close to the wooden wall and taking in its soft musty smell. Ristun began to stir and sat up, his cot creaking beneath his weight, and let out an enormous yawn as he stretched his arms. "What a night!" he said as he twisted his torso hard to the right. *Crack!* "Awwww, that feels so much better!"

"Your morning ritual makes me uneasy," Dralo said as Grace watched him rub his weary eyes. "Must you crack your back like that?"

"Of course. And you should too. You would not believe how refreshing it is as the bones shift and pop."

Crack! This one came from Dralo's other direction. And then, from Gildareth's.

"Oh no! Not you too."

Grace found it impossible not to giggle. Dralo and the others turned in her direction and she popped out from her hiding place. "You all are so silly," she said as she took a seat next to Dralo. "Here, let me show you how it's really done." She twisted with a quick jerk. *CRACK!*

"Oh my!" Dralo said as Grace remained in the twisted position.

"Most impressive!" Ristun cheered.

Gildareth applauded. "Well done, child. Well done!"

She stood and curtsied. "Thank you my good sirs. Now, what would you all like for breakfast?"

All three warriors' eyes grew bright. They gave her their orders, and she skipped out of the living room and headed toward the kitchen. Though they'd lowered their voices, as she prepared their food, she could still hear them as they spoke.

"Remarkable!" Gildareth said. "That dear girl was mercilessly tortured last night by a vulgheid, and now look at her! It's as if it never even happened."

"I haven't seen anyone recover that quickly from an attack for centuries," Dralo remarked. "Normally, those bitten by a vulgheid walk in misery for weeks before they're able to conquer the depression."

"It doesn't surprise me," Ristun added. "You should have heard her last night after you sent me upstairs. When we and her mother got into Dibbs' room, she insisted I let her go to her room so she could get her illumina. I obliged, and when she returned, she began beseeching the king for the two kidnapped boys with fervency I haven't seen since the Battle of Illuminara. Her light grew so bright, it nearly blinded me. Even her mother seemed shocked."

Grace set a plate on a counter and smiled, hoping the men didn't know she was listening. But she could hardly contain her delight at how highly they seemed to think of her.

"That *is* interesting about her illumina becoming that bright," Gildareth said. "And how did the boy react?"

Ristun looked away, seeming a little embarrassed. "He hid under his covers and whimpered."

Grace rolled her eyes. Dibbs *had* been rather pathetic.

"That's not good," Gildareth said. "I'd hoped the urgency of the situation might resonate with the lad. It was so pressing, I believe all of Woodend could feel it."

"Indeed," Dralo said. "When I looked out the window last night, I saw the light of the king twinkling in many a window. But I could also sense a great anger rising up within the town. *They* could feel it too, and now know that some in Woodend are capable of direct communication with the throne. All ties to the king haven't been cut off, as *they* undoubtedly planned."

The men were speaking more softly now. Grace abandoned the food and slunk closer to the kitchen's entrance, careful to knock a spoon against the plate she was holding every few moments. The men either didn't notice, or didn't care that she heard.

"I feel that Wrathar is prepared to begin his attack upon this forest and this town," Gildareth said. "It will come in many forms, both direct and indirect. But every battle he'll wage will have one purpose: to destroy this city and pave a way to the north, while eliminating any chance of the prophecy's fulfillment."

Dralo said, "Do you believe he's beginning to take the prophecy seriously now? In that, perhaps he's trying to determine the identity of the three servants and three warriors?"

Gildareth nodded. "And thankfully, their identities haven't yet been fully revealed to anyone, even me. Wrathar, like us all, can only guess at who the six will be. This is both to our advantage, and against it. Since he doesn't know their identities, he can't seek them out and destroy them. But neither can we hide them and protect them. Though, even if we did know who they were, it's not the king's will that we shelter them. They must ally themselves with the king on their own accord, and fight their own battles on his behalf. We may help them when the need arises, but we cannot fight for them."

Stirring sounds came from upstairs. Grace returned to her food preparation, knowing her parents would be down soon. But she wondered at the men's strange talk. Who was Wrathar? And what of these six? Did it have something to do with what happened to her last night, and the stories she'd overheard the day before?

"I must leave after breakfast," Gildareth said, speaking loud enough now that Grace didn't have to strain to hear him. "I'll meet with one of the emissaries of Macalum. She's searching for the way the drilockk have been getting into the city, but I believe she's searching for something more. I intend to help her find it."

"And what of Jebin?" Dralo asked. "Will he be safe left alone?"

"I can do nothing more for him at the moment. He is under a curse of his own making now, and can only escape it when he wills. For now, Dralo, keep watch over his chamber and ensure that no more shadows enter his room. Ristun, please go to Kandis' household and see how they fare. If they are in need of aid, give it to them."

Grace stirred the fire in the stove and set down a pan. With a few quick flips of her wrist, she had four eggs sitting yolk-up on the iron.

✝ ✝ ✝

Will and Lianna descended the stairs. He could smell food, and knew Grace was already busy in the kitchen. The thought of his daughter lightened his heart.

He walked by the living quarters, offered a bow to his guests while Lianna slumped into a nearby chair, and hurried to see how Grace was faring after the previous night.

He entered the kitchen, and their eyes met. They stood for a moment, both smiling, and she ran into his arms. "My perfect little princess," he said as he kissed her head. "How are you doing this morning?"

"Excellent, Father." She slid out of his arms and went back to the stove. "I've made you and the guests some breakfast. It'll be done soon."

A scoff came from the direction of the stairs, then some mumbling. "Perfect little princess, ridiculous. They don't know what a brat she really—"

"Dibbs, come to breakfast," Lianna called from her chair. Will had a good mind to run over and smack the boy, but forced the thought from his mind. Instead, he walked over and stroked Grace's hair. "I wouldn't talk to Dibbs this morning. Sounds like he's in a bad mood."

"Typical."

"Now Grace . . ."

"I'm sorry, Father. I'll be nice." She climbed onto a stool to fetch another plate.

Will entered the living quarters as Dibbs took his seat and began mumbling to himself, words Will couldn't make out. Aside from that, few words were spoken, and when Grace brought out the food, even fewer. When the northerners finished eating, which they did remarkably fast, Gildareth and Ristun took their leave while Dralo excused himself to Jebin's room. Now Will was alone with his family, and none of them, not even Grace, looked cheery.

"Why did that stupid fellow have to come into my room last night?" Dibbs asked though a mouthful of sausage. "I barely got any sleep."

"He wanted you, Grace and me in the same room, so he could make sure nothing bad happened to us," Lianna answered. "Something terribly odd was going on last night."

"What was it? I didn't notice anything out of the ordinary," he cut his eyes at Grace, "except for her stupid conversation with that illumina of hers."

"I was asking the king to help the lost boys!" she snapped. "And you should be too. After all, you were kidnapped with them for a while."

"Yeah, and left to die," Dibbs said, shooting an angry glance at his father.

"Again, I'm so sorry for that," Will said. "When Hamlin informed me you were kidnapped, I panicked, and my mind . . . well, shut down. I wandered around for a while completely disillusioned, until Ella found me in the alley and told me monsters were prowling about on our road. My fear for you all overwhelmed me, and I went to help."

"And you completely forgot that I was already kidnapped by those monsters! You obviously don't care much for me."

"Dibbs, I care about you. I'd just had too many things hit me at once that evening. But that's no excuse. I failed you. I admit it. And I'm sorry."

"Sure you are," Dibbs muttered, poking at his last piece of bacon.

"If it makes you feel any better, last night I realized how terrible a person, and father, I've been lately. I've let my worries for this town take up far too much of my time and energy. But not anymore. Your mother and I are asking the king to help me do better."

"A lot of good that'll do. He's never helped yet."

Will's eyes grew wide with anger. But before he could rebuke Dibbs, Lianna gave him a stern glance of warning.

"And what do you mean by that, Dibbs?" he asked softly. "How has the king failed you? You've never before wanted anything to do with him."

"You wouldn't understand. And you never will. You'll always be too busy with the town, or somebody else, to know what I've been going through the past year." Tears shone in his eyes. "They . . .Never mind."

"*They?* Whom are you talking about?"

Dibbs shoved his plate away and ran upstairs. Will and Lianna looked at each other in bewilderment. Grace, on the other hand, sat pensive. "Mother," she said softly. "I think I might know what's making Dibbs act that way."

"Really, Grace?" Will said, trying to sound respectful. "So, what do you think's making your brother act the way he is?"

"He must've seen one of those shadow creatures. The ones that give a person terrible nightmares. I saw one last night, and it was awful."

Lianna glanced at Will, worried.

"I saw it last night, with Jebin," Grace explained. "It was like a shadow, but there was no one around to cast it. And it had nasty yellow eyes. Sort of like a cat's. And fangs too."

"Fangs?" Will said, surprised.

"Yes. And when it bit me—"

"It bit you!"

"Yes, it bit me. And when it did, I saw all sorts of terrible things. If it wasn't for Mr. Gildareth and his friends . . . I wasn't sure if I'd be able to forget all those things I saw. But after last night, and after Mother and I talked to the king in Dibbs' room, I can't remember much of what I saw. I just know it was awful."

Will grew quiet. "Did you hear any voices . . . threats, perhaps?"

Grace thought for a moment. "Yes."

"Would you allow your mother and me to speak privately for a moment?"

Grace nodded. "I'll start the dishes." She picked up her empty plate and headed toward the kitchen.

Will whispered, "Lianna, do you remember what Gildareth told us, about the drilockk and the vulgheid?"

"Yes, and do you know what I think? I think Grace saw a vulgheid last night."

Will nodded. "That's exactly what I thought too. But it seems out of the three of us, only she can see them. After all, I'm fairly sure there were some on the roof the night the drilockk attacked you two. They were invading my mind somehow." He thought for a moment. "But she didn't mention seeing them then."

"No, she mustn't have. We've talked about that night numerous times now, and she's mentioned nothing about shadow creatures."

"But apparently she's seen one of them. And it was in the room with Jebin. Sounded as if it was trying to harm him further, if that's even possible."

"What are they so interested in Jebin for, and how do they keep getting into the house?"

"I don't know, but I intend to find out. I think it's time for me to start asking our guests some questions. Gildareth's told us much, but I'm not satisfied. He keeps saying there's a battle brewing on the horizon, but one that isn't just physical. And it certainly seems he's right. Jebin's fallen prey to a strange curse while in the forest. Our daughter is seeing shadow creatures—"

"Dibbs keeps getting those scratches on his back," Lianna said.

"Yes, that's right! I'd forgotten." Something began burning in his pocket. He grimaced and pulled out his illumina. By the time he got it out, it had cooled. "What's that all about," he muttered.

"What do you mean?"

"It just . . . started burning."

She scooted her chair closer to his and gazed at the illumina. "When did it start?"

"When you mentioned Dibbs' scratches."

Lianna leaned forward, looking excited. "Exactly! That must be it."

"What are you talking about?"

She stood and pointed up the stairs. "The vulgheid must be the ones scratching Dibbs each night! It has to be them. What else could be sneaking into his room but some sort of invisible phantom?" She began pacing. "That's why Gildareth had me, Ristun and Grace stay together in Dibbs' room. He figured that with all the evil going on last night, Dibbs was in even greater danger than usual."

"From the vulgheid?"

"Yes. That has to be it." She sat back down and leaned toward him. "Something strange *was* going on last night. I could feel it. Couldn't you? It was so oppressive."

Will thought hard. "Yes, I certainly felt something. But I thought it was my fear at hearing Grace's screams, and watching the northerners running every which way."

"It was more than just that. It was the vulgheid." She looked out the window. "I'll bet the forest is full of them. They're probably not only here, but in Lockspell, and Mahotholin as well. From the way Gildareth's been talking, I think all of Arvalast is a hive for the creatures."

"But Gildareth's said the walls are supposed to keep them out of the cities. Although he mentioned they've been weakening. . . ." He remembered something he'd heard the emissaries of Macalum say at the council meeting. "Aliah and Dirfin," he whispered.

"What?"

He'd forgotten she was still in the room. He shook his head. "Aliah and Dirfin. Two members of yesterday's council. They said they were going to inspect the wall. I thought it was for a hole the drilockk were using to get in. But perhaps it was for . . . perhaps they're looking for where the vulgheid are getting in."

He looked around to make sure they were alone and continued. "You know, Bolard was always worried about the wall before he went crazy. Remember?"

Anxiety swept over Lianna's face. "You're right."

They sat quietly for a moment. Finally, Will spoke. "Where's Dralo?"

"He's attending to Jebin."

He picked up his illumina and held it tight. "Although Gildareth has told us some things, I want to delve deeper into this unseen war we're clearly becoming part of." He blinked a couple of times, and his eyes grew misty. "My family's been attacked enough, and it's got to stop."

He brushed away the tears and managed a smile. "I wish those warriors of the prophecy were here right now. We could certainly use them."

Lianna chuckled. "Don't forget, the servants must come first."

"Wish that ridiculous prophecy would change its mind. Warriors then servants, that would be better."

"Oh, get out of here and talk to Dralo, you silly man. But don't forget, tell me everything. I don't like it when you leave me out."

He gave her a tight smile. "I don't think Gildareth does either. Nor the king. And I'm agreeing more and more with them each day. We need to act as one to get through this. And not just us. Our whole family."

"We will," Lianna said softly. "We will."

With that, he patted the illumina and put it back into his pocket. With a sigh, he turned and headed toward the closed door to Jebin's room, wondering how responsive Dralo would be to his prying. It didn't matter; he needed answers.

THIRTY-SIX

"Get up, my little ones. Get up! Hurry, the morning's getting old. Look, the sun's already nearing the treetops. Time to go."

Tarin bolted upright, and the first thing he felt was the aching in his back. After the tower had fallen, he, Thief and Sarky had set up camp on a boulder similar to the one he and Sarky climbed the day before.

Nearby, Sarky groaned and tried to rub away his own stiffness. "Who picked this idiotic spot?" he mumbled.

"You did, my little master," Thief said while he followed a path off the boulder. "Thought it would be safe. Wouldn't listen to poor Thief's advice to get back to the road."

Sarky gave a groaning sigh. "With all the monsters prowling around, it doesn't matter where we are. Eventually we're going to be skewered by a drilockk, eaten by that winged beast, or driven mad by a vulgheid."

"You shouldn't speak so lightly of these matters," Thief scolded as he reached the bottom of the boulder and began picking up sticks and banging them on the ground.

"And why should I be careful what I say about vulgheid and such? It isn't going to change the fact they want to kill me and Tarin, now is it?"

"Perhaps not. Perhaps not." Thief bounded back up the boulder, wielding a new walking stick. "But it likely wouldn't hurt to take the evil in this land more seriously. After all, I'm not sure how you two have survived so long, considering how foolish you are. Allow me to demonstrate."

With a quick swing of his arm, he knocked Sarky alongside the head. The boy slumped to the ground unconscious.

"Really, my little Rat, you're too quick to trust." He turned to Tarin, smiling meanly. "You probably should have set up guard around me during the night. After all, I threatened to kill Rat when we were trapped on the tower. Who's to say I wouldn't do it again?"

He bent over Sarky's body and retrieved his dagger, then pointed it at Tarin. "All right, Mouse. Looks like little Thief is the master again. And this time, I plan to stay the master."

Tarin stared at Thief through wide eyes. "I . . . I thought you'd changed after the tower collapsed." He stepped forward and glowered at the scrawny man. "I thought you were grateful we saved you!"

"Stay where you are!" Thief yelled. He leaned over Sarky's body and placed the dagger against the boy's throat. "Look familiar? Yes, yes it does. Again, if you want your friend to be all right, you need to cooperate. There's something special about you, Mouse. It's not every day I meet someone who can fend off the crimson light."

"What do you mean?"

"Do you think I'm a fool? I know who you are. You're a servant of the king."

Tarin's face grew red at the same instant he sensed the minute weight in his pocket. He realized it was the illumina he'd picked up while escaping the collapsing tower.

"Though I'm still not sure how you were able to escape the sentinel."

To distract the man while he tried to think of a way out of this, he said, "Sentinel? What's that again?"

"It's a vulgheid lord, and more evil than anything you'll ever come across. Had to be one of those on the tower last night. Only they and their human servants can wield the crimson light."

He pulled Sarky to his feet and held his limp body close. "So, how did you do it anyway? Most people, even those who follow the king of the north, succumb to the crimson light without a fight. Its lure is overwhelming to most. Even my father, the seer, was near overcome by its power."

"I don't know how I escaped," Tarin said honestly. "There was this big orb of light that came and surrounded me and the sentinel. Then . . . I don't know, I just came to my senses."

Thief gave a knowing nod. "Ah, the others."

"What others? What do you mean?"

"Certainly you don't think you're the lone servant of the king living in these woods."

"I'm not even his servant . . . not really."

Thief began cackling, so hard he almost dropped Sarky to the ground. "Yes, yes, you're a funny one you are. Not a servant? No mere man can stand against the crimson light and keep his sanity as you have. Though, you now provide an argument against that." He laughed even harder.

Tarin frowned. "Go ahead, make fun of me. Everyone else does. Even that boy you're holding right now sometimes."

"What, you mean you two aren't friends?" Thief asked through blood-shot eyes.

"Well, yes. I suppose. But we certainly didn't use to be."

Thief looked at Tarin and grew solemn. "Hmmm, you act like friends. Oh well, I don't care what you two are. All I know is that when I hold Rat hostage, Mouse listens to whatever I say. So Mouse, here is our plan. I don't like these woods. I thought I would. Thought I might be able to get away from the drilockk up here. But no, no, no. The stupid beasts are here too, and even more aggressive than the ones down south. So, time to return south, then look for some secluded area to steal, eat, and hide."

"I don't want to go south with you. I want to go home!"

"Oh, you *do* want to go south. Otherwise," he held the dagger closer to Sarky's neck, "*slit*. Blood everywhere. I don't like the sight of blood. Never have. So don't make me do it."

Tarin's face grew hot, but he knew there was nothing he could do except wish he and Sarky had thought of keeping watch on Thief rather than believing he was repentant. "All right. I'll do what you want," he said, though inwardly, he kept planning how to later rescue Sarky and escape Thief for the last time.

"Good, good. You'll be useful to me, as will Rat. With you two, I'll be able to avoid the shadows *and* the drilockk, and with a little luck, the bostt."

"I'm not as strong as you seem to think," Tarin said. "At home, I'm considered the most timid boy in Woodend, and the biggest coward."

"You're too modest. I know what you're capable of."

He was pleasantly surprised by the compliment, even though it was coming from a complete scoundrel. So when Thief pointed out the direction he wanted him to follow, he obliged, forgetting that poor Sarky's unconscious body was being dragged around by a scrawny lunatic holding a dagger.

After an hour of walking, Sarky stirred. "Tarin ... what's, what's happening?"

Thief shoved Sarky forward. The boy rolled along the ground a few times before coming to a stop.

"Hey!" Tarin yelled, rushing to Sarky. "Why'd you do that?"

"Because I can." Thief glared at Sarky. "So Rat, you're awake. Good, my poor arms were getting quite tired, yes."

"What's he talking about?" Sarky asked, still seeming disoriented.

"Thief's in charge again. He's got the knife. We have to do what he says."

Sarky pulled himself to his feet and rubbed a large knot on his head. "Ouch! How'd that get there?"

Thief snickered. "My walking stick's not fond of you, no, no."

"Why you—!" He wobbled toward Thief, anger masking his obvious pain.

Thief pointed the dagger at Sarky. "No, no, no! Don't come any closer. My dagger doesn't like you either."

Sarky stopped. "Tarin, we don't have to take this. Let's just get out of here."

"And where will you go, I wonder?" Thief said. "For the last hour, I've taken you deep into the forest. How will you find your way home without me? Yes. How will you keep from getting lost?"

"We were doing just fine before!" Sarky blurted. "All we have to do is head northeast, and we'll eventually get back to Woodend."

"Yes, but how do you know you're west of Woodend? You could be east."

"Then we'd have crossed the road while I was out. Tarin, did we cross?"

Thief laughed. "The road connecting Woodend with Lockspell is dirt and not easily spotted. I might've taken you both across, and Mouse would never have noticed."

A lump formed in Tarin's throat. Thief was right. Many dirt patches they'd crossed could have been the road to Woodend.

"Ahh, Mouse has gone silent. Yes, he must know Master is right."

"Sarky, I'm . . . I'm sorry. I'm not sure if we crossed the path or not."

"How could you be so stupid! Any idiot could tell if we crossed the path. It would be a big dirt road heading in two directions!"

"We crossed a lot of dirt patches. I just didn't happen to think to look both ways to see if they were roads."

"Your stupid head was down, wasn't it? It's always down when you're feeling scared, or afraid of people. You didn't look up once during the last hour, did you?"

"No! I didn't! Thief had a dagger to your throat, and I was trying to think of a way we could escape!"

Sarky groaned. "And now we have the chance, and we can't! Great thinking, Tarin. Great thinking."

"I . . . I hate you Sarky!"

"I couldn't care less!"

In an uncommon fit of rage, Tarin lunged toward Sarky, fists flailing. They started to tussle. Thief hurried over to break them up. "Rat, Mouse, stop it! Stop fighting! They're going to hear—!"

"You're never going to insult me again!" Tarin roared. He pulled back his arm, preparing to hit Sarky in the jaw, when Sarky spun out from under him and kicked Thief in the shin. Thief howled in pain and toppled over, and Sarky was on top of him, biting the hand holding the dagger. When he dropped it, Sarky snatched it up and placed it against Thief's chest.

"Sorry, Tarin. I didn't really mean all that stuff. Just wanted to be master again, that's all."

Tarin watched in awe as Sarky pulled the now whimpering Thief to his feet. "Won't make the mistake of not keeping an eye on *you* anymore," Sarky said.

"But . . ." Tarin stuttered.

"Don't worry about it. I'm good at getting out of tight spots. Got to do it all the time in Woodend."

"No, not again!" Thief screamed. "I won't listen to you anymore. I won't serve a rat!"

"I'm afraid you've no choice, you little—"

Thief punched Sarky in the jaw and bolted away. Sarky grabbed his mouth and spat out some blood. "Tha' filthy piece o' no good. . . . Go ge' 'im 'arin."

"Why? Let him leave. He's been nothing but trouble from the start."

"Bu' how will we find our way back?"

"Go north, like we were doing before."

"Bu' I don' really know if tha'll work. We could come ou' miles from home."

"Shut up Sarky, you sound ridiculous."

"My mouf is blee'ing, s'upid!"

"Then keep it shut. Let's just rest for a little while, then head back north. I'm sure we'll be able to find our way."

"Why the sunnen faith?"

Tarin wasn't sure how to respond. He simply felt more assured than normal. Then, at the side of his body, he felt a warm touch. Only it wasn't a touch, because no one was close enough to touch him. He felt the warm spot and noticed a lump. Then he remembered. He was carrying around his own illumina. He hadn't thought about it much since picking it up. But now his mind, searching for answers, gave him no choice but to pull the little glass object out.

It glowed gently, discernable even in the sunlight breaking through the trees. Other than the light within, it was rather plain. Just a phial, transparent and without a scratch. He dangled it in front of his eyes, wondering what secrets lay within.

"Hey, where you get tha'? I didn' know you 'ad one'a those."

Tarin's eyes locked onto Sarky's, suddenly sheepish, he stuffed the phial back into his pocket and turned away.

"Sure, don' wan' to 'ell me anything, huh? Fine. Bu' unless tha' lil flask can help us find our way, i's worfless."

"I wish you'd realize how stupid you sound right now."

Sarky growled and began nursing his wound. After about an hour of quiet rest, he was able to speak without pain. They turned north, or what they thought was north based on the sun, hoping to this time finally get back to Woodend without meeting any annoying thieves or terrible enemies.

They traveled steadily for about three hours before reaching an impassable region of thickets. At last, they chose a bypass that seemed to go uphill, found a raspberry bush and greedily purged the entire plant of its ripe berries. Their hunger pacified for the moment, they pressed on up steeper and steeper hills, until at last they stopped before what might have once been a large path, though it was now overgrown with high grass.

"Do you think this is the road to Woodend?" Tarin asked.

"Of course not. The road to town is well kept. This hasn't been traveled for years. But look, it seems to go from north to south. If we follow it that way," he pointed north, where it skirted up a sharp incline before disappearing over the top, "we should eventually get out of the forest and into the flatlands. From there, we can work our way back to Woodend."

So off they went, their tired legs groaning beneath them as they started the climb. Fortunately, the road became more level later on. Every now and then, whenever there was a break in the leafy canopy toward the west, they could see the tall hills that made up the Forest Mountains.

The path began to descend sharply into a particularly dark patch of woods. Tarin could feel his heart begin to race as the light of the late afternoon was stripped of its power by the heavy foliage surrounding him. Sarky also seemed nervous, because he'd slowed down.

"Hey Tarin, why don't you try to use that light of yours? It might actually be of a little use here."

Tarin reached into his pocket and pulled it out. Unlike before, it wasn't warm, and only the faintest luminance flickered within.

"What's wrong with it?" Sarky groaned.

"I don't know."

"Don't you know how it works?"

"I'm not even sure how I got it. I'm not even sure if it's mine."

"Well put it away then. It's worthless."

But Tarin wanted to try something first. He brought it close to his lips and whispered, "Gildareth." The flicker within grew steady and bright, chasing away the murkiness of the forest along with his apprehension.

Sarky felt it too. "Tarin, what did you *do?*"

He said nothing, only smiled.

"Fine, keep your little secrets. Just come up here with me, and we'll walk together. I don't like the feeling of this place. I want to stay as close to that little light of yours as you'll let me."

Tarin obliged, and together, they pressed onward. After less than a mile, they walked into a thinner area of woods full of young trees. A little farther on, they entered a vast clearing. Both boys stood agape at what lay before them. In the treeless valley were the ruins of what looked like a city. Battered remains of houses lay everywhere, covered in vines and thorns. Roads long ago devoured by greenery wound through the labyrinth of demolished buildings. To the west, the Forest Mountains cast their deepening shadow over the old city.

"Undertree," Sarky whispered. "This used to be Undertree."

THÍRTY-SEVEN

W ill knocked on the spare room's door. A moment later, the door opened. Dralo stood in the entrance.

"Uh, hello," Will said. He could feel beads of sweat on his forehead.

"Something tells me you didn't come here just to say hello," Dralo replied.

"Well, no. That's right. Actually, I came to . . . well, to ask you some things."

"Hmmm, I can think of many things you'd likely wish to know." Dralo looked behind him at Jebin's slumbering form. "Not the nicest place to talk, considering your sheriff's plight. But I have to stay in case he's attacked again. If not for your daughter's unintentional intervention last night, he might already be dead."

"You mean he's going to die?"

"If things don't change, yes, he will. We've tried to help mend his great wounds, to no avail. Something else is needed, something hidden to us."

Will looked at his sheriff, feeling both concern and confusion. He looked up at Dralo. "I've come to ask some questions, some of which are about Jebin's sickness. May I inquire of you?"

Dralo stepped aside. "Come in. Gildareth said he thought you were near ready to learn more about the unseen war. Mind you, I won't be able to answer everything you ask. Some things, I don't yet know. Others, the king might desire for you to discover on your own."

"I'll take whatever information I can. I've known for a while something terrible was looming on the horizon. I just didn't realize from how deep those troubles came."

Dralo's shoulders stiffened. "What do you already know?"

"Gildareth has already told me of the prophecy, and how Wrathar is planning to destroy Maplelake Forest, particularly this town." At Dralo's waved hand, Will took a seat in the darkest corner of the small room. "And

I know something Gildareth doesn't. I know how Wrathar will likely carry out his plot."

Dralo raised his eyebrow. "Perhaps I will have some questions for you too." He sat on a bench near Will. "But I will answer first. Where shall I begin?"

"Start with Jebin, and this curse he seems to be inflicted with."

"He's no longer under the curse. Gildareth lifted it a few days ago. Now, he is under a curse of his own making. Despair has overwhelmed him. He wants to die. And death would take him, if not for the flicker of life deep within him. It refuses to succumb to the sheriff's wishes. *It* does not want to die."

"And what is *it?*"

Dralo hesitated only an instant. "We've searched and searched, but haven't been able to discover what this bit of hope is stemming from. The king refuses to reveal it. It appears we won't find out until the time is right. But all of us, including Gildareth, believe that when the source of this hope at last reveals itself, Jebin will awaken. Then, he will have choices to make. To be exact, will he abandon the king for good, or return as a loyal follower?"

Will shook his head in confusion. "Why would he want to forfeit his allegiance to the king? He's always been a devout servant."

"Jebin's been under the constant affliction of the enemy's lies for years. That, at least, we could determine. Wrathar seemed to have implemented a long-term plan of torture for the sheriff some time ago, and is now trying to consummate it. If he succeeds, he will wholly defeat Jebin. And by doing so, will strike a terrible blow to our cause. It seems Jebin is vitally important not just to you, Governor, but to the throne as well. He is to play an important role in the battles to come. If he survives."

"What can I do, then?"

"Seek the king on behalf of your friend. Plead with the throne to allow the remaining flicker of hope to grow into a burning fire. Only then will the sheriff be capable of coming out of this terrible state of despair."

Will stared at Jebin's pale face. Though it looked calmer than it had in some time, the eyes were still clenched shut, as if he was in much pain. He didn't avert his gaze until Dralo interrupted the silence.

"Have you other questions?"

Will shook his thoughts from Jebin and remembered something else he'd wanted to ask. "What's wrong with my son? Gildareth told us to begin seeking the king on his behalf, and we have. But it's not helping. Instead, he's getting worse, and he hates me more than ever. He's terribly angry with me for not looking for him after he was kidnapped. I tried to explain that

I'd all but lost my mind after the riot. Too much happened at once. I was overwhelmed. Is that such a sin?"

Dralo grinned. "If it were, all men would be doomed."

Will wasn't amused. "Seriously sir, why can't Dibbs understand that I love him? Why doesn't he realize that I've been pressing him to give his loyalty to the king for all these years for his own good?"

"He is angrier at the king than he is at you. In fact, he blames the king for your seeming disinterest in him."

"I'm not disinterested in him! Why would he think that?"

"Because the village has kept you so wrapped up in its many meaningless problems and squabbles, you've spent little time with your family, particularly your son."

"But . . . it's my duty. I'm the king's servant."

"Indeed. But the king expects a father, even one that is a governor, to first look after his family. Nothing, save your loyalty to the king, should ever get in the way of that."

Will began fidgeting with his hands, wanting to grab hold of something to calm his rising anger. "Don't I have enough problems without getting rebuked all the time? First my wife says I'm not doing enough, then Gildareth, now you. I'm trying to do better . . . no, not trying. Gildareth says that's part of my problem. He says to simply rely on the king to help me. So I've been practicing that, but certainly I can't improve overnight."

"But you have."

"What?"

"Gildareth informs me that the king is pleased with you. You must be doing something right."

"Huh?"

"Does a compliment surprise you? I said what I did only because you asked what was wrong with your son. So I told you what *was* wrong with you. If you continue on your current path, you are no longer the problem. A monumental battle has already been won, and Wrathar was dealt a terrible blow. You, Governor, dealt this blow. He meant to destroy your family, and by doing so, destroy you. Woodend would then be without a leader in the upcoming times of trouble. Wrathar would be handed the entire forest without resistance. Now, things will be different."

Will couldn't help but feel a little pleased. He hadn't been directly complimented for so long.

Dralo leaned closer to him. "Though there is still one more battle to be won before all is well with your family. Your son now has to have a change of heart. That is why you must seek the king's aid. You cannot change Dibbs' heart on your own."

Will fought anxious tears. "Is there hope for him?"

"Hope is something that can never be fully defeated."

Will felt renewed strength rush into him, invigorating him. Suddenly, seeing Dibbs changed wasn't just an impossible dream. He stood and began to pace the room.

"All right. So my family's starting to come together. Or at least, I'm not hurting it anymore. That's good, quite good. Now we can start planning for Wrathar's less subtle attacks. For instance, why did he attack my family on the roof that night and kidnap Dibbs in the first place?"

"I think it is because of Gildareth's coming. The enemy foresaw that his plans to quietly destroy you might fail. His hand was forced. Though he would rather have seen you torn apart from within. He loves to see the king's servants at war with one another, particularly within the family unit. But he will settle for simply killing his enemies when his more intricate plans are on the verge of failure."

Willerdon suddenly felt less elated. "You mean my family's still in danger?"

"Yes, but not just yours. Anyone who serves the king right now stands out in the enemy's eye as a plague that must be eliminated. Kandis and his family are in danger, along with Clooney and all others serving the king in this forest. You must all stand together under one banner if you wish to resist Wrathar's attacks."

"But Gildareth told me not to fear the attacks from the drilockk, or to worry about the armies rumored to be south of here."

"He wanted to first ensure your family was your ally, rather than a distraction. During battle, you don't want to be stabbed from both the front and back. You always want to focus on what's coming at you."

"Then drilockk are coming, and vulgheid?"

"The vulgheid are already here. They've been here for some time. But, they aren't yet rallied as one. At present, they're simply bent on causing as much unrest as possible within Woodend. Consider the riot. They were involved, I am sure. And the people's dislike for you? Again, the work of vulgheid. Though they cannot force people to adhere to their commands, the hearts of this town are blackened enough to give them great strength. Many in this village are nothing more than the creatures' pawns. The shadows speak, and they obey. Yet, who these people are isn't always easily determined. So be wary."

"Why can't we see them?"

"Some can, but not all. There used to be a powerful group of warriors of the king called the spectril. All spectril could see them, but they're now extinct. The last one died not long ago."

"But my daughter can see them. How? Is she a spectril?"

Dralo smiled. "No, but she certainly has the courage of one."

"How can she see them if she's not a spectril?"

"Some are more in tune to the shadow's devices than others, enabling them to see the cloak of darkness in which they often conceal themselves. I don't believe she saw them in their true form though." His eyes became distant. "It is much more hideous."

"Why was it here anyway?"

"To kill Jebin. Apparently its master, an even more powerful vulgheid, could sense that Jebin was still holding to fleeting hope. Given time, the vulgheid would have been able to stamp it out."

"So Grace saved him?"

"In a manner of speaking, yes."

"Still, I wish she didn't have to go through that. I'm really not sure how she's taking it so well."

"Even Gildareth is astonished. The beast bit her, which means it discovered her greatest fears and flooded her mind with terrible images of their fulfillment. Yet, she seems to have forgotten them all. That, my friend, is a remarkable feat. Even the spectril would take many a month to forget the bite of a vulgheid."

Will smiled. "My little princess. Stronger than a spectril. That's amazing."

"Yes, it is. But guard her carefully. The enemy now knows she is of much tougher make than he imagined. Until last night, he only saw her as a means to destroy you. Now, she is a threat to him."

"If he ever tried to hurt her again I would—"

"Allow the king to aid you, I hope. You cannot fight these shadows on your own."

"Yes, yes, of course. Then together, we will tear the filthy things to pieces."

"Do not take them lightly, Governor. They're much more horrible than you realize. If the need arises, they will abandon their shadow and be quick to demonstrate what they're capable of. They, along with their master, destroyed the greatest city in Arvalast once, Illuminara. They can and will destroy Woodend unless we resist. But I don't think they will attack the forest as they did Illuminara. At least not at the start. Wrathar has learned that subtle schemes tend to work better, as you've seen. Before he permits an attack, he will try to destroy Woodend from within."

"And as I said earlier, I think I know how he plans to do it."

Dralo's face brightened. "Ahh, yes. Now it's time to ask questions of my own. So Governor, what do you believe Wrathar will do?"

"Have you heard of the governor before me? Bolard?"

Dralo nodded. "And I know of his Royal Decree and Jebin's victory against him."

"Temporary victory, I fear." Will peered around the room, looking to make sure they were alone. "Bolard is coming back."

Dralo remained emotionless. "And how do you know?"

"The townspeople have been talking about him being in the forest for quite some time now. First, some merchants told me of a man named Bolard residing in Mahotholin. Their description fits him perfectly. They said he'd come from the south on secret business. That was a few months ago. Later, I heard he'd come to Lockspell. And sorry to say, others did too. Rumors began spreading throughout town, creating unrest. Animosity against me grew as people thought they might again be governed by their precious Bolard. It is almost as if they've forgotten about the Royal Decree."

Dralo considered this. "Not all in this town are followers of the king. They would not care about those with illuminas having to give them up."

"Yes, I understand. But even some with illuminas want Bolard back. This is what disturbs me most."

Dralo nodded. "Please continue."

"The last piece of evidence of Bolard's return came from the emissaries from Macalum. At the council meeting, they told me of their captain. He had led them and a group of drilockk slayers into the forest to defend the towns. That's where I heard of the drilockk army. If the occasion were different, it would've brought me some peace to know Macalum had sent warriors to protect us from an invasion. But when I heard the name of their captain . . . it was Bolard. He's apparently worked his way into a position of power in Macalum, and now he's returned to take back what used to be his: the governorship of Woodend. And he's not alone. He's got a whole battalion of warriors with him, two of which are within the town as we speak."

Dralo ran his fingers through his hair. "I will tell Gildareth this when he returns. At this moment, he's looking for the two you mentioned, intent on helping them find something."

"Help them? Why?"

"Don't be concerned. It is with a matter that will help protect your city from Wrathar, not help Bolard retake it. And even if these emissaries are loyal to Bolard, I don't think they know of any malevolent plans on his part. He's likely using them."

"Still, I don't trust them. Anyone who serves Bolard is not my friend."

"Be careful, Will. Even Bolard is but a pawn of a greater evil, as you well know. I must confirm to you that the emissaries are correct about the drilockk army south of here. I myself saw it once, before it disappeared."

"How could an entire army disappear?"

"Wrathar is more cunning than any other creature in Arvalast. Somehow, he's found a way."

Willerdon pictured Woodend surrounded by a sea of red cloaks. Lightning flashed overhead, and at the gate, tall and thin, Bolard stood, grinning menacingly. At last, he looked back up at Dralo. "Without Jebin, without aid of some sort, I have no idea how to prepare for what's to come. Dralo, I'm going to need help. Obviously, I can't simply wait for Jebin to wake up and become sane again. I need a helper *now*. I need a new sheriff."

Dralo returned the governor's gaze and smiled. "Then find one. And I suggest doing it quickly."

"But who? Who out there is stout enough for the job *and* a devout servant of the king?"

"Have you considered Kandis? He certainly fits the qualifications you specified."

"The lumberjack? Well, no. But come to think of it, he would be good." He rubbed his chin. "Yes, he would be good. Exceptional."

"Then go to him. Ristun is at his house right now. Perhaps he can help you persuade him to become sheriff."

"Right now?"

"You'll want to speak with him before he goes searching for his son again."

"You're right." Will stood.

Dralo lifted his hand. "Don't give up if you meet some initial resistance.

Willerdon patted his pocket. "I'll let the king do the persuading. If Kandis is the right man, the king will find a way to convince him."

He left the room, and decided to tell Lianna of his plan before leaving for Kandis' house. He found her in the kitchen with Grace. He drank some milk, devoured a piece of toast to calm his nervous stomach, left the house and headed east along Willow Road.

THIRTY-EIGHT

Will passed many a villager as he drew closer to the main road of town. Some nodded and gave him a pleasant hello. Other ignored him. Some even shot him cruel expressions, muttering unintelligible insults under their breath. This was nothing new, yet as he crossed the main road, butterflies came to reside in his stomach. He wasn't sure how Kandis would react to his request for him to become sheriff. He wasn't even sure why he'd decided to ask him. Did he need help that badly?

But as he received a deluge of frowns from a group of gruff-looking men, he realized he wouldn't be able to govern much longer alone, particularly if Bolard returned or Woodend was attacked by an army of drilockk.

At last, he reached Kandis' house, remembering it from a few months ago, when they'd met about starting a new lumber camp. Which they had, abandoning an old one so new trees could replenish it. But as he walked to the door, another man was already there, a young man he immediately recognized, looking nervous and holding a bouquet of flowers.

"Jak, is that you?"

Jak looked over. "Governor Willerdon! Um . . . hello! What are you doing here?"

"I'm here to talk with Kandis about something." He nodded toward the flowers and smiled. "Ah, I wonder whom those might be for."

"Oh, no one . . . really."

"You mean you just like carrying around flowers?"

"No, I . . ."

"Well, they're lovely. Anyway, have you knocked yet? Because it appears no one is getting the door." As he spoke, Will reached up and banged on the door.

The door opened. Ella, wearing a look of surprise, stood just beyond it. "Oh, hello," she said.

Will gave Jak a chance to respond, but after a long silence, decided to speak. "Hello Ella. Could I speak with your father?"

"Certainly. He's at the table with Mother and Ristun right now."

"Thank you," Will said. He stepped inside, but before heading farther, he turned around and winked at Jak, whose face turn an even brighter hue of red, and left the two young people together.

Smiling, he walked to the table across the room where Kandis, Raina and Ristun were in deep discussion. At first, he thought he should leave them be. But before he could tiptoe away, Kandis noticed him.

"Governor! Hello! What brings you to my house?"

"Uh, hello, Kandis. Good afternoon Raina, Ristun." He returned his eyes to Kandis. "I . . . was wondering if I could discuss something rather important with you."

"Certainly. Have a seat." Kandis pulled one out and patted it with his hand.

"Thank you. Thank you. I'll be quick. I've been talking with Dralo, and he and I agree that I need to fill the position of sheriff . . . seeing we're in some difficult times right now, and they're likely to get worse."

He let these words sink in before continuing. "I'm looking for a man with a stout heart who is a servant of the king. Few, I'm afraid, fit into this category."

At this point Ristun leaned in, interest on his face.

"And what has this got to do with me?" Kandis asked.

"Do you know of anyone I should ask?"

"No."

"Hmm, I thought you might." He'd hoped Kandis would jump to the occasion. Inwardly, his hope sank.

"Perhaps I could recommend someone, Governor."

All eyes turned to Ristun, who continued. "I think the man you're looking for is sitting right in this room." He turned to Kandis. "You, Kandis, are both hardy in spirit and a strong servant of the king."

Kandis laughed. "Me? Sheriff? I'm a lumberjack. Never had any status in this town. No one would take me seriously."

"I don't agree," Ristun said. "I heard you demanded a great deal of respect during the riot. In fact, you are the one most responsible for scaring away the ruffians who started it."

"Well, I suppose . . ."

"And you have the respect of all the lumberjacks in town. The guards now hold you in high esteem as well."

"Yes, but—"

"You would be a great asset to Willerdon."

Kandis sighed. "But many still hate me for not giving up my illumina during the decree. Certainly people won't forget that I was jailed for it, or that I supported Jebin when he fought against Bolard."

"That's the type of man I need!" Will said, realized he was almost shouting, and lowered his voice to a whisper. "Bolard is returning, you see."

"What!" both Kandis and Raina had shouted this.

He held up a hand for quiet. "I don't want this to leave the room. Yes, Bolard is coming back." He told them all he knew about the emissaries from Macalum and their captain, and why they were in the forest. When he finished, he found himself surrounded by stunned faces. Even Ristun looked surprised.

Kandis said, "I've had no idea how deep our problems were, though I wondered. I will consider your request after talking with the king, and of course," he looked to Raina, "my wife." She smiled nervously. "But right now, I need to look for my son. I have a search party of lumberjacks who are going to help me today. We plan to search into the night."

At that moment, Jak and Ella walked into the room, smiling. "Good morning sirs, ma'am," Jak said.

Kandis and Raina smiled when they saw Ella holding the flowers.

"I was wondering if Ella might accompany us on our search today," Jak said. "From what I heard, she's an excellent tracker, and just because she's a girl, I don't think we should overlook her."

Kandis glanced at Raina, who gave a nod of approval. "Certainly," he said.

"You two keep a good watch on her," Raina said sternly. "I've already lost one child."

"Don't worry, ma'am," Jak said. "We'll take good care of her. And when we get back, you'll not only have your daughter back, but hopefully your son as well."

Raina's eyes teared. "I'm sure I will."

Kandis filled the others in on his plans for the day. He would head toward Lockspell, having the party fan out on either side of the main road in search for signs of the boys. If they didn't find anything before nightfall, they'd return and set out again the next day. "I'll search all the way to Lockspell if needed," he said, "but that would require we camp in the woods. I don't want to do that unless absolutely necessary."

After a quick lunch, Kandis, Jak and Ella prepared to leave for the search. After bidding Raina goodbye, Will and Ristun accompanied them to the main road.

"Well, here's where we part," Kandis said, then leaned in close to Will. "Don't worry, I've not forgotten your request. I will consider it carefully. Just do me a favor. Seek the king for us today. I want my son back safely."

Kandis clasped hands with him before heading toward the main road, followed by Jak and Ella.

"Are you going too?" Will asked Ristun.

"No. Gildareth will want me back at your house to help Dralo watch over Jebin." He fell into a whisper. "The enemy is fervently seeking his demise."

Will nodded. "I'm glad you and Dralo will be there to look after him tonight."

"And perhaps more nights, until he recovers."

Will and Ristun hurried to catch up with the others. At the main road, they said their final farewells and watched the search party head south. In the distance, Will was just able to make out the gate, and beyond that, the forest. It seemed to grow more foreboding as each new day passed.

✝ ✝ ✝

Wearing her regal huntresses' garb, her blonde locks tied behind her head with a leather thong, Aliah stood outside Woodend's north wall. It rose in front of her to about the height of some of the young trees growing near it. Most of that end of the hill, on which the northern portion of the city stood, looked to have been cleared of trees many years ago. But they hadn't been hewn without dropping their seeds; now, their young were beginning to reclaim the area. Behind her, the hill descended to a vast, seemingly endless plain that stretched beyond the horizon into the north. Produce fields looked like little patchwork quilts as they spread out over the grasslands.

Near each field, huts and a few barns stood. Willerdon had told her that though the farms on the outskirts of the city produced enough food for Woodend and trade with some of the other forest cities, that year, most of the fields were flooded by excess rain. When she'd come out of the greater forest on her trip to the northern wall, on which Dirfin and she had followed a cart path around the western edge of the city, she'd noticed pools of water drowning many of the low-lying fields. She pitied the poor farmers, who'd be even poorer that winter. Yet, as she studied the wall, her hand in an inner pocket near her waist, she knew the winter would be the least of Woodend's problems.

"I still don't see any place the drilockk could get through," Dirfin said, punching at the wall with a dagger. "I'm starting to think we're not going to find anything."

Aliah stood silent, glaring at the wall, angry that she'd yet to discover its weakness. Then, on the same path they'd taken to get to where she now stood, she heard hooves approaching at the same instant her protector did.

Dirfin jumped in front of her and fixed his eyes on the path. "Who goes there?" he demanded in his high voice.

A white-and-black patched horse came around a curve in the wall. It carried a cloaked man who held up his hand in a gesture of peace. "It is Gildareth. Hold down your weapons."

Dirfin ran up to him, smiling broadly. "Well, well. And what brings you here, northerner?"

"I've come to aid you in your quest, for your success will greatly assist the town."

"How do you know what we're doing?"

Gildareth chuckled. "It was fairly obvious. You left traces all along the wall. Cut vines, scratches on the wood. You're looking for the way the drilockk are getting in, likely so you can set a trap and slay them before they enter."

Dirfin grinned. "Ah, you're a smart one, you are. Aliah, did you hear that? He knows what we're up to."

Aliah's smile was for Gildareth. "Yes, I'd expect nothing less from a northerner. Dirfin, continue searching the wall. I need to speak with Gildareth a moment."

"Whatever you wish to tell him you can also tell me," he said sternly.

"Dirfin, I am in no mood to argue. Look for rotting wood, a gap, anything. And continue doing so until I tell you otherwise."

Dirfin mumbled under his breath as he slashed away a grouping of vines. Gildareth dismounted and followed Aliah into a stand of trees.

"You are only partly right, Gildareth."

"What do you mean?"

"About the wall. Yes, Dirfin thinks we're looking for a break where drilockk are getting through. But I already know how they are entering."

"And how is that?"

"Last night, I went out alone. Found a shack on the eastern edge of the village. A light was on inside, so I went over to investigate. Within it, a low voice was speaking to someone. Someone who hissed back. I couldn't make out the words of either. But when it ended, I heard a door creak open within the shed and then close again. A short time later, a man left the shack, looking nervous, and headed south. When I thought it safe, I picked the lock and searched inside. Beneath a rug on the floor, I found a trapdoor. It led to a short tunnel. I followed it until I found a ladder leading back up.

It exited into the woods. When I retreated from the opening, I found some large boot prints. Those of a drilockk."

Alarm shadowed the herald's face. "So someone from within Woodend is *letting* them in?"

"Yes. And I intend to find out whom. But first, I have more pressing worries. You're from the north, so you'll understand. I fear something far worse than drilockk are getting into Woodend, and they are finding it easy to do so."

She reached into her cloak and pulled out a phial that glowed brightly. "I've seen it back at home. Our walls look secure, but when the light of the king falls on them, you see them for what they really are. I've tried the same thing here, all along the wall. Yesterday I tried the inside, whenever Dirfin wasn't looking my way, that is. But I found nothing."

"Why do you hide it from Dirfin?"

A second's hesitation preceded her reply. "Though I feel he would be indifferent to my having one, the people of my land . . . are not friendly to the king. They feel he has failed them. In these dark days, all they trust are the sword and shield. I am one of the few who still hold true to the king's way. If Dirfin were to tell Varla about my loyalties, I might meet with much grief. I might even be sent home. And if my father found out where my allegiance lies, he'd be furious. And above that . . . best not speak of it at the moment."

"I shall keep your secret then."

She looked up at him with grateful eyes. "Thank you."

They returned to the wall, where they discovered that Dirfin had decided to stop working and take a nap.

"I tell you, that imp is hopeless," Aliah said, and sighed. "But at least this gives me a chance to demonstrate my difficulty." She held her illumina toward the wall. It immediately went dim. When she pulled it away from the wall, it grew bright again. "It is as if the wall's been cursed somehow."

Gildareth stared at the wall. "This is Wrathar's new tactic. He doesn't want anyone to know the wall is weak. Otherwise, if someone with an illumina happened to bring it close to the wall, it would reveal its frailty. But I wonder how strong the curse is."

He brought out his own illumina. "Hold yours close to mine." She obliged, and as the lights met, they grew brighter.

Dirfin began to stir as the light fluttered upon his eyelids.

"Hurry," Aliah said, "before he wakes up."

They walked toward the wall. At first, the lights grew dim. Gildareth whispered words under his breath. They flickered a moment, looked as if they might go out all together, then grew bright again. Immediately, a vast fissure running from the top of the wall to the bottom crept from the wood. "Come," he said, watching it. "Walk this way."

They headed east. Other fissures, some larger, some smaller, crept along the wall. Then a massive gap, the width of two men, opened up before them about halfway up the wall.

Aliah gasped. "Even at home, I've never seen a gap in the wall that big. Where do you think it leads?"

As she spoke, a house rose up alongside the wall, a little window just above it.

"I must get back to the governor," Gildareth whispered, and turned concerned eyes to Aliah. "That's his house. Wrathar has not been idle the past three years. He now has the wall broken, to the point it's of no more worth than a hedge."

Aliah's face showed alarm. "I . . . thought the Lord of Shadow was just an old wives' tale, a phantom that some claim rule the vulgheid. I find it difficult to believe that such creatures would bow to anyone. Are you saying Wrathar is real?"

"Yes, though the vulgheid loathe him as much as everything else. They only follow him knowing that with him as their head, they can do far more damage to the king than if they fought individually."

"What then of the drilockk?" she said. "Who commands them? They often seem more of a threat than the vulgheid."

"Wrathar controls them too, through lesser servants." He looked curiously into Aliah's eyes, noted their sudden pain. "Can you see the vulgheid, young one?"

"No. But I know they're real."

"And how is that?"

"They reveal themselves to me in nightmares, and . . . sometimes in visions. All who profess loyalty to the king in Macalum have these nightmares, unceasing. Often, they threaten to harm our dearest friends. And if we ignore the threats, our loved ones fall into terrible despair, and their eyes become . . . hideous. Sometimes, their hopelessness grows so strong that . . ."

"They die?"

She nodded. "Yes. That's why we keep our loyalty to the king secret. For our own safety, and our loved ones'. It's the real reason I hide my illumina from Dirfin. They told me . . . if I show it to him, or he sees it in any way, they would slay him. I believe them."

"They tell the truth about that," Gildareth said, his voice gentle. "They would indeed try. But there is a defense against this red curse of theirs. For that's what it's called in the south: the hopeless despair. Is it not?"

Her eyes grew wide. "Yes. Do you really know a cure?"

"I can teach it to you when time permits. But I must warn you, it involves the person cursed more than anything else. That person must want to be free. And unless you can find that tiny speck of hope, one that keeps him from willingly giving up his life, there is no hope."

"I only wish . . . you see, my—"

"Hey, Aliah."

At Dirfin's call, she shoved her illumina under her cloak.

"Sorry, I fell asleep. It's just such a nice cool day. Any luck searching the wall?"

"Yes. I found what I was looking for."

Dirfin swiveled his head and studied the wall, tapped it with his dagger. "Looks like it might be starting to rot. But no drilockk's getting through there."

"I know. It's not here. But I just remembered something I saw yesterday. A trapdoor of sorts on the east side of town. I'll show you."

He rose to stand, rubbing his eyes. "I'm starting to think you just brought me out here to admire these scrawny trees." He let out a war cry and slashed at a sapling with his dagger, hewing it from its tiny trunk. "Aha! Take that, you ugly little—"

"Dirfin, please! You know how I hate it when you talk like that."

"Sorry, my lady. Just can't help it. That was the ugliest tree I've ever seen. Thought I'd put it out of its misery." He turned to Gildareth. "So, did you help her find this trapdoor?"

Gildareth ran his fingers through his beard. "Dirfin, I feel obligated to tell you something important."

Aliah eyed Gildareth, sudden worry in her eyes.

"Based on some evidence I've just discovered, I feel Woodend is about to be attacked by your enemies, and soon."

Aliah sighed.

Dirfin's eyebrows rose. "You mean the drilockk."

"*Your* enemies, Dirfin. I'll leave it at that. I'm not sure when this attack will come. But since the town is without a sheriff, could you ensure the guards are well armed and prepared for an assault? Perhaps even begin training them in some of your arts?"

"Arts, eh? I *am* pretty good with a sword. And, with a dagger."

"Certainly! Now, I wonder, can you use a bow?"

Dirfin grinned. "Can I use a bow? I'm hurt. Who can't use a bow?"

"Some of Woodend's guards, I'm sure. Train them in archery as well, if you'd be so kind."

"I'd love to. It's about time *some* people began to respect my talents."

"Just remember this. When you get to the northern guardhouse, and I suggest going there first, mention you're a warrior from Macalum, and that you are in pursuit of a band of ruffians that have come into the forest from the south. Say you need the guards of local towns to be ready, in case their villages are attacked. This should sway them to listen to every word you say. Most of the guards in Woodend rarely see action, as was demonstrated during the riot. I'm sad to say that many died due to their ill-readiness."

"Don't worry, when I'm through with them, they'll be a battalion worth reckoning with!"

"Excellent! Now, I shall take us back into town. Please, allow me to help you onto Rapstag."

Dirfin's head jerked toward the horse. "Onto that! You want me to ride that giant beast?"

"Don't worry. He's an excellent horse—"

"Don't care, I'm not riding it."

"Dirfin, please," Aliah said. "We must get back to the village. It would take more than an hour to reach the gate on foot."

Dirfin grumbled, then at last agreed. They hoisted him into the saddle. Aliah sat in front of him, holding the reins; Gildareth sat behind them both. "Back to Woodend," he said, and prodded Rapstag with his foot. The horse lurched forward. Dirfin screamed in terror, but calmed when Rapstag began a smooth gallop.

Soon, they reached the gate. But as they did, a hunting party was just leaving town. Kandis was leading them.

"Gildareth, what are you doing here?" Kandis asked. He, Ella, and the thirty others in the group halted, eyeing the three on the horse.

"I was out inspecting the wall with Dirfin and Aliah," Gildareth replied. "Are you preparing to search for the lost boys?"

"Yes, we plan to search until nightfall."

"You're a bold one, that's for certain," Dirfin said from his perch. "Don't you remember that monster we heard the night we met in the forest? It could be out there right now. And likely, it's hungry."

The search party members who'd heard no such tale started murmuring. Kandis' face became thunderous. "Please," he whispered, "I've warned them there might be danger. And together, we're stout enough to handle such a beast."

"Unlikely."

Kandis ignored the imp and turned to his party. "Let's be off. We've got a lot of ground to cover before nightfall." The group, which was laden with axes, knives, bows and even pitchforks, clattered and clanked past Rapstag.

"Looks like they could use a little training themselves," Dirfin mocked. "I've never seen such a ragtag group of peasants."

"They'll be fine," Gildareth assured him. "Kandis is a strong man, and has a strength you wouldn't understand."

"Try me."

Gildareth glanced at Aliah, and she sent him a pleading expression, hoping the herald would do like everyone else who knew the small fellow and ignore him.

Gildareth smiled and nodded, then turned back to Dirfin. "I cannot explain Kandis' courage at the moment," he said, "but soon, you'll learn more than you ever imagined. Trust me."

"Sounds good. But for now, just let me off this stinking animal and point me to the guardhouse. I want to get this training started."

Gildareth dismounted and helped Dirfin do the same. Aliah watched from Rapstag while Gildareth introduced him to Clooney. The old lumberjack heartily agreed to take the Eastmonting to the northern guardhouse and explain to the guards why he was there.

After the others left, Gildareth took Rapstag's reins and looked up at her. "Would you accompany me to the governor's house?"

"Certainly, but why?"

"I would like to introduce you to someone there. A young boy who might find your experiences with nightmares . . . interesting."

She measured him with her eyes. "Is this why you arranged for Dirfin to be away? Did you think he wouldn't approve—?"

"Not at all, Aliah. I only asked for his help, which I truly want." He smiled. "Of course, it makes it easier for you to say yes to my request if your feisty little protector isn't around. Just call it a bit of serendipity."

She sighed. "Even if he were here, I'd rather not dwell on those terrible dreams. Every day, I try to forget them."

"Please. I believe this lad is plagued by similar dreams, and harmed physically by their makers. It might hearten him to know there are others who understand his plight."

She reached for her illumina and held it tight. It grew warm in her hand. She closed her eyes, growing weary at the mere thought of remembering her terrible past dreams, but knowing her duty as a follower of the king. "I will help him," she finally said, and opened her eyes.

Gildareth smiled, jumped onto the saddle in front of her, and nudged Rapstag.

It took half an hour to reach the governor's house on Willow Road. Grace was knitting outside.

She looked up from her work and smiled. "Mr. Gildareth! You're back!"

"Yes dear, I am." He dismounted, and Grace wrapped him in her small arms. "I'm so glad to see you again," she said.

"As I am to see you."

Aliah dismounted next to Gildareth and looked around, uncomfortable.

"You're the pretty lady I saw when Dibbs came home," Grace said. "But I forgot your name."

"Aliah. And you're Grace, right?"

"Yes! How did you know that?"

"I rarely forget a name. I remember your father introducing me to you a couple of nights ago . . . though we were too busy to talk at the time."

"That's all right, I'm glad to see you again too." Grace jumped forward and hugged her. When she released her, she said, "Quickly, come inside. Supper is almost ready. We've already made enough room at the table for many guests." She smiled. "We always seem to have a full house lately. Even Raina's here tonight. She's the mother of one of the kidnapped boys. Tarin, I think."

She tugged at Aliah's shirt and pulled her toward the door. Gildareth followed.

Inside, they were greeted by Dralo, Ristun, Raina, and the rest of Grace's family. Except a boy who sat, scowling, in a chair near the fireplace in the living quarters.

"Is that the boy you want me to talk with?" Aliah whispered to Gildareth.

"Yes, he's the one."

"He seems . . . cheery."

"You have no idea."

Dibbs looked up at her, and their eyes locked. As they did, Aliah felt unease crawl up her spine. *He looks so young and innocent, yet at the same time, full of something quite terrible. Evil.*

She closed her eyes hard, calmed herself, then opened them. Now, terror greeted her. In the corner, behind Dibbs, a dark shadow stood. Its long, spidery fingers rested protectively on the boy's shoulder, and it stared at her with large pale eyes.

Please, no, not here, not now, her mind screamed. She opened her mouth to call a warning, but the shadow vanished, leaving the pitiful boy still sitting, looking at her sadly. She stumbled a few steps back. Gildareth steadied her.

"Is all well?" he asked.

Grace walked by carrying a kitten. Aliah held up a hand. "May I sit?"

Grace pointed at a chair near Dibbs, but she shook her head. Not questioning her refusal, Grace directed her to a little stool in the adjacent dining room, which was full of people and well lit. Aliah hurried to the stool, and welcomed her hosts' light conversation that followed. She managed to push aside the terror she was fast gathering for Dibbs, but dreaded the inevitable meeting with him. Even so, she had agreed to the meeting, and it was unthinkable for her to back out. She was a warrior, after all.

Thirty-Nine

"**S**o this is Undertree?" Tarin said.

"It's also called Rock Valley," Sarky replied. "Because of the abandoned quarry nearby. Remember, Father said it used to be the chief city of the forest before it was destroyed."

"Do you think those red-cloaked creatures in the story were drilockk?"

"What else could they have been?"

Both stared at the ruins below, proof that the beasts haunting the forest so long ago was no longer just rumors.

"The sun's going down," Sarky said, looking around. "We should find a place to spend the night. Maybe one of those houses down there is still sturdy enough to use as shelter."

The boys descended into the valley. Soon they reached the remnants of an ancient wall, likely, Tarin thought, once similar to the one surrounding Woodend.

"I wonder if this is what will happen to Woodend," he said softly while visions of his town, smashed up and in ruins, flitted through his head.

"Of course it won't! Don't talk like that. The people of Woodend are tough. They won't let the drilockk or . . . or any other enemies bring them down. No, they'll fight." Sarky gave him a hard stare. "And so will we."

Tarin felt a lump form in his throat. Fight? Him? Is that what it might come to? He couldn't stomach the thought. He felt his legs give way under him, and knelt on the ground.

"What's wrong with you?" Sarky asked.

"I . . . I just don't think I want to actually fight."

"What are you worried about? I'm sure you could fight if you needed to. Look at what you did to those vulgheid a couple of nights ago."

"That was different. Something came over me. *People* do this to me." He held out his hands to show Sarky how badly they were shaking. "You see? That's why I hide in the alleys. Regular people scare me. How in your right mind can you think I could ever fight monsters?"

Sarky was quiet a moment, then said, "I don't know. I'm not even sure *I* could. But if one of them was trying to kill Father, or one of my friends, then I'd at least try to fight."

"But me?"

"You've already fought, Tarin! Those vulgheid . . . you scared them away with your flaming hands. They were terrified! I'm actually jealous of you. I wish I could do the things you did, and I kind of wish I had—"

"Had what?"

"Never mind."

From his kneeling position, he looked up at Sarky. "No. What do you wish you had? The ability to see the vulgheid? Is that what you want? Well, if I could give that gift away, I would. Or maybe," he patted his pocket, "maybe you want one of these illuminas. Is that it? Well fine."

He pulled the phial from his pocket and held it toward Sarky. "Go on, take it. I don't know why it came to me anyway."

Sarky eagerly reached for it, wrapped his fingers around it. As he did, the light within grew dim. He withdrew his hand and scowled. The flicker within the phial returned.

"Why did the light go out?" Tarin said.

"Are you a dolt? It happened because I'm not a servant of the king. You are."

"But . . . I didn't even realize I was his servant."

"Come on. Everyone knows that only those who've pledged their loyalty to the king can have his light. I'm sure you pledged your loyalty at some point. How couldn't you have?"

Tarin searched his memory, but couldn't recall ever giving the king his loyalty, or even wanting to. Then he recalled the night on the tower: his fear, his hopelessness as the crimson light seduced him.

"I did," he whispered, surprised by the memory. "It happened on the tower, while Thief was holding you captive."

"What happened down there anyway? We were too busy with Thief to talk about it."

Tarin prepared to speak, but closed his mouth when he saw the sun's last rays burst over the mountainous western horizon. A moment later, the sun's orange glow disappeared behind the mountains. A cold breeze swept into the old city. "It's getting pretty dark," he said, holding himself in his arms to stay warm. "Don't you think we ought to find shelter before we talk any more?"

Sarky peered out toward the mountains and nodded.

Together, they headed deeper into the ruins. But as they walked, both watched for movements, hoping not to end up in the clutches of another drilockk, or something even worse.

They searched for nearly an hour, finding houses with walls, and some with an intact roof, but none with both intact.

They worked their way to the western edge of town, where the wall had once stood against a solid rock face that spanned most of that end. Above it, the terrain rose sharply into one of the smaller outer mountains of the nearby range. They traveled along this stretch for a while before reaching an archway of sorts, leading into a gap within the rock.

"What do you suppose this is?" Tarin said.

"Looks like a cave. A manmade cave by the look of that arch. But hey! It's actually got a roof and walls. I think we've found ourselves a home."

"Let's look inside." Tarin pulled out his illumina, which was dim, but bright enough to allow them to see around in the cave.

In the light, it no longer looked like a cave, but a room. The four walls, though stone, were smooth and flat, with the exception of the arched doorway carved into the nearest wall. The archway looked to have once contained a wooden door, though it had long ago fallen from its hinges and decayed. The ceiling stood about twice their height. On the far wall, a single shelf still fought to carry its load of one large old book. Below it, a metal chest rested on the floor, a bulky lock fastening its lid on tight.

"Look at that chest," Sarky said as he walked toward it. He ran his hand over the top and wiped off the dust. "Hey, it says something on the lid, but I can't make it out."

Tarin drew closer. Indeed there was writing on the lid, but it was faded. He held his illumina directly above it and squinted. As if coming out of a mist, the words grew clearer.

When darkness comes, and Shieth again awakens, three shall come, servants of the king, three more will follow, warriors of the LIGHT.

The last word was written larger and bolder than the rest. Tarin muttered the phrase so Sarky could hear.

"That's a load of nonsense if I ever did hear any," Sarky scoffed. "Three servants of the king, three warriors of the light. What a bunch of—"

"It's a prophecy."

Sarky turned dubious eyes on him. "A what?"

"A prophecy. A description of future events."

"I know what a prophecy is! What I meant was, what's a prophecy doing written on some old chest? And what does it mean?"

"I'm ... not sure. But I've seen it before. In *The Annals of Illuminara*." Tarin sat down on the chest and fiddled with his illumina.

Sarky pointed to the shelf above him. "I wonder if that book up there could tell us anything."

Tarin peered up at the shelf.

"I think I can reach it if I stand on the chest." Sarky jumped up next to Tarin and grabbed the book. Then he lost his balance. Before he tumbled off the chest, Tarin steadied him.

"Thanks," Sarky said. "But I think I could've handled it."

"Sure," Tarin mumbled.

"Anyway, let's have a look."

"Be careful, it might fall apart when you open it."

But remarkably, it was able to handle Sarky's less-than-gentle touch as he flipped through each page. "No pictures in this book," he moaned. "What kind of book doesn't have ... oh, wait."

A single page glided out of the book and landed on the floor. Sarky snatched it up. "Hey, there's a picture. Looks like your light, Tarin, only ..."

Tarin glanced over, and his heart thudded in his chest. Indeed, the page contained a drawing of a phial similar to his, but deep crimson ink smeared the insides of the orb and even spewed out onto the rest of the page. At the bottom were scrawling words clearly written in great haste.

Beware the light of crimson. It is not what it seems, nor are those whom wield it.

He lifted his eyes to Sarky's. "I saw that light on the tower."

The phial in Tarin's hand became suddenly hot. He grimaced and let it fall. Even as he did, he yelled "No!" His fears that it would shatter were pointless. It landed with a dull thud, but not one crack formed in the smooth glass.

"Hey," Sarky said. "What are you trying to do, destroy the only light we got—?"

The illumina became a brilliant white light, blinding them.

"What's going on?" Sarky screamed.

Tarin shielded his eyes and bent down, carefully touched the illumina with the tip of his finger. It was scorching hot, but didn't burn him. Wary, he picked it up.

His eyes began to adjust to the light, though now the underground room looked as if lit by the sun.

"What's it trying to say?" Sarky asked.

"Huh?"

"The illumina. It's trying to tell you something. Why else would it have suddenly gotten so bright?"

"I don't know," Tarin sputtered. "I haven't had it that long, in case you've forgotten." He raised his eyebrows quizzically. "And why do you think you know so much about it? You don't have one."

Sarky lowered his head and stared at the floor.

"What's wrong with you?"

Sarky looked up and locked eyes with Tarin. "I . . . I do have one." He reached into his pocket and pulled out an old, dirty phial. "But look, the light's gone out. It disappeared a long time ago, after . . ."

"After what?"

Sarky didn't answer, just returned the empty phial to his pocket and lumbered over to a corner, where he sat, looking miserable.

"Well, you could at least tell me why you think mine's so bright right now."

Sarky didn't answer.

"Sarky! Come on! Tell me." He peered around. "I'm starting to think we're in danger."

"Is that what he's telling you?"

"What do you mean—?"

Sarky's entire body jerked upright on his sudden rush to the archway. He peered out and whispered, "Put it back in your pocket. Hurry! We don't want to get spotted."

Tarin stood dumbfounded, unsure if Sarky was being serious.

Angry at Tarin's hesitation, Sarky grabbed the illumina. Upon touching it, he howled in pain, but managed to force it back into Tarin's pocket. The room went black.

"Stay quiet," Sarky whispered. "I heard something out there."

Tarin nodded, and he and Sarky looked out at the darkened old city.

He was just about to whisper that he didn't hear anything, when he heard it: a faint cry, coming from the far end of the ruins. Then, above them, something dark swept past the moon. He looked up, but saw nothing. Again, someone, or something, yelled. This time, Tarin could make out a single word: "Help!"

FORTY

They continued listening for the faint cry to repeat, but it didn't. They looked at each other, nodded, and ventured a little farther from the cave, straining their ears harder.

"Help!"

The cry was back, carried by the wind from somewhere north of them.

"Someone's in the northern part of the city," Sarky whispered. "What should we do? Try to help whoever it is?"

Tenacious curiosity gnawed at Tarin, but fear of meeting up with a drilockk or vulgheid quenched it. "I think we should stay here. It could be a trap."

Sarky nodded. "Yes. They know we're out here, the drilockk and vulgheid both. They might be trying to lure us out of hiding so they can capture us, or maybe even kill us."

"I love how you're so blunt."

"Ah, sarcasm. A rare treat coming from you."

"Now's not the time to be a fool, Sarky. Listen. I think I heard it again."

They went silent and continued to stare into the dark city, toward the noise. A steady, cold breeze made Tarin wish for warmer clothing.

A familiar roar pierced the night sky far above their heads. Both boys looked up, searching for the same hideous thing: the flying monster that Thief had called a bostt.

Their eyes caught sight of it as it soared beneath the wispy night clouds.

Tarin whispered, "Let's get back inside!"

Sarky started backing up, but then stopped and pointed toward the bostt's swooping form. "Something's wrong with it."

Tarin directed his eyes to where Sarky pointed. The beast, which appeared about the size of Sarky's thumb from their vantage point, looked like it was trying to dive to a particular point in the northern edge of the old town. But each time it drew near the ground, it snarled, flapped its wings, and returned to the sky. The boys watched as it circled the place and roared, though it didn't venture back down.

"Wonder what's stopping it," Sarky mused. "Hey, look, is that an orange light over there?"

Tarin peered harder toward the north. "Yeah. It's flickering. There must be a fire." He glanced back up at the flying beast. The bostt was now so high, it appeared a speck in the night sky. His heart raced as curiosity devoured his mind like a ravenous animal.

"Help," the voice cried again, faintly but frantically. Tarin could stand no more. "Let's go," he said, and hurried toward the voice.

"Stop!" Sarky quietly yelled. "We'll get killed if we go over there. That thing will see us."

"No it won't. Something was blocking it."

"Curse your stupid curiosity!" Sarky groaned, but followed.

They traveled over a broken doorframe, crossed a few shallow, dry canals and hurried behind a dilapidated wall. Once there, Tarin knelt. From the looks of the rusty tools lying on the ground and the nearby anvil, he thought the wall once belonged to a smithy.

He looked around the corner and located the distant fire with his eyes. Now, he saw the shadows of cloaked figures standing around it. "Let's get closer," he said. He pointed toward a still-standing shed about three hundred paces away, nearer to the fire. "Over there."

It took them many minutes of carefully crawling through debris, ducking into the dry canals and hiding behind rubble, to reach the shack unnoticed.

Tarin took in their surroundings. They were at the extreme edge of the town now. Collapsed a short distance in front of them was the northern segment of the ruined wall. And beyond that, a sight that made his heart stand still.

A tall drilockk paced by the fire. By its leather suit and iron breastplate covering its massive torso, Tarin recognized it as the commander he'd seen before, the one that had escaped the bostt at the cowardly sacrifice of its entire battalion. His red cloak was slung over his shoulders like a cape. The hood was off, and the scales of his lizard-like face glistened in the moonlight. A fat tongue occasionally slid across his lips in a disgusting fashion as the beast strode back and forth.

At least thirty drilockk tents, similar to the one he'd seen before, spread out toward the north and into the forest. Drilockk, some wearing cloaks, others only leather with bits of armor, milled about, sharpening swords and stringing bows. Five of the largest drilockk sat near their tall commander, fully covered in their red shrouds.

Sarky began to pant. "Tarin . . . I'm starting to feel sick."

Tarin looked around. "Like when the vulgheid are around? I don't see them. Are you sure you're not just overwhelmed by the drilockk? There must be over a hundred of them out there—"

"It's not that. I'm telling you, the vulgheid are here."

The drilockk captain stopped pacing and glanced up. Tarin followed his gaze. "I hope that foul animal remains where it is," the captain hissed. "It got too close last time. What do the shadows think they're doing? I thought they were supposed to be holding it at bay."

Tarin squinted into the night sky. The winged creature swooped back and forth, swinging its massive arms and flapping wildly, as if being stung by bees. Then Tarin saw them: little wisps of darkness blacker than the night sky, circling and darting into the monster.

"You're right, Sarky," he whispered. "The vulgheid are right above us. They're the reason the winged monster wasn't able to get down. They're stopping it somehow."

Sarky managed a weak smile. "They probably don't want it eating their entire army like it did last time."

The captain's raspy voice interrupted. "We march in less than an hour. Thornkill, muster the others. When I give the order, I want them ready to leave."

"Yes, Master," Thornkill, a broad-shouldered, rather fat drilockk said, and walked toward the tents. He drew his sword and shouted orders to the other drilockk, who immediately began to withdraw into their tents, where the clanging and clashing of armor being handled resounded throughout the remains of Undertree.

The captain put on his own helmet and continued to pace. "The sentinel commands us to kill as many as we can before the withdrawal. Woodend will realize that we are a mighty foe. We must strike fear into their hearts, or the plan will fail."

Tarin and Sarky shot each other terrified glances, but Tarin whispered, "Keep listening."

The captain walked up to the fire and began prodding it with his sword, making sparks fly out of its center. Above the drilockk, the bostt roared in misery. The captain laughed. "Looks like the shadows might be doing their job after all. Wish they'd just kill the thing though, rather than leaving it flying around after we leave. They say the sentinel thinks it might ultimately be useful to our cause. Not sure how, though."

He pulled his sword from the fire and held it in front of him as he observed the sharp, glowing edge. "I am eager to go into battle. It's been so long. I only wish we could pillage the entire city rather than retreat early. Bolard better be there. If he's not, I say we burn the whole town and kill all those within! Women, children, everybody!"

A chorus of cheers erupted around the fire. The captain grinned and sheathed his sword. "If not for the king's orders, I'd kill Bolard too. I loathe these foolish plans the shadows persistently thrust upon us. We could use a more worthy foe for our armies. Even now, our power could easily overwhelm this entire forest if the army was unleashed. And after our long and weary trek through the plains and having to hide for weeks in the mountains, our restlessness would bring us quick victory. But what pleasure would that be? I'd rather have a fight. And it will come. Oh, yes. It will come."

A short drilockk ran out of the woods and up to the captain. "Sir," it said in a high-pitched, raspy voice. "I've just received orders from one of the sentinel's shadow messengers. It informed me that the family of the sheriff must be slain immediately. We are to send one of our own with word to the three assassins in Lockspell."

"Why must one of us go? Why not one of the shadows?"

"The shadow told me they're too busy up north. The light is more powerful than they foresaw. The governor is beginning to grow in strength, as are others. And as you know, Gildareth—"

"Never say that name in my presence!" the captain bellowed, striking the messenger across his scaly jaw.

The little drilockk fell to his knees and quailed. "I'm ... I'm sorry sir. But there are no shadows to be spared. They're going to attack the governor's house within the hour, through the damaged segments of wall. We must send one of our own."

"Then you go!"

"Sir?"

"Go! Waste no time. Do as your precious shadow commanded."

"But ... but ..." It glanced toward the sky, and its eyes caught sight of the flying beast. "What if I'm caught by the winged creature?"

"That is not my concern. Take what provisions you need and leave!"

"But if I fail, the shadows will blame you."

"Why, you filthy ..." The captain reached for his sword, but his eyes suddenly grew wide. "Fine! Take two others with you. Get to Lockspell quickly. Make sure the assassins get the message. Do not dare fail me."

He drew out his sword and held it at the messenger's neck. "If you fail, we shall see how well you fare without a head."

"Yes, Master." The small drilockk gulped.

The captain sheathed his sword. "And make sure the assassins know to make their deaths painful. I want the sheriff to know his family suffered greatly before they died."

The small drilockk gave the captain a cruel smile. "I shall." It got up, saluted, and ran toward the tents.

Tarin began shaking. They were talking about Jebin's family: Rosie, and her three children. He'd seen them many times in Woodend, though he'd never spoken to them. Like everybody else, he was rather afraid of them for their odd behaviors. But once, the little girl had noticed him lurking in a corner as he was traveling toward the inn for some stories, and smiled at him as if she'd known him her whole life. It had made him feel warm inside . . . before he shoved the feeling away.

Within his pocket, his illumina grew warm with the memory. He pictured Rosie and her children safely in bed, dreaming pleasantly, when heavy breathing and scuffling came from outside a nearby window. A head concealed by a red cloak rose up behind it, and the glass shattered. A sword was drawn. Rosie and her children woke up as three hooded figures climbed through the broken window and lifted their swords.

He shut his eyes, trying to force the images from his mind. They wouldn't leave. He put his hand into his pocket, and when his fingers touched the illumina, he felt, not comfort, but urgency surge through his veins, a call to aid four people he'd never even spoken to before.

No! he inwardly screamed. *There's no way I'd get there in time. The drilockk will reach the city before I ever could. Rosie and the children . . . there's nothing I can do for them. Surely you have a servant in Lockspell. You could warn them. That would work much better—*

The job is for you, a quiet voice spoke to his heart.

I can't. I just can't. And besides, didn't you hear? The drilockk are marching against Woodend. It's Woodend I should be warning.

But the urgency to go to Lockspell didn't subside. Rather, it grew stronger. Frustrated, he shoved his illumina into his pocket and withdrew his hand, panting.

"Tarin," Sarky whispered. "Look, they're preparing to march. We've got to do something! That army's going to attack Woodend. And that wicked little drilockk's going to Lockspell to have Sheriff Jebin's family murdered. What can we do?"

Tarin grabbed his shoulders and looked into his eyes. "We can't do anything until the army leaves. Otherwise we'll get caught and won't be of any use at all."

Renewed urgency to hurry to Lockspell rushed through him. He tried to push it away, but it wouldn't budge. In his thoughts, he said, *If you want me to go to Lockspell so badly, and there's no one there you can use to warn the sheriff's family, you'd better find a way to get me there faster than the drilockk.*

Immediately, peace fell upon him. He sighed. *Finally, you realize there's no chance of me being able to help Jebin's family in time.*

The drilockk captain suddenly began running to and fro, shouting commands as the battalion formed ranks around him. "All of you, follow me! Swords to the front!"

When they had all assembled, the captain addressed them. "We head toward the road to Woodend. From there, we travel toward the gate. When we break through the gate, don't disperse throughout the city. Let them come to us, and kill all who do. When Bolard arrives, sacrifices will have to be made. Do not cower away, or you will feel my sword! That is your order until you receive the signal. At the signal, retreat south. We'll regroup with the rest of the army at the rendezvous point in the mountains. There, we will wait for the signal to begin the true assault upon this forest. Then, my friends, we shall see bloodshed as we haven't in many a year!"

Cheers resounded and feet stomped in approval. Out of the crowd, two drilockk emerged with the scrawny form of a man bound head to foot. They threw him onto the ground before the captain and backed away.

"Ah, our prisoner," the captain said. "You are fortunate, my little fool. Normally, those who attempt to steal from a drilockk meet with a quick fate. You, though, shall receive a more pleasant end." He peered toward the sky. "Right now, at least five phantoms of shadow are holding a monster at bay. The moment my army is safely away, the shadows shall leave, and the beast will descend upon this place in search for food." He lowered his head, and his eyes were filled with malevolent glee. "But I'm afraid all it will find is . . . you."

Bellowing laughter, he kicked the scrawny fellow in the stomach. The man squeaked in pain, "Somebody, please . . . help!"

From their hiding place Sarky and Tarin looked at one another, then back at the man. It was Thief. His voice was unmistakable.

The captain threw his hood over his scaly head and wrapped his cloak around his armor. "To Woodend!" he shouted, and charged east into the woods. The earth shook as a hundred heavy pairs of boots followed into the trees and toward the road leading to Woodend. All the beasts, concealed in their red cloaks, surged into the forest like a red tide. When they at last disappeared into the boughs of the trees, and the thunder of their running gave way to quiet, Sarky turned to Tarin. "Hey, my stomach's better—"

A wild roar pierced the sky, and Tarin looked up. The vulgheid had apparently followed the drilockk army toward Woodend. The bostt was now free. It circled a few times in the sky, lifted its head and bellowed triumphantly at the moon, then surged downward.

"Quick!" Tarin shouted. "We've got to help him!"

"Who, Thief? Why? He tried to kill me."

"We can't just leave him there to be eaten!"

"Why not? The monster won't be hungry anymore then. He'll leave us alone—"

"Sarky, *think!* That creature ate at least twenty drilockk last time we saw it. I'm sure it's capable of eating Thief and us too."

"But if we move, it'll see us."

"That's why we've got to go now!"

Sarky looked up at the beast, then at Thief. The man was thrashing wildly, trying to break free of his bonds. "No, no, no, no, no!" he kept screaming. "I don't want to die! Please, no!"

Sarky grunted in disgust and leaped up. "Let's get this over with."

Tarin smiled as they both rushed toward Thief. The monster growled, and with a powerful thrust of its wings, surged downward even faster.

Tarin and Sarky reached Thief and began to work at the cords binding him.

"Rat! Mouse! My saviors! I love you forever and ever and ev—!"

"Shut up and be still," Sarky hissed. "How do you expect us to help you if you keep wiggling?"

"It's no use," Tarin said. "They won't loosen. Let's just get him out of here."

Sarky nodded and grabbed Thief's feet. Tarin took his shoulders, and they hoisted him up and lumbered over to the town's broken wall. Nearby was a dry canal leading out of the city. It looked about as deep as they were tall.

"Throw him in there!" Sarky shouted.

They heaved Thief into it, then jumped in after him, landing hard onto Thief, who squeaked as the breath was knocked out of him.

"Don't move!" Tarin ordered as he watched the monster swoop toward their hiding place. With a powerful thump, it slammed down next to the trench, folded its bat-like wings behind its hairy back and peered in.

On its huge bear-like head, angry black eyes searched the hole for movement, but Thief and the boys remained motionless. It took in air through the large, crusty nostrils at the end of its snout and roared, revealing large fangs and sharp teeth stained with the black blood of drilockk. It tried to thrust its head into the trench, but the opening wasn't big enough. Then, with its massive three-clawed hands at the ends of its log-like arms, it began to try to dig its way in.

Tarin and Sarky clenched their eyes shut while dirt spewed all over them, covering them with a thick layer of grime. Tarin knew they'd soon be forced to wipe it from their faces or risk suffocation, and the beast showed no signs of stopping its digging. But right before Tarin thought he'd have to move, the monster reared its head into the air and snarled.

Its attention wouldn't be diverted for long. Tarin pushed the dirt from his face while the other two did likewise. Then he noticed a fist-sized rock. He grabbed it up and threw it out of the trench as far as he could.

With the loud thump he'd hoped for, the rock hit the ground some distance away. The beast turned to face the direction of the noise, sniffed a few times, and lumbered toward it. Tarin and Sarky mopped the remaining dirt from their faces and helped Thief into a comfortable position.

"Thank you," Thief whispered as tears poured down his face.

"Thank us when we're safe," Sarky growled.

They listened while the winged monster trudged around above them. Apparently, the stone was enough to make it forget about the trench, because it hadn't returned. But it wasn't leaving either, and all the trio could do was wait, quiet and still, and hope the beast would eventually lose interest and go elsewhere in search of food.

Tarin's legs began to grow stiff, but the bostt still sniffed around, getting into the bones and rotting meat left over by the drilockk army. Right now, it sounded as if it were chewing on something hard and crunchy. After a few more chomps, a noxious belch exploded from its mouth.

Sarky began to snicker, and Tarin slapped his hand across his mouth. Sarky shoved Tarin's hand away, groaning, "Gross! You've got sludge all over your hand."

"Be quiet," Tarin scolded. "We don't want it coming back here."

"No, no, no," Thief whispered nervously. "That would be bad."

Sarky muttered something as Tarin felt a sudden familiar warmth in his pocket. He reached for the illumina, and pictures of Jebin's family materialized within his imagination. The little girl was playing a game with her two brothers in a large room with a window overlooking a lake. Her mother was knitting in a rocking chair in the corner. Behind the woman, looming just beyond the window, three figures swept out of the fog and approached the house. They were cloaked in red and held long, crooked daggers in their hands.

No! Quit showing me that! I can't do anything about it. Send somebody else. There's got to be someone in Lockspell who can get there much faster than I can.

But the old urgency returned with a vengeance.

Fine! I'll go! But only if you make a way. I don't know how to get there in time, especially with that bostt lumbering around up there.

From deep within the woods, a male moose let out a deep bellow. The winged beast stopped chewing and grunted with interest. With a mighty thrust of its wings, it soared into the sky in pursuit of a meal fresher than the drilockk scraps.

Tarin's heart beast faster. Again, the illumina burned within his pocket. He looked down, could see its gentle glow through the threads. *No, No, I can't do it. I just can't go.*

"Hey Tarin, it's gone! Let's get out of here." Sarky wriggled away from the others and jumped for the edge of the trench. But he couldn't quite reach it. Soon his rump was back in the dirt.

Thief saw a sharp rock near Tarin and squeaked as he sidled over to him and began furiously rubbing his bindings on the object. Tarin rolled his eyes, but to his amazement, the cords snapped. Now free of his bonds, Thief stood and tried to jump out of the trench. With a thud, he slammed against the wall. But as he came sliding back down, he managed to grab hold of the top of the trench and hoist himself out.

"Look at that runt," Sarky said. "He's running off again! And after we saved him—"

Thief peeped back over the edge and looked in. "Looks like all is well, my little Rat and Mou— I mean, friends. Here," he reached down, "jump up and grab my hand."

Sarky looked at Tarin. "Should we trust him?"

Tarin sat in the dirt, recalling his earlier challenge: *I'll do it, but you have to make a way....*

"Fine, don't answer." Sarky peered up at Thief, who was still smiling. "You aren't going to try anything funny again, are you?"

"No, no, no. Not again. You saved me. Now, I will help you."

Sarky leaped into the air, grabbed hold of Thief's hand, and though he nearly pulled Thief back into the trench with him, the little fellow, sweat beading up on his forehead as he strained, managed to pull Sarky out.

Thief bent over the edge and reached for Tarin. "Master, quickly, grab hold. I'll help you out."

Tarin didn't reply.

"My arm's getting tired, Master, please grab hold."

But still, nothing. Finally, the little man edged away and shrugged at Sarky. "The other master won't come. Why don't we just leave him?"

"No." Sarky's head appeared over the trench's edge. "What's wrong, Tarin? We've got to get out of here."

"For what? What will we do then? Warn Woodend?"

"Of course, what else would we do? And why do you sound so angr—?"

"Did you forget about Jebin's family?"

Sarky grew silent for a moment. "Is there really anything we can do for them? The drilockk messenger left over an hour ago. And I'm sure they move much faster in the forest than we do."

Tarin sighed. "My thoughts precisely. But . . ."

"But what?"

"Never mind, just pull me up."

Sarky reached down and hoisted him out of the trench.

When Tarin finished brushing himself off, Thief walked over to him and smiled. "I couldn't help but overhear, you need to go to Lockspell, yes?"

Tarin looked at him. "Uh, that's right."

Thief giggled. "If you think the drilockk move fast, you haven't seen me make haste. I fly through the trees like a deer."

"Then how did the drilockk catch you?" Sarky questioned.

"My dear master, they trapped me while I was trying to steal some of their food. There was nothing I could do. If I'd been able to run, things would have been different. But of course, you would never have saved me then, and I'd not be your servant now. Yes, if things had gone differently, you'd have no way to get to Lockspell in time to save the filthy sheriff's family."

"How did you know Jebin was the sheriff?" Sarky asked with narrowed eyes.

"No matter. No matter. But for you, my dear masters who saved my valuable life, I will even go so far as help you save the family of one of my most-loathed enemies."

"Why's Jebin your enemy?" Sarky asked.

"Because, Master," Thief said with just a hint of annoyance, "I am a thief and he is a sheriff. Is that so confusing?"

"Oh, I see."

"Good. Now," Thief turned to Tarin, "little master, do you want me to take you to Lockspell?"

Tarin muttered, "Yes."

"I can't hear you, little master."

"Yes! Take us to Lockspell!"

Thief's lip began to quiver, and he looked as if he might cry.

"Tarin," Sarky whispered. "You're being ridiculous. He's our only way to get to Lockspell in time, and look, you've hurt his feelings."

"But what about Woodend? Who's going to warn them about that army?"

"You're confusing me," Sarky squeaked. "First, you seem to want to save Jebin's family. Then you want to warn Woodend. We can only do one, and honestly, I think we should go to Lockspell. Woodend still has enough guards to hold off that army, and Father will warn them in plenty of time when he sees the drilockk approaching the gate. Jebin's family only has us. Although, if it were Jebin himself in danger, then . . . never mind." He lifted up his palms and shrugged. "So what do we do? You choose."

Tarin began to shake as he pondered his choices. But the persistent urgency drawing him toward Lockspell simply wouldn't relent. In his pocket, the illumina grew hotter and hotter. Surrounded on all sides with pressure to make a decision, he blurted, "Lockspell! Let's go to Lockspell! Just take us there, Thief. And hurry, we have to get there before those drilockk do."

Thief puffed up his chest. "Then try to keep up, my little masters. Following me will be like following a wild buck in search of his love, or like a bird as it soars through the trees, or like—"

"Let's just *go*," Sarky ordered.

Thief nodded and lunged southward, back through the old city of Undertree. Tarin and Sarky worked with all their might to keep up, amazed at how easily Thief dodged all the rubble without slowing. Fortunately, Thief seemed to be choosing the smoothest path through the ruins, which allowed Sarky and Tarin to keep up.

They traversed the entire city in what seemed like little time and reentered the woods. "We shall run straight to the road, young masters," Thief yelled behind him. "The drilockk try to avoid the road if they can. We will make it to Lockspell before morning if you manage to stay with me."

Tarin felt his side begin to ache, and doubted his new comrade's confidence.

FORTY-ONE

Aliah took a seat at the dinner table in Will's house, surprised they were able to squeeze in an extra stool at a table already surrounded by more seats than it looked to comfortably accommodate. Dibbs sat across from her, the black rings beneath his eyes making him look as if he'd not slept in weeks. The few times he happened to glance up at her, she felt her illumina grow cold in her waist pocket and greater unease swept over her. Though she'd not again seen the phantom. That, at least, was something.

As they ate, the conversation remained light. Soon all that was left on the table was a single roll in a woven basket in the center.

Gildareth peered out the window, then leaned toward Will and whispered, "Could Aliah and I speak with you and Lianna privately for a moment?"

Will and Lianna shot each other worried glances, then nodded. Raina excused herself to the living room, saying she would teach Grace some new knitting techniques. Dralo and Ristun went to look after Jebin. Dibbs skulked upstairs.

Aliah felt a lump in her throat when Gildareth asked her to explain her nightmares to the governor and his wife, but obliged.

"Are you saying these nightmares aren't uncommon?" Will said.

She sighed. "Not where I come from."

"Then by all means, talk with Dibbs. Maybe he won't feel so alone. We certainly haven't been able to get through to him. But ... he's still so angry at me. It's best if you talk to him alone. I'll only be a distraction."

Aliah smiled, though couldn't shield her discomfort about such a talk. She followed Will upstairs.

"Don't pay too much attention to his sour face," he whispered when they got to his door. "He's looked this way ever since he got back from the woods." He knocked on the door.

"What?"

"Dibbs, ah, there's someone to talk to you."

Slow footsteps, then the door opened. Dibbs' eyes grew wide at the sight of Aliah.

"Um . . ." Aliah stammered, "your father thought it might be nice if we talked. I think we have some problems in common. Nightmare problems."

Dibbs glared at her, then turned to Will. "I don't want to talk about anything to anyone." He prepared to close the door, but Will stopped him.

"I want you to give her a chance to tell her story. I'm sure you'll find it interesting."

"Do I have a choice?"

"No."

"Typical. Well, you might as well come in, miss," he said with a mocking bow.

Aliah gulped and entered the room. Will shrugged and closed the door behind him.

She sat on the corner of Dibbs' bed. He pulled out a little chair and sat in the corner, refusing to look at her. She reached down to fidget with her sword, then remembered she'd left her weapon and armor downstairs. Why was she here again? *Oh yes, to discuss nightmares. But first . . .*

She gave him her brightest smile, the smile that made even Varla lose his bad mood. "Your name is Dibbs, right?"

Silence.

This is ridiculous, she thought, and rose from the bed to leave.

"You're not from here, are you?"

The weight of resignation lowered her back onto the bed. "No. I'm from Macalum. It's a country south of here."

"I didn't think so. You're too pretty to be from the forest."

She smiled again. "Why, thank you." Then she raised an eyebrow. "But I've seen many girls here prettier than me."

"Your face is fairer. Not like the lumberjack's daughters, or the farmer girls."

"Oh."

"So why did Father want you to talk with me? It isn't about the king, is it?"

"It's more about me, really. I've gone through some things you might find interesting. Nightmares similar to ones I've been told you are having."

Dibbs grimaced. "You don't even know what a nightmare is."

"I think you're wrong."

He peered at her.

"Would you like me to tell my story?" she asked.

He turned away for a moment, but returned his gaze to hers and nodded.

She told him about the dreams plaguing her land, described the beasts that threatened her in her nightmares, the fears that overcame her. She told him how the beasts had threatened her dearest friends, including Dirfin.

Her eyes grew teary, and she found herself telling him something she hadn't told Gildareth. "When I was little, perhaps a little younger than you, I had my first nightmare. A great dragon-like beast came upon me while I was standing in a dark forest, sneering at me while other dragons laughed from somewhere within the trees. With a single beat of its horrid wings, the beast knocked me to the ground. Then it leaned in close, and spoke to me. Would you like to know what it said?"

The answer was a sullen shrug . . . but then, a nod.

"It said— No, it hissed, 'We shall take this land from your father. Many shall fall to our blade, and your father will be made weak, and humiliated.' It pulled me up by my hair and stood me in front of it. And then it hissed, 'But first, a sacrifice must be made. Your mother, child, shall die before the full moon.' Then it spun me around and swiped at my back."

Aliah wiped tears from her eyes. "I woke up feeling pain on my back, and a stickiness I knew was blood. I ran to my mother's room. She was unharmed, just sleeping."

"So it was just a dream," Dibbs whispered.

She sighed. "The next day, I heard rumors of an army coming to attack us from the south. Soon, the enemy took our gateway city of Ferion. Many in our land began to get similar nightmares, and a . . . a curse entered our country. Whomever it took fell into despair. Night after night, I had the same nightmare. And day after day, I went to Mother to make sure she was all right. And she was. Until one day I noticed a red gleam in her eye, and she started acting odd. The color left her face, and she became sadder each day. Eventually, she never left her bed.

"On the night before the full moon, I had another nightmare. This time, all I heard was laughing in the forest. I ran to Mother. She was lying still in her bed, as always. But her eyes were wide open, staring at the ceiling, full of a terrible crimson color. Father . . . even today, twelve years later, he still mourns her death."

She looked up at Dibbs, her tear-soaked eyes hot with anger. "The night she died, I vowed I would avenge her. Varla—he's my bodyguard—

taught me the ways of warfare. When I was old enough, he helped convince Father to let me fight in the war."

She smiled at Dibbs. "Consider yourself fortunate. You have both a mother and father."

She was surprised to see that Dibbs' eyes were waterlogged.

"My father's going to die," he said. "I've been having the same nightmares you had. And the dragon phantoms say he's going to be destroyed, along with me and the whole town." He stood and showed her his back. "I have the same scratches." He put his shirt back down and turned around. "And *my* father doesn't even care."

All the fear she'd earlier had of the boy turned to pity, and she walked over to him and put her arm around his shoulder. "Just because my nightmares came real doesn't mean yours will. I know many in my land who had similar dreams, and nothing happened. I believe they're meant more to terrorize us than anything else. My mother would have died whether I ever had a nightmare."

"But," Dibbs said, "I don't care anymore if he dies, or if the town is destroyed. Since I got back from the forest, I don't care about anything." His face contorted with anger and he pulled himself from her arm. "There's only one thing I still care about."

"What's that?" she asked. The unease returned full force.

His eyes lit with rage. "I want to see the king dead on a blood-drenched throne!"

She drew back, stumbled and landed on the edge of the bed as Dibbs laughed manically.

"What's wrong, servant of the king?" he growled. His voice no longer sounded like his. He tilted his head until his neck made a popping sound.

Aliah pointed at him. "How did you know I was a servant of the king?"

He stood in the middle of the room, panting. The pupils in his eyes had turned to slits that pierced her with their hideous stare.

"Say something!" she demanded.

He ignored her command, held out his arms and lifted his head toward the ceiling, then hissed. The room grew inexplicably cold and damp as he lowered his eyes, and drew her into his gaze. Her mind began to cloud, and she saw the same forest she saw in her nightmares. Within it, wispy, shadow-like creatures approached her.

"We have come to fulfill our master's wishes," they chanted. "All those with the light will die."

She tried to scream, but couldn't.

"There is no hope," they hissed.

Her body quaking, she collapsed onto her back, paralyzed. Dibbs approached and stood over her, eyes not his own gleaming at her with a terrifying delight. "A shame that one so beautiful must come to such an end. But do not fear. Your mother welcomed us when we came to retrieve *her*."

He reached for a pillow on the bed. With a cruel thrust, he brought it down onto her face. She tried to inhale, but her immobilized body refused to even struggle. Then, she felt her illumina grow warm, and her right arm moved. She reached for the phial and wrapped her cold hand around its warm glass. With a convulsive shuddering, her body freed itself of the paralysis.

Dibbs snarled and pushed harder on the pillow with strength unnatural for a young boy. She tried to push it away, but couldn't. Feeling herself blacking out, she held up the illumina, seeing its glow even through the pillow across her eyes.

Dibbs howled and stumbled back, fell to the floor. She jumped from the bed and looked around.

"The heat!" he screamed, writhing. "It burns!"

As if through a fog, hundreds of dark shapes darted around her in a frenzy, smashing into walls and crawling around on the floor. She caught sight of yellow orbs with black slits swimming inside them.

But then her light began to dim, and the shadows disappeared. Dibbs stopped writhing and pulled himself to a standing position. "You should not have resisted," the voice not his own hissed. "Your death shall now be infinitely more terrible."

She backed away, toward the door. Again, her mind started clouding over.

"No!" she managed to scream before falling to the floor, her limbs once again frozen.

✝ ✝ ✝

Gildareth reclined in the living room, watching with a smile while Raina and Grace played a game in which they manipulated a loop of string into various designs. Lianna leaned against Will, who was reading a proposal Siller had sent him on food distribution for the winter. At Aliah's one-word cry, all eyes gazed toward the stairs, and Gildareth leapt from his seat and ran toward them. Grace headed up the stairs after Gildareth.

"Wait!" Will shouted. "Don't go up there!"

She continued ascending. Groaning, he followed.

At the top of the stairs, he saw her staring into the open door of Dibbs' room. Gildareth was shouting into the room in a foreign-sounding tongue.

"Grace!" Will yelled, "what are you doing?"

"I ... wanted to see if Mr. Gildareth was all right," she said, staring into the room as if in a trance.

"Will," Lianna said, coming up behind him, "I don't feel well."

Raina stood behind Lianna, clutching her stomach. "Neither do I."

Gildareth stopped shouting and turned to them. "An army of vulgheid is within your house! They've come through the breach in the wall just outside Dibbs' room. Even now, others are likely attacking Ristun and Jebin downstairs. If he doesn't receive aid, Jebin will die. And," he pointed into Dibbs' room, "if Aliah and your son don't get help, they too will die."

"Will," Lianna gasped, "what does he mean?" She ran past him, down the hall, and entered Dibbs' room. Will hurried after her, and when he brushed passed Grace and Gildareth, he saw Lianna doubled over.

"I ... I can't breathe," she panted.

Will looked around the room in horror. Dibbs was in the corner, holding a chair above his head, slowly walking toward Aliah, who lay unmoving in the middle of the floor.

"Dibbs," Lianna moaned in pain, "what are you doing?"

Will felt something strike his face. He spun wildly, but couldn't see the source of the blow.

"Governor!" Gildareth shouted from the doorway, "the prophecy spoke of three servants rising up against the darkness, then three warriors." He lifted his arm and pointed at him. "It is time to demonstrate to Wrathar whom the first of the three servants is!"

Will stared at him in confusion.

"Willerdon, you are the first servant of prophecy!"

Will took a step back. As he did, he felt something grab at his ankles, trying to pull him to the ground.

"The prophecy's fulfillment has begun," Gildareth said. "Now go. The king has chosen you to command these foes and drive them from your house. Only you can perform this task."

Will's heart raced. Sweat trickled down his forehead onto his cheeks. Raina and Grace stared at him. "Do it, Father," Grace prompted. "The king will help you." She held out her illumina.

Raina glanced at the girl and did likewise. "You're not alone, Governor," she whispered.

Will turned to Gildareth, weaving while invisible hands continued to strike him and pull at his feet. Yet a power surged into him as Grace and Raina's illuminas grew brighter. "Help Jebin," he said to Gildareth. "The king and I will deal with this."

Gildareth smiled, stepped into the room and embraced him. For a moment, the invisible forces stopped their assault on his body. "The king is pleased," Gildareth said, released him, then hurried away, drawing his sword.

The invisible forces in the room renewed their assault. Will spun around, pulled out his illumina and stumbled forward, shouting, "Dibbs! This time I'm not going to forget about you!"

It was like walking into an invisible mist, and his boldness began draining away. In response, he lifted his illumina into the air. The first thing he noticed was his wife, bent over next to him, struggling to breathe. He placed his free hand on her back and shouted, "I command you in the name of the king to unleash my wife!"

Lianna gasped and straightened as if something had just let go of her throat, and grabbed onto his arm. He kissed her forehead, then leaned into her ear. "Get out your illumina."

She did so, and together, they stared into the invisible mire.

In the center of the room, Dibbs still held the chair over Aliah's head. From his mouth, a snakelike voice began to speak. "Leave, Governor, you cannot command us."

Will and Lianna held out their phials, the light within each burning as if one. "I am the king's servant of prophecy," Will responded, "and as such, have authority over you."

Dibbs lowered his chair and walked up to Will. "Prophecy? There is no merit to the *Annal's* rantings. You have no power here, or anywhere." He spat into Will's face. "Now go!"

"Son, what has happened to you?" Will said, tears welling.

"You have no son," the voice in Dibbs snarled. "He is ours now. He is hatred, he is refuse, he is shadow."

"You may not have him!" Will bellowed.

Lianna's illumina quaked as she began to sob.

Dibbs lifted his head toward the ceiling, hissed, and strode back to Aliah, again lifting the chair.

Will grasped his light tighter and approached, preparing to again address the creatures in the boy. What emerged from his lips was instead a whispered language, similar to the one Gildareth had just spoken.

Lianna looked at him, confusion on her face. Will kept talking, surprised but feeling such a renewed sense of strength, he feared to stop speaking.

Dibbs looked up at him, eyes wide. "How do you know the ancient language of the seers?"

Lianna began to speak along with Will, as if in translation. "Fear not, my servant," she said. "I am here. Do not speak to them. Do not converse with them. In words, they have power. Order them to leave by my authority, and stand fast. They will obey."

Will stared at Dibbs, lifted his voice and shouted, "In the name of the king, *leave this house!*"

Dibbs erupted into laughter so wild, he fell down and began rolling on the floor. "He . . . He thinks he can command us!"

The cold fog in the room grew. Will didn't move. Nor did he listen to the voice speaking through Dibbs. His heart was full of an inexplicable peace, and he knew the darkness was bluffing its merriment.

"What is it, Governor?" Dibbs panted in that horrible voice. "Why are you now so short on words? Afraid, perhaps?"

Lianna prepared to say something when Will pulled her closer to him. "Don't speak to it."

"But . . . it's our son."

"No it isn't!"

"Oh?" the voice hissed at her. "Are you so wise now?" The eyes within Dibbs grimaced as if in pain. "You . . . you have no power over us." Suddenly Dibbs screamed, "Get rid of that light, fools!"

Will looked around and noticed the room had become brighter. Behind him he saw Grace and Raina at the door, hand in hand, holding their illuminas into the room. Tears were in their eyes, but joy colored their faces.

"Daddy, we're here!" Grace said.

"Curse you, girl!" the voice in Dibbs screamed. "I loathe you! I loathe you! I'm going to come in the night and bite you again!"

"Don't listen, Grace!" Will shouted to her.

Though tears dripped from her chin, her hand holding the illumina remained steady.

"How can this be?" the voice in Dibbs shouted. "They were supposed to be destroyed! Their lights were almost dead!"

Will pulled Lianna forward and thrust his illumina onto Dibbs' back, screaming, "Get out of my house!"

There was a hiss, and the phial burst into such a brilliance that Will had to close his eyes. Dibbs writhed and squirmed, shrieking, "Heat! Stop! STOP!" Then, he went limp. As he did, the fog in the room subsided and the illuminas diminished to a soft glow.

Will pulled the cold, sweat-soaked body of his son into his arms, leaned in and listened for breathing. Moist air greeted his cheek.

"He's alive!" he shouted. Sobbing, Lianna collapsed onto them both. Grace added her warm presence, and Will pulled her close and planted kisses onto her cheek. All his family was near, and he wouldn't let them out of his arms, ever again.

FORTY-TWO

Tarin clutched his side as a knife-like pain pierced it. "I ... I need a break," he panted, and slumped into a patch of leaves. He and Sarky had been following Thief at a fast pace for hours, and his endurance was on the throes of death.

To his left, he heard the sound of a creek and smelled cool water in the air. Sarky slumped down next to him, wheezing as if he was being throttled by a drilockk. Thief continued prancing forward, until he turned around and saw the boys resting on the forest floor. He sprinted back to them and rested on all fours, staring at them through weariless eyes.

"How ... how on earth are you not tired?" Sarky squeaked through struggled breaths.

"I run a lot, young master. And I mean *a lot!*" He slumped onto his side and propped his head on one of his hands, still looking at them. "You do realize that if we stop, we might not beat your enemies to Lockspell."

Tarin felt his hand sliding toward his illumina as his heart, already beating hard from the run, pumped even faster. When he touched the phial, he felt two things: a sense of great victory, but from where he didn't know, and a growing urgency to save the family in Lockspell. He knew the urgency couldn't be his own, for he'd never cared about anyone as much as he now did about Jebin's family. He had to help save them. He didn't know why. He just knew he did.

"But why me?" he panted aloud.

"*Our* enemies?" Sarky didn't hear his question. His eyes were on Thief. "Yours too."

Tarin slapped the pocket holding the illumina, then started beating the ground in anger. He cursed. "Why is the king sending me on this fool-hardy mission to save a family I hardly know? I'm a pathetic child! He has better servants. Like Dralo. Like Ristun. Like Gildareth for heaven's sake!"

He stopped his tantrum and sat up, letting his shoulders droop in misery. "I don't want to do this, Sarky," he said, looking up at his friend. "Even after all that's happened, I don't want to continue. I just want to go home and hide like I've always done. I want to listen to stories from beneath a bush, or under a window. I don't want to actually be part of one."

Sarky came over to Tarin and put his arm around his shoulder. Tarin allowed it, for the first time ever relishing the comfort a simple touch could provide. Thief watched them intently, as if in wonder.

"First off," Sarky said, "you're not pathetic. Second, you're not alone. If the king has some special mission for you, like in Lockspell to save Jebin's family, well . . . I'm coming too, whether he likes it or not." Sarky patted his back. "Neither you nor he can get rid of me that easily."

Thief whimpered and shook his head as if in sad disbelief. "I've never seen such friendship, such care." He pointed at the boys, pursed his lips together to fight back oncoming tears. "There's something special about you two, no doubt in my mind. If my father was here, he'd be making you both his apprentices."

Thief crawled closer, stood, and beckoned for the boys to do likewise. They pulled themselves to their feet and looked up at him. For the first time since meeting the strange fellow, Tarin saw confidence in his eyes, determination even.

"I'm going to help you with whatever plans the king has for you," Thief said. "And if that means getting you to Lockspell to save that fool sheriff's family, or even more once we get there, so be it! But I must insist, if this quest is truly as urgent as my young master professes, we must shake off our weariness and run to the city. We have little time before daybreak, and if my judgments are correct, even less before the drilockk get there."

He held out his hand in the direction they needed to go. "So, shall we be off, little masters?"

Tarin looked at Sarky, who was grinning. He couldn't help a smile at those crooked teeth, for he knew that beneath that bizarre exterior lurked a fearless and loyal friend, one who was earning his respect with every passing hour.

He lifted his chest in one more deep breath, then let it out with a nod. "Let's go!"

Sarky whooped, and lifted his fists into the air.

As if a signal, Thief clapped his hands together and shouted, "We're almost to the road! After that, young masters, our travels will be easier." He sprinted forward and began the race to Lockspell. Tarin and Sarky, with renewed vigor, sped after him.

Printed in the United States
131865LV00002B/2/P

9 780615 232010